STORIES FOR CHIP

A TRIBUTE TO SAMUEL R. DELANY

Praise

"I read *The Jewels of Aptor* in 1962, when I was fourteen. Samuel Delany had written it when he was nineteen, and I totally got that, the fantastic youth of the thing, but I was also blown away by what I didn't yet understand was the style. It induced one of the most persistent and global somatic memories of reading I've ever had, to the point that I can actually use it as a sort of time-travel device. And yes, I know he's written many novels since then, including *Dhalgren*, but I've always wanted a chance to say that about *The Jewels of Aptor*!"

—William Gibson, author of *Pattern Recognition*

"Samuel R. Delany sits at the crossroads of the story of SF. Explore any path—why SF matters, how, to whom—and he is there, beaming, either in person or reflected in the writers forging ahead. This book of beautiful, brilliant stories, fiction and nonfiction, shows us why he matters so much—and how, and to whom. All of us, of course."

—Nicola Griffith, author of *Hild*

"This anthology rocks your mind, rolls your heart, and makes you tingle all over. Nisi Shawl and Bill Campbell have curated an entertaining and provocative volume, a whirlwind tour of the mythic, science fictional landscape that Delany engendered. These stories, essays, and memoirs are sensuous encounters with Delany, an ongoing conversation in the delanyesque universe. A polymath geek fest! *Stories for Chip* is a perfect tribute to a creative genius, a theoretical titan, and a great adventurer."

—Andrea Hairston, author of *Redwood and Wildfire*

"This lovingly made tribute to Samuel R. Delany is packed with tiny delights. Stories that are as diverse as they are refreshing to the palate. A blend of so many different voices and takes on the influence of this great author--one could only dream that in the winter of one's career such a collection could be constructed in one's honor."

—Jennifer Marie Brissett, author of *Elysium*

"A powerful testimonial to the impact Delany has had in inspiring so many of this generation's diverse voices."

—Tobias Buckell, author of *Arctic Rising*

"A tribute to one of the great geniuses of science fiction, this diamond of a book has stories as multi-faceted, brilliant, and wickedly sharp as Delany himself."

—Ellen Klages, author of *The Green Glass Sea*

STORIES FOR CHIP

A TRIBUTE TO SAMUEL R. DELANY

EDITED BY NISI SHAWL AND BILL CAMPBELL

ROSARIUM

Published by Rosarium Publishing
P.O. Box 544
Greenbelt, MD 20768-0544
www.rosariumpublishing.com

International Standard Book Number: 978-0-9903191-7-7
Library of Congress Control Number: 2015943602

Acknowledgement for permission to reprint the following:

"Haunt-type Experience" by Roz Clarke first appeared in *Black Static*, Witcham, Cambridgeshire, UK, February 2009.

"Nilda" by Junot Diaz first appeared in *The New Yorker*, New York, NY, USA, October 1999. It was subsequently reprinted in his collection *This Is How You Lose Her*, New York, NY, USA, September 2012, Riverhead Books.

"Real Mothers, a Faggot Uncle, and the Name of the Father: Samuel R. Delany's Feminist Revisions of the Story of SF" by L. Timmel Duchamp first appeared in *Cruising the Disciplines: A Symposium on Samuel R. Delany*, Kenneth R. James, editor, Annals of Scholarship, Aliso Viejo, CA, USA, Volume 20 (2013).

"Michael Swanwick and Samuel R. Delany at the Joyce Kilmer Service Area, March 2005" by Eileen Gunn first appeared in *Foundation*, Kempston, Bedfordshire, UK, Winter 2007. It was subsequently reprinted in her collection *Questionable Practices*, Easthampton, MA, USA, March 2014, Small Beer Press.

"Guerilla Mural of a Siren's Song" by Ernest Hogan first appeared in Pulphouse, Issue 4 (Summer 1989). It was subsequently reprinted in *Alien Contact*, Marty Halpern, editor, San Francisco, CA, USA, November 2011, Night Shade Books. A Polish translation appeared in *Nowa Fantastyka*, Warsaw, Poland, January 2013.

"Empathy Evolving as a Quantum of Eight-Dimensional Perception" by Claude Lalumière first appeared in *Suction Cup Dreams: An Octopus Anthology*, David Joseph Clarke, editor, Charleston, SC, USA, November 2013, Obsolescent Press.

"Kickenders" by Kit Reed first appeared in *monkeybicycle*, Montclair, NJ, USA, Summer 2014.

<<Légendaire.>> by Kai Ashante Wilson first appeared in *Bloodchildren: Stories by the Octavia E. Butler Scholars*, Nisi Shawl, editor, Seattle, WA, USA, January 2013, The Carl Brandon Society.

"The Master of the Milford Altarpiece" by Tom Disch first appeared in *The Paris Review*, Paris, France, Spring 1969. It has been subsequently reprinted many times, including in *Getting into Death and Other Stories*, New York, NY, February 1976, Knopf.

Contents

Introduction

Kim Stanley Robinson

I was in a dusty used bookstore in downtown San Diego, looking at its science fiction shelves, when I pulled down a little book titled *City of a Thousand Suns*. Author one Samuel R. Delany. I had recently discovered science fiction and was on the hunt for new writers, so I opened this book and started to read. It was February 12, 1972. I know that because I wrote the date on the flyleaf after taking the book home, and in all the years since I've held on to that volume, despite my frequent cullings of my library, because it means something to me. It brings back the feeling of that time: a twenty year-old reading another twenty year-old (more or less), discovering science fiction and the world.

Because the book was the third in a trilogy, I read it with some confusion, but when I was done I went looking for more Delany. Soon I had found all of it, and Delany had become one of my favorite writers. He was, I gathered, a young writer traveling the world, his life an adventure that was vivid and romantic and filled with literature. My own life became more exciting because of his writing: this was an intense feeling, a kind of joy.

I see versions of that feeling in all the stories and essays collected here. Delany's writing is beautiful, which is rare enough; but rarer still, it is encouraging, by which I mean, it gives courage. People respond to that encouragement with pleasure and thanks, as you will see here.

These tributes mostly don't try to imitate Delany's style, which is good, as it is a very personal style, one that has morphed through the years in complex ways. Imitation could only result in pastiche or parody, forms of limited interest, although a good parody can be fun, and I've seen some pretty good ones of Delany's work elsewhere. A "Bad Delany" contest would be at least as funny as the famous "Bad Hemingway" and "Bad Faulkner" contests. But a better tribute, as the writers gathered here seem to agree, results from considering not style but substance. Delany's subject matter, his mode or method, involves a characteristic mix of the analytical and the emotional, the realistic and the utopian. By exploring this delanyesque space (and I think delanyesque has become an adjective, like ballardian or orwellian or kafkaesque), the stories and essays here make the best kind of tribute. They perhaps help to make the Delanyspace a new genre or subgenre. However that works, it's certain that Delany's work has effected a radical reorientation of every genre he has written in. Time and other writers will tell the sequel as to what that means for science fiction, fantasy, sword and sorcery, pornography, memoir, and criticism. Here we get hints of what that will be like.

It was a persistence of vision that created the Delanyspace, over decades of hard work. It's both theoretical and material; it pays attention to sex and bodies more than most fiction, but also it is often more social and political. It is, remembering what Virginia Woolf said about George Eliot's books relative to earlier English literature, "a literature for grown-ups." Reading Delany provides us with new cognitive maps, which reorient us to our experiences and to our own thoughts. This is what literature should always do, but it's rare to experience the effect so distinctly and joyfully. Even when emerging from his books chastened, or alarmed, or shocked, or even appalled, there is something deeply positive in Delany's vision. His books are utopian in a sense bigger than politics. They make you bolder. Their greatness includes a great generosity. This volume is one sign of their impact.

Michael Swanwick and Samuel R. Delany at the Joyce Kilmer Service Area, March 2005

Output from a nostalgic, if somewhat misinformed, guydavenport storybot, in the year 2115

Transcribed by Eileen Gunn

Their journey took place in verdant March, when the sun was not yet so high in the sky as to be dangerous. The New Jersey Turnpike was redolent with the scent of magnolias, and the trees in the Joyce Kilmer Service Area were clad in exuberant green. What brought them, the nascent politician and the noted philosopher, to this place, in a vehicle that shed its rich hydrocarbons liberally into the warm, clean air?

The truth was that Michael Swanwick and Samuel R. Delany shared a taste for animal flesh, and had come to this bucolic waystation to satisfy their common need. "I'm a burger kind of guy," said the future ruler of Russia. "So am I," said the white-bearded semiotician, and they chose an imperial meat-patty palace for their repast.

As they stood in line, contemplating a panoply of burgers, fries, and blue raspberry Icee®s and basking in the cool green glow of fluorescent lights, Swanwick was struck with nostalgia for a time long past.

"I miss Howard Johnson's," he said. "Not the food, of course—I miss the orange-roofed temples, celebrated by Jean Shepard as sirens of the highway. Once upon a time, every rest area on the Jersey Turnpike had a Howard Johnson's. 'A landmark for hungry Americans.'"

Though Swanwick had spoken the words, each man, involuntarily, heard the chime of the ghastly jingle. "Funny thing," he continued quickly. "It was capitalism that killed it. Marriott bought it for the real estate."

"Red in tooth and claw," said Delany. "I miss the pistachio ice cream cones, that's all.... But *here*," he added in a soothing tone, "*here* we have trading cards with robots on them." He accepted a trading card from the cashier. It depicted Cappy, a sleekly androgynous silver-metal lover. "I want a different one," he said.

"Have it your way," said the cashier, shrugging. He handed Delany another card, this one featuring Crank, a grubby makeshift robot with rust under his gnawed fingernails.

Delany laughed, a musical sound somewhere between a snort and a giggle. "I'll keep this one," he said. He ordered a beef patty made with real beef, medium rare, topped with horseradish and Béarnaise sauce, kosher dill slices on the side.

"Have it your way," said the cashier again.

"Are you a robot?" asked Swanwick, suddenly concerned. The cashier did not reply.

"I would like a big, sloppy, greasy double cheeseburger with lettuce and tomato and all the trimmings," Swanwick told the cashier. "I want ketchup, mayonnaise, mustard, and Russian dressing with beluga caviar. Hold the pickle."

"Caviar is available only at the Walt Whitman Service Area," said the cashier, frowning. "You can't *always* have *every*thing *your* way." He gave Swanwick a trading card depicting Aunt Fanny, a matronly, pink, lipstick-wearing robot with a protuberant posterior. Swanwick accepted it with bemusement, wondering whether Burger King offered the same card in the United Kingdom. "Can I have another, too?" he asked. The cashier handed him a card with a pigtailed Lolita robot on it. "Another?" The third was Madame Gasket, who was a bit scary, frankly, for a trading card. He couldn't get *anything* his way.

"Lucky in love, unlucky at cards," said Delany.

"They hand these things out to children?" Swanwick asked, glancing again at Madame Gasket.

They paid for their meals in the devalued currency of the late-period religio-capitalist hegemony, and took their food trays to a small table at a window overlooking the Sunoco station.

"Bon appétit," said Delany, gesturing with his hamburger as one would with a wineglass.

"Priyatnovo appetita," replied Swanwick with a similar gesture. He had recently returned from the Urals, where he had been the toast of Ekaterinburg.

At first they ate in hungry silence, gazing out at the gas station, as languid pump attendants with huge palm-frond fans hailed approaching automobiles and waved them toward available fueling bays as though they were New Jersey's famous zeppelins. Then, having taken the edge off their appetites, the two men continued the conversation they had begun in the car, the one great debate that writers and thinkers everywhere have carried on since writing and thinking first evolved: the debate about the ultimate futility of writing and thinking.

"I'm a cult writer in Russia," said Swanwick, "and I'm a cult writer in the United States. And I'm sick of it."

"Nothing so terrible about being a cult writer," said Delany. "Christianity started out as a cult, and look at it now."

◊

"I want to make some *difference* in the world, communicate with the mass of *humanity*, have an *effect*." He gestured toward the crowded freeway. "I want to change *entire lives* for the *better*."

"Have you thought of a different career?" asked Delany gently. "Perhaps emigration to a land of greater opportunity? You speak some Russian, do you not?"

"Nyemnoshka," Swanwick answered, with a modest shake of his shaggy head. "A smidgeon," he translated.

"Maybe you should consider pulling up stakes, retooling for the new millennium. As a cult writer in the US, you're nothing. You have considerably less effect on how the world fares than a Hollywood screenwriter, which is low indeed in the social hierarchy. But as a cult writer in Russia, you'd have some clout. They are afraid of writers in Russia, and with good reason. You could leverage your celebrity into a political career, take control of that long-suffering country, and change the world. Of course, you could also get killed." He sighed. "It's a sad thing, but nobody kills writers in the U.S. They just don't matter enough."

"I will consider that," said Swanwick, and did. It would not be so difficult for him and his wife to create new lives in another land. She was a public-health scientist, although, when provoked, she sometimes described herself as a career bureaucrat. Russia had jobs in either category; like everyplace else, it needed scientists more, and paid bureaucrats better. And Michael had always enjoyed caviar and sour cream, however difficult they were to obtain on the Jersey Turnpike. It could work.

But, he thought, it was time to get back on the road. They gathered up their things, recycled the trash, slapped on their canvas hats and a heavy layer of sunblock, and hit the road.

They continued north in Swanwick's chartreuse 1959 Thunderbird, past service areas named for the heroes of New Jersey: Allen Ginsberg, Paul Robeson, William Carlos Williams, Frank Sinatra, Bruce Springsteen, Jimmy Hoffa, Yogi Berra, and Jon Bon Jovi. Soon enough, they found themselves at the most intellectually exciting stretch of highway in the United States. Between exits 16E and 13A, the New Jersey Turnpike at that time passed over the Passaic River. The General Casimir Pulaski Skyway, a masterpiece of Depression-era engineering, soared off to one side, crossing the Passaic and Hackensack Rivers in great lattice-work leaps. As the car approached New York City, the primeval Meadowlands swept off on the left, balancing the demands of nature and of solid-waste disposal, and the darkly crystalline rectangles of the Manhattan skyline arose to the right. Gleaming networks of railroad tracks recalled to them the glorious empire, created by commerce and forced labor, that had, until the new century and its disasters, sustained the American Dream. Where the towers had been there was still, in 2005, negative space.

◊

The car containing the two men sped across the George Washington Bridge and made its way, under Swanwick's instruction, to Delany's residence. Chip Delany, ever hospitable, invited Michael Swanwick to come upstairs and continue their conversation, but Swanwick, by now lost to American literature, made a hasty excuse in mumbled Russian, and disappeared into the gray fog of urban twilight.

Billy Tumult

Nick Harkaway

Billy Tumult, psychic surgeon, with six shooters on his hips, walks into the saloon. There are dancing girls dancing with dancing boys and dancing boys dancing together, and women behind the bar in hats made of feathers. There's a fat man at the piano and a poker game in each corner. Up on the balcony there's some comedic business involving infidelity, but no gunplay, not yet. Billy swaggers over and gets a beer. And make it a cold one, miss, okay? The barkeep leans across the shiny surface and prints a perfect lipstick mark on his cheek. Rein it in a little, cattle hand, she murmurs, you're cute but this here's a civilized sort of establishment.

Yeah, sure, Billy mutters, you can tell by the nice clean bullet holes in the furniture, I bet you dust 'em nightly, and the barkeep actually laughs and says she likes his style. She sounds too much like Chicago, almost a moll, and Billy adjusts the filter a few notches to the left. Doesn't do to mix your conceptual frame during a house call.

I'm lookin' for a man, Billy Tumult says, probably comes over like a gunslinger. New in town, a solitary sort of fella, not much for talking. He'd be my height or more and looking to keep things quiet. Barkeep says she doesn't know nothing about that, maybe talk to the fat man, fat man hears everything, and Billy Tumult knows she's lying and she knows he knows and she blushes: talk to the fat man, and he says okay.

Billy turns his back on the bar and lets his hands fall down by his sides. Six shooters be damned, they're for show and to take care of any ambient hostility, the real weapon is invisible to these good townsfolk, the Neuronoetic Interference Scalpel 3.1.a holstered in the small of his back. He can clear and fire it in under seventy subjective milliseconds, literally faster than thought unless the thought is a really bad one. Patient in this case presents with anhedonia, and that's pretty damn bad.

He looks around at the room, and has to hand it to the guy: these are well-imagined people, and there's a decent ethnic mix. He's pretty sure that cardsharp is supposed to be a Yupik, for example, which may not be authentic—you surely didn't get a lot of Eskimo hustlers in the Old West—but it speaks well of the patient's interior life. Most of Billy's patients are assholes, by definition. Billy has no problem with assholes in the abstract. It is everyone's God-given right to be an asshole, in fact it's basically the default setting and you evolve your way up from there, but that does not mean Billy particularly enjoys spending time in worlds created by assholes, which is his working life. So this guy has problems but is less of an asshole than most and that is acceptable.

Billy walks over to the fat man. Fat man can't see him, surely, not from this angle, but he shifts to a minor key, staccato. Mood music? Billy wonders if he should just flat out erase the guy. Better not. Don't want to be talking to a patient's lawyer about how you came to delete his memory of nine thousand nine hundred hours of music tuition. Never a good scene, there are lawyers and all that but the worst is the crying. Billy hates emotional display, he's a fucking surgeon for crying out loud, not a therapist. You want to break things and scream about your momma you can go see one of those wishy-washy liberals on the East Coast. You want your problem hunted down and shot, you call Billy: mind medicine, open-carry style. Your psychological issue will bleed out and die and you carry right on with your life. It appeals to traditional men with sexual dysfunction, executive types who've suddenly discovered their humanity and want it gone, that kind of thing. Occasionally he does memories for divorce cases and once the State of Alabama had him kill a man's whole history from the present back down the line, leave nothing but the child he'd been before he became a crook. They raised that fella back to manhood inside the system, and he's a productive citizen now, although Billy went back and met him out of sheer curiosity and he's kinduva a jerk, basically a boring-ass wage slave of the dehumanizing statist system. Not Billy's problem, but he doesn't take government work any more. One time they asked him to do espionage. Fucking torture bullshit. Billy said no, turned those fuckers in to the real law, the sheriff's office, made a helluva stink, man from the *New York Times* came to interview him. Weirdest month of his life, so-clean liberal actresses draping themselves over his arm and whispering sweet nothings in his ear, sweet nothings and some really outré shit Billy was quick to take fullest advantage of because those chances do not come along twice. Weird, but really satisfying, sexually speaking. Got to hand it to the Democrats, they know from orgasms.

Hey, fat man, Billy says, you playing that for me? Fat man shakes his head. No, he says, I play what's on the hymn sheet is all, and sure enough there it is written out. Turn the page, Billy says, give me a preview. Fat man does and growls, it's a fight scene. Brawling or guns? Well, that's kinda hard to tell, you better ask me what you want to know in the next few bars.

Where's the new guy, Billy says. Lotsa new guys in town, fat man replies. No, Billy says, there ain't, there's only one. My height and taller, black hat, solitary fella don't like to make friends. Oh, that new guy, fat man says. That new guy got hisself a room above the hardware store, has

Missus Roth bring him food and all. He armed? Billy Tumult asks, and the fat man says that a patron that tough don't go about without some manner of weapon but the fat man don't know what kind.

Fat man turns the page on his hymn sheet and one of the poker tables flies up in the air. Fistfight, bottles flying and you goddam cheating bastard and blahsedyblahs. Dissolve to later.

Billy Tumult, walking down the street. Tips his hat to the ladies, bids the fellas good afternoon. Going to the Marshall's office. Want to be in good with the local force. No stink-of-armpit law-keeper, this one, but a high buttoned pinstripe and waistcoat number, almost a dandy. What are the chances, Billy Tumult growls. Man might could be Billy's brother, might could use him for shaving around that dandy moustache. Patient's been thinking about coming to see Billy Tumult for long enough that he's got hisself a tulpa in here, a little imaginary robot doing what the patient thinks Billy'd do. Ain't that just the sweetest thing?

Marshall William says hello, and Billy says hello right back and they shake hands. It's like icebergs colliding. The Marshall's got two shooters on his hips, of course, just like in the brochure. What's behind his back, Billy wonders, maybe a third gun, maybe a humungous nature of a knife. That would figure. But when they get into the Marshall's office and the fella takes off his coat, mother of Christ, it's a dynamite vest, a bandolier. The guy so much as farts wrong and they're all in the next county over and fuck if he doesn't actually smoke. Laws of sanity have been suspended for Billy's oversold publicity-and-marketing hardassery. Thank God if the thing goes up the worst that happens to Billy is a damn reset and the whole surgery to redo from start, pain in the ass, but if this was the real world or if Billy was really part of this whole deal then he'd be pasta sauce.

Pasta sauce is inauthentic. Billy tweaks the filter again. He prefers the gangster aspect, can't keep this horses-and-mud shit straight in his brain. Well, if the patient can have Eskimos, Billy can have pasta sauce, call it fair play.

I'm Billy Tumult of the Pinkertons, he tells Marshall William, come lookin' for a dangerous man. We got plenty, says the Marshall, which one you want? Or take 'em all, I surely won't miss 'em. I want the new guy, Billy says, the one in the black hat living over the store. The one Missus Roth has an arrangement with. Now hold on, begins the Marshall, no not that kind of arrangement, the feedin' kind is all I mean, I got no beef with the Widow Roth.

Widow my ass, parenthesizes Billy Tumult, if I know how this goes, but never mind that for now.

He's an odd one, sure, says the Marshall. Odd and I don't like him and he don't much like me. But I figure the one he's looking out for is you, now I think on it. He offered me a whole shit-ton of gold, I saw it right there in that room, to tell him if a fella came askin' about him. You say yes? Billy wants to know. No, Marshall replies. 'Course not, he says, and rolls his shoulder.

Cutaway: a thin man naked in a room full of gold, lean like a leather-gnarled spider stretched too tight on his own bones. He tilts his head and listens to the sound of the town, and he knows someone's coming. Slips down the gold rockface into his pants and shoes—demons evidently need no socks—and buckles on his gun. Not much of a thing, this gun. Small and dirty and badly kept. Buckles it on, long black coat around his shoulders. Tan galàn on his head: bare-chested Grendel in a hat, and that's as good a name as any. Arms and legs too long, Grendel spidercrabs out of the golden room and into shadow, gone a-huntin'. Too fast, he's under the balcony across the street, flickers in the dark alley by the blacksmith, by the sawbones, by the water tower. Too fast, too quiet. All of a sudden: it's not clear at all who's gonna win this one.

Billy Tumult doesn't exactly see all this, not being present in the mis-en-scène, but he gets the gist because that's the benefit of narrative surgery. You pay a price in hella stupid costumes and irritating dialogue, but you get it back in inevitability. Sooner or later they will stand in the street and one of them will outshoot the other, and Billy can do it over and over and over and over until he nails it; the other fella has to get it perfect every time. That's the thing about your average cognitive hiccup or post-Freudian crise: they just don't learn. That said, on this occasion there's a sense of real jeopardy, contagious fear, and it takes some stones to go out on Main Street and walk down the middle, spurs clankin'.

Billy Tumult has those stones. He surely does.

Half-naked Grendel comes on like blinking, like he doesn't really understand physical spaces. Which he don't, but all the same he's fast and he's focused, he sees Billy the way they mostly can't, sees him as an external object rather than part of the diorama. Not your common or garden mommy issue, this fucker, but a real nasty customer, maybe even a kink in the standing wave. Blink! Walking outside the smithy. Blink! Hat shop, dressmaker. Blink! By the trees outside the mayor's place. Blink! Right there, dead on his mark where he should be for the showdown, except it's too soon. Can't draw down on him, not yet, the patient's mind will fracture him away. It's not the right time. Got to earn your conclusions. This is the chit chat segment, bad guy banter.

Heard you might be in town, Billy says, figured I'd come and see if you were that stupid.

White teeth under thin lips. Patient presents with anhedonia: can't feel joy, can't even feel pleasure, just nothing. Only pain and less pain, sadness and more sadness. Whole top half of his spectrum is missing. Grendel is stealing all the best stuff like a leech, keeping it in that room back there above the store.

Figured you'd stay out in the wilderness, Billy suggests, figured you had maybe a cave out there, livin' on human arms and all, figured you'd feel safe being a wild beast. No place for you in here, you have to know that. It's time to give it up. I'll go easy on you. Like hell he will. Ugliest fucker Billy's ever seen, standing there without moving his eyes, turning his head like a goddam owl. The weird face twists and tilts, and off somewhere behind there's a laugh, an old woman cackle. Billy looks for her, can't find her. Always check your corners.

Patient says he's being watched, all the time, can't shake the feeling, paranoia with all the trimmings.

There is no patient, Grendel whispers—Billy can hear it like he's right there behind him, and then he is, actually is right there, cold breath on Billy's neck—there's just us.

Oh, shit, Billy Tumult thinks, like a lightbulb just before it pops.

◊

This is the cave where Grendel lives. Right now it's in a room over the hardware store, but it could be anywhere because it's basically a state of mind. It's a cave because Grendel lives in it. If you went in—well, if you went in you'd probably die, but if you went in without dying—you'd see it as a great dripping space full of twisting faces drawn in black on shadow, lit by the glimmer of a solitary camp fire and the reflected sheen of bullion. By the fire you'd see Grendel, crouched in his long coat, roasting fish for his mother for her dinner. On a stout stick you'd see a head that looks a lot like Billy Tumult's. It would be unclear if it's a trophy or a dessert.

What Grendel sees, if Grendel sees or even thinks at all, we do not know.

◊

Billy Tumult, on his stick, takes a moment to contemplate the forgotten virtue of humility.

Goddammit.

He was operating on his own self. How did he ever get that stupid? And why can't he remember? Well, he can think of reasons, reasons for both. Can't be much of a psychic surgeon if you've got your own crippling issues, can't exactly trust the competition much, can't be seen to go to a therapist. How'd that play on cable? Not well.

And as to forgetting, well, that could be a mistake or a choice he's made, maybe the stakes are high and he doesn't want to cramp his decision making. Maybe he wanted to be sure he'd do what it took, deliver a cure even if some of the loss was painful. Maybe Grendel's got roots in something Billy'd ideally like to hang onto, good memories from the old days, whatever. But clear enough: this fucker needs to be got, because he is one terrifying sumbitch.

Which is going to be hard to arrange from the top of a goddam stick in a goddam cave.

◊

Top of the morning to you, Missus Roth, Marshall William says, tips his hat. And to you, twinkles the merry widow on her horse, thirty five years of age at most, sure in the saddle and a fine figure of a woman. William wishes she'd stop and pass the time a little but she never does. I hear there was some excitement earlier, she tells him, I hear it was quite unsettling. Oh, well, yes, there was some excitement, William says, but it's all done now. A man come to town lookin' for a fugitive, your Mister Grendel as it happens, but it was all a misunderstanding if you can believe it, and the fella's gone on his way and no harm done. Is that right, says Evangeline Roth, is that right, indeed? And Marshall William assures her that it is, misses the flicker in her eyes, the hardness that says he's just fallen in her estimation, fallen a good long way and may now never resurface. That's fine, she says then, for Mister Grendel is a gentleman I'm sure. And she goes on her way to market. That's a fine figure of a woman, William murmurs, and bold for a respectable widow to wear a vermillion chapeau to go out riding, bold and quite suitable on her to be sure.

Evangeline Roth married a young preacher in Spokane, Missouri, when she was only twenty, loved him more than life, saw him die on the way out west of a snake bite. The thing had lunged for her and he put out his hand to take the strike, the wound festered and that was that. They had no children: they were waiting for the right time. She learned to shoot from a carnival girl, learned to sit a horse the same way, has no intention of being a second class anything, not here or in any other town. Owns the hardware store in her own name and takes in lodgers when it suits her, knows fine well there's a darkness in her house now, a bad place that needs dealing with the way you'd bag a hornet's nest and put it in the river. Looks back over her sharp shoulder at Marshall William and growls. Useless.

But speaking of the river—she taps her heels to the flanks of the horse—well, now, wasn't there a place once? A wide strand where all manner of things wash up, jetsam and littoral peculiars. Yes, indeed, some distance out of town, a half day's riding and a little more. Widow Roth, with a few necessaries in her saddlebags, makes her way along the old mule trail and past the abandoned mines, across the yucca plain to the very spot, where the wide blue water winds about the sand, and removes her clothes to work magic. She has no idea if nudity is requisite, but likewise no intention of making a mess of things for the sake of crinolines and stays.

That night on the white sand she draws all manner of significant ideograms, according to her strongly-held opinions. She dances—furtively at first, for it is one thing to be discovered nude by a river where after all anyone might reasonably bathe, but quite another to be seen cavorting—but eventually she stretches out her hands to the world and spins and leaps with her whole remarkable self. She invokes angels and local gods she has heard about from local people, performs whatever syncretist rituals are in line with her understanding of divinity. Overall, indeed, she does the best she can with what she has, promising a small sheep if such is required, or good strong whisky and tobacco, or a life of virtue and contemplation on the other hand, and heartfelt apologies for this behavior. The point is, this thing must be done, she repeats over and over to the wind. It must be done.

The night seems not to care. In the end, she lies exhausted and dusty on her back and just shrieks at the sky, conscious that here at last she has perhaps finally come to an understanding of what magic and religion truly are. And at dawn, through gummed eyes, she sees the result of her exhortations and exertions washed to shore by the breeze: a strange contraption like a sword or flintlock, to be worn as near as she can tell in the small of the back. Inscribed upon the hilt are occult symbols: Combine Medical Industries: NIS 3.1.a.

This is a river in a dream, and as such washes through all caves and all valleys, and will in good conscience respond to such desperation as it can.

◊

Grendel springs from his sleep, from his golden bed, jointless neck twisting. Snatches up his coat. Pauses to strike at Billy Tumult's living head. Ow, Billy Tumult says in the empty cave, and hears Grendel's mother chortle from the dark. She must be able to fly, thinks Billy Tumult on his stick. That must be it. She's never where she should be and always where you don't want her.

No time for that now: through the shadows skitters spidery Grendel, owl eyes bright and fingers grasping. Blink blink here and blink blink there, but he has no idea what to look for, knows only that something is wrong. Peers in through the high windows of the saloon, looking for another lawman. Perhaps Marshall William's found his steel? But no. There he is, stuffed shirt presiding over a poker tournament, the Yupik winning, yes, of course. Where away?

So very close, did he but know. Evangeline Roth stands in her boudoir, scant yards from the door she rents to Grendel, the entrance to the cave. A sensible jacket and good trousers are important in such moments. She doesn't bother to put the scalpel in its holster, doesn't propose for one moment to let it out of her hand until she's done with her task. No idle oath, this, but pure practical terror, which she feels sure is a better guide to questing behavior than any bold pledge or pretty couplet.

Amazing, she considers, how impossibly hard it is, in a nightmare, to open the doors of one's own house.

But she does.

On the roof of the mayor's mansion, Grendel gives a shriek and spins in the moonlight, spins for home like a compass needle. Scrabbles across the tiles and leaps. Never touches the sandy street, just folds away. In a real hurry now, is Grendel.

◊

Evangeline Roth takes in the cave, the cackling dark, and the head of Billy Tumult on a stick—and all this existing somehow inside the confines of her guest room, for the rental of which she charges a few dollars including soap and hot water for washing. Two seats by the fire, she notes, laid in front of all that lustrous gold, but only one shows any sign of occupation. Before the other, decaying and uneaten baked fish, peppered with flies.

This all is, she acknowledges, more odd than she was prepared to contemplate before stepping through the door she painted last summer in duck egg blue. All in all, though, she would handle it very well if only the dismembered head would stop giving her instructions. Just like a man, she considers, to die absolutely and then hang around to offer his useless experience to a female person who is so far still alive.

Charity, she thinks firmly, putting the head in her bag. Charity begins at home.

Billy Tumult stares up at the interior space of the handbag and considers this a new low. Rescued by a merry widow from a monster's cave, dumped into a perfumed clutch filled with the unmentionable secrets of females. No, he promises more loudly, he will be quiet, there is no need to stuff that—somewhat used—monogrammed lace hanky in his mouth for hush. But how hard is this for the bold adventurer? Quite hard, indeed, and that must be his very own scalpel in her other hand, prudently unholstered and charged. If Billy still had that—and arms and legs and so forth for its deployment—this story would run differently, that's for sure. But here, this is the way things are, and he's reduced to... what? Baggage? At least, surely, early warning system, canary in the mine. And yes: warning, indeed! Scuffle and titter in the dark, rat-roach rustle. Christ, Billy says, it's the mother! Look out behind you!

This being his advice, and he being in his present place—and having resolved in her mind the curious clue of the undevoured fish repast—Evangeline sweeps up the scalpel directly in front of her and thumbs the trigger. No monster takes her between the shoulders, no great vasty mother sups upon her spine. The tittering and cackling carries on regardless as the blue white stream emerging from the scalpel licks just in front of crabwise Grendel, cloaked in shadows, and brings him scritching to a halt. There is no mother, Evangeline has reckoned, not really, just a chittering landscape. There's Grendel, and he must have his sound effects, but in the end—just as she is—he must be alone.

So there they stand: widow and monster, each paradoxically in their own place of power. His cave, her house. A darkness walking meeting a patchwork saint of practical technology and improvised magic in this altogether unanticipated explosion of Billy's Wild West operating table, on which apparently he is himself presently anaesthetized.

High noon, she realizes, as somewhere a church bell begins to ring. Grendel drops his hands to his sides and waits for the twelfth chime. She can feel the shadows smirking. A ridiculous mismatch. After all, he can step behind her on the strike. Take her, just as he took Billy Tumult. It wants only the right moment.

She shrugs, and uses the scalpel to remove his head. Watches the body fall. Listens to the chimes run out: bong bong bong bong. The right moment, Evangeline the widow remarks to her spare bed and washing china, now returned from whatever reality they occupied while the cave was in residence in this space, is when I bloody say it is.

She puts the head in the bag and, on a whim, attaches Billy Tumult to the fallen corpse. The body rises. Job done. I'm alive, alive, shouts the resulting personage. Well, yes, Evangeline replies, judicious, but best you wear some sort of neckerchief until the scar is properly healed. And for God's sake put on a shirt.

◊

Marry me, Billy Tumult says, opening his eyes on the operating table to the first pleasurable feelings he has known in half a decade, Jesus Mary and Joseph I'm cured and I thought I was screwed. Marry me, Evangeline, I swear to God!

The object of this proposal is a fine figure of a woman, a temporary hire in the practice, recently arrived in town and filling time while she looks for an apartment. Hell, no, replies Evangeline Roth, I don't even like you and frankly going by this one observation your specialism's a crock. That in mind and with some reservations regarding your ability to understand the literal truth of what I'm about to say, you can buy me a platonic drink while we discuss my bonus.

And with this offer, Billy Tumult has to be content.

Voice Prints

devorah major

1.

Well, first of all, you must understand I am one who loves people; I mean I love humans. I love our smells, and the way we lounge around, how we throw out an arm or pull in a leg, the way this one tilts his head and that one scrunches up her nose. And the voices, oh how I love them—especially in song. Let others have their pianos and saxophones, let others crave the beat of the drum or the strumming of an acoustic guitar; for me always it was the voice humming and becoming a bird or a windstorm—the notes of love flying, the essence of the singer if you will.

Of course it was that love that brought me here, caged by you who have no center. My only solace is that I know others will discover that too. Perhaps they already have.

The thing is, I really don't know how I first started to know, or when. To tell you the truth, I wish I never had found out about you. Well sometimes, anyway, once in a while, or at least once. Oh, you do smile. How nice, one with a small sense of humor. But sometimes I wonder what it would have been like if I never found out. I mean, now that I know you intend to keep me here until I die. Oh yes, it is pretty on this mountain cliff and the air is so incredibly clean. But it is snowed-in so many months of the year and I am alone most of the time, or else served by one of you.

How I miss humans. It's been eight years. Three years since you found out I knew the truth and five more spent up here. Odd, isn't it? I never was one to believe in aliens. After all, there is enough evil in humans; why try and make some extraterrestrial beings to explain evil away? Mmm, of course, I don't know where you come from. Perhaps you are actually Earth creatures. A different species than Homo sapiens, amazingly similar in external structures, but fundamentally different where it counts. Yes, I do, I do know for sure that you are not human in the way we are human. I know I am right because you have put me out here and spent years trying to find out how I know. Of course I keep telling you, but, er, you don't believe me.

Ah, but I prattle on. Forgive me. Thank you for bringing the teas, and the ingredients for the curry too. The scent of fresh ground coriander is wonderful. Let me make you a cup of tea while I grind the spices. You said you preferred honey, didn't you?

Now, as to your first question, yes I will tell you exactly how I know you are not fully human. I have told you, I am telling you. I know you think it is more complicated, and that you can teach each other how to protect yourselves from my talent, remake yourselves and again be completely hidden from me, from us humans. But there is no technological solution that can keep people from finding out the truth. A turtle without its shell is still a turtle, after all. And a turtle inside its shell may be better protected, but it cannot move quickly; it is a turtle.

I am pretty sure that if you fail, you are eliminated. Am I right? Don't look away. It's obvious how fearful each of you gets as the contract end grows near. Obvious.

You don't wear a cologne. Most of you do. Because of that sour smell, like a mildly infected scab, just a bit of pus leaking from its edge. Have you gotten better at concealing that, or have I simply gotten used to the scent, no longer able to smell it as readily? But there it is sliding out underneath your sweat.

Of course you are uncomfortable with me. You all are. That is why they change caretakers so often. But I must say, you do have a nice smile. How old are you? Twenty-nine, thirty, or maybe much older, but benefitting from their surgeries? Don't be nervous. Er, what did you want me to call you—Marcus? Right? A very good name, Marcus. Lots of human history. I'm glad your kind is beginning to read. You were so boring before that. Everyone I was sent had nothing to talk about, and of course your kind tries to speak endlessly, especially since I have told you about silence.

It was that fact that got me out of the cage. *It is your silences,* I said, and then they put me through all kinds of lie detectors and truth serum treatments and discovered that I was always telling the truth, nothing but the truth. It was then that they decided to put me up here. And now it's been five long years with only your kind for company. But you know that, don't you? They realized that I had told them silence since the beginning, so the deprivation and torture weren't working. That's when they decided to put me here and try treats and seduction instead. Oh, treats and seduction and the occasional torturer. Hmm.

They send one of you every few months with a box of treats, fresh fruit, a real book, cake. And you, you brought it all plus the teas I asked for and what you claim is an underground tract to boot. You say it is written by a fellow prisoner. How amusing. Don't worry, I'll read it, if only to see what you want me to believe. Your hands are quite soft-looking. But you still look quite virile, nice muscles. Is that imprint in your jeans real? If so you are quite well-endowed despite your short stature. Or perhaps it is because of it, short torso long....

Oh my, I've embarrassed you. How sweet; you are just light enough to blush. Are you supposed to woo me? Hoping for a bit of loose pillow talk? But I have already told you all there is to know: It is your silence. In some of you I can tell by the way you breathe, so you may as well start talking again. Three sentences and you were done. You are trying to be quiet to hear what I hear. But you cannot. Maybe with machines and tracking, if you can measure silence, but you are unable to hear the difference. That is why so few of you are singers; few are even competent.

Yes, yes, how can I tell? Of course I will tell you. I will tell it all. I have waited for the right time and the time is now. I, er, tire of this cat and mouse. I tire of this mountain. Even though you have been here less than a day, I tire of you. You are trying to figure out what part of your silence reveals your essence. Squirming, shifting, frowning, shooting out the briefest of smiles, silently. Totally silently.

That was my important discovery, the one which brought me my original sentence of the living death of silences in a dark dry cage with powdered nutrients given four times daily and drugged water available whenever I wanted it and a video screen where I could see all the TV drama replays of news that never happened mostly performed by you empties. Sometimes humans got the roles; they are far better actors. You flatter yourselves because you have infiltrated so deeply. But it is simply that most people are so unobservant, so careless with their attention, so mediocre in their desires. But for those who are awake you aliens stand out like a swath of chartreuse in the middle of a white-on-white dress suit.

You smile. Yes, I know how chartreuse scares you all. In fact, all greens seem to make you nervous. Why is that? Of course I notice; I have nothing to do but notice you and your kind. None of your silly movies ever take place in meadows or forests. You love old westerns and interminable war pictures, and snow, what little of it is left, lots of snow. But you do like reds; my, you enjoy blood. To my knowledge I've never seen you bleed. Is your blood red? Or is it green? Is that why you flutter so at the very thought?

It was my observational skills that got me here. Those and my big mouth. Mindfulness was supposed to come with circumspection, but no, I'm blabbing all over the place. Yes, most humans laughed at me, ignored me, but your kind—they knew I spoke the truth and they trembled. They needed to figure out how I knew, how I could recognize you. And so quickly, too.

Yes, yes, I know what you are thinking. Get to the point. How can I tell? How? Not even a grunt, my handsome outlander? No, you are trying silence just now. Measuring me. Yes, I know you are trying to learn all that I know before you return me to my cage. You are so smug in your supposed values. You don't kill, you say. Unlike humans, you don't murder. You simply use humans to murder each other. And then of course you starve populations, create new diseases, destroy our ecology. You kill. You simply don't do death in a one-on-one fashion.

I must admit you provide some small amusement with your supposedly friendly interrogations and stoic quiet. These past years are so tedious, only one of your kind at a time to talk with. No communication with the outside, no communication with humans, so that my heretical ideas will not be spread. Oh, you frown so deeply. Not very convincing. You are clenching and unclenching your right hand. Yes, that's it. Relax.

Come, let me massage your shoulders. I love to touch flesh, even alien flesh. And you love to be touched. Most of you, anyway. Come on. We are stuck here, you and I, until the next envoy is sent. Until they decide you have failed. Tell me, do they really eliminate you if you fail? Oh, I am not to ask questions. The one before you was very strict about that. They sent a woman, you know, an older woman pretending to be Romani. She had long dark hair and bronze skin and crooked teeth. She swore she had lived on the streets of Sarajevo before being captured and sent up here, but it was a lie. Oh, yes, they had even given her tarot cards, so cliché, as if all Romani read cards or palms. Your kind has so little imagination. Of course, it was clear she was a fake right away. She called herself a gypsy. That's like me calling myself a nigger.

Again, you smile, halfway. Of course, you are supposed to be black, are you not? American black at that, so I suppose you think nigger may be acceptable. But I'm not a nigger, at least not your nigger—but are you mine, my pretty yella nigga? Ah, a bit of a bigger smile there. Come on, lovely almost-man, sit between my legs and let me run my fingers across your shoulders. They are close to your ears; they must ache. Let's not play games. I know what you are and you, well, you know as much of me as I let you. But we are here for a time. Let's enjoy ourselves. I'm sure that is the instruction you were given. Carrot, stick, stick, carrot. That is the way. I've had three sticks, it's about time for a carrot. And such a fine, long limber carrot, definitely good for the eyes. And maybe the teeth too. If you are very nice I might just nibble on your earlobes.

Goodness but you are tight. Don't you do anything but work out? Now back to your question. You slipped, you know. You said, "How do you know us?" not "How do you know them?" The last male they sent kept pretending to be human for a full week. We had some wonderful sex before he gave up. Simply wonderful. Your kind can be quite attentive. Oh, you move away. Please come back. You are too impatient. Are you a torturer, then? They are so much less patient, so much less patient.

Yes, I do suck my teeth. I picked the habit up from one of my aunts. She always sucked her teeth when she was frustrated or mad and didn't want to show it. But I don't grind them like you do. You are such a tight knot. Lovely, but stiff.

Come, let's walk outside. You'd best get something to cover those ears. You have no fat to keep you warm. You say you have a sled outside. Wonderful; we will go for a ride and have a snow fight and you will pretend to lose and I will feel very proud of myself and we will laugh and fall into bed and then I will whisper sweet nothings into your small flat ears. That is what you are waiting for, is it not? The secret, that one thing I have told no one before. Come, take a chance. I tell you what, if I like the ride I will tell you all of it. All of it. And you will promise to let me free because once you know the secret I am no longer a danger. We will both be happy. Come, let us frolic. I love that word. Frol and lick. Yes let us frol a bit and lick a lot, and then I promise we will talk. I will talk. How does that sound?

2.

What a wonderful sled, what a wonderful ride. Now I see why I did not hear you arrive. Instead of a copter they had you come in on a sled. I didn't hear its quiet motor until you were a few feet away from the door. And you were able to carry so much on the sled. I love the new coat and the wool socks and finally, some coriander seeds and turmeric. Umm.

But why a sled? Are some of your transports being shot down? Has the resistance grown? Ah, your silences destroy you. Yes, there it is. You see I have told you all you need to know. The last male they sent, he wanted me to call him Buck. Is that hilarious? I called him Jimbo. My little joke. He was so taciturn. When he became exasperated with my answers he would bellow and scream and his cheeks would turn red and make tiny beads of sweat rise under his eyes. The veins on his neck actually shivered just a bit and there was even the slightest sound of breath between his words, the breath of a winded man running too long.

No, I don't want to make love yet. You know, just for the record, we can't really make love. You see, you don't love me, and I detest you. It is such a shame because you are a fox, with your smooth caramel skin and thick full lips. Your nose is a bit pointed, but that's all right; it balances the slits of your eyes. Usually I like full round eyes, but your eyes make you look rather Indian. Very pleasant.

I tell you what: We will eat, we will drink tea and sit by the fire and nap a bit, and then I will tell you all you want and need to know. Of course

I already have, but I will be clearer. You will understand completely.

You need not remind me of how it was before. How could I forget, the way there was no time, only the endless gray. I never knew if it was three hours, three days, or three weeks in between interrogations. It was one long continuous drone, a light that never went out, a cot that I was allowed to see and sometimes even allowed to lie down on and fall asleep just long enough to be awoken. Then your kind would parade another through when I was half- asleep, in the middle of a dream when I was running arms spread down a long green hill eating the air and the nectar of honeysuckle blossoms as I ran free. Or sometimes I was put in a small dark hole in the wall looking out of a sideboard mouse hole opening and able to see only the scuffed hard-toed black boots that walked back and forth. Sometimes the guards would feed me and bring torturers in to question and harass and sometimes they would starve me and bring them in, always with one question: "How do you know?"

They would parade folk past me: human, alien, human, alien, and I would be fed only if I got every one right. And I always did. They began to suspect the humans were giving me signals, so they put me behind a one-way mirror.

The aliens would talk with the humans, who never knew the difference, but I always knew. Then they made everyone be quiet and all I could do was watch your breath, listen to your silence. And there it was; I would know the truth.

And you need not remind me of your gifts, how you made crops grow so much faster and thicker, how you gave us ways to kill unwanted insects and clean the water. Ah, but at a price; more and more of us die, and more and more of you arrive. You do arrive, don't you? I mean, if you were really simply a different kind of human, wouldn't someone have discovered it long before me? So many books have been written and movies produced about aliens with big black almond eyes and smooth white bodies that humans began to believe that that was what aliens truly looked like. But what if that was a subterfuge you invented? What if they looked just like us, but were simply different in the way they breathed, in the way they smelled, in their silences? Maybe the real aliens had no reverence for the human condition or humans and created ways to slowly kill us off until only they and their kind—you and your kind—were left.

Or are you simply more able to live in this environment, fewer types of animals, fewer numbers of trees, but more of you and fewer and fewer of us? Ah, but enough talk about death and dying.

Come, let me feed you. No, not just cook for you. Let me place these sweet morsels into your mouth. My hands are clean, my nails scrubbed. Yes, it is chicken. I know you are not supposed to eat flesh, but you love it. You all do. Come, no one but you and I will know. It will be out of your body in three days. That is why you must eat some tonight, in case they come to check on your safe arrival before the week is out. You will have the pleasure of the forbidden meat and you will have glory in knowing the truth. I am tired of the lies. Tired of the games. Come, I will give you what you want but it must be on my terms. I have spent five years trying to deny the simplest of information. And you, my Toussaint hero, you will be the one I finally open for. Come, it is a curry. A red curry. I know spices make you a bit drowsy. We have time. We can sleep, and later we will touch and sweat and groan and sigh, and still later I will tell you. Or perhaps before we wrap our limbs around one another and I listen to the silences around your moans, maybe then I will tell you.

Yes, lick my fingers. Hmm, they are sweet you say. Or is it the meat? Or is it the coconut milk? All of it. Every bit. I see your eyes are becoming heavy. Don't despair. Let me pick up these dishes and then I will bathe your feet and rub them until you fall asleep. No one knows but you and I what you have eaten. No one will know but you and I that you slept before I revealed the truth. What glory you will have. What honor. Come, my sweet guard. Drink this tea. Is it bitter? I made a special brew. Let me put a little more honey in, to soothe a savage beast. Yes, to soothe.

Give me your foot. So soft, you do not walk without shoes do you? Yes, you see this spot here? It is connected to where you digest your food. And this one over here? It connects to your lungs and keeps the air flowing. I know many things.

Yes, my dear, please, do sleep. I do know many things, how to brew teas, how to cook meats, how to rub feet. Oh yes, before you sleep, hold this thought: It is your silences that set you apart. That is all, your silences. Yes, sleep. Sleep. Ah, your head is becoming heavy. It was in the teas, you know. The teas and the liquor I have made from the rice given to me. I know your kind is so vulnerable to liquor. But it relaxes you, lets you appear more human. So I put some in the tea. Not poison, just a brew that with your metabolism would put you in a deeper sleep. I tried it on a few before you. I had to be sure it would work. Put you in a deep sleep. And you so obedient, my serious keeper, don't even snore. Always quiet, ever quiet.

You will not be the first I have bound. You will be the first I do not release. I will pull you outside and hide you in the snow cave I fashioned before you came. Bury you in layers of snow. How I have waited for the right season and for a man small enough that I could manage it. How I have waited for one young enough to be vulnerable to my touch. How I have dreamed that you would come. And I am sorry I did not have time to have sex with you. I would have enjoyed the release. But I cannot spare the energy.

Did you know I begged to go on a sled ride? Lied and said that it was one of my favorite childhood memories. Cried that winters were so hard, if only I could go on a sled. And here you come. How wonderful, how perfect.

So now that you are trussed and bound I see you are stirring. Yes, a bit awake, not fully. Do you dream? If so, perhaps you think this conversation is a dream, an invention. Well, let me tell you then. You see, I am a woman of my word. Hear me breathing in your ear, softly, so, so softly. Softly, but not silently. You, my attractive gremlin, have no sounds between your words. You are silent. There is a way we humans breathe and whistle between our words, pause and grunt or stumble and click. They are almost musical, the sounds between our words. When you remove the words, more than breath, there is a cadence almost like a fingerprint, individual and unique. I can even recognize different people without hearing them speak, just by hearing the sounds between the words.

But your kind, your kind are nothing but words and silence. For humans, it is the soul that fills the spaces between our words, it is more than breath, it is soul. And you, my alien compadre, are without that breath, without that soul. So, I have always told you all. It is your silences that tell me. I have always told you the secret. Umm. Always.

Foolish boy pretending to be human man. Such a foolish one. When they find you your legs and feet will be bound, your mouth tied shut. And you will be frozen in the snow. They tried everything. I knew one day they would slip. I have waited these years for them to slip and they did. In your terms, I too do not kill, my sweet pretender. But I know the truth, it is my hand that leads you to death.

Before your dreams turn gray and then black I will have packed what stores I built up over the past year, along with the new stores you have brought, set out on the sled and escaped. It was not easy rationing my food and burying it a mile away from the hut so no one would suspect. It was not easy, although it was fun, teaching myself how to make rice wine to cover the tea's bitter taste. Years of planning, my dear. Years of patience. Years of sighs and tears and so much patience. Things you would know little about, my alien breeder.

If I am lucky I will find a human outpost and be given sanctuary. I heard a human yodel last winter. I had always found yodeling most irritating, but I tell you when I heard the breath in between each phrase I was so excited. I laughed and laughed. I knew it was coming off of a mountain miles away. Who knows? It may have come from another captive. What do I care? Then there will be two of us. Two to struggle, to survive.

Yes, I could be recaptured and returned to a cage. But I will have some days of freedom. And I will take my freedom. And while I am free I will sing, and in between each note there will be the peaks and gullies of my spirit punctuating my breath. Always I am sound, even in my silences. Always you are silent even while you speak. So you have your glory, if only just before death, you have the secret. And I have my victory if only to be recaptured. Of course, there is always the chance that I will stay free. I take that chance. Ah. I will savor that chance. Ahhh.

Delany Encounters: Or, Another Reason Why I Study Race and Racism in Science Fiction

Isiah Lavender III

"Why study race in science fiction?" I have answered that deeply personal question a couple of times now without including the influence of Samuel R. Delany's work on me as a science fiction scholar.[1] My previous replies were sans Delany because I knew at those points, as I know now, that Delany deserves special consideration. In terms of my personal experience reading Delany, the dual nature of his influence as a thinker and as a creative writer requires my full self-awareness.

◊

Samuel R. Delany at his finest—black, gay, and erudite—remains a creative and critical force in science fiction. This opening statement encapsulates my many encounters with Delany's writing in my time pondering the significance of race and racism in the science fiction genre, although I first came across the work of Octavia E. Butler and Steven Barnes much earlier. Believe it or not, my first ephemeral encounter with Delany occurred during my initial grad school days at Louisiana State University in the mid-1990s. Science fiction scholar Carl Freedman had something posted about Delany on his office door.[2] It may have been a placard advertising Delany's essay collection *Longer Views: Extended Essays* (1996), or the Wesleyan University Press edition of *Trouble on Triton: An Ambiguous Heterotopia* (1976; 1996); I cannot be sure. Though we are now colleagues at LSU nearly twenty years later, I regret not having taken a class with Carl. However, I did not think of science fiction and fantasy as an academic pursuit at that time, only as a category of pleasurable reading and viewing. Besides, I was courting my wife Heather when not studying various facets of black American literature. My time was occupied.

I was also enthralled, though to a lesser extent, by the Dakota-verse and its black superheroes, particularly Virgil Hawkins, a.k.a. Static, which seemingly has nothing to do with Delany. I identified with

Virgil because he was locked in the "friend zone" with his best friend Frieda Goren and had no luck with dating, much like me in high school. However, his sharp-witted Static alter ego gifted him with self-confidence. Now, I could not channel electricity, but my intelligence worked to my own advantage in college through the bad poetry that I wrote from time to time. Imagine my fury and pain upon learning that an aunt of mine had thrown my cherished Milestone Comics collection (*Static, Icon, Hardware, Blood Syndicate, Kobalt, Xombi,* and *Shadow Cabinet*) in the trash when she moved to Atlanta! I practically owned every issue of that seminal line. In fact, my first publication was a letter of the month in the *Hardware* fan column *Hard Words*. Milestone even sent me a gold-foiled issue of *Hardware*. I'd love to get my hands on one of those again.

I could have sworn the letter appeared in issue 15. My chagrin at learning it was not hit me pretty hard. I bought a copy of this issue online and it was not there!

In hindsight, I should have never stored my comics and baseball card collections at my aunt's apartment in Baton Rouge.

Anyway, I had no idea that Delany wrote two issues of *Wonder Woman* and was so heavily invested in comics as a paraliterature. In his own words, Delany has "always liked comic books—which is the understatement of the age" because "of the unique things that comics can do" in providing the "visual realization" of storytelling (*Silent Interviews* 85-6). I did not discover this fact about Delany until much later in my doctoral studies at the University of Iowa, when I bought and read some of Delany's philosophical works at Prairie Lights Books in Iowa City, such as *Silent Interviews: On Language, Race, Sex, Science Fiction, and Some Comics* (1994) and *Shorter Views: Queer Thoughts & The Politics of the Paraliterary* (1999). My scholarly inclinations and ambitions might have turned to the speculative much sooner if I had known this information about Delany sooner. I would not have been so intimidated by the man's brilliance as a thinker and would have discovered his penchant for beautifully crafted sentences as a fiction writer so much earlier.

*Unbeknownst to Delany, he came to my rescue during the fall semester of 2000 at the University of Iowa. I was newly married, trapped in a particular way of thinking about mainstream literature, and taking a particularly intensive early twentieth century readings course in American fiction with a top professor, who I thought was tough, fair, and even likeable in his altruistic, colorblind way. The class had to read twenty influential texts in a fourteen-week semester. When you have to read Theodore Dreiser's *An American Tragedy* (1925), an eight-hundred-fifty-six page naturalist novel, in the forty-eight hours between your Monday and Wednesday class meeting times while teaching two courses of your own, you know the class is tough. I must say that I tremendously enjoyed Dreiser's book because of its influence on Richard Wright's classic black social protest novel *Native Son* (1940).

Nonetheless, I painfully recall the moment I discovered my professor was racist. A silver Ford Taurus had just backed into my wife's raisin-pearl 1999 Honda Accord. A dear white friend and classmate of mine, who carpooled with me from the Emerald Court apartment complex for the class, made for the perfect witness as the police accident report was filed. I did not know that he would be witnessing two events on that day. Needless to say, we arrived late for class with the most valid of excuses. My friend was treated with respect upon entering, while I received a cold shoulder and an unnerving glare from this white professor. Bear in mind, I was the only black student in this particular class of fifteen. It made me extremely uneasy for the rest of the class period and reticent to participate, which was unusual, given my gregarious nature.

Class was over when the moment of micro-aggression burst forth. While I was standing next to my friend, this particular professor had the temerity to say, "Never mind the car accident, Mr. Lavender." (This was the only time I was ever called "Mr. Lavender" by an Iowa professor instead of "Isiah"—which was more typical of the campus's laidback Midwestern atmosphere.) He continued, "I'm concerned with your insistence upon using reader response theory in your journals, whereas your peers are offering much more sophisticated arguments utilizing the likes of French and German philosophers such as Foucault and Derrida, as well as Nietzsche and Heidegger." Reader response theory focuses on the individual reader and his/her experience of the text, whereas other literary theories focus on the form of the work or its content or the author or the period in which it is written, or any other number of esoteric ideas. This professor implied that I was not smart enough to apply more popular theories to texts such as post-structuralism, with its emphasis on the destabilized or decentered meanings of authors separated from their texts in order to investigate others sources (like readers, culture, class, politics, race, religion, gender, etc.) for value in the books at hand. His remarks were belittling to me, as if to imply that my level of education was on a ninth grade level like Richard Wright's[3]—that my education was inadequate at best and that I didn't belong at Iowa.

Talk about a gut punch! This man utilized all the power and privilege granted him in everyday life by his white skin to reduce my intellect, to make me feel small, to humiliate me in front of my friend, and to alienate me from the program. And I am certain he was unware of the power of his words and the extent to which they harmed me because further classes went on as before, with the exception that I no longer participated in discussions. I no longer had the desire to try out my ideas in a roomful of my peers—a devastating thing for the intellectual growth of a budding scholar. I am definitely not Frederick Douglass, but he acted like the slave-breaker Mr. Covey! Douglass captured exactly how I felt at that moment in his monumental *Narrative of the Life of Frederick Douglass*: "My natural elasticity was crushed, my intellect languished, the disposition to read departed, the cheerful spark that lingered about my eye died...and behold a man transformed into a brute!" (73).

I remember the stunned and sympathetic look my friend gave me; I remember leaving the classroom and sitting in the stairwell feeling stupid, inconsequential, and disoriented while my buddy tried to console me with an expletive-laced diatribe against that particular professor's intellectual abuse; and most of all I remember discovering Delany's essay "Racism and Science Fiction" (1999) a short time later, reprinted in the back of Sheree R. Thomas's *Dark Matter: A Century of Speculative Literature from the African Diaspora* (2000), while writing my first ever book review for *Science Fiction Studies*.[4] Delany scrutinizes racism's systemic structure while tracing his own predecessors and successors in speculative fiction. He then shares a couple particular examples of racism from his own early career before offering possible ways of dismantling racism in science fiction by encouraging minorities to participate at conferences through panel discussions, open race dialogues involving writers and readers of different races, and confronting white comfort zones established by centuries of oppression.

Delany explains two moments of straightforward racism in his early career. First, the legendary editor John W. Campbell, Jr.—commonly recognized as the shaper of the Golden Age of Science Fiction (1939-1948) through his editing of *Astounding Science Fiction* magazine and handling his stable of writers (Isaac Asimov, Robert A. Heinlein, and A. E. Van Vogt)—rejected Delany's novel *Nova* (1968) for serialization because it had a black main character. Campbell spurned *Nova* after Delany won two consecutive Nebula Awards for best novel in 1967 (*Babel-17*[1966]) and 1968 (*The Einstein Intersection* [1967]) simply because Delany was black. In fact, Campbell was publicly hostile to conceding "civil rights for African-Americans" according to Albert Berger (187). Likewise, Gary Westfahl reveals how everybody in the science fiction community knew how "Campbell was a racist, a bigot, a sexist, and an anti-Semite" (50). At that point in American history, Delany was forced to accept Campbell's racial intolerance in order to have a long and illustrious career.

The second occasion occurred when Isaac Asimov flippantly called Delany a Negro in a private conversation at the 1968 Nebula Awards Banquet. Context matters here, because Delany had just been pilloried by the award presenter (who had not yet read Delany's winning novel *The Einstein Intersection*) in front of science fiction's leading lights as well as the author's mother, sister, friend, and wife. Delany's short story "Aye, and Gomorrah..." (1967) won the next award to be presented at that ceremony, too. While everyone applauded Delany as he left the podium and made his way to his banquet table, Asimov pulled him aside, leaned in and stated, "'You know, Chip, we only voted you those awards because you're a Negro...!'" (390) According to Delany, Asimov merely attempts to lighten the mood and ironize the tension with his well-known acerbic wit and really meant that race had nothing to do with Delany's victory, only the writing's high quality. Still, Delany never forgets this moment and recognizes that "the racial situation, permeable as it might sometimes seem (and it is, yes, highly permeable) is nevertheless your total surround" (391).

This notion of total surround applies to all people of color, particularly blacks in America. Delany's essay brought it home to me in stunning clarity. Consequently, I now understood what had happened to me in that English Philosophy Building classroom. This professor apparently did not realize the nature of his assault on my spirit, but I had yet another racial awakening and this time in the ivory tower of academia—the totality of this racial surround is profoundly real everywhere!

Delany's words proved the salve my nascent critical mind needed for recovery from this most bitter experience of my otherwise halcyon days on the U of I campus. "Racism and Science Fiction" changed the course of my graduate career. Truthfully, his brave decision to record these instances has clearly influenced generations of writers, readers, and scholars; it teaches us to stand up and speak out. Just consider his Clarion Writers' Workshop student Nalo Hopkinson, and the confrontational and instructional nature of her chapbook *Report from Planet Midnight* (2012).

I happened to be at the March 2010 International Conference of the Fantastic in the Arts, where Hopkinson first performed "Report from Planet Midnight" as the Guest of Honor speech. (In fact, I, along with Patricia Melzer and Kim Surkan, proposed the conference theme that year—Race and the Fantastic.) With a bunch of blue alien people/creature images from various films flashing on the screen behind her as she stood at the podium, Nalo looked up at us. Then her chin bounced of her collarbone and she was possessed by this alien ambassador. Here's a partial transcript of her speech:

Since none of the images of real people from your world show blue-skinned beings, we can only theorize about what these images symbolize or eulogise. Perhaps a race of yours that has gone extinct, or that self-destructed. Perhaps it is a race that has gone into voluntary seclusion, maybe as an attempt at self-protection. The more pessimistic among us fear that this is a race being kept in isolation, for what horrendous planet-wide crime we shudder to imagine; or that it is a race of earlier sentient beings that you have exterminated. Whatever the truth of the matter, we're sure you realize why it is of extreme importance to us to learn whether imprisonment, extinction, and mythologizing are your only methods of dealing with interspecies conflict.

Here are some of the other communications with which we're having trouble:

You say: "I'm not racist."

Primary translation: "I can wade through feces without getting any of it on me."

Secondary translation: "My shit don't stink." (36)

I was riveted by her performance and by her courage in delivering this fierce message to those particular members of the science fiction community, a largely white audience of writers and scholars. Surely some people did not understand the importance of this moment, but she received a standing ovation. And I believe that somehow, in some kind of way, Samuel R. Delany laid the groundwork for that moment.

*Of all Delany's writing "Racism and Science Fiction" unquestionably has had the greatest, profoundest, most emotional impact on me as a human being. But the essay which yielded the most influence over my critical thinking is "About 5,750 Words," published in Delany's first critical text, *The Jewel-Hinged Jaw: Notes on the Language of Science Fiction* (1977). I return again and again in my own thinking and scholarship to his notion of subjunctivity, the word-by-word corrective reading process used to analyze the literal metaphors of science fiction. Delany models a literalized metaphor with the sentence "The red sun is high, the blue low," by examining each word of this sentence through subjunctivity and how it only makes sense as science fiction (*Jewel* 7). He does the same thing with the image of a "winged dog" and the images of other writers like Heinlein and Philip K. Dick (*Jewel* 12). As Delany argues, "The particular verbal freedom of SF, coupled with the corrective process [subjunctivity] that allows the whole range of the physically explainable universe, can produce the most violent leaps of imagery. For not only does it throw us worlds away, it specifies how we got there" (*Jewel* 12). In this respect, comprehending science fiction comes down to understanding its language and how words are used differently from mainstream literature to create alien environments. Delany's critical writing functions as one of my ideal sounding boards for my explorations of race and racism in an otherwise white genre in my own book *Race in American Science Fiction* (2011).

*Mark Dery irks me (and I think Delany too) just a bit because he coined the neologism "Afrofuturism" after interviewing three astute black intellectuals (Delany, Greg Tate, and Tricia Rose) who establish some of the parameters for Afrofuturism. More than once, Delany indicts Dery's "interpretative idiocies" for lifting a book, in this case William Gibson's *Neuromancer* (1984), "out of its genre" (195), which indicates Dery's "historical misunderstanding about the history and tradition of science fiction" (202). Even more problematic for Delany, Dery uses "White writers for [his] science fiction template for thinking about the problems blacks have in America" (195). For me, Dery misappropriates the philosophical verve of Delany, Tate, and Rose by wrongfully taking credit for the term Afrofuturism. Delany, Tate, and Rose do the heavy intellectual lifting in the set of interviews, where they make trenchant observations about science fiction's relationship to black cultures and vice versa.

Unfortunately, Dery's limited definition has become the benchmark against which all other competing ideologies are measured. Dery states, "Speculative fiction that treats African-American themes and addresses African-American concerns in the context of twentieth century technoculture—and, more generally, African-American signification that appropriates images of technology and a prosthetically enhanced future—might, for want of a better term, be called 'Afro-futurism'" (180). Yet Afrofuturism is not just about technology and black uses of technology but is a way of viewing the world. That is to say, "our imaginings of the future are always complicated extensions of the past" (Nelson 35). Afrofuturism preserves "peoples of African descent, their ways and histories, [and ensures they] will not disappear in any credible future" (Kilgore 569). This sentiment is exactly why Delany believes that "if science fiction has any use at all, it is that among all its various and variegated future landscapes it gives us [black people] images *for* our futures" (*Starboard Wine* 31).

A case in point: It is Delany who first links slavery with Afrofuturism in "Black to the Future," not Dery. Slavery as the foundation of the US depended on the "systematic, conscientious, and massive destruction of African cultural remnants" according to Delany (Dery 191). (This parenthetical citation, Dery 191, is what vexes me so—some rich, white guy defrauding Delany's thoughtfulness, not to mention Tate's and Rose's, and defining my science fiction for me.) Delany gets it exactly right in identifying how the vestiges of the Atlantic slave trade have formed and reformed black cultures on both sides of the ocean, something readily apparent in science fiction written by blacks in the Americas and increasingly on the African continent. In this regard, Afrofuturism means speculative writing by black people in a global context. Consequently, hope becomes a core Afrofuturist concept embedded within the still-oppressive conditions that blacks face on a daily basis going all the way back to antebellum America.

Hope fuels the fundamental emotional drive that foments resistance, rebellion, and subversive writing by and for black people. Hope unsettles the white order of things. Hope also makes allies between the races. That's why I greatly admire the work of Mark Bould and Lisa Yaszek on Afrofuturism, among others.[5] To paraphrase Yaszek, there are three basic goals for Afrofuturism: tell good stories, recover lost black histories and their influence on contemporary black cultures, and think on exactly how such recovered pasts "might inspire" black future "visions" (2).

As I see it, Afrofuturism provides a set of race-inflected reading protocols designed to investigate the optimisms and anxieties framing the future imaginings of people of color. It's the first of the alternative futurisms related to race and ethnicity to emerge and disrupt the colorblind future envisioned by white writers, but not the last by any stretch of the imagination: Indigenous Futurism and Chicanafuturism have now gathered critical masses along with Asian American futurisms that refute yellow peril science fiction and techno-orientalism. Such a rich intellectual legacy belongs to the greatest Afrofuturist of all—Samuel R. Delany.

In truth, I have debated writing this penultimate section of my Delany encounters and re-encounters. This internal dispute centers on one question: "Who on Earth would want to hear about my favorite Delany novels?" Yet, the essay feels somehow incomplete without it. I think John Pfeiffer nailed my feeling for Delany's fiction nearly forty years ago with this declaration:

> Delany's work is a rich lode awaiting discovery by the socially conscious general reader. It could not exist apart from a bonefelt knowledge of the past and present Black experience. It extrapolates this history, rather, and its vision is of encounters with the racisms of a post-revolutionary age, subtle to the point of being metaphysical, presaging a future in which certain sociological problems of the present, then solved, must be met once again on the level of the individual. (37)

If Pfeiffer didn't do it, then Jane B. Weedman did thirty-two years ago when she declared: "Delany uses the distancing technique to approach his white audience with the realities of black culture...as the product of his double-consciousness" (11). And if the essence was not captured by Weedman's incisive remarks, then Sandra Govan's did so thirty-years ago when she opined, "Delany parades black characters across the spectrum of his speculative fiction not simply to attest to black survival in the future, but to punctuate his social criticism of our present" (48). If Govan didn't, then Takayuki Tatsumi surely did articulate my feelings twenty-seven years ago when stating, "As a writer, [Delany] has certainly been concerned with genres of minority literatures, for instance, science fiction, science fiction criticism, feminist literature, sometimes pornography or gay literature, and of course black literature" (269). Or if these older pronouncements on Delany's magnitude fail to capture my sentiments, then Jeffery A. Tucker did so a mere five years ago by testifying that "In Delany's work, science fiction presents itself as a genre that is particularly suited to, even a necessity for, contemporary African American intellectual inquiry, with Delany as a specific and exemplary model who guides his readers through a variety of webs—epistemological and semiotic as well as electronic" (251).

It seems I have no words of my own. Delany is a living genius, rendering identity politics in all of its manifestations and vagaries. For me, his portrayals of race and racism make all the difference in science fiction. Others treasure his representations of gay identity and alternate sexualities, his descriptions of social and political class designations, his masterful use of critical theory. My own list of favorite Delany novels follows in reverse order, in true David Letterman style.

#5 *The Einstein Intersection* (1967): Humans have left the Earth, and an alien race has settled down on the planet to live among the remnants of human culture. The story is told by Lo Lobey, a brown-skinned simian-like humanoid, who has the gift of music: he plays on his machete. The functional members of this alien society have titles such as Lo, La, and Le, denoting purity and normalcy among the race, whereas the unfunctional are caged, cared for, and killed when necessary. Lobey learns his music through old recordings of groups like the Beatles and by listening to his elders make connections between 60s pop culture and Greek myths such as Orpheus. The story centers on Lobey's search for his lost love La Friza through the debris of human culture as he encounters a giant bull underground, a feminine computer named Phaedra, killer flowers, dragon herders, and other functionals who are different such as Spider, Green-eye, Dove, and Kid Death. Delany suggests that we break away from entrapping myths through this absolutely brilliant race novel.

#4 Dhalgren (1975): I enjoy the challenge of *Dhalgren* and understand it as an ironic commentary on segregation. *Dhalgren* forced me to take my time, reading in five- to ten-page spurts on a nearly daily basis in order to absorb its many textures. Kid, a half-Native American drifter-poet-criminal in search of his forgotten identity, enters the stricken imaginary Midwestern city of Bellona, a city where the fabric of reality unravels. Some nameless disaster impacts this city to the extent that entire city blocks burn one week and are unharmed a week later; time dilates and does strange things; two moons rise on some evenings, or a gigantic sun rises and sets. For Kid, Bellona "is a city of inner discordances and natural distortions" populated by youth gangs, rapists, and murderers, as well as gays, transvestites, and local celebrities, in addition to questionably sane individuals (14). While othering himself in the process, Kid finds no resolution in this broken city despite trying out many identities not his own. The novel culminates at its beginning and continues to challenge me.

#3 Trouble on Triton (1976): The reformed Martian prostitute Bron Helstrom, immigrates to the Neptunian moon Triton in search of happiness as some kind of masculine ideal, as near as I can figure. Political and economic tensions escalate between the inner planets (Earth and Mars) and the solar system's outer moons, eventually leading to interplanetary war. Against such a backdrop, Bron does not find happiness, because of his self-absorption and the difficulty he has in forming meaningful relationships. He meets and falls in love with a theater woman known as the Spike, and loses her in his desire to possess her. Ultimately, he becomes a woman by undergoing sexual orientation reassignment and body modification in the hope of finding the male that he desperately wanted to be before the change. Bron as man or woman cannot be happy. This novel taught me a great deal more about identity politics beyond racial parameters.

#2 Babel-17 (1966): Galaxy-famous "Oriental" poet Rydra Wong is enlisted by the military to decode an alien language known as Babel-17 and help fight the invasion of alien humans. She puts a spaceship crew together herself to decipher the language from the site of the next incident. From the start of the mission, things go wrong: her ship communications are sabotaged, she realizes that there is a traitor among her crew, an important military official is assassinated in her presence, her ship is tampered with again, and she and her crew are taken captive, then rescued by a space pirate working for the alliance. While participating in the fighting, Rydra teaches a murderer named the Butcher the concept of "I" in language. Somehow, Rydra's mind becomes linked with the Butcher's through Babel-17, whereupon Rydra figures out that the language of Babel-17 is a flawed weaponized language. The novel ends with the Alliance turning the tables on the Invaders with the corrected language. Delany conveys that racial antagonisms can be overcome through communication—either that or violence.

#1 *Stars in My Pocket Like Grains of Sand* (1984): While many fans and scholars consider *Dhalgren* as Delany's masterpiece, I deem *Stars in My Pocket Like Grains of Sand* his magnum opus. I very much like the neo-slave narrative vibe of its opening sentence "'Of course'...'you will be a slave'" (3). The Radical Anxiety Termination technology that strips Korga of his identity to rid him of antisocial behavior and sexual deviance in conjunction with corporate slavery plain scares me. Rat Korga is the lone survivor of a cultural fugue event, a holocaust caused by socioeconomic collapse and competing political systems, that destroys his home world Rhyonon. Of course, the far-future setting, intergalactic empire, and love affair help me choose this novel as my favorite of favorites. Delany turns gendered language on its head with one simple change: every human being becomes "she" regardless of biology unless a person is the object of sexual desire and then becomes "he," again irrespective of sex. Thus, he creates something profoundly alien about gender by defamiliarizing language. The love affair between Marq Dyeth, ambassador to alien worlds and industrial diplomat, and Rat Korga threatens to bring about a second planet-wide destruction on Dyeth's own home planet Velm. The novel involves identity politics in every conceivable way—race, gender, sex, class, and family—and strips from us all forms of intolerance. Now that's powerful artistry.

*I hope my continuing self-reflection on why I study race in science fiction demonstrates my commitment. As the only black Grand Master of science fiction, Delany's work inescapably infuses my own. Indeed, Delany's worlds are fully occupied by all kinds of minorities, especially people of color, and I quite simply love that.

End Notes

[1] See my introduction to *Black and Brown Planets: The Politics of Race in Science Fiction* entitled "Coloring Science Fiction" (2014) and my essay "Black Grit: or, Why I Study Race and Racism in Science Fiction" (2014).

[2] See Carl Freedman's *Critical Theory and Science Fiction* (2000) as well as *Conversations with Samuel R. Delany* (2009).

[3] See Chapter VIII of Richard Wright's memoir *Black Boy* (1945), where he drops out of junior high after being named the valedictorian of his ninth grade class and refusing to read the speech provided for him by the school's principal.

[4] See my review of *Dark Matter*, "A Century of Black SF," in *Science Fiction Studies* 28.2 (2001): 140-3.

⁵ See Bould's essay "The Ships Landed Long Ago: Afrofuturism and Black SF" (2007) and Yaszek's essay "An Afrofuturist Reading of Ralph Ellison's *Invisible Man*" (2005).

Works Cited

Anderson, Sherwood. *Winesburg, Ohio*. 1919. New York: Dover, 1995. Print.

Berger, Albert I. *The Magic That Works: John W. Campbell and the American Response to Technology*. San Bernardino: Borgo, 1993. Print.

Bould, Mark. "The Ships Landed Long Ago: Afrofuturism and Black SF." *Science Fiction Studies* 34.2 (2007): 177-86. Print.

Delany, Samuel R. "Aye, and Gomorrah...". 1967. *Aye, and Gomorrah: and Other Stories*. New York: Vintage, 2003. 91-101. Print.

---. *Babel-17*. 1966. New York: Vintage, 2001. Print.

---. *Dhalgren*. 1975. Hanover: Wesleyan UP, 1996. Print.

---. *The Einstein Intersection*. New York: Ace, 1967. Print.

---. *The Jewel-Hinged Jaw: Notes on the Language of Science Fiction*. 1977. Revised Edition. Middletown: Wesleyan UP, 2009. Print.

---. *Longer Views: Extended Essays*. Hanover: Wesleyan UP, 1996. Print.

---. *Nova*. 1968. New York: Vintage, 2002. Print.

---. *Shorter Views: Queer Thoughts & The Politics of the Paraliterary*. Hanover: Wesleyan UP,
    1999. Print.

---. *Silent Interviews: On Language, Race, Sex, Science Fiction, and Some Comics*. Hanover: Wesleyan UP, 1994. Print.

---. *Starboard Wine: More Notes on the Language of Science Fiction*. Pleasantville: Dragon Press, 1984. Print.

---. *Stars in My Pocket Like Grains of Sand*. New York: Bantam, 1984. Print.

---. *Trouble on Triton: An Ambiguous Heterotopia*. 1976. Hannover: Wesleyan UP, 1996. Print

Dery, Mark. "Black to the Future: Interviews with Samuel R. Delany, Greg Tate, and Tricia Rose." 1993. *Flame Wars: The Discourse of Cyberculture*. Ed. Mark Dery. Durham: Duke UP, 1994. 179-222. Print.

Douglass, Frederick. *Narrative of the Life of Frederick Douglass*. 1845. New York: Signet Classic, 1997. Print.

Dreiser, Theodore. *An American Tragedy*. 1925. New York: Signet Classic, 2000. Print.

Fitzgerald, F. S. *The Great Gatsby*. 1925. New York: Scribner, 1995. Print.

Freedman, Carl, ed. Conversations with Samuel R. Delany. Jackson: UP of Mississippi, 2009.
    Print.

---. *Critical Theory and Science Fiction*. Hanover: Wesleyan UP, 2000. Print.

Gibson, William. *Neuromancer*. New York: Ace, 1984. Print.

Govan, Sandra Y. "The Insistent Presence of Black Folk in the Novels of Samuel R. Delany." *Black American Literature Forum* 18.2 (1984): 43-8.

Kilgore, De Witt D. "Afrofuturism." *The Oxford Handbook of Science Fiction*. Ed. Rob Latham. New York: Oxford UP, 2014. 561-572. Print.

Lavender, Isiah, III. "Black Grit: or, Why I Study Race and Racism in Science Fiction." *Deletion: The Open Access Online Forum in Science Fiction Studies* 7 (2014): n. pag.
Web. 6 October 2014.

---. "A Century of Black SF" review of *Dark Matter*. *Science Fiction Studies* 28.2 (2001): 140-3. Print.

---. "Coloring Science Fiction." *Black and Brown Planets: The Politics of Race in Science Fiction*. Ed. Isiah Lavender, III. Jackson: UP of Mississippi, 2014. 3-11. Print.

---. *Race in American Science Fiction*. Bloomington: Indiana UP, 2011. Print.

Nelson, Alondra. "AfroFuturism: Past-Future Visions." *Color Lines* (Spring 2000): 34-37. Print.

Pfeiffer, John. "Black American Speculative Literature: A Checklist." *Extrapolation* 17.1 (1975): 35-43.

Tatsumi, Takayuki. "The Decomposition of Rock and Roll: Samuel Delany's *The Einstein Intersection*." *Extrapolation* 28.3 (1987): 269-80.

Thomas, Sheree R. *Dark Matter: A Century of Speculative Fiction from the African Diaspora*.
New York: Warner, 2000. Print.

Tucker, Jeffrey A. "The Necessity of Models, of Alternatives: Samuel R. Delany's *Stars in My Pockets like Grains of Sand*." South Atlantic Quarterly 109.2 (2010): 249-78. Print.

Weedman, Jane B. *Samuel R. Delany*. Mercer Island, Washington: Starmont House, 1982. Print.

Westfahl, Gary. "'Dictatorial, Authoritarian, Uncooperative': The Case Against John W. Campbell, Jr." *Foundation* 56 (1992): 36-61. Print.

Wright, Richard. *Black Boy*. 1945. New York: Harper Perennial, 1993. Print.

---. *Native Son*. 1940. New York: Harper Perennial, 2005. Print.

Yaszek, Lisa. "An Afrofuturist Reading of Ralph Ellison's Invisible Man." *Rethinking History* 9.2/3 (2005): 297-313. Print.

---. "Race in Science Fiction: The Case of Afrofuturism and New Hollywood." *A Virtual Introduction to Science Fiction*. Ed. Lars Schmeink. Web. 2013. 1-11.

Clarity

Anil Menon

After the untimely death of his wife, elder-brother sold his apartment, gave me the proceeds, handed his eleven-year-old Chandini to our safekeeping, and took off for Kampala, where he owned a modest sports store. He hadn't been able to find a buyer for the glass desk and so that too had moved into our home, or rather, my bedroom, since it was too big for anywhere else. Three months passed and elder-brother hanged himself, may God rest his soul. It was only some six months hence, after Chandini had slowly but surely begun to count herself sister to my other two darling girls, Lakshmi and Parvati, that I let myself worry about trivialities such as an unwanted glass desk.

I will be blunt. There is something unpleasant about being able to see one's lower limbs as one works. There is such a thing as too much clarity. My missus had found this claim amusing but had to admit I was right after trying it for herself. Strangely enough, I enjoyed watching her work at the glass desk.

This amorous detail is an instance of the desk's inauspiciousness. That morning, had I not been thinking about the missus, missing her, looking forward to picking her up at the airport in the evening and the long chit-chat we would have thereafter, had I been paying attention to detaching the laptop's cord from the power socket, I would not have knocked the back of my head sharply against the desk's glass edge.

I must have cried out because Chandini came running into the room. What is it, younger-father, she cried, what is it? Her fright brought me to my senses. Does it hurt badly, she asked, and I said jovially: No, no, I just banged my head and finally calculus makes sense.

"You should get rid of the desk," she said, smiling. "It's a useless burden."

"Yes, first chance I get."

I bit my tongue only later. She had been seeking reassurance, and fool that I was, I'd flubbed the opportunity. I fired off a worried email to the missus who responded almost immediately. Single line, all caps: RE-

LAX, CHANDINI KNOWS SHE IS NOT A WRITING DESK.
I was less sanguine. A life can change in a look, a word, a gesture. Later, after making sure my girls were safely on the school bus, I set off for Somaiya College. Each day I take the harbor line from Dadar to Vidyavihar, and this morning, as with other mornings, the platform was crowded with the same set of familiar faces. Everyone had their favorite positions on the platform. Mine was to stand under the large railway clock. When the train reaches the platform, some of the younger, less-experienced office-goers lose their nerve and begin darting up and down the platform, trying to spot a relatively empty compartment. This makes professionals like me smile. Our friends are already holding places for us inside the train, just as we'll hold places for others further down the line. The secret to a comfortable journey, in commuter trains as well as in life, is having people look out for you. In any case, I enjoy the few minutes' wait.

As a mathematics professor, it hadn't escaped my attention that there were many nice mathematical problems waiting to be solved in this act of rearrangement, but it also hadn't escaped my attention I wasn't going to be the one cracking them. For instance, everyone knows it isn't surprising to spot a familiar face in a crowd of mostly familiar faces. But how do we spot a particular familiar face in a crowd of familiar faces? That is what happened. In the crowd of faces milling to catch the morning train, I spotted Martin-sir, my wife's old mentor and former Honorable Justice of the Bombay High court, now a resident of Nagpur. Martin-sir had made time in his very busy schedule to officiate at our civil marriage, a gracious act for which I will be eternally grateful.

The old gentleman had seen me as well, because a smile lit up his noble face. It had been several years since we'd last met, but he seemed to be exactly the same. We exchanged pleasantries and when I inquired about his well-being and that of his family, he told me that families, like gardens, were always in a state of becoming. His ghostly tone left me nonplussed. Was Nagpur very cold this time of the year, I queried. Martin-sir laughed, punched my shoulder jovially and said, Damn it lad, it's a wonder you managed to lasso that wife of yours. He promised to come for dinner, his mobile number hadn't changed, we would catch up at leisure, et cetera.

At the math department, I found the staff room in a hubbub. Ramki-sir, our probability guru, had been asked to be an expert witness for the defense in the Zohrab rape case. The actor was accused of assaulting his mother's nurse; the hospital had collected DNA evidence from the victim, but apparently hadn't handled it properly. Ramki-sir's articles in the Indian Express on the contamination of DNA evidence and the misuse of DNA matching had led to the present honor. He would have to shave his beard; he always shaved before a court appearance.

"But it's an open-and-shut case," said Mrs. Patwardhan, Statistics. "Zohrab confessed. He was drunk he says, but he remembers raping the nurse. He confessed. The police released the tapes."

"The police!" snorted Ramki-sir. "You'd trust *our* bloody police. It's a frame-up, I'm telling you. What you're seeing and hearing is all an illusion."

"Come on, Ramki-sir, she has a point," said Mrs. Balamurali, Linear Algebra. "The man did confess. Don't you feel the least bit guilty? You have a daughter."

That struck home. Ramki-sir slammed his hand on the table.

"It is because I have a daughter," he said dramatically. "I want the right man punished, not some poor idiot roped in by the police to satisfy the public's blood-lust. Rape and murder? No sir! Seduction and suicide. It doesn't matter Zohrab confessed. We can be made to remember anything.

"Take the case of Bradley Page, nineteen years old, accused of murdering his girlfriend. Not a shred of evidence, no motive. Nonetheless, the police lied to him, told him he'd been seen near the body, that he'd failed the lie-detector test, that his fingerprints had been found on the murder weapon. Sixteen hours of interrogation. Young Bradley begins to wonder if he could have killed his girlfriend and somehow 'forgotten it'. The detective interrogating him tells him 'It happens all the time,' and together they recover his lost memory. Imprisoned for nine years before the real murderer is caught. The bloody police—"

"But he confessed!" insisted Mrs. Patwardhan, looking around piteously for support.

"Yes!" echoed Mrs. Balamurali.

"I rest my case," said Ramki-sir. "You have just confessed to being idiots. Are you?"

Hubbub and *halla*.

"Confession or not, he will go scot-free," said Rajan-sir, Discrete Maths. "The entire system is rigged. Ramki-sir will do his *chamatkar*, the slut nurse will withdraw her complaint, the hospital will admit it mishandled the evidence, and we middle-class fools will continue to believe there is law and order in the universe. Why should we fight over what has already been settled?"

"It's all an illusion," repeated Ramki-sir, finger-combing his beard.

Noticing my silence, one of the teachers tried to draw me in.

"What do you think? Is Zohrab guilty or not? Or is it just an illusion, as Ramki-sir says?"

"Everything can't be an illusion if some things are to be an illusion. Even in a story, at least some things have to be facts. The Fixed-Point theorem says—"

"*Please* do not teach me the Fixed-Point theorem, sir!" begged Ramki-sir.

"The Fixed-Point theorem says—"

"Sir Isaac Newton to the rescue," crowed Mrs. Patwardhan.

"Actually, it's Jan Brouwer," I corrected her, "The Fixed-Point theorem says—"

"Please do *not* teach me the Fixed-Point theorem. I can prove you're biased, I'm warning you; I have a Brahmaastra and am prepared to unleash it."

"Ramki-sir, I wasn't aware we were locked in combat. All I'm trying to clarify—"

"Here's my clarification," said Ramki-sir. "Who is prosecuting the Zohrab case?"

I remember the silence in the room, the triumphant expression on Ramki-sir's highly punchable face, the puzzled expressions of the others slowly turning to surprise then excitement.

"His missus!" shrieked Mrs. Balamurali. "Really? Is that true?"

I had to admit it was true. I was almost as surprised as they were. To be honest, I had put it out of my mind. It is not the sort of thing I like to think about. These are the times I wish the missus were an LIC agent or some such thing. How such a decent Brahmin woman, devoted mother and loving wife, could also be a bloodthirsty piranha of a prosecutor is beyond logic.

My wife had only been gone for two weeks, but for all that, it had taken a toll. When I met her at Arrivals, I was very glad but strangely unable to show it. Perhaps she felt that way too, because we talked in a rather stiff way, as if the two parts of a whole had become enjambed. How was the flight? Did I have a cold? Was it still raining in the evenings? However, my daughters had no such reservations. They made a scene. They clung to their amma, loudly complaining of all my misdeeds. I was pleased to see the missus pay some extra attention to Chandini.

"Let's get going," I barked. "We can shoot the breeze at home."

"Oh, daddu can't wait to pinch amma's waist," said my eldest, and the other two monsters laughed.

"It is his waist to pinch," said the missus, cool as cucumber. "Your father has lost weight. I thought I told you all to take care of him."

In the Indica, with the girls squashed in the back, whispering God alone knew what amongst themselves, as I adjusted the gear the missus moved her hand over mine. And just like that, we were connected again.

"I want to go nowhere this weekend," she murmured, "Go nowhere, see no one, except you and the girls. Maybe not even the girls."

I smiled. "That is my plan as well. But what if I told you I met Martin-sir at Dadar this morning?"

She sighed. "That is not funny, please don't crack jokes about the dead like that."

The moment she said, "the dead," I felt a strange shiver run through me. Of course! Martin-sir was dead. He had died two years ago. We'd attended his funeral in Nagpur. Yet the memory of the morning's meeting was—then I wasn't sure any longer. Was my memory of an earlier meeting?

"He said that families, like vegetable gardens—" I began.

"Are always in a state of becoming. Yes, yes, I remember your telling me the day you met him. Martin-sir was really saying he didn't expect to be around much longer. We should have invited him for dinner. But what to do? It was my first big case; he himself called to tell me not to worry, that we'd all meet another day. Now it's too late."

I didn't turn my head because I had a terror of taking my eyes off the road while I was driving, but I knew without inspection that I had unintentionally hurt my wife. What on Earth had come over me to bring up that meeting?

"I'm so sorry," I said, quite vexed. "I don't know what possessed me."

She smiled, poked me in the waist. "Don't feel so bad, sir; it is simply the excitement of seeing me."

Yes, perhaps. Nevertheless, I resolved to tend to my family better. I considered the matter settled but Chandini, who must have overheard us, considered it otherwise. The missus came to know I'd bumped— "cracked" is the word she used—my head on the glass table. She and the girls took turns to inspect the area, and though their combined expert medical expertise could find nothing wrong, their recommendation was that I schedule a visit with our GP. I rejected their advice, but a few days, I found myself in the GP's office, with Chandini as guard, waiting to learn about the results of the MRI report.

The doctor's office had a TV tuned to the news channel, since there are few other things guaranteed to induce a desire to live. Zohrab had been released on bail. Per usual, the news item was an excuse to display a salacious album of violence the victim had had to allegedly endure. Or rather, had failed to endure.

"What is this rubbish?" I barked at the receptionist. "There are children here. Please change the channel."

She resentfully switched to the MTV channel, and since I'd spent my aggrievement quota, there was no choice but to endure this new form of violence.

The tests had confirmed, we eventually learned, there was nothing detectably wrong with me. Four thousand rupees down the drain.

"I hope you're now happy," I told Chandini, somewhat bitterly.

"Actually, younger-father, I'm now a bit hungry. Udipi?"

I always loved it when she wanted something. We stopped at an Udipi, not far from the quack's clinic. Once the waiter had taken our orders, I cast about for a suitable topic. We had been able to chat like old friends once. I asked Chandini whether she still kept a diary. She said she didn't and I sensed the distance between us increase. Stupid question. It's a fact that a girl whose mother had been raped and murdered would lose interest in recording reality. The fact seemed strangely unfamiliar, like I had avoided thinking about it and had just become aware of it. Yet I had to admit the fact, just as I also had to add an "allegedly," since whether Chandini's mother had been raped and murdered or had been seduced and committed suicide depended on which side of the courtroom one stood.

I stared at Chandini, as if I were seeing her anew. This innocent child, my brother's only daughter—no, my child—how she'd suffered. I was overwhelmed with emotion.

"It's okay," she said quietly.

I nodded, unable to speak. Some homes are protected by silence. My elder-brother, may God rest his soul, had been the strong-silent type. I had decided when the missus and I had gotten married that I would not have such a home. My home would be protected by conversation. I would say what I wanted to say. My children would say what they wanted to say.

"Chandini, your mother—your new mother—she is only doing her duty. She cannot prosecute without sufficient evidence. Hence the delay. His fame or influence has nothing to do with it."

"I know that," she protested. "Who cares about the Zohrab case? I don't hate anyone."

I looked at her closely. "Do you really mean that?"

"Younger-father, I'm old enough to see things clearly. Anything can happen in this world, I know that."

"Yes, but we all need justice—"

"Younger-father, that I can love is the only justice there is."

"My dear child." I didn't care if I embarrassed her; I grasped her palms. "How did you become so wise?"

"Amar Chitra Katha," she said humbly.

She smiled when I laughed, and we talked more easily. She liked history, considered the ACK series a reliable source, and as someone who taught history for a living, I was torn between encouraging her interest and shattering her illusion. When I eventually remembered that the missus would be waiting to hear about the MRI results, Chandini said she'd already SMS'd that I was fine.

I was less sanguine. I felt fine, physically. I slept well, ate well, and moved my bowels regularly. I was virile as ever. Nonetheless, there were these odd slippages in my life. Like the morning I got up convinced I had three daughters instead of two.

"Where is Parvati?" I asked, at breakfast. "She'll be late for school."

"Who is Parvati?" asked the missus, baffled.

"Our child, who else?"

They goggled at me. I sympathized with them. I knew exactly how they felt. I only had two daughters. What Parvati, who Parvati? I knew as well as I knew the five fingers of my hand that Parvati existed only in the gaps in my head. My wife developed this amorous little smile that said: my dear sir, we can discuss a new baby but not in front of the children! Ha-ha and hee-hee from my two monsters.

It was all very entertaining for others, but for me, a terror began to haunt my soul. How can I describe this terror, especially in an age where the existence of the soul has been disproved? My wife sensed some of this turmoil. How could she not, when what happens to one happens to us all? Or has science disproved that too?

"Is everything all right?" she asked, touching my forehead. "Ever since I decided to drop this accursed case, you have been out of sorts. You understand why I had to drop it? In the absence of evidence, Zohrab is innocent. I cannot manufacture evidence. Even if the man is suspected of raping and murdering my sister-in-law. It is a sacred principle, the foundation of law and order. Tell me what I did was right; give me clarity."

"You did the right thing." I saw her in the battlefield of life, face resplendent, bow in hand. Life had assigned me to be her charioteer. I would drive her wherever she wished. "What is the use of a principle if we abandon it the moment it becomes inconvenient?"

"Then please tell me what troubles you," she begged, her voice wobbling. "I want my jolly husband back."

I confessed then that I feared I was going mad. I told her I remembered things, bits and piece of things, things that had never happened. For example, I had this crazy idea we had three daughters. I was terrified, I told her, I would awake one day to find that I only remembered having a wife. Her face relaxed slightly, as if I'd confirmed something she'd been suspecting for a while.

"What nonsense you talk," she said tenderly. "As if you will ever lose me. I know what the problem is. I have been working too hard, we don't see each other much, that is why. I will cut back. It pays really well, but let this job get over, I will cut back."

We talked for a bit, she made some hot chocolate, we took out albums, we perused the photos of our family, birthdays, sports days, holidays, remember this, remember when. After a while I began to see the stupidity of my concerns. I told her so, and she sighed with relief.

"They're not stupid. Let me tell you a real incident that happened with me also. It will blow your mind."

She told me of a pet poodle she'd remembered loving greatly as a child, then discovering in a conversation with her father that the family had never had a pet anything, let alone a filthy dog. My mind stayed in one piece and her story comforted me. She'd recounted this incident once before, only it had been a pet cat in that version. If her mind could forget, then so could mine.

In the bedroom, post-ablutions, I waited for her to get into bed, then turned off the light. The missus said in a sleepy voice: watch your step. But I didn't need the light. There was a full moon. The glass desk, a ghostly blue in the limpid moonlight, guided me to my wife's side.

"Are you still looking to sell it?" she asked.

I had placed ads both online and in print. No takers. I rewrote the ads, made the desk sound more tempting, re-shot the photos. No takers. Eventually, I lost all sanity and began to post completely imaginary details. Once I gave the desk fluted golden wings. Another time I claimed I'd found it buried in a Peruvian rain forest. Still later, I boasted it was Samuel Delany's personal writing desk and the real reason behind his success. I gave the desk clawed feet, headphone jacks, iPhone chargers, scaled it to golden rectangle proportions, and photoshopped religious symbols on its corpus. No takers. There did not exist a fiction that could sell the glass desk. If I threw it from a six-story building, it would probably bounce like a rubber ball and settle back in my bedroom.

"Don't sell it." My wife was almost asleep. "The desk has no duty to perform whatsoever and that somehow comforts me."

My wife had been fond of the desk. I remembered her request. I told my brother I'd been able to dispose of everything but the glass desk. He and his wife would shortly arrive to take me to the airport and take Chandini with them. I sat at the desk, neither here nor there, neither in time nor outside it, caught in the twilight of all things. Chandini came into the room and stood by my side. Seeing my poor darling, I still felt compelled by duty, if not belief, to offer hope. I reiterated, I advised, I comforted. I failed.

"I'll be all right, father. There is no need to worry about me."

"Yes, yes," I told her, clasping her hand to my cheek. "Let me set things up in Kampala and I will send for you."

"When, father?" she asked.

The quaver in her voice stabbed me to the core. The Buddha, it is said, touched the Earth so that she would bear witness to his words. Oh, for solid ground. I took her hand, touched the glass desk.

"As soon as things are a little clearer."

When Two Swordsmen Meet

Ellen Kushner

"Writers who (as it were) fetishize straightforwardness, yes—and see high style as a way to achieve it. That's [Sir Thomas] Browne's legacy. But not clarity."
— Samuel R. Delany

1.

When two swordsmen meet, no one knows what to expect.

It's a cold night in a cold city. Cold stone under cold starlight. He walks down a deserted street, sure of himself, sure of the weapon he bears. He's not altogether surprised when the stranger steps out of the shadows.

"Hey," he says to the newcomer. "You hungry? I'm going to friends with a fire and a big pot always bubbling on it." By which we see that it's not just his sword that defends him, whatever he may think.

The other stands very still. "You're not what I thought you'd be," he says flatly.

"Why not?" the swordsman asks, curious.

"The way they talk about you, I thought you would be all embroidered gloves and studded leather."

The swordsman nods. He's used to being misunderstood. "So are you hungry?" he asks again.

"Not for friends. Not for a bubbling pot of stew."

Slowly, the swordsman nods. "Fame and glory, then. Studded gloves and embroidered leather."

Without another word, he draws, and the other man does, too.

It's almost too easy. This kid—he can see it's a kid, now—is sure of his own moves; he was clearly top dog in all his classes. Good ripostes, full of verve and aggression. But he's not always sure how to respond. He should be thinking more about defense. That's something you polish with time.

The kid's got his lower lip caught in his teeth. *Relax your jaw*, the swordsman thinks; but he's not his teacher. Instead he says, "Fame and glory? There's no one here to see you. No one will know. Ah! Nice move."

"Thank you. You'll know."

More aggression now. The swordsman is having to enlist his own flawless defense. Not what he expected.

"No silks," the kid pants, coming at him the length of the cobbles. "No leather—"

Was there something underfoot? Too dark to see what it was, or if it was, or if it's just a kid who badly needs to win making him give way; but the swordsman finds himself on his back, with his opponent's point at his neck.

"What I want," the kid says. He pauses. "I don't think the word has been invented."

"Maybe it's not a word." He's never been able to be anything other than himself. If the kids wants him to die, here, that's what will happen. But he doesn't think that's what the kid wants.

"When I hear it, I'll know it. You're not it."

On his back, he nods his head—submitting, acquiescing, but also asking permission.

The other grants it with a similar nod.

He reaches into his jacket, pulls out a card, a Deuce of Lions. Across the corner is scribbled:

The House of Nine Doors
KOLHARI

"Here," he tells the kid. "Go here. They'll know what to do with you. Strip down, and you'll be shouting more words than you ever knew before."

Without a word, the kid takes the card, sheathes his sword, and walks in the direction he wasn't coming from. The swordsman gets up, and, without dusting himself off, proceeds to the place of food and friends.

2.

When two swordsmen meet, no one knows what will happen.

He's thinking of jewels. Which is not surprising, since he has them secreted all about his person. And *secreted* is the *mot juste*: It is a secret, a big secret, that he has even met with the one who gave them to him. (They are rumored to be mortal enemies.) A secret that he has been trusted with them. Him, and only him.

The idea is that no one could imagine them being transported thus, without a cordon of security—and that he alone has the requisite skills to ensure they reach their destination, anyway.

It is well done, and neatly thought of.

He tries not thinking about jewels. Jewels in little pouches, sewn into special pockets all over his person, here, there, and everywhere, by a master tailor who knows every trick, so that not a single bulge reveals itself.

He whistles a tune he heard a girl sing once, something about sack and sherry. He doesn't remember the words. But better not to whistle; don't want to draw attention. On the other hand, any implication that he doesn't want to draw attention could draw attention to him. This is a city of thieves. And he is passing through the higher reaches of the town, streets of fancy shops. He needs to look like a man without a care, like he belongs there—no, as if he's on his way somewhere pleasant, not important, a picnic, or drinks with an old friend, on the other side of town. Just passing through. No jewels, no intention.

> *I gave her cakes, I gave her ale*
> *I gave her sack and sherry. . . .*

A woman coming from the opposite direction. Singing the song he was just whistling. A coincidence? Maybe. He has his eye on her nonetheless. She is small and lithe, grey-eyed and dark-haired. She isn't looking at him, though; she's looking at the shops, their wares laid out on boards elaborately carved and gilded, because this is that kind of street, trays of goodies depending from the sides of the shops themselves. When night comes, the display tables will be drawn up as shutters and heavily bolted. Right now, though, they're open and displaying just a fraction of the lovely things inside, each one guarded by a self-important apprentice wielding a heavy baton.

His reflexes are too good. When she stumbles, crashes into a board, sending strung pearls and carved lapis tangling to the ground, when the 'prentice goes for her with his baton, the swordsman throws himself in the way, shouldering the 'prentice off, letting her grasp his forearm before she can go down.

He thinks she'll make a run for it. But to his consternation, she just stands there, looking every bit as haughty as a woman that small can do. The 'prentice is torn between seizing her, and catching up all the precious wares before anyone else on the street can grab any.

"Here," she says to the apprentice, "I'll help."

She hasn't apologized for the fall. But before too long, everything is back up on the boards, nested in their velvet as before.

"Count it," she tells the flustered apprentice. "It's all there."

The swordsman should have gone his way; but that would have

looked suspicious. So he stays.

A little crowd has gathered, of course. "Should I call the guard?" someone says.

"Count it," the woman says again. "Or call your master if you will, and let him do the work. I weary of standing here under the implication of insult."

Despite himself—or maybe because of it—the swordsman smiles. She doesn't smile back; she doesn't even look at him. She hasn't thanked him, either.

"It's all here," the apprentice says at last. He nudges a final pearl back into perfect place. "Everything is as it should be."

She continues to stare at him, her grey eyes sharp like steel. The unspoken word *And?* hangs in the air.

"And I'm very sorry, miss—milady."

Finally she smiles, showing good white teeth. "Never mind," she says. "A natural mistake. It could happen to anybody."

The crowd parts to let her pass on down the street.

Relieved, the swordsman walks on the way he was going. What an odd woman! He wonders if he'll see her again. He's a bit shaken; this little excitement was not part of his plans. It will take him a while to start whistling again.

Especially when he touches one of the secret pockets of the sequestered jewels, and finds it empty. There is a small slit in the side.

3.

When two swordsmen meet, no one knows what to expect.

One of them is bearded, the other clean shaven. Each bears a long and elegant weapon with a surgeon's point and a razor's edge, each hilt a work of art, guards scrolled like the fine script of a legal document.

They meet at a crossroads. That is where significant things happen; everyone knows that. Encounters at a crossroads are rarely by chance, and never inconsequential.

The clean-shaven man says nothing. He is slim and young. He draws his weapon, for no apparent reason.

The bearded man has been around awhile. He knows his worth. "I don't fight with strangers," he says, and the other says, "But you've seen me before."

"Where?" asks the bearded man.

"In your dreams," the younger swordsman replies. He wears no gloves. His hands are chapped, rough, the veins rising on the back where his right fingers hold tight around the grip.

He has a companion, a weedy-looking fellow, dark like a crow, who cradles some kind of funny harp in his arms. The musician stands well back, at the edge of the point where two roads meet and form a V.

The bearded man, the dreamer, examines them both. He hasn't seen them in his dreams—or if he has, it was so long ago he has forgotten—but he wants to, from now on.

Still, it doesn't do to look weak. Speak first, or thrust last, but always maintain the upper hand.

"I don't want to kill you," he says.

"Don't, then." The hard-handed man throws back his head, showing off his bare neck, a pillar of light and shadow. "But by all means engage."

"A playful duel? A duel of skill?"

The other nods. "That's right. A game, only."

"What are the stakes?"

"Let's play for luck. Let's play for memory."

The bearded man inclines his head. "And him? Your friend?" When he sees him from the corner of his eye, the strange musician does seem to mean something to him. But how? So young.... "What does he play for?"

"He plays for love. Some of us do."

It's a beautiful fight. They each want the other to win. Not so much duel as duet.

Halfway through, the young musician lifts his device and plays. The air is full of the scent of cinnamon, of city streets, of cigarette smoke and diesel fuel; of baking bread and new-cut oranges.

When two swordsmen meet, no one knows what will happen.

But something always does.

For Sale: Fantasy Coffins (Ababuo Need Not Apply)

Chesya Burke

The sign outside Hello Design Coffin Works read, FOR SALE: FANTASY COFFINS. But the little girl imagined more ominous words floating just below the other letters, *"Ababuo Need Not Apply."*

Many people in Accra bought these beautiful caskets on time, and often took many months and even years to pay off one of their expensive death homes. But no matter, her credit in that city was worthless and Ababuo knew she could never get one. The girl chided herself, but she stopped at the storefront, and stared into the window. Without being able to suppress the urge growing inside of her, she entered the threshold of the tiny building. Fantasy surrounded her within, proudly displayed. Closest to her was a giant, man-sized statue of an eagle. The bird's head was held high, its eyes large and knowing. The bird's body was adorned with feathers, brown and beautiful, its beak and talons yellow and bright. This was a strong bird, proud. That meant that the (more than likely) man who would be folded and stuffed into the narrow opening in the back of the carcass was also strong and proud. Perhaps he was a bird lover or pilot. It didn't matter. Although the coffins often represented people's professions, they just as often represented the wants and desires of the people entombed within them. Across from the wide-eyed bird was a hammer, standing almost twice as tall as she, and more than half as wide around. Its owner would likely have been a carpenter or something. Only a person with a love of tools would want to spend eternity in that thing. Ababuo smirked. It wasn't that the hammer was ugly, per se, but it was not what most people would choose out of admiration or simply a love of the craft—instead, this tool represented honor, skill, pride.

Then she saw it, sitting across the room in a corner as if forgotten. A beautiful, small white elephant. Ababuo made her way over to the coffin, touching it carefully. It was striped like a tiger, with ears too big for its head. But it was lovely. White Elephant was barely large enough for the tiny body that would grace its shell for all eternity, but Ababuo wouldn't mind leaving a limb or two behind to find peace within the belly of this gorgeous creature. She stood for a long moment touching the tiny white tusks and then the thick sturdy legs. The girl patted the elephant's side as if it was real, closing her eyes, imagining that this coffin actually belonged to her. How morbid it was, she knew, to long for nothing more than to choose her death bed. But the truth was that in this room, nothing mattered to Ababuo because nothing was real, nothing was solid, tangible. She wasn't cursed within this room of fantasy coffins—simply because she could never possess one. Perhaps knowing her life was so short caused her fixation with death, her eternity.

"What are you doing here?" Ababuo slowly opened her eyes. She didn't have to turn around to know who had spoken. It was one of the owners of the coffin shop—the son. Too bad; the father was much nicer. "You can't be here. You have to leave." He walked up to her, but didn't touch her. That was the rule.

"I was just looking. No harm in that."

"No point in that either, is there, girl?"

"I can look. I just want to see them. That's all."

"Not here. You're a *Nantew yiye* child. You must go." Then he whispered, "It's dangerous." As a "safe journey" child, Ababuo knew all too well her position. This man did not hate her. In fact, in his own way he probably simply wanted to save her the effort of wanting something she could never have.

Behind her someone spoke. "Dangerous? Pft!" Ababuo recognized the woman speaking as Accra's first lady, the wife of the newly appointed mayor.

The son backed a respectable distance away. "I was just...trying...."

She walked up to him, closing the distance he had set between them, "I know what you were doing. You should be grateful to this child. You're disgraceful."

◊

Most of the world will never know the sadness of an unfulfilled desire to have a fantasy coffin. Most of the world doesn't even know what a fantasy coffin is. And most will not care. Thus is not the case with Ababuo. Her strongest desire in the entire world was to have her tiny body crammed into the frame of one of those monstrous carved wooden boxes and get buried in the earth of her precious Ghana when she died. Well, that wasn't entirely true. Her foremost desire was to never need a fantasy or any other coffin.

But neither of these was the fate for Ababuo. Her soul was not pure enough for burial, and the earth would reject her body, and punish those who had offered her as a gift to it. The last time a Nantew yiye child had been buried in the Ghanaian soil, the clouds had opened up and flooded the land, killing crops and several people in the process.

And not dying would leave the people of Ghana without her protection. That couldn't happen. No whole group should suffer for the wants of one person. Ababuo understood this. Her job was to protect the people of Ghana, not harm them.

Either way, her thirteenth was coming and she had to make a decision.

The girl closed her eyes, hoping to clear her head of those thoughts. As if in answer, someone knocked on the door of the home she shared with her caretaker, paused, and then knocked again. Ababuo opened the curtain and looked down at the man from her bedroom on the second floor. The man glanced up at her and looked around as if he didn't want anyone to see him there. Ababuo was sure that she saw shame displayed across his face.

After a moment the man was let in and Ababuo's caretaker tapped on her door, then opened it. "It's for you, child."

The girl sat very still, "This is ten, you know? Only three more."

"We all have a burden, Ababuo. This is yours." The woman sounded harsh, but she did not meet Ababuo's eyes. They would lose each other soon.

Without further discussion, Ababuo sauntered down the stairs, taking one at a time. She was in no hurry to do what was needed of her. At eleven, Ababuo shoulders were broad and strong, as if hinting at the woman she would never become, but she was still just skin and bones.

While she followed him, Ababuo let her mind wonder about the girl she had seen just the day before. Ababuo had never met anyone else like her, but this child had been chosen to take over after Ababuo had fulfilled her duty. She was only seven years old, so tiny, so frail looking. So much like Ababuo had been a few short years before. Ababuo hated the thought of what would happen to this little girl when she had fulfilled her own duty to Accra; she felt guilty and ashamed.

The man led her to a path through the woods. Without looking back, he entered the tree line and the dark swallowed him fully. Ababuo hated the woods at night; she always seemed to get bad feelings in there. The trees seemed to whisper to each other and though she felt she knew them, she never fully understood what they were saying, as if there was a big secret that they kept from her. She hesitated at the woods' opening, which seemed to suck all light into a vacuum. The hole looked endless. Nothing but blackness greeted them, despite the moon that shone directly overhead.

This was not good. Ababuo had always gotten feelings about things. She just saw things more deeply than others. It was second sight, her caretaker told her. Ababuo was special. She had been born with a caul covering her face, so that she could always see the way, the old woman had said.

Ababuo knew by experience that this void that she saw now was a sign. One that she couldn't ignore. She looked back, took a deep breath, and then followed the man into the darkness.

Half a mile later, the girl could see the light of the moon shining through an opening in the tree tops. Past the tree line at the woods' end and across the railroad tracks it followed the pair, silent as they were. Just as the man reached the railroad tracks he stopped, looked at her. She never really knew how to react when people needed her services, never knew what to do or even what they wanted. She walked closer to him, and he pointed to the tracks. She hesitated for only a moment, and then reached out and touched the cold steel with the tip of her right sandaled toe. Suddenly she was transported into another time, not long before this night, but not completely on the same plane on which she had arrived either.

In this parallel place, there were children. Ababuo counted them. Seven. Four girls and three boys. They had all snuck out of the house to go to the graveyard just across the tracks, through the trees. Ababuo watched the children, simultaneously wishing she could be one of them and fearing what was to come. She would not be there if something terribly tragic hadn't already happened.

"Look," one of the little girls yelled. She was a twin of another child there that night, a little girl. "There it is." The kids loved the way the moon shone on the cold, marble tombstones. The way the beams bounced on the writing made the words look almost as if the names were dancing on the light. And that the dates were the amount of time that they'd been going. It was magical. They loved this place.

The forest was dense, and they'd had to walk single file just to get through the trees. They all had played in these woods since they were able to walk, as had Ababuo, so they weren't in fear of getting lost. But that didn't stop their minds from running wild in this place every single time they ventured here. The night, the trees, the moonlight, the grave stones, the polished train tracks, the dead.... It was spooky. But the kids seemed to relish this in a way that Ababuo never had; she could feel their anticipation growing, while her own fear made her cower.

The distant moon seemed to do nothing for the darkness in these woods and only served to make the surrounding trees look more sinister. As the group entered a clearing, Ababuo looked up at the stars in the sky and closed her eyes. She had been getting increasingly nauseated since entering the woods and now she couldn't ignore the feeling any longer.

Something was wrong. More importantly, something was going to happen. Something she felt down deep. Something bad. She swayed, lost her balance, falling to her knees, reaching out to touch the tracks with her free hand. The world around her swam as if she were trapped in a pool of water, drowning. She began sinking in its unknown depths. She couldn't breathe. Couldn't see. She was in the dark place, though her eyes were open. She had been here before. Exactly nine times before. She would experience it another two times before it was all over. She knew the pain, the fear, the sorrow. But she understood now that this pain was doubled. Two souls would be released tonight, and she was one soul closer to death than she had been only a few moments ago. The total was going to be eleven, not ten as she had expected.

Knowing what to do, Ababuo spasmed and began falling deeper into the dark place, letting it consume her completely until she was there, that night. The world around her spun out of control. To the children, she appeared as if out of nowhere. As she appeared, she saw that the younger of the two twins' legs had gotten stuck on the track and she couldn't move. Her sister worked desperately to get it out, but it just would not budge.

The train approached.

Ababuo could hear it charging forward: a constant chug-chug-chugging coming closer, like the minute hand on a giant clock ticking down to destiny. The other children were screaming, but Ababuo did not focus on them. She could not. She was not here for them. They had survived that night.

With the train chugging nearer, the bright headlight getting brighter, Ababuo grabbed the twins, and pulled them both close to her. A spark of energy went through the group, as if though a live electric wire. Just as the train reached them, she held out her hand to stay it, not letting it demolishing these children again. She spoke with words that weren't her own but were honest and sincere.

"Your grandma," Ababuo said to the girls, "misses you. She's waitin' to see you both again. Tonight. Finally." To those around her, Ababuo's voice sounded very much like her own, but to Ababuo her voice sounded like an old woman full of years she had yet to see.

"Who are you?" one of the twin girls asked, as her sister held onto her, not wanted to let go. Ababuo understood why: they had been born together, and they would leave the same way.

"Ababuo, a Nantew yiye child. I came to help you."

"You can't, we do this always. The train." The girl looked on as Ababuo strained to still the locomotive destined to tear through the children. "It's okay. It doesn't hurt much anymore."

Ababuo fell to her knees again, feeling the weight of the heavy train, but not letting it go. Her eyes showed only the whites of time that passed as she spoke, "You must go."

The older girl shook her head, "We don't have anywhere to go."

"Into me. Come into me. I need you as much as you need me."

The train was so heavy now. So very heavy.

The older girl looked to her sister, ever the protector. "Will we breathe again?"

Ababuo smiled. "With your mind, your heart. Never again your lungs. They hurt too much."

Without warning the girl's foot was released, and the two took each other's hand and merged into Ababuo's body, swallowed by her essence. She consumed them fully. They no longer suffered, but they were not extinguished. Instead they breathed, without lungs or the need for air at all.

At that moment Ababuo forgot about the train, letting it go as she relished the girls' within her. The steel bullet slammed into her knocking one of her shoes off, throwing her backward twenty feet. She opened her eyes to the girls' father standing over her, holding back tears.

He seemed to want to help, but he was not allowed to touch her. She was considered too pure to touch, but really she just thought that people were afraid of her, and that suited her just fine. She could stand on her own. That was why she had been chosen. She said simply, "They belong to me now. They're free."

The man nodded and walked away, his face downcast. Ababuo stood there a long time after the man left, not really thinking about anything. She didn't really *want* to be thinking about anything, least of which those little girls who were now somewhere beyond their father's reach, the father who would not see them again for many years. The father who had loved them.

The girl made her way home, alone. She could barely walk, as she had taken on the real injury of the memory train and it would take a long time to heal. She died a little more with each of these souls, as she helped to lessen their pain. That was the worst of it, she thought. She suffered for them, she suffered great pain for them, and yet they never even seemed to notice. They never seemed to care. But she didn't want to think about it anymore. She was too tired. Too young, too worn.

◊

Accra, Ghana was Ababuo's first love. She loved it and in its own way, it loved her too. Accra was a part of Africa, like every other city on that continent, but Accra did not represent Africa, speak for it, or call it as one. Just as Ababuo didn't represent the people of Accra, and she only helped and complemented them as any part does its sum.

But if Accra was her first love, then the waterway extending from Lake Volta held her heart within its waves and calm, still surface in a way the land could not. Lake Volta was said to be the largest man-made lake in the world, and if you followed it far enough, it emptied out into the Black, White, and Red Volta Rivers. Ababuo had never seen those rivers in person. In fact, she had never been outside of Accra or even seen the whole of Lake Volta in all its glory. This waterway was the closest she had gotten. It was tiny and pathetic; most fish or marine life couldn't survive its shallow depths. But she didn't care; she liked the idea of this underestimated water source flowing silently into the biggest manmade river in the world. It was connected to both man and nature in a way that Ababuo herself understood. If no one else in the world did, Ababuo understood.

Behind her, rhythmic song disturbed the silence of the day. She turned to see a group of people leading a procession through the small wooded area beside her precious waterway. Although she realized this was a funeral, she momentarily resented the interruption. Most people didn't come here, as no good fishing could be done from its shallows. But besides the Gulf of Guinea on the other side of the city, this was the closest one could come to a water source. And that was the point, it seemed. The mourners were followed by a group of men who carried a giant, blue-painted, wooden whale on their backs, its tail curved high toward the sky. Ababuo stared as the procession marched its way to the final burial site somewhere beyond her sight. The man stuffed into the whale-shaped box was probably a fisherman, and they had chosen the site near the water to honor him. Although death is a time for mourning in Accra, it is also a time for celebration. People celebrate the life and accomplishments of the dead so as not to forget that they were loved, and a valuable part of the community. This was what they did for this man now. This was what no one would do for her.

After a moment, Ababuo turned to face her water again. She closed her eyes and allowed the calm waves to release her frustrations. There was no point in being angry at anyone, and jealousy was simply unacceptable. What sense did it make to envy a dead man? She who lived every day hoping not to die.

Ababuo didn't realize that someone had walked up behind her until they had been standing there a full minute or longer. She turned and saw the mayor's wife in her colorful attire. The woman had a way of showing up unannounced. "I thought I saw you here, Nantew yiye." The way most people spoke her title was scornful, but on this woman's lips it was lovely, valuable.

"I didn't mean to disturb you. I'm sorry."

"Why should you be sorry? You were here first. I'm Serwa. We weren't properly introduced the other day." The woman looked back toward the festivities. "My son. He was a fisherman." Ababuo nodded. She figured the woman simply needed to talk and it didn't matter who she spoke to. "All we have left of him is his wife and unborn son." A tear fell from the woman's face; she wiped it away quickly. "Why are you here alone?"

"I like the water."

The woman stared at her. "I'm sorry for you, Nantew yiye. I saw you go into the coffin shop the other day...and I was curious. There are so many rumors...about you. The things you can do. But still, I pity you." The woman wasn't being rude. Ababuo had experienced worse things than being pitied by her neighbors.

"Have you ever thought about escaping? Leaving all this behind?"

Ababuo didn't answer for a moment. Perhaps Miss Serwa was testing her loyalty to the people of Accra. "Why would I do that?"

"Freedom, dear! Everyone deserves that."

◊

Miss Serwa came for her that evening. Something had gone wrong in the delivery of the mayor's grandson. Perhaps the woman had known something was wrong, or perhaps it was simply a coincidence that the two had met prior to this. Ababuo supposed it didn't matter.

The woman walked into her room without the benefit of a knock, then closed the door before her caretaker could enter. Ababuo stood to her feet and let the woman speak: "I will not take from you without giving." She paused for a moment, was silent as Ababuo had been earlier, lost in thought. "Most people can't offer anything in return, so they suffer without coming to you. But I offer you freedom if you help me tonight. I will take you away, help you escape, if you save my son's son."

The city passed by her automobile window in quick, bright flashes that were almost unrecognizable. When Ababuo reached the house, Miss Serwa took her hand and led her to the room where the doctor stood over the mother, his hands between her bloody legs.

"What is she doing here? I told you none of that witchcraft while I'm here."

"And I told you, doctor, that you do not make decisions for me or my grandson."

"Send her away, I warn you." The man was angry. He stared at Ababuo as if he had never hated anyone more in his lifetime than this girl.

But before he could speak again, the pregnant woman screamed and pushed, her face bloating with air, her eyes bulging in pain and fear. After a moment, the baby slid into the doctor's hands, its breathing rushed and rapid. Without a word to inquire about her child, the mother closed her eyes, unable to hold them open any longer. She and her son were in distress; neither would survive. Ababuo could sense it from where she stood in the doorway.

"Send her away," the doctor demanded again.

Ababuo looked up at the mayor's wife, untwined her fingers from within the woman's grip, and walked over to the mother and child. All she had to do was save the kid and get whisked away to *freedom*. That word sounded so sweet, so peaceful.

As she reached the other side of the room, the doctor stood and moved out of her way, as if she carried the plague. Ababuo touched the mother's stomach, feeling the blood and energy flow too rapidly from within her. The baby was just as bad. His head was warm and his mind was unfocused, cloudy. Ababuo could sense the life slowly drain out of his body. Ababuo could not save them both.

Thirteen. That was it. That was how many souls she was allowed to save, both dead and alive. She had only two left within her to save. But she had to save one for herself. She had sacrificed enough. She hesitated for a moment. Without giving it another thought, she grabbed the child, placed her mouth over his, and sucked all of the illness and cloudy residue in his mind away. She held the child to her, her entire mouth covering his nose and lips. She breathed in, feeling all of the sickness within the child enter her body, fog her soul, overwhelming her senses. He was so tiny in her hands, so cold and scared. Newborns, she had learned, understood little and feared nothing but light diminishing from their too-new souls. When she released him, he began to cry, loud and strong. Miss Serwa smiled and lifted the child from her arms, hugging him. Crying, she laid the baby in his mother's arms and caressed the woman's face. The dying woman did not move, or hear her son screaming within her arms.

"You must go." Miss Serwa kissed Ababuo. "My men will take you to a secluded farm. You can stay there as long as you want. Thank you." She looked back at the screaming child: "I'll take good care of him."

Ababuo walked to the door, stopped, and looked back at the mother still unable to hold her child. Then her eyes fell on the soon to be motherless child. She had lived thirteen years without a mother. A caretaker was no substitute. Before she could regret her decision, she ran to the bed and took both the mother and child into her arms. She placed her mouth over the woman's nose and gave her life away. Death slowly left the woman and entered Ababuo, her body becoming weak. When her knees gave out her body slumped to the floor. She drifted away before knowing whether to regret her decision.

This was her thirteenth. The same number of years she had been allowed to live, only to die and not be buried in Ghanaian soil, but burned, as if a witch in punishment.

◊

The mayor's wife carried Ababuo's body down stairs and laid her on the sofa. The following day she commissioned a fantasy coffin for Ababuo. A sarcophagus: such a lovely, tiny thing, reminiscent of those of Ancient Ghana's kings and queens. Miss Serwa had only one requirement: that the coffin remain buoyant in shallow waters for no less than thirteen days, keeping her promise not to bury Ababuo in the soil of Ghana. The mayor, his wife, and their family celebrated in a private ceremony by setting Ababuo's body to sail on the waters of the small waterway which led into the Volta River, so that when the earth quaked only the depths of the sea life felt it and mourned for this beloved and simultaneously unloved child.

Holding Hands with Monsters

Haralambi Markov

I learn early that some children are born to be stalked in the dark.

The monster comes when the last light in the house is turned off. He smells of musk and forbidden thoughts. I fear him first as he makes his entrance from below the bed. He sounds like a breath pushed through an unstable telephone line: hazy, warm, and ripe with the threat of some danger that leaves me wet and marked with gooseflesh.

Then I see the light from his eyes as he slides from underneath: bright and golden like the sheen of crumpled candy foil wrappers, sweet and inviting.

Don't look at him as he leans over and smacks in your ear, waiting patiently.

This is how you survive the night. This is how you survive the monster in the dark.

Something I've had to do for years now.

◊

A rustle comes from behind my back.

I'm a grown man now. I live alone in a small apartment with a small bedroom that doesn't allow me to place my bed against either wall, unless I want to sleep beneath the window or block the bedroom door.

The sheets peel off my back and the bed creaks underneath the additional weight, trying to find a new shape to accommodate the second person.

The monster.

It's the first time he comes to bed and he's not bothered by the lamp on my desk in the corner. He's human, or at least that's what he feels like when his skin touches mine and our legs entwine as if they've belonged together since before the kingdoms of eras past rose to power and fell. His breathing finds a steady rhythm, lapping at the small of my neck.

This shouldn't be real, couldn't be real, and I imagine my therapist in his crisp pants and a white shirt that's somehow so tight around his chest the fabric around the buttons warps until tiny crescents reveal his skin and hair underneath. His words ring clear as if he says them to me right now: Monsters don't exist. Open your eyes. Confront what you think is there. Then the Latin words flow from his mouth, scientific poetry that transforms into colored pills in orange bottles—rattling in my hand as I chase away my demon.

Monsters aren't real. I relax my eyelids in preparation to fight, reestablish my boundaries and claim my bed back. A chilling breath laps at my nape again and I squeeze them tighter, until it hurts so bad it feels as if I've gone blind.

His breath is cold and sharp and reminds me of those winter games my father and I used to play in the park near our house—a small plot squeezed between several apartment buildings where the winds would fall, wild and sharpened by their January travels. The gusts would bite and freeze, have you pant with frosted exhaustion and pray the electric heater would chase their bite marks off your flesh.

Nothing happens that first night. The monster lies spooned against me cold as a corpse, but I catch my breath every time I try to make my lungs work. My heart pumps faster than I have ever known it to. I want to tear the sheets and run; every muscle twitches with the desperate desire to escape and although I freeze, my insides burn with the strain to keep myself from screaming. This tension stretches into infinity.

I let a steady breath out, eyes squeezed shut, and wonder what changed. How did the monster change? He's behind me and I mustn't see although I want to, so I let my body act as a pair of eyes. Yes, there's the cold, but against my skin I feel every line cut through me. Fuzzy hair presses against me and his chest is firm, rigid, and tough. Perhaps he's chiseled, or taken with rigor mortis.

That's not how I imagine it would happen. There are no teeth. No hands wrapped around my throat to turn me around and face him. No dirt-stained nails that crumble soil on the sheets to pick my eyelids apart and look into his eyes. Acknowledge his existence. End it all. That first night sleep doesn't come. Nor does it come the following nights for he joins me every single time afterwards, pressed against me, the big spoon in the relationship and technically I am up all night with a man in my bed.

I joke around the office about him, index fingers always at the bags under my eyes. Every mention of him makes him more real at night; the bed dips lower under this newfound weight, this unholy gravity he accumulates from my words. I don't perform so well at work, though.

Harsh computer light punctures my eyeballs until all the boxes in the spreadsheet fill with a nauseating shade of red, like diluted menstrual blood. And when I rest my eyes at my desk I see a face outlined. I catch it as I blink and the thought that I'd actually see his face scares me into blinking less and less. Infection claims my eyes by the second week, and I'm given a sick leave. The company doctor fails to hide his surprise at my condition and I feel less again, like those times in high school when all the other kids knew what I was. It never had to be spoken. It never had to be admitted. They knew. An instinct told them I was off and now the same happens here. The doctor spreads the news about my infection faster than a used needle spreads a blood disease.

In the meantime I learn how to sleep with the monster that comes into my bed every night. He continues to spoon against me. Sometimes when I go into the bathroom and the lights in my bedroom are already turned off, I can spot the shape of him in the bed, patiently waiting for me to assume my place in front of him. I can see the golden glow cast on my pillow. That's when my breath catches again and I consider sleeping in the bathroom, but that never happens. I turn off the switch and I close my eyes, the one rule that's saved my life for so many years looping in my mind—Don't open your eyes. Those are the nights when I bump into furniture and stumble into my bed, which is colder than normal. It's always cold as I lie on my side and wait for him to press against me, his breath a regular meter, a constant, the throaty beating of a clock in the dark. He smells of a fresh grave, which I feel is where I belong. That thought is too scary, though, and my therapist, whose shirt is still too tight around his chest, recites his verses in Latin again. I want to trust him. I want to believe he's capable enough to remake me, to rewrite my chemistry, to reconfigure my brain. Make me not hurt. Make me not hide.

He tells me to imagine the monster's breath is the breeze on the pier during a visit to the funfair with my family on a late summer afternoon. Imagine the lamps and the carnival music, the smell of greasy carny food and chatter of people who speak of love, affection, and brighter futures. Imagine all these layers over this breath that hisses like the ocean before a storm and reeks of sweet rot.

I try and try.

Sooner rather than later I catch pneumonia and a nasty ear infection. I can't explain the truth about how I got them. The doctors can't explain it themselves. As a patient I'm guilty, defeated and yellow.

"We'll get you fixed up, bro," my brother says with forced cheer as he arrives with packed suitcases. He's the younger one, yet life somehow has assigned him as my caretaker. Always there to mend my life, the sinking boat. No matter how much I empty it, it continues to fill and sink. I can't talk to him about what's happening. When we were little and he used to trust me, I'd tell him about the monster, but childish interests don't last, and my stories held his attention less and less until I stopped talking.

"Are you all right?" He breaks the cheerful act eventually. He has that hurt look that says "I can't go through this again." "Answer me honestly. Otherwise, I don't know what I'm doing here. Is this your new way of hurting yourself? Like that time...." He can't even say it, say I swallowed a whole bottle of pills.

No. I shake my head, too sick to form words. The pain and exhaustion catch up with me. He goes into my kitchen to play vigil, while I lie in my bed wrapped in blankets. The monster doesn't show for a month while my brother is here on leave; an act of kindness he'd remind me of in the future. I should be in a hospital, but I don't have enough to pay for the bills, so my kind brother takes care of me day in and day out. I gradually get better, but then he leaves.

He has a family now, one that doesn't come with baggage as heavy as mine and I'm alone in my bedroom, without a job or a future. After the eye infection, I've lost the endurance to stare at screens for too long and all I have to do all day is to stay at home and sleep. The monster keeps me company, his limbs intertwined with mine.

Sometimes he nuzzles at me and I feel his nose like an ice cube, circling at the small of my neck until I'm stiff with pain. Every morning and every night I spend hours in hot baths. I boil water and pour it in just to feel my blood rush and the pleasant sting as it scalds me.

I fear hypothermia might settle in.

Soon he progresses from doing nothing to foreplay. His fingers creep down my waistband and I shiver from the touch. It doesn't matter if I cover myself with a blanket. He always finds a way and he's there, resting his hand on my cock. Fingers play until I get hard, because by then I am used to it and I hope for the touch of his fingers. In the dark, they feel like icicles so I can't say if they're stubby and fat or long and bony. All I feel is the freeze, but they still get me excited. I still get hard.

It's been a long time since anyone dared touch me and eventually I turn to lie on my back, so the man-monster-freak leans over me, his cold hard chest pressing on my left, his face resting in the nook of my neck. I look out when I'm sure I can't see his eyes and my body gleams a golden hue, as if I've embraced a neon liquor store sign.

Stubble rubs my neck raw as he moves his face with the rhythms of his hand. I come in his grip and he brings his hand to his mouth first before presenting his half-licked fingers to mine. The nails, sharper than anything I've ever come in contact with, cut my lips as I accept the offering, and my mouth fills with the taste of life and death at the same time: savory, sweet, and bitter. His digits are cold and he doesn't seem to mind when I bite down to the bone and grind my teeth sideways in a cruel game to get them to warm up. Pain apparently doesn't register with him. His breathing doesn't change. My tongue plays with his nails, my tip lacerating on them until my mouth fills with the taste of blood and it's not bad. Whatever this is.

My brother calls to see how I am. Somehow I sound better. As if the nightly emissions with the monster have given me some measure of health. The lies I tell my brother make him stop calling. Yes, I'm fine. Yes, I'm healthy. Yes, I'm looking for a job. So easy to tailor a reality that couldn't be more different, but I do feel happy and I have grown to expect the hours the monster spends with me. His breath changes now as I run my hands all over his body and touch him the way he touches me. His cock hardens in my hand, which goes against everything I know of dead bodies, because technically he is dead. I can see the death in the mornings when he is gone and the sunlight shows the stains. The smell doesn't bother me. Neither do the sounds when we fuck. I dream of his kisses. First limp and tentative, later hungry and violent. Devour me, I scream at him and he does, in a way. He sucks and bites on my flesh, tender from a lifestyle behind the computer screen, down and down until he takes me whole in his mouth. I run fingers through his coarse hair, which is tangled and snags when I try to roam, but that never disrupts his rhythm.

In the mornings I follow the bloodied flowers he's left me on my body—red angry scars as thin stalks and deep bite marks that bloom in purple. They don't hurt though, these wounds of love. My skin has been anaesthetized by his cold and all sensation is periphery, yet somehow he makes me climax harder than I could make myself with my hand or a dildo. We graduate to penetration four months in.

I see the faint golden shine through my clenched eyes as he pushes into me relentlessly, his hands like vises on my ankles held high and spread. We don't speak and I can't say whether he loves me, though I think I may have fallen in love with him. He finishes in me and his deposit is cold as it leaks out. Sickness has abandoned me. Existence has abandoned me.

Sustenance matters now. I remember to open the fridge at one point and see only mold. How long has it been since I ate anything other than the products of our love making? I still take hot baths to remember what it's like to feel warm. The rules now have me do them with the lights out and the bathroom door locked. Towels cover the windows and it's as dark as a womb. A slice of cold cuts through the scalding water and a splash announces his appearance in the tub. His flesh almost takes on the warmth of the water as he grabs me by the shoulders and pushes my head under the water.

His palm rests on the top of my head as I struggle to get out and when I'm ready to give up he allows me to chase for air and kisses me then, his breath filling my lungs. I test his limits and he allows me to push him around, strangle and submerge him in the soapy water. That makes me burn inside in a way I never have before.

He doesn't protest. He's just there. He takes it and it's good. Soon, though, all the thrills become as cold as his body.

I try catching more glances of him. In the bathroom, I leave the door open so I have a sliver of light in the room, but otherwise it's complete darkness. He still comes in twilight to take me from behind, and I see the outlines of his body. In the glimpses I catch of it, his skin looks dusky with decay but otherwise intact, and I see tattoos run up his arm. His hairy knuckles carry symbols that remind me of spells and rituals caught in the flesh, made for those who would become enraptured by him. I drape around his right arm and embroider it further with my kisses, bites, and scratches. Just to see whether I can damage him, affect his reality. Do I have any power over him or not? There is no blood in him and my attempts to make him feel something add scars, but nothing more. There are no weeping wounds.

"I love you," I say to him in the bathroom and he places his palms on my hips and we dance in slow circles on the bathroom floor, feet bare, and as we circle I see more of him as he crosses the light. I expect him to dissolve or burn.

No smoke, no sizzle. Just cold white light on cold dead skin. He changes, though. I know his bodies. He comes to me in many men. Whenever I'm in the mood, I've envisioned him with skin in every color created by the human genome. I have felt him short. I have felt him tall. I have felt him with a different size in me.

Now I believe he is pale with a hint of some other shade that death has bleached. The tattoos, their lines distorted by decay, even wrap his feet, which to me seem bony, flatter than my own. Bigger in size to keep his body balanced.

The dance ends with us in the bathtub where we push the limits of how long I can hold my breath underwater while he's pounding away. It's the burning pain in my lungs that's the only warmth I feel anymore. Yes, I see the burn marks from the scalding water as it claims my skin in red, but there's not much sensation there. Warmth and pain have been winking out. The only thing I can feel now is the hard freeze of his touch and the nonchalant arousal that he brings to my life.

"Say something," I beg him, but he only gives me a smile I can sense curving in the dark. Maybe his breathing will change, but he never says a word. Do monsters speak? His language so far is one of kisses, bites, and scratches. A Morse code written in sex, and I lack the vernacular to express my thoughts—not that I haven't tried.

One night he comes to me in the kitchen. I keep it dark on purpose. Just a few candles to bring outlines to the tools I've prepared. All the knives, peelers, and graters in a neat sterilized line. I have boiled them so they're pristine—a makeshift surgery playroom for us. I introduce his shoulders to the peelers, his legs to the graters, his buttocks to the knives, tracing love lines that elicit old blood way past its expiration date. Yes, there is some in him, deep down, and I try to draw it out like that time I tried to make a summer lantern out of a watermelon with my cousin. The watermelon was dry, but still released milky pink liquid.

He doesn't protest as I do this to him and we do it on the table, me covered in more of him than any other man, a different taste in my mouth now. Ever since that night I smell off in a way I can't wash away and it changes me more than having sex with him ever has.

I feel guilt. I feel inhuman. I feel like a monster.

All I have is darkness and golden light staining everything. It's a maddening sensation to be in such a trap for so long. One day I want to see him fully. A flashlight sits at the base of my bed and a thin long rag is in my fist. As he comes without fail, I wrap the fabric around his eyes so they don't end me and I grab the flashlight in my hand. Time to face my nightmare and see what this thing really looks like. My finger slides over the button and my muscles twitch as if I'm forbidden to exert my right to know. The light is weak and it doesn't belong in my room any more at night.

His face is beautiful. Sharp features, soft skin rippled with blond fuzz that at a certain angle looks red as if he's lapped up blood recently and couldn't get the drops out of his beard. His skin reflect the light with a tan that may be the perfect bronze of too much life in the sun or carry the hue of some other ancestor. Nevertheless, he knows my preferences and allows me to illuminate him in this limited environment. Light in small doses, especially an artificial light doesn't, can't hurt him. And I've tried.

Months pass and we've fucked in every way. Ever since that time in the kitchen, I sweat a lot but what my pores secrete is something else— thicker, and sweet. He loves it and laps at me until the sensation of his tongue on my skin makes me insane. The love I think I feel turns out to be a yearning of the body that messes with my mind. I'm tired of holding hands with monsters.

Eventually I know I can't do this anymore. This has to end and killing him won't end it. Summer announces itself, and I soak up the warmth during the day. The searing heat feels good. I remember slowly what it is to live. My brother visits me at the beach and I bathe my pale skin in the light, but I never burn.

I start working again. Freelance design, something I promised I would do long before I had to settle for practicality and the expectations others set for me.

The money I make goes into buying floodlights I install in my room. All contain bulbs that imitate sunlight and as I lie down with a sleep mask tightly placed around my eyes, the bed no longer creaks and I learn sleep. I learn warmth. I learn peace.

The sweating continues and smells even stronger.

I smell it on myself. A strange scent that marks me as off to the others. Then I sense it on my sheets, a discharge from my pores that lets me slide and slither, until I find myself on the floor in a puddle. The landlady complains and no matter how much Febreze I buy, I can't mask it. I change flats, spend time to scrub myself clean, get in a tight diving suit, and rub oils on it to mask the smell. The new landlord doesn't notice and the room is isolated.

There I see my fingers grow harder nails and my teeth sharpen until I stab my mouth a little every time I chew. Then the scales come. I imagine they're rot at first, transmitted by him, but then I see the pattern and feel the texture.

It's then I know that what he gave me wasn't death and that he wasn't just a corpse.

I'm a monster now. I crave blood. I dream I eat the landlord's black lab over and over. Crunch its neck and swallow the animal whole. My jaw flexes open and my throat expands and squeezes the body the way my anus did whenever he changed sizes mid-thrust.

The day I see the dog and my mouth waters is when I turn off the lamps and wait for him, more monster than human. He does come. I see the golden light spill underneath my bed as he makes his entrance and it's a special sort of entrance as I can now see his true form, not the shapes he'd present for my sake. I can now see in the dark as if it's day and the shape of him is glorious, human but not quite. It is as if I'm seeing a creature humans once battled or once were. His eyes glow with burning intensity as he stares, but he doesn't devour me when he sits on the bed.

I try to say something, but I can't. The teeth have all grown to the point where my mouth has lost its mobility. He takes my hand, which now belongs in his.

Darkness is water we submerge ourselves in and he guides me as I dive into the black pit beneath my bed and go to his place.

Song for the Asking

Carmelo Rafala

Day 5

Mutiny is a swift predator: brutal, bloody, an entity without mercy. We had been locked in the hold of the ship for our own safety. From the decks above our heads, shouts, gunshots, and the sound of running echoed down the stairwells and airshafts to pummel the steel door that kept us alive.

Me.

The boy.

The woman in the cage.

When the bloodshed is finally over, we are let out and assemble on deck with the remaining crew. A few men, hand-picked by Master Hautalo, stand with weapons drawn.

The bodies of the dead are wrapped in white sheets and carried upon shoulders. As a Brother of the Church I am asked to say prayers over the departed, and the dead crewmen are dropped into the sea, one by one.

The few who remain loyal to the captain sit in one of the skiffs, now hanging over the side of the ship. Hautalo speaks to them in a low, steady voice; then he steps back while Jenko and a crewman named Marl, a plump and red-cheeked Northern man, lower the craft into the water. Oars in hands, the men push themselves away.

Their chances on the open sea are slim.

Out here.

Where the raiders of Estua-Nin roam.

I watch the men row toward certain death, and offer them a silent prayer.

The boy is looking up at the cargo crane, mouth open, face ashen. Tied high upon the beam is the captain's bloodied corpse. It is a sign of his shame—and Hautalo's newfound authority.

"Avert your eyes, my son," I tell him.

He bows his head without a word.

◊

I take the boy back near the stern of the ship, behind the bridge tower, where the deep thumping of the engines vibrates through the deck like a heartbeat. He does not look at me, but continues to stare down at the decking. I can sense his fear, and I squeeze his arm gently.

Deck gunners are sitting at their weapons, scanning the horizon. And holding positions behind us are the five remaining sister ships of what had once been a convoy of nine.

Hautalo follows us back and slumps against a deck gun, chewing his cigar, deliberating.

I do my best to remain impassive. "Is there a problem?"

His cigar smoulders between his lips. He looks haggard. But his eyes, bloodshot as they are, are alive with suspicion.

"You know there is," he says.

"I paid for transportation, *and* privacy. In advance. Your former captain accepted."

"For you, a boy and a woman."

"And that is what you have."

"What I have is a woman under a blanket in a covered cage, Brother Sunde. Unlike our captain, I want to know why."

"Suddenly a merchant takes issue with the type of cargo he ferries across the deeper sea. How strange."

He ignores my quip. "Well, Brother?"

"So you are a moral man, are you?"

He folds his arms across his chest. "Brother Sunde, we've lost three ships and our fair share of comrades. Our captain was not prepared to do what was necessary to protect the men. I am."

The subtle threat does not go by me unnoticed. I try not to fidget with my robes.

"Her semiconscious state is meditative," I say, "self-induced, not chemical. She is processing. Normal after periods of heavy tuition."

He nods. "A seminarian."

"Yes," I say. The boy looks up at me, his face tinged with unease.

Hautalo eyes the boy; then me. He chews his cigar some more. "So you are saying the cage is for her protection?"

"Yes. Appropriate enough, considering her condition and our long journey."

He holds up our documents. "Your papers could be forgeries."

"Are you suggesting I'm a slave trader?"

"You're not Cityfolk."

My ears burn with offense. "You are addressing a Brother of the Church of the Everlasting, and I serve the Abbot of Rik-Tarshin with the utmost devotion."

"Devotion." He turns the word over in his mouth several times. "A Hinterland convert. Many of you would sell your own daughters if the price was right. Many have done so."

"If you are as brave as you are bold, I can arrange an audience with the Abbot upon our arrival," I say. "You may take up any of your meaningless reservations with him."

Hautalo seems to be deliberating again, then flicks the cigar overboard.

"Very well, *Brother* Sunde, I will take you at your word."

"You will honor the terms of our original agreement?"

"Yes."

I thank him and prod the boy to do the same.

Hautalo scowls. "Remember, Brother, that as long as Estua-Nin's raiders infest these waters I cannot guarantee your safety."

"The conflicts between the city-states of this region are not my mission. We must be in Rik-Tarshin in seventeen days."

"Seventeen days, *if* the raiders allow it." He calls out to the new first mate: "Jenko!"

The new first mate is standing near, slicing a piece of apple away from its core with a long knife. He tosses the rest of the fruit away and replaces the blade in the sheath on his boot. "Aye, sir."

"Prepare to get under way."

Deck gunners prime their weapons. There is the click of artillery shells locking into place.

"You know, Brother," says Hautalo, "if we are boarded I doubt that cage would stop a determined man. I take no responsibility for her. Or the boy." He walks off.

The boy utters a deep trilling sound. He does this when confused or frightened. He does not understand the sounds of our common language any more than I do. But at least he can make these few sounds. I was taken far too young to remember how.

The breeze tugs at my cassock. Pulling my robes about me, I glance at the darkening sky. The wind does not carry whispers now; there is no song in its currents, only a deep hissing.

"The past is a dead heart, my son," I say. "We make the sounds of Citymen now."

His voice shakes: "Forgive me."

I place my hand on his shoulder. "Faith teaches us strength. And how do we approach faith?"

"Trust in the church."

"And?"

"Fealty."

"These bring us peace of mind." I pinch his arm gently. "You would do well to remember your catechism."

Despite his lapses he is a dedicated boy, eager to please. More than what he had been when the authorities in Faulk brought him to me: a street urchin, an orphan of the Hinterlands, living hand-to-mouth like an animal. Much like I had once been, before Abbot Diyari had taken me in.

And I want to encourage him, guide him with a more gentle hand than I ever knew. I bristle at the memory of my tuition, and the scars of penance that still live in deep pink lines across my torso.

"What's wrong, Brother?" The boy is peering at my face.

I realize I'd been staring at him, and my eyes are filled with tears. "Nothing," I say. "Just tired, that's all."

He stands, gazing up at me, considering my answer. I tousle his hair, and he smiles. It makes my heart sing to know that soon, when he completes his first catechism, I will give him a name, just as the Abbot had named me.

He casts his eyes to the hatch that leads down into the ship, to the hold, and to the caged woman waiting below. That strange woman who does not speak, or cry out in her pain.

It is forbidden to give a Cityman's name to a nonbeliever, to someone who has not passed through catechism. But she must have an identity. Secretly, I call her Rydra.

"What we bring the Abbot is a great prize," I say. "The faithful will read about what we've done for ages to come."

He says nothing but leans closer to me, as though true comfort lay not only in my words but in my close physical presence. Like a son to a father.

◊

...many mornings I would stand at the back of the great hall in Rik-Tarshin to watch the faithful crowd into the sanctuary, watched closely those who would hope to touch a scrap of the robes of Theosis, the First Abbot, and acquire wisdom. For a small tithe some are granted an audience with the Skulls of the Sacred—remnants of the first, great Citymen—in the hope of obtaining vitality.

I was envious that the Abbot had been brought such wonders of the ancient world by Brothers who had proved their devotion. And they had been rewarded in various ways, as true sons would by a proud father.

And so forsaking comfort and all aid—and with the blessing of the Council—I left the cathedral, and Rik-Tarshin, and set out on the

Pilgrimage.

I walked the deserts and prairies of the Hinterlands, suffered many hardships, lived frugally, prayed relentlessly.

But I never found any holy relics...

Day 6

Rydra spends most of her time sleeping. During her semi-conscious moments, I feed her bread dipped in condensed milk. Sometimes she gazes out through half-opened eyes, irises the color of desert sand.

I pull the blanket back ever so slightly (and true to his tuition the boy turns away, and does not look upon her exposed flesh). The gas lamp suspended above highlights a network of cuts and bruises. Her skin is pale, ghostly. Her hair, as fresh and as clean as white linen, flows softly about her shoulders.

Without turning his head, the boy hands me a cloth dabbed with ointment. As I clean her arms the boy begins to chant the Creed of Theosis. I listen carefully as I work. When he is finished I smile with satisfaction. He's remembered every line. Every word.

Reaching behind Rydra I brush the grazes there, careful to avoid the two distinct folds of skin that run the length of her back on either side of her spine. They look like layers of calluses, folded in on each other. The wounds bleed a little as the scabs come free.

I don't know where she was found, or how she came to be in a slaver's market. But I understand for what purpose she would've been sold.

I first set eyes upon the woman while travelling back to my parish in Faulk. Taking a short route through the valley, I passed through the town of Mordia. The slave market bustled and stank of blood and faeces; slavers shouted above the din.

And there she was, a Hinterland woman, lying on a slaver's cart, naked, unmoving, bruised body chained to the wooden flatbed, wrists bound. Her breathing was so shallow I'd almost mistaken her for dead.

And something stirred within me. A deep pain I had not known before. I hadn't thought of my mother since being sent away to Faulk. But I thought of her in that moment: a slight woman, flowing yellow hair and a smile like rays of sun.

What I did next shocked even me. I took my leather purse, pregnant with the tithes of desperate believers, and dropped that hefty bag of coins at the slaver's feet.

It was only later that I came to recognize the type of binds that tied her wrists together: numinous cords from ancient days, fashioned by the First Citymen to bring low the people of cloud and air.

Our ancestors.

The People of the Hinterlands.

As I finish cleaning her wounds I am struck by a sudden awareness. She is awake.

Sitting back on my haunches I stare down at her face, her ethereally beautiful face. She is looking beyond me, to the boy. She tries to lift herself up on one elbow, and flops back upon the floor of the cage.

"It's time, my son," I say.

The boy sighs heavily; then passes back to me a small ceramic demitasse. Taking a small bottle from my satchel, I pour out the correct amount of sedative. As I bring the cup to her lips she turns her head, and her whole body convulses violently. I pull back, spilling some of the sedative on my robes.

"Brother..." The boy wants to turn around.

"Stay as you are."

Her chest heaves and she pushes herself into a sitting position. Swaying like a drunkard, she holds out her bound wrists to me.

Can she see the fear in my face? I cannot tell. Her expression is unreadable.

She collapses to the floor again.

Hands shaking, I pick up the sedative bottle and pour out another measure.

The boy, back still turned, has become anxious and whimpers something, some tonal phrasing.

The woman looks to him and puffs air from her mouth, a series of subtle breathy sounds, as if trying to respond.

Day 9

We lost another ship in the night.

In the morning the cramped mess hall heaves with boatmen lining up for breakfast. The men do not speak. Silence lives between them, a reflective, solemn quiet.

Receiving our bowls I lead the boy to a long table, where Hautalo sits at its head. He motions to an empty space near his end of the table and I sit, the boy squeezing in next to me.

I ask about the missing ship, the *Sea Dawn*.

Hautalo chews his food but does not look up. "Brother Sunde, if our aid would've changed the situation I would've ordered it so. That ship was hit hard with concentrated weapons fire. A generator was knocked out, the engines were a hopeless pile of scrap, and they were bleeding fuel."

"What of the men on that ship?"

Hautalo looks into his bowl. "I gave the order to cut loose."

"You mean you fled?"

The men stiffen, spoons frozen in mid-air.

Hautalo fixes me with an icy glare. "And what would you have me do, Brother, with these simple cargo carriers? Attack raiders? Survival is the first order."

"Captain never would've left comrades behind," says a man named Crist. A few men mutter amongst themselves.

Hautalo points his spoon at the man. "You are here, mister, for one obvious reason: lack of space in the skiff. You would do well to keep that in mind."

"And I am grateful you spared my life by allowing me to remain aboard," says Crist. "But he *was* our captain. By *law*. His brother died on one of the ships we lost. He was mad with grief. If given more time we could've talked him down. He was almost ready to listen."

"Almost is too late," says Hautalo. "We needed to act. And I will not waste any more time explaining that simple fact to you."

There are voices of agreement, prodded along by Jenko's agitations.

The boy speaks: "But you have bigger ships. Theirs are small."

"And built for speed," says Hautalo.

The boy nods, slowly.

"Ships that small need a supply chain way out here, boy," says Jenko. "Our former captain said he knew of a depot in this region, at the Uvalu Atoll. He wanted to storm it, break the chain."

"But these men are merchants, boy," Hautalo adds, "not military."

"Tis true, dat is," says Marl, the fat Northern man. Other men raise their voices in agreement.

"You are men of Rik-Tarshin," I say. "Appeal to the Council. They will provide you escorts."

Crist scoffs. "Just like that, hey? You've been away a *long* time, Brother."

"And this conversation is over." Hautalo glares at him.

Crist thrusts his spoon into his bowl, stirring its contents rather violently. "The Abbots once raised armies to subdue the new lands, and to apply and uphold the law among Citymen—"

"Crist."

"—and what do they do now? Collect remnants of ancient days to remind themselves of how impressive they once were. And while they brood on past glory, the world they built collapses upon itself."

Hautalo slams his fist on the table. The boy flinches. I place my hand upon his leg, to calm him.

"Master Jenko," he says, "take this man into custody. Assemble the crew on deck in one hour to watch Crist receive punishment for insubordination."

"Aye, sir." Jenko rises from his chair, hand on his holstered weapon.

Crist glares at Hautalo across the table. Then he puts his spoon down gently and gets up. Jenko escorts him from the room.

Some men exchange hard glances; others continue eating, slowly, cautiously, as though waiting for something. Utensils scrape bowls. The ship gently rocks. No one utters a word. It remains like this for some time.

It is the boy's voice, soft and melodic, that first breaks the silence. "The raiders. How many are there?"

"If we are vigilant," says Hautalo, "and disciplined, we shall make it through."

"Not ta worry, lad," says Marl. "Da Brother will pray ta da Everlastin' for us. Maybe dose raider bullets will simply pass urs by."

Some of the men snicker.

I clear my throat. "I am always happy to offer prayer, individually or corporately."

"See here," says the fat crewman. "Ya really want ta offer sometin', why don't ya rouse dat girlie ta give urs a dance."

The men, seemingly revived by the jolly spirit of this fat man, whoop and clank their spoons to the sides of their tin bowls.

"The seminarian never dances," says the boy, indignant; he looks to me. "She processes."

"Ah!" The fat boatman chuckles. "Well, ya think, Captain Hautalo, ya can give me permission ta go down dar? I got some of me own processin' I'd like ta do."

The men roar with laughter.

"Take no notice of our bloated comrade, boy." Hautalo leans forward. "After pulling a double shift and enjoying half-rations tonight, Marl is going to scrub the sanitary closets."

The men jeer loudly at the fat boatman and bang their fists on the table.

Day 11

The wail of the siren penetrates through the body of the great ship, and down into the hold. Guns rumble overhead. There is a muffled explosion and the vessel shudders.

The boy looks uneasy, as he did in the early days of our journey, before he found his sea legs.

I'm pouring out a measure of sedative when Rydra utters a discordant note. I drop the cup and throw myself back against the bars of the cage.

"She speaks!" I whisper. "By the Everlasting, she speaks."

Another explosion, this one nearer and louder. The ship rocks violently, and the boy utters something. It is the sound of fear.

Rydra reacts to the boy, calls to him in a long, drawn out wail, a sound so lamentable gooseflesh rises on my arms.

The boy cocks an ear and wraps both arms around his chest. He is terrified, of her, the guns, or both. In this mad rushing moment I cannot tell.

The ship pitches to one side. I grab hold of the bars in an effort to remain upright. The boy falls sideways, howling as he hits the deck.

And Rydra reacts, letting out a riotous screeching, like a bow dragged across the strings of a violin. It's so loud and so terrible I'm almost deafened by the noise as it slices through my head. The boy claps hands over his ears.

She does this several times, until she falls unconscious again.

Day 12

"All right," says Hautalo. "I want to know who you *really* are, and what the hell you've brought aboard my ship."

Wisps of black smoke roll across the deck in slow, phantom motions, strangely illuminated by the orange and gold of the morning sun. A ship, the *Marigold*, is badly damaged, and sits close to our port side.

When everything had calmed, Hautalo's armed men had stormed the hold, and dragged us all topside. The armed men now keep their distance, weapons cradled in their arms. Crist and the gunners stand at their posts, frozen with uncertainty.

"I am Brother Sunde," I say. "From Faulk."

"And this is a seminarian?" He points to the woman lying unconscious on the deck. He covers her with his long coat.

Jenko is leaning forward, as though about to step out of his own overcoat. By his side is the boy, on one knee. He has the child gripped firmly by the arm.

The boy's eyes appeal to me for help. I hold up my hand to him and make the sign of faith.

"Bother Sunde," says Hautalo, "I will not ask you again—"

"I am who I say I am. The Abbot will vouch for me."

"And who will vouch for her?" says Jenko, letting the boy go. He rushes to me, grips my robes, and sobs quietly.

"What creature makes a sound like that?" says Hautalo. "A sound to freeze the spirit and send men running?"

Like the boy, I, too, am frozen with fear.

"Brother," Hautalo continues, "we had twelve raider ships bearing down on us. *Twelve*. And when they heard that sound—and it was *heard*, as though it thundered from the very air around us—they turned and *fled*."

"I didn't know. I didn't know," I babble. "That she could speak. I thought her mute. I didn't know..."

"*Brother*," says Hautalo, the very tone of his voice is a threat.

I try to compose myself. "I...am a Brother of the Church. And she is...and she...is—"

"Syrmulus." Jenko says the ancient word, ancient in the tongue of Citymen.

The crewmen speak in terrified whispers.

"The elemental peoples of the Hinterlands," Crist says wildly, "brought low, kept in a cage; ancient from the time of the First Citymen. This is what you bring the Abbot? *This?*"

Crewmen shout: "Kill it! Kill it!"

Panic overtakes me. "No! Those binds are holy, and will keep her grounded. We are in no danger." I look to Hautalo. "I thought she was mute."

There is a shuffling of feet. I can see fear in every weather-beaten line of the men's faces. Hautalo sees it, too, and signals his armed men. They move among the crew cautiously, gripping their weapons as they go.

"It is foolhardy to keep her on board," says Crist. "You must get rid of her."

"Shut up!" Hautalo snaps.

Marl bounds through the hatch and onto the deck. He rushes to Jenko, places something in his hands, speaks in a low voice.

Jenko looks at it; then holds the sedative bottle up for all to see. "I suppose, Brother Sunde, she is quite passive. At least for the time being. Yes?"

I nod, slowly.

Hautalo and Jenko exchange knowing glances. My eyes move from one to the other, searching their faces.

"The boy," Hautalo says to me. "You said he cried out, and that's when she began to speak."

"Yes," I say.

Hautalo casts his gaze out to the still morning waters. "Master Jenko, call the bridge. I want to know how far we've travelled from the Uvalu Atoll."

Jenko hands him the bottle and moves to the intercom.

"Marl," says Hautalo. "Put the boy in my cabin. Secure him there."

I pull the child closer to me, and hug him fiercely. The burning in my lungs reminds me to breath. "Whatever your intentions I beg you, keep the boy out of it."

Crist's face is pale. "You think you can control a creature like that, Captain?"

"No," he says. "But our passengers can. They've been doing it for weeks." He twists the bottle between his fingers. "With *this*."

"I didn't know she could speak," I protest. "And the boy doesn't understand—"

Marl pulls the boy from me. The child struggles, begins to squawk. Hautalo steps over and grips his jaw.

"No talking," he says, "until I say so. You wouldn't want anything"— he pulls out his gun and points it at the woman's head—"*unfortunate* to happen to the woman."

The boy looks to me for help, tears streaming from his beautiful eyes. I want to speak words of comfort to him, but they fail to come from my mouth.

The boy's shoulders droop forward and he hangs his head, breath sporadic through quiet sobs. He allows himself to be led below.

My stomach twists. "Captain, I implore you. Honor our agreement. *Please.*"

He ignores me. "Medic!" A small man comes forward. "The woman goes back to her cage. And take care of this." He hands over the sedative. "It's vital the drug is administered at the correct times. Brother Sunde will...*assist* you."

The medic calls to another man, and together they lift her gently from the deck. I watch her being carried slowly to the hatch.

Jenko returns. "The Atoll is eight days away, north-by-northwest. Six days at full speed. Fuel reserves are fine. We can do it."

"Signal the *Marigold*. She is to continue her course away from here," he says. "The *Venture* will be her escort and provide cover. Inform the *Daystar* and *Azoria* to remain with us. We're going back."

"Back!" Crist says. "Hautalo. *Captain*. You are deceived."

Hautalo sneers. "What's the matter, Crist? You fought with our former captain against the raiders. Now suddenly you don't have the belly for it?"

The armed men chuckle at this; the crew smile nervously and hold on to their belts.

Crist sidles up to Hautalo. "You'll still have an inquest to face, *if* we make landfall. Don't forget that. I won't."

Hautalo considers him for only a moment, and then breaks the man's nose.

Day 17

I am not allowed to be alone with Rydra. An armed guard stays with me in the hold. When he is needed to attend to other duties, I am locked in a sanitary closet.

Rydra makes no sound in her semiconscious state, but stares with empty eyes at the spot where the boy used to sleep. She keeps her back to me.

I finish administering balms to Rydra's wounds and close and lock the door to her cage. The medic takes from me the key, the sedative, the salves, and the cloth and puts them in my satchel. He slings the bag over his shoulder and leaves.

The guard suddenly snaps to attention.

Hautalo is standing in the doorway.

The guard greets the captain with a salute.

"He salutes you," I say. "So this is a military operation now?"

Hautalo rolls a cigar between his teeth.

"I want to see the boy," I say.

He sucks hard and blows out a puff of thick, white smoke.

I should choose my words carefully, but the affront to my person chokes me with indignation. "I cannot, in good conscience, be a willing part of this, nor can I allow—"

"Good conscience?" Hautalo takes slow, deliberate strides toward me. "You hardly have the moral high ground here." He points a finger at Rydra. "You came aboard under false pretenses, and talk to me of good conscience."

I feel my cheeks flush. "I merely withheld information. For a very good reason."

"You people have no good reasons for anything you do. I said you're not Cityfolk, didn't I?"

I'm consumed by both my failings in these matters and my resentment that he could so callously dismiss me.

"I am a Brother—"

"—of the Church of the Everlasting," he spits out. "So you've said."

"Raised in the Rectory at Rik-Tarshin! Instructed by Abbot Diyari *himself*—"

"—but still not a Cityman."

"—and I will not allow you..." I swallow my next words, for I know how hollow they will sound.

Hautalo leans casually against the doorframe. I obviously amuse him.

"A Hinterland convert." He shakes his head. "Who heads a mission in Faulk. *Faulk*. Not exactly a place of inspiration. But you have done one good deed, convert, though unintentionally. You've created for me an incredible opportunity."

"You took command to save the men. I understand that..."

He grunts. "I'm still going to save the men. And many more. We're heading for the Atoll. No doubt it will be heavily guarded. If you want to survive this, and take back your trophy to the Abbot, you'll cooperate. You don't have a choice in the matter."

"Captain Hautalo, *please*. For the love of the Everlasting, don't do this. Stop this madness!"

"Yes," he says, "for the love the Everlasting, I will stop this madness."

He shuts and bolts the door.

◊

...I've never overseen mass conversions to the faith, nor contributed to the sacred history of the church through Pilgrimage. I'd been assaulted by my Hinterland brethren on more than one occasion, endured a volley of stones, and fled a mob under cover of darkness to a neighboring village—shameful incidences which had me recalled to the Rectory to give account of myself.

Considering my many difficulties, Abbot Diyari decided it best to send me away, to Faulk.

I begged him to reconsider. Faulk was a small community: safe, reliable in its meager but steady support, conservative, uninteresting.

He told me our talents and our appointments must not be mutually exclusive; that they must complement each other.

I resisted, and declared there was so much more I wanted to do, so much more I could do. For the church. For him.

He told me, yes, yes there was.

And I would do it in Faulk.

◊

Day 19

The ship's portside guns thunder into the dying light of day. Raider ships are there, black needles cutting through the water, advancing upon our convoy with great speed.

The medic helped me guide Rydra up on deck. We are escorted by two guards. Jenko is there, holding the port railing as the ship rises and falls. A storm is brewing. A thin rain sprays our faces.

The *Daystar* and the *Azoria* begin fanning out, forcing the enemy line to fracture. A group of raider ships break away and head straight for us.

Jenko signals a crewman, who disappears into a hatch. The boy is brought on deck, struggling in Marl's clutches.

"What are you doing?" I say, cradling Rydra with one arm.

Jenko waves to the men, who haul the boy across the deck and tie him to the cargo crane. Marl works a lever. The arm rises up. The boy dangles there, howling discordant notes.

The horror of perception grips me. *"Jenko, no!"*

Rydra, eyes half open, turns her head to the boy and twists in an attempt to break free. The medic stumbles, crashes into the railing, taking me and Rydra with him.

The raiders are closing on us. Sporadic gunfire lights up the night. The *Azoria* is on fire.

A speaker crackles and Hautalo's voice booms through the air: *"Target atoll, dead ahead. All hands ready. We're going to make a break for it."*

I can just make out Hautalo at the bridge window. He turns and says something to the helmsman. I feel the engines increase their pounding. We pick up speed, pulling ahead of the other two carriers.

I begin to tremble, not just my hands or legs, but my entire body. I feel as if I am suffocating. I see my prize slip away: a revered place among my honored Brothers denied, and the proud father turning his back on me, as he did all those years ago.

I stare at the boy. A cold, slow fear drips down my body, trickles over my scars.

I cry out: *"Give me my son!"*

Jenko signals Marl. He turns the wheel, and the crane arm rotates and swings out over the sea. The boy's panic-stricken song pierces through the sounds of crashing waves.

Rydra convulses and looks up, eyes now wide. And from her throat comes a terrible sound: deep, dissonant, like a church organ growling.

Jenko comes over, one hand resting on the pistol holstered at his side. The medic's face is a sheet of white. "I'll take her." Jenko reaches out and grips Rydra's arm. The medic moves back to stand with the guards.

Jenko shakes her with fury. "Come on, you monster. You can do better than *that*."

Swallowing the bile in my throat I gather my courage and shove my elbow into Jenko's face. He lets go of Rydra and stumbles back; the woman wobbles and falls over, and I let her weight take me with her. Before he can act I reach out, snatch the long blade from the sheath on his boot, and cut the holy binds around her wrists.

Now free, she loses the pale color of her nakedness and her body changes, becomes less substantial, almost translucent, as though she is but a wisp of illuminated cloud.

She draws herself up to her full height; the soft features of her face alter and she is something altogether different, a creature both beautiful and terrifying.

In one swift motion, Rydra extends her arms at the elbows, flexes her fingers, and from her body comes a great swooshing sound, as though a gas primer had just been lit. A wall of air, only visible by its trail across the water, speeds outward to shatter the advancing raider ships into kindling.

Gunners abandon their posts and run for the deck house, mid-ship. Jenko sways between rage and horror. He pulls out his pistol, but I spring up to block his aim. Knife still in my hand, he must think I'm trying to kill him. There is a popping noise and my shoulder explodes with fire. The vessel heaves up under me and my face hits the cold, wet deck.

A scream. I look up just in time to see Jenko and the armed guards being flung overboard in a gust of wind. Three more armed men stumble forward and raise their weapons. Rydra emits one discordant sound, a grinding of notes, and the men are hurled against the bulkhead of the deck house. Cracked skulls smear red and gray across white paint.

Hautalo is scrambling down the stairs of the bridge tower, rifle in hand. He stops, lets off a warning shot into the air, and continues down.

Rydra ignores him, and me, and moves toward the crane and the boy, still hanging over the sea, crying and wailing. Marl has no chance. With a flex of her fingers, Rydra sends him flying into the storm.

"*Stop!*" Hautalo runs ahead of her, lets off another shot. She halts and looks at him, eyes slits. He begins to walk backward, slowly, toward the crane controls. Working the crane's wheel he swings the boy back over the deck. The child hangs there, crying in fractured arpeggios.

I pull myself to my knees. The sleeve of my robe is heavy with warm blood. Pain travels in waves down my arm.

The sea near us is full of debris and dead bodies. The other raider groups are concentrating on our sister ships in the distance behind us. The *Daystar* is taking heavy fire. The *Azoria* is listing. In minutes, she will sink.

Hautalo remains where he stands, rifle in hand.

Rydra's throat grumbles with dark tones.

"Captain," I say into the rain. "I'm sorry...."

His face is pregnant with loathing. "You filthy Hinterland son of a bitch!"

I can hear the rifle cock.

The creases on either side of Rydra' spine ripple. In a motion as rapid and as fluid as a bird's she extends great wings, thin membranes that glow with a silver-white light.

I swallow a deep helping of air, like an infant taking its first breath of life. If terror has gripped Hautalo he doesn't show it.

Hautalo is no fool. He knows the convoy is lost. His hope has died, along with all the souls he's needlessly committed to the deep. There is nothing he can do now. Except, maybe, flee the area, and if we make it home, face an inquest for murder and mutiny.

"I should kill you, Sunde!"

He raises the rifle.

But he aims it at the boy.

Rydra rushes him with a speed that is inhuman, lifts him up into the air. The gun goes off. A shot into the darkness. They hover above the ship for only a few seconds; then she pulls him up into the sky with her, into the whirling tempest, wings flapping furiously.

His screams are lost in a cacophony of cyclonic arpeggios.

Day 31

A gull cries somewhere overhead, and the smell of land is in the air. Our vessel limps toward the dock at Rik-Tarshin, bleeding smoke, engines emitting a sickly groan.

My shoulder still aches. The medic could not remove the bullet, but at least he has stopped the bleeding....

Crist is in command now. Crist, the man with the broken nose who stood by one doomed captain, and stood up against another.

And we've received no word of the *Marigold*, or the *Venture*.

Days of anxious sailing, and we finally met up with another convoy. Together, we made landfall only once, at a small port town whose name escapes me. A few crewmen got off. The boy went with them, the boy I'd cared for, nurtured. The boy I'd hoped, one day, would be a seminarian, a scholar of the faith, and ordained as a Brother. The son of a proud father....

I hang high above the deck now, tied to the cargo crane. As the ship nears the dock I cannot cast my eyes upon the Rectory, standing tall and proud on a hillside. But I can almost feel its heavy shadow reaching out to me.

And I know Abbot Diyari will be there, waiting, that foreign man who instructs me in strange ways and guides me with strange motives and calls me son.

Sweet arpeggios, swift and bright—the language of my people, the people of the Hinterlands—play along the gusts that come forward to touch my beaten face and taunt my ears.

I rest my head into the wind, wishing I knew how to respond.

Kickenders

Kit Reed

"I dunno, Mel, who do you think we should get to end this?"

"End what?"

I love Melanie, but she doesn't always get it—unless she is pretending. I jerk my head at The Sanctum, the closed door, the man behind it drooling over our secret places, that lascivious toad. "Him, you idiot. *Him.*"

We both know who but she says, "Oooh, Dumbo," because she loves the way it sounds. That overbearing, lecherous piece of crap Chester Underworth, whose X-ray eyes strip you down to your Bikini wax, a.k.a. the boss. Correction. The default boss because Cecil Underworth is in bad shape and the job fell into the hands of his only son. Mel tries, "Sexual harassment suit?"

"I said *end* this, not drag it out." It's so late that we're the only two still here, and it won't matter how late we stay. Every night Dumbo outwaits us, so it's a wind sprint across the parking lot to the safety of our cars night after night after night; we could show you bruises on certain soft places as proof. We have to put up with it, for Dumbo is our boss. Fortunately, his precious open office plan, wherein our cubicles are open on three sides so Our Leader can see up our skirts, does not include his. The Sanctum has teak walls chest-high. Two-ply frosted glass covers the rest. He's in there early and late, probably trolling the Internets for incriminating particles—our emails, text messages, and, for God's sake, subversive tweets, hoping to find scantily clad selfies of me and Mel and Sophia on the web, and she's *old.*

"What if we torch the place?" Mel and I are colluding outside the women's bathroom—naked babe silhouette stenciled on the pink door that Dumbo special-ordered, with frilly letters reading: GIRLZ. Like that puts us in our place. If he emerges in the middle of this discussion, we make like we're either coming out or going in.

I say through my teeth, *"Keep it down."*

She says brightly, "Or we could quit."

"And *lose our jobs?* Don't make me spell it out, Melanie. We don't go. *He* does."

Like *that* she says, "I know a guy."

"And he'll..."

"Take care of the problem." She is poised. "Senski."

Thus she drives the stake into Dumbo's heart. Even her tone creeps me out. Everybody knows about Senski, but nobody knows what he's famous for. All we know is his watchword, **I am very good at what I do,** the problem being that nobody will tell you exactly what he does. I blow off the idea with a what-the-fuck shrug. "Can't afford him."

"Sarah..." Mel sags.

"But we have to do something or UNDERWORTHOVERWRITE goes belly up. Dumbo's bleeding us dry." The percs alone! High-end trips to exotic spots, "company" cars that only he can drive, on-call limo with salaried chauffeur to take him home whenever he's too drunk to drive home with his hooker *du jour*. Plus high performance bonuses. Every Thanksgiving, New Year's, Presidents' Weekend, on every known and made-up holiday, Dumbo writes a big fat check to the most valued employee: you guessed it. Him.

"Sophia says we're running in the red and it's only a matter of time. If the company goes under, we're kaput."

"*Sarah, shut* up!"

"In this economy, we're screwed." Face it, there are no other jobs out there for engravers like us. UNDERWORTHOVERWRITE is the last of its kind. Only high rollers can afford U.O.'s services. We incise your calling cards/wedding invitations/letterheads into precious metals with this diamond stylus that other companies abandoned years ago. We've been replaced by machines. Only UNDERWORTHOVERWRITE creates hand-engraved designer one-offs like ours, a unique design on hand-crafted plates that, after we've produced your order on creamy stock finer than silk and stronger than steel, will self-destruct. You can't get that just anywhere. Without these jobs, we're shit out of luck. Gulp. "So this is it."

And if Mel and I are alone in the office at this hour while Dumbo lurks, he has his reasons, and ours? Long hours, no overtime, or Edgar starts training the first popsy smart enough to learn and maybe a little more willing to let Dumbo...oh, never mind.

Mel nods. "Understood."

"Whatever it takes."

Oh, yes we do despise the man. His father used to come into the office every day, back when he could still walk. Cecil Underworth was a real craftsman, stopped by your bench to admire your work. He built this business, and kept designing until it got so bad that he couldn't see. He used to run his hand over the design you were working on, reading it with his fingertips. Then he'd say "Lovely, lovely," and back away with the smile that signified a performance bonus on your next check.

Then Chester Underworth got home from his trip around the world on the company dime. "He brought special chocolates from Thailand and we had a celebration," nice old Cecil told us the next morning, but all the excitement wore him out and he had to go home. It was the last time he came in. When he got better he called three lawyers to his bedside and turned the company over to Dumbo—signed and sealed the papers and lapsed into a cathartic state.

Now he spends his days strapped in a wicker wheelchair, according to Sophia after she went to the house with the company books. The felon Chester hired to take care of him parks in the one patch of sunlight in that cavernous old house and comes back when it gets dark. Then he doses poor Cecil with *something,* and puts him back to bed.

OK, this is weird. Until Dumbo came back with those special chocolates, Cecil was in charge.

Now Chester is. No, Mr. Underworth, I will not call you Chet. In addition to being an incompetent and a failed murderer vacuuming up money like an aardvark on an anthill, he's a lecherous fuck, riding herd on an office filled with women because we're cheaper than men and—groan—easier to replace, a fact Dumbo uses to push us around.

It is what it is, which means that most days I get done after midnight if I'm lucky, and if I can't outrun Dumbo he'll cop another squeeze, spraying whiskey and gross endearments at me on the eternal footrace to the car.

Oh, yes I am despairing. "It's him or us!"

Mel shakes her fist. "It's him or us."

"Damn straight!"

"Shit, Sarah, here he comes!"

The rest, we will have to do later. That, at least is agreed.

"Ladies," Dumbo smarms, while his eyes strip us like a TSA scanner. "Let's knock off early and go somewhere quiet for some nice, get-acquainted drinks." Evil grin. "Us three."

I forget what we blurted but I remember how fast we ran—it's easy to elude Dumbo if you can race the elevator down five flights of stairs. We were in our cars and out of there before he crunched through the front hedge, lumbering our way.

We regrouped at Mel's.

A little wine does wonders. Melanie says, "I bet Senski would do it if we had the money."

"If we knew what Senski does."

"Whatever he does, it works. I heard if you put down ten K, Senski solves all problems!"

"Like we have that kind of jack. Like it works."

"Don't be so negative, Sarah. Remember, 'I am very good at what I do.' It's true! Really. All we have to do is get the..."

"Jack." Then I hit rock bottom. "And we're raising that—how?"

Just like that, she comes back with: "Jumpfunders!" Clever witch.

Still it makes me uneasy, don't know how, can't say exactly why; an old story pops into my head and digs in its claws, hanging upside down like a bat. You know, "The Monkey's Paw?" In the end you get what you want, it's just not what you meant when you said you wanted it. "Like, we're crowd-sourcing funding for a...hit man?"

Mel says, "As if! We could go to jail for that. Ask the wrong person in some bar and they go all 911 on you. Trust me, Senski is the positive solution."

"Try that on jumpfunders.com and see what you get. WE WANT MONEY FOR A GUY. It totally won't wash, so forget it."

She looks ready to hit me. "We already have a guy."

"That we don't know what he does." Even saying it makes me despondent.

"My point."

"I'll think of something, just give me time."

"I've already thought of something!"

We're like puppies trapped in a gerbil wheel. Five more minutes and we'll start to fight. "OK, OK."

But Melanie sags. "But who wants to fund somebody that they don't know what he does?"

"Idea, idea!" Late as it is, nasty as my mouth tastes right now, I have to grin. "We're crowd-sourcing a movie called EUPHEMISM!"

"Oh," says Melanie, who is most impressed. "My. God."

Picture two exhausted thirty-somethings doing a happy dance in Mel's living room. Gawd we designed a great movie, sure to raise a few bucks and maybe, just maybe, attract an actual producer, although that was my private dream, for it is I who sat down to write:

JANE and GAYLE, two friends on a road trip, are tricked into taking along genial TIFFANY from the office. They don't like her all that much, but she's cheerful, and offers to pay for dinners and first-rate motels. TIFFANY is too big for those print dresses, but she loves those flower prints, heavy jewelry, and heavy perfume; at the beginning of the trip TIFFANY's all happy riding along in the back seat, making jokes and having little accidents, e.g. falling off her platform shoes, comic relief until they stop at secluded Overmount Overlook. JANE and GAYLE put quarters into the 360 binoculars at the edge. JANE swivels to see: TIFFANY unzipping the print dress, the fat suit, to reveal DUANE, lithe and sinister in his black unitard— transvestite, transgendered, who knows? Only time will tell. DUANE has blood in his eyes. Or something worse.

Well, you can imagine the rest. OUR PROJECT TAKES OFF!

I think it was the cat-and-mouse rollercoaster ride when they all get back in the car, intent on violent sex plus nonspecific violence (DUANE), or escape (JANE and GAYLE). Partly it was friends pledging tens and twenties, partly it was strangers happy to gamble a few bucks just to see a movie about trans whatever-it-is, not even close to our goal which was Senski's ten thousand, but, hey. The thermometer climbed up to the thousand dollar mark the first night!

Then the project caught fire.

A thousand ten, forty, sixty dollars on Thursday and then, wham, Zot. On Friday, a MYSTERY BACKER pledged the rest. Overnight, the red on the thermometer hit the top. Somebody had kicked in nine thousand! Interesting. In addition to funding pledged, our mystery backer had a cashier's check, made out to Mel and me, FedExed to my house.

Senski's price, on the button.

That's not a patch on the hundreds that came in to Jumpfunders later, so the thermometer went up like Krakatoa, and that was only the beginning. Guys, hey, guys, a real producer pledged big money, along with Lady Gaga and Miley Cyrus, who have feelers out to Ryan Gosling and Joseph Gordon-Levitt as we speak, so you'll get your movie as soon they sign up Lars Von Trier or John Woo to direct, depending on who pledges the most, and they can begin casting. Turns out our producer wants to go out to the studios with a package and pick up the balance, but that comes later.

Mel placed a blind ad on Craig's List the day the cashier's check came, and surprise, the next day, bingo, voila, Senski sets a meet and names the place.

That night we pull on sweats and hoodies and go to Millie's Roadside Dine and Dance at 11:45 p.m. exactly—Senski set the time. He's at the dimly lit far end of the bar; we're sure that's him—tall, shrouded in a black trench coat, I think; could be a cape. The place is so dark that you can't even see what you're drinking, but there he is, in a slouch hat that totally hides his face, although I think Mr. Senski has a strong jaw and an even stronger face. I whisper, "There!"

Mel sidles closer, "Are you him?"

As if he'll acknowledge. Handsome, I think, but who knows? He cuts to the chase. "I know what you want."

Mel says, "We have this problem."

For a second I see a point of light in the shadow of that felt brim—the eyes. Glinting. A flash of white teeth. "And you want me to get rid of it."

Forgive me, Mel. I blurt, "As long as you don't hurt him!"

"Shut up, Sarah." Mel is like steel.

He says, "You want him off your backs and out of that office."

Anxiety makes me stupid. "Without us getting life?"

"Or the chair?"

The shadows shift: Senski wheels to go. He doesn't have to say, **I am very good at what I do.**

Is that really me pleading, "Wait!" It's that magnetic field.

He turns back. It isn't just the slouch hat, or those eyes, visible even in shadow. Like *that*, Mel hands off the money. Cash, neatly bundled. He takes it and wheels, striding away.

"Wait," Mel says. As if that will keep him here.

"Later. Done deal."

"When? And how?"

"You don't need to know."

Drawn and scared because I am, I go all business on him, like that will slow him down. "How do we know you'll make good?"

"You'll get what you want," he says, slipping the bundled bills into his messenger bag. Over his shoulder he adds, "Whether or not you want it."

Then he's gone. He just is.

Leaving me gnawing my knuckles, conflicted. Is Senski the devil and we look the same, but he put our souls inside that messenger bag along with the bills? "Well."

Mel grins, sort of. "I guess that's it."

"Unless it isn't."

It didn't happen overnight. It didn't happen the next day or the next one, either. We kept watching the office door for signs; we kept checking back at Jumpfunders; the mercury was still at the top, cashier's check notwithstanding, so our benefactor didn't de-pledge. And the big money that made the thermometer explode into the ether and jump-funded our imaginary movie so it's actually heading for a theater near you?

That comes later.

Then there's the $10K cashier's check. The meeting with Senski. Maybe our mysterious benefactor is just that. Someone with no interest in funding made-up movies. Somebody who knows what we really need that ten thousand for.

It's been days, more like weeks, since our mysterious meeting with Senski. **I am very good at what I do.** Well, dammit, start doing it! We hit a new low near midnight on a Monday; Jumpfunders thermometer stable. No more pledges, and unless we find some way to start our imaginary movie, we'll never get the cash. Standing outside GIRLZ with Dumbo sealed inside that office doing God knows what, Mel mutters exactly what I am thinking. "Looks like we should have kept that check."

Then the hairs on the back of my neck rise up and tremble. The air in the room changes, signifying a disturbance I don't know about.

Mel feels it too. "We need to go."

It's odd. At 11:45, Dumbo's usually glued to his computer, searching body parts on the web. Instead he's up and running. We can see his big, restless shadow through the frosted glass: Dumbo, pacing back and forth. "He'll come out and hit on us."

"Again."

"It's too late," I say again, without knowing why, only that it's true. This is the nadir. "We're stuck."

"Us and him."

But behind that glass, something is happening; we're just too depressed to see Dumbo's outline changing, changing. "Out ten K and what do we have to show? 'I am very good at what I do.' Yeah, right."

Mel says bitterly, "Ten thousand dollars and he hasn't done shit. What's that?"

Behind that glass, there is an explosion of ugly guttural noise, like nothing human makes. "He's up to something. Run!"

She grabs my arm. "Wait. Something's happening."

Whatever it is, it's tremendous. There is much flailing, much crashing of furniture, muffled sounds that mean nothing or everything. Senski at work? Is that Senski, wrestling Dumbo to the mat, or is something worse going on in there? We don't know.

We want to leave. We have to stay.

Mel and I have been here all night and except for the pizza guy and the UPS guy, who left as soon as they made their deliveries—food, new clothes at this hour?—except for them, nobody went into that office. Dumbo has his own bathroom with the fax in there, and enough food in that mini-fridge to keep him going for as long as it takes.

If it really is Senski, how did he get in, and what's he doing in there to cause all the thrashing and the gurgling? Strangling Dumbo or stabbing him or some worse crime that will end us up in jail? Will there be blood and we'll have to explain it to the cops?

Clinging to each other's biceps with white knuckles, Mel and I grit our teeth and wait. Dumbo's shadow seems to get bigger and bigger—unless it's two shadows, grappling to the death. It's hard to know. Near morning the shadow gets huge. Then something happens and the whole, shapeless mass drops to the floor. There's groaning and gasping followed by a long pause and then a strangled, genderless shriek. Then it stops.

By this time Mel's fingernails are so deep in my arm that I gasp. One look at her grim, lockjaw squint tells me that we're hurting each other, so we let go and sag against the wall, settling on our haunches to wait. For a long time, nothing happens. It may have been minutes. It seems more like hours. No, like days. We roll our desk chairs into the long aisle between GIRLZ and the sealed, silent office, and we keep watch, waiting for somebody or something to come out that door. No Senski. Was he ever here? No Dumbo. What is he, dead in there? We sit and watch until sunrise warns us. We need to act before the morning shift comes in and calls 911, meaning that whatever happened behind that door, they'll blame us first.

Should we stay? Should we go?

Mel and I sit riveted, too tired and anxious to talk. In the long silence, everything I know about pacts with the devil runs on a loop inside my head, along with every detail of "The Monkey's Paw." Oh fuck, I think, and that's all I can think, just. Oh, fuck. We go in there and find out that we got what we wanted and it's not what we wanted at all.

Then there is a stir. The shadow rises behind the frosted glass. It's Dumbo, but not Dumbo. There are unexpected noises, outline of distressed creature forging back and forth behind that glass, reaching for things. There are muttered curses that sound like Dumbo, except they don't, but before we can get out of those chairs and shake sensation back into our legs and feet, before we can turn to run, before we can think...

The office door opens and this huge, flailing, genderless *being* comes shambling out. It's Dumbo all right, but Dumbo miraculously morphed into a shapeless, hideous version of Chester Underworth, our hated boss, except it's a sort-of woman so fat that she could play TIFFANY in our movie, hideous in a garishly flowered muumuu with hairy legs rising above huge plush bedroom slippers that look like Hobbit legs or Wookie paws. H/she, or it, is simultaneously stuffing pizza into its face and gnawing on a cigar, while it runs sausage fingers through a new growth of hair on its head that's, I don't know. Puce, I think, a mass of artificial girly curls. Whatever this creature is, it isn't interested in sex or power any more.

It wants one thing only. Huge, shapeless, and barely recognizable, Chester Underworth lunges right past us and out the office door with such urgency that I think it's after either whiskey or more food, raw meat or all three.

So nobody died on our watch and we won't be charged with this—insult or transformation or whatever Senski did to him. You bet he is very good at what he does. Furthermore, although the office closed for the day, it turns out Cecil Underworth signed the order. He arrived next morning first thing, in his right mind after all, and under his own steam. Dumbo's hired thug was gone, along with the drugs and whatever else they were giving him. He came up in the elevator in a dandy motorized scooter and rolled back into our lives. His eyes were clear—no pills and no explanations. He took over the reins at UNDERWORTHOVERWRITE, so not only is Senski very good at what he does, he's not about to turn up later and demand our souls.

Mel and I got what we wanted and, you know what? It's exactly what we wanted after all.

Walking Science Fiction:

Samuel Delany and Visionary Fiction

Walidah Imarisha

My second meeting with Samuel Delany was one of those near-perfect moments. One of those "I could die right now and I wouldn't have any regrets" moments.

It was 2003, at the Franklin Institute Science Museum's Planetarium (a locale I as a Black nerd was more than passingly acquainted with). For Black History Month, the Institute had assembled a panel of Black science fiction writers that took my breath away: Samuel Delany, the late Octavia E. Butler, Tananarive Due, Steven Barnes, and Touré. I think I got there at least an hour and a half early, to ensure that I got the best seat in the house. Spellbound by the impact of not only seeing so many of the writers whose work touched me so deeply it lived inside me, but seeing them all on one stage, I barely moved a muscle during the program.

In the middle of the event, when the lights went down and they turned on the planetarium overhead, I leaned my head back, staring at the miracles of space which seemed close enough to touch, while the voices of visionary Black writers filled my ears. I remember thinking, "Okay, life, you are gonna have one hell of a time trying to top this."

After the event all of the writers stayed to sign books and chat with fans. I approached Samuel Delany tentatively, and was shocked into speechlessness (a singular rarity) that he remembered me from an interview I had done with him for a local weekly years before.

He talked for a few moments, then asked, "Have you met Octavia yet?" When I mutely shook my head no, he smiled brightly and said, "Well, come on then." I have no idea how my legs carried me trailing after him, up to Octavia Butler, who smiled graciously and thanked me for coming.

This was the only time I met Octavia Butler, and in my mind it is so fitting that my interaction with her came about through Samuel Delany, as that is the role he played figuratively for so many. So long seen as the lone Black voice in commercial science fiction, Delany held that space for all the fantastical dreamers of color who came after him. The space he held was one in which we claimed our right to dream. To envision ourselves as people of color into futures, and more, as catalysts of change to create and shape those futures. To recognize that, as Avery Brooks, who played *Deep Space 9's* Captain Sisko, said in an interview several years ago, "Brown children...must be able to participate in contemporary mythology, must use the imagination, to see themselves whole some eons hence."[1]

Delany was instrumental in supporting the decolonization of my imagination, truly the most dangerous and subversive decolonization process, for once it has started, there are no limits on what can be envisioned. This type of science fiction/speculative fiction, "visionary fiction"—as opposed to mainstream SF that reinforces dominant paradigms of power and oppression—is the foundation of my work now, thanks to visionaries like Delany, Butler, Due, and many others.

As I said, though, the Planetarium event wasn't the first time I met Samuel Delany. That was in 2001, at a crowded Philly Center City diner. Less than a year into my migration to the so-called City of Brotherly Love, I had moved up from just-out-of-college intern (read: grunt) at *City Paper* to freelance reporter. When my editor asked if I wanted to interview Delany, who was touring for the re-release of his seminal work *Dhalgren*, I blurted out "Yes" before my editor even finished asking the question.

But as I got off the El and walked toward the diner and the interview, I felt shaky. Were my questions too simplistic? Or were they trying too hard to be clever and original (because I was trying my damnedest to be clever and original when I wrote them)? What if I couldn't think of anything to say in the beginning? What if this went down as the worst interview he had ever done in his life?

I was so ridiculously nervous because Delany's work, his presence, and his clarity around the intersections of identities meant the world (in fact, multiple worlds) to me.

His work was vital to me even before I had a framework through which to articulate its vitalness. As a Black radical nerd in high school, I felt that Delany's work connected with me via race; I had found only a handful of Black science fiction writers at that time, and I treasured each one as a reinforcement of my very right to exist in a world that often made me feel like I shouldn't. A reinforcement of my right that Brooks spoke of, to re-imagine this world, and to imagine many others.

I've since taught courses on science fiction in which I assign students the iconic *Dark Matter* anthologies, edited by Sheree Renée Thomas. Delany's essay "Racism and Science Fiction" in the first collection is a powerful articulation of racism as a system of oppression, rather than just individual acts of prejudice, an exploration of how racism functions

---

1

within the science fiction genre and community.

His writings in general, but especially Delany's nonfiction, modeled for me that I didn't have to engage in a politics of respectability (really a politics of assimilation) as a Black writer. I did not have to write what felt safe to the mainstream, what was expected of me by those whose ideas had been shaped by shallow stereotypes. Rather than bemoan the fact that the larger white society labeled me a "Black writer," which to them meant fitting me into a very narrow box, I was able to claim the mantle as fully mine, and know that mantle in no way constrained my vision or my work. If anything, it allowed me to stand in concert with ancestors, elders, and contemporaries who were showing that Blackness, like space, is vast, seemingly infinite, and continually expanding. As hip-hop emcee Q-Tip put it simply, "Black is Black." [2]

Part of Delany's *Dark Matter* essay intones the names of those Black writers before him who used the fantastic to explore conditions of identity and power, honoring their work and connecting it to his. In the same way I connect my writing, work, and vision to Delany, to Butler, through them I also connect to Black folks enslaved in this country, who were the ultimate science fiction creators, alchemists, miracle birthers. I co-edited the anthology *Octavia's Brood: Science Fiction Stories from Social Justice Movements* with adrienne maree brown, another Black woman, and we carry with us strongly the idea that we are walking science fiction.

By this we mean that we are living, breathing embodiments of the most daring futures our ancestors were able to imagine. Enslaved Black folks had no reason to believe generations without chains would ever exist. In fact, every part of society screamed it was unrealistic to hope for an end to slavery; the most they could hope for was reform, "a kinder, gentler slavery." But our enslaved ancestors dreamed of freedom, and they bent reality and reshaped the world to create us, all of us Black people who walk the Earth today. We believe all of us who come from communities with historic and institutional trauma and oppression are walking science fiction, and that the ancestors' futuristic envisioning does not culminate with us.

We must not only look forward when using visionary science fiction to build new worlds, but we must engage in the concept of Sankofa to create the future. The Andinkra symbol for Sankofa, used in Ghana, is a bird moving forward but with its head looking behind. It is often connected to the proverb that translates, "It is not wrong to go back for that which you have forgotten." [3] We must go back for the dreams of those

2
3

who came before and sculpt the future from this breathing clay. We have the right, the responsibility, and the privilege of continuing this collective dreaming towards total and true liberation into the future, and to build it in the here and now.

It is this level of real-life world-building and transformation adrienne and I hope to add to with our book. Offering visionary science fiction as a process for engaging in liberatory collective dreaming, and then pulling those dreams down from the stars and making them a reality. Adrienne has been traveling the world facilitating Octavia Butler emergent strategy sessions, asking, "What lessons for our movements for justice can we learn from Octavia's writing, from science fiction?" One of our contributors, Morrigan Phillips, developed a science fiction and direct action organizing workshop that uses science fiction worlds as testing grounds for real life-tactics and strategies. We have been holding collective storytelling/visioning workshops, asking how we can imagine the social issues we struggle with into the future and prepare for those worlds now, centering them in humanity.

Much of my work has focused on alternatives to incarceration, and I believe this work serves as a prime example of why our movements for justice need science fiction. We have been told for so long that prisons and policing are all we have to address harm done in our communities, told that there are no other options. Visionary science fiction allows us to mine our pasts for knowledge and solutions, and use those to envision systems of justice and accountability that prioritize wholeness and healing over retribution and punishment. Centering conversations about race, centering communities that have been marginalized and oppressed, allows us to create institutions that will make our communities stronger and safer.

In his *Dark Matter* essay, Delany also offers visions of alternatives to the oppressive systems that shape all of our lives: "Because we still live in a racist society, the only way to combat it in any systematic way is to establish—and repeatedly revamp—anti-racist institutions and traditions."[4] It is not enough to just write well as Black people to somehow dispel racism; we actually and actively have to dream of and build alternative systems. Science fiction is one process that allows us to step outside of everything we think we know. To stop asking the question, "What is realistic?" and begin to answer the question, collectively, "What do we dream of?"

In my *City Paper* article about him I wrote, "Delany's determination to discuss issues of sexuality, race, and gender in the context of his liquid, complex writing sets him apart from authors who offer easy solutions.

4

Delany's writings are a reflection of life, where there are no easy problems, let alone well-defined answers[5]."

I am thankful for the questions Delany's work raises, especially the visionary question, "What do we want?" His creations give us so many opportunities to question—well, everything. These convoluted futures he gave us, these "ambiguous heterotopias," allow us to see race, class, gender, sexuality clearly. And perhaps more importantly, they allow us to see the intersections of these identities and their oppressions, the ways systems of oppression interlock, thus allowing us to understand that any alternative institutions and traditions we create must do the same.

My first encounters with Delany's work also showed me how these larger conversations are an external manifestation of each person's internal realities. Like light expanding as it moves farther from its source, touching and illuminating, that far-reaching light is still the same tiny spark at its core. His memoirs and essays, what he calls "promiscuous autobiography," framed around his intersectional analysis and experience of being a Black gay man in America, fundamentally changed my thinking around sex and power and identity. They show in practice what Delany writes in his *Dark Matter* essay: "...transgression inheres, however unarticulated, in every aspect of the black writer's career in America.[6]" Delany's work, of course, articulates it so clearly you could hear it on Triton.

Delany's promiscuous autobiography also gave me the space to include myself in my work, to see my life, in all its messy complexities, not as my private shame, but as composed of pieces of larger issues we are all holding and exploring. Because it is only when we bring into our work ourselves in all our contradictions, at our most human, that we are useful in imagining new futures and systems of visionary wholeness.

My 2001 interview ended up going extremely well, mostly because Samuel Delany was one of the most gracious, open, and welcoming folks I've ever had the pleasure of interviewing. He was gentle with my fumbles, helpful in providing context when I didn't know to ask for it, and generous with his time. The story actually ended up being my first (and last) cover story with *City Paper*, though that is more to his credit as a fascinating subject rather than to any journalistic ability on my part.

Samuel Delany's work, in every genre and every way, stands as a testament to the scope of imagination, highlighting the idea that you can both create the fantastical as visionary and also view the everyday through a visionary lens. And his words remind us that, ultimately, they are one and the same, for those of us who are walking science fiction.

5

6

Endnotes:

Interview. "Avery Brooks and Justin Emeka discuss 'Death of a Salesman' at Oberlin." Filmed at Oberlin on September 1, 2008. Produced by Daniel Schloss. https://www.youtube.com/results?search_query=Avery+Brooks+and+Justin+Emeka+discuss+%22Death+of+a+Salesman%22+at+Oberlin

[2] "Black is Black." The Jungle Brothers featuring Q-Tip, *Straight Out the Jungle*, 1988, Idlers/Warlock Records.

[3] "African Tradition, Proverbs, and Sankofa." *Sweet Charity: The Story of Spirituals*. Retrieved Feb. 11, 2015. http://www.spiritualsproject.org/sweetchariot/Literature/sankofa.php

[4] Thomas, Sheree Renée, ed. *Dark Matter: A Century of Speculative Fiction from the African Diaspora*. New York: Aspect Books, 2000, pg. 396-397.

[5] Imarisha, Walidah. "Sex, Race and Outer Space: How being black and gay influenced groundbreaking science fiction author Samuel R. Delany." *City Paper*, Philadelphia, June 21-28, 2001. http://citypaper.net/articles/062101/cs.bq.delany.shtml

[6] Thomas, Sheree Renée, ed. *Dark Matter: A Century of Speculative Fiction from the African Diaspora*. New York: Aspect Books, 2000, pg. 392.

Heart of Brass

Alex Jennings

All of us have special ones who have loved us into being.

—Fred Rogers.

Brass Monkey finished off the last of the Hate City gangsters by stuffing him into a dumpster in an alleyway off Jackson Avenue and crimping its lid closed. The blow she'd dealt to the nerve cluster at the base of his neck had shorted out his powers—which weren't so hot to begin with—and he'd be helpless long enough for the police to arrive and cart him off to Powered Holding.

After taking a quick look around to see who was watching, Monkey pulled the Mask from her face. It came away easily enough, and Althea Dayo bloomed back into being.

It was just after eleven on a Sunday morning. Monkey had spent all night chasing those Hate City assholes across town after they tried to spring a trap on her in Wallingford.

In human form, Thea's senses were not as keen—which was good, since this alleyway smelled of burnt hair and human waste. Even so, Thea felt an angry rumbling in her belly and knew she must have skipped dinner again last night. She shook her head, irritated with herself, as she opened her leather satchel and slid the Mask inside. She dug around a little, hoping for an energy bar, but all she found was a couple of crushed M & Ms.

She shrugged and popped the candy, considering what to do next. If she'd thought before changing back, she would have made her way home to Capitol Hill first, but now she'd have to bus her way there, which would take longer than she could safely wait to eat.

Thea bent a little and clutched her belly, grimacing. Her period was at least a week away, so she knew she must have missed lunch, as well. Transforming back and forth used up a lot of energy, and without fuel, Thea's body couldn't help but register its protest. We gotta take better care of ourself, Thea thought.

Brass Monkey didn't answer.

Thea grabbed her cell phone and flipped it open as she slid into character. She dialed 911.

"Please state the nature of—?"

Thea cut her off. "Oh my God! Oh God! I just—! There was a guy in a fez and sunglasses, and he shot beams or something out of his hands and Brass Monkey hit him, and they went into an alleyway, and I heard them crashing around! Send cops! Send everybody! He's got powers!"

◊

Thea was nearly broke after paying rent on Thursday, but Cham and Diep at Green Leaf usually let her eat for free. Besides, it was Sunday, which meant Simon would be working. Thea hadn't seen him in days. As she walked, Thea considered the events of the previous night.

Honestly, she felt a little sorry for the Hate City Boys. With their leader dead, they didn't seem able to get it together anymore—their powers had dulled, and they hadn't executed a successful crime in months. Not even so much as a bank job. Every time Thea ran into one of them (in the old days, they'd never traveled alone) his suit looked slept-in, his fez looked half-squashed, or his mirrored sunglasses were all scratched-up.

But who was she kidding? A little despair wasn't a tenth of what those jackasses deserved. The only reason they'd never killed anyone was because Brass Monkey stopped them at every turn. Besides: anyone who needed a father figure so badly that he'd place himself under the influence of Chairman Bombast had failed at life as far as Thea was concerned.

Thea turned down 8th Avenue South, rubbing her belly as she went. The restaurant was a hole-in-the-wall, but Thea loved it. The furniture was cheap and ill-matched, as were the dishes, but everything was immaculately clean. As soon as Thea walked in, she smelled meat and herbs sizzling on the grill, heard the kitchen staff yelling at each other in Thai, saw Simon bump his way out of the kitchen balancing a broad platter piled with dishes.

He cast Thea a quick smile as he began serving a large family gathering.

Since neither Cham nor Diep were out front at the register, Thea crossed the room to sit at a table by the kitchen door and watch Simon work. His skin was dark—almost bronze—and while he was slight of frame, he had an unobtrusive fighter's musculature that made him look carved from wood.

◊

Thea and Simon first met after the Olive Way Massacre, when most of Seattle still seemed asleep on their feet, trying to drag themselves out of a terrible nightmare. People tended to lose track of their words, trailing off in the middle of sentences, or to stop on the sidewalk, staring up into the sky as if some vision there could make sense of what had happened. Thea felt a pang of guilt every time she saw someone struggling that way: After all, it was she, as Brass Monkey, who had seized their minds and drawn them to aid her in her battle against the King of Cats.

Simon, though, was one of the few who'd escaped the Call's effects. He'd strolled into Coffee Messiah and ordered a soy mocha latte, and though they exchanged not a word, the grin he gave Thea as she handed him his drink made her heart skip in her chest. He'd started coming in every day after that, and whether he bought a drink or not, he always tipped Thea at least five dollars. Finally, Thea had asked him out dancing, and they'd spent a sweaty Friday night writhing together at a Belltown club.

She would have gone home with him. She'd wanted desperately to go home with him, but the noise of twisting metal and shattering glass from the street outside had told her she had work to do. An awful roar rolled through the city and the techno beat stuttered to a halt: A Chinese dragon had tossed a city bus into Key Arena.

Cursing her luck, Thea headed for coat check to grab her satchel and her Mask.

◊

Simon cast a smile at Thea over his shoulder, and when he'd finished serving his table, he crossed to join her.

"Hey, Lovely. What brings you by today?"

Thea blushed and looked away. "Well, I came to see you."

When she glanced back at him his smile had become a grin. "Oh, yeah?"

"Listen," Thea said. "I'm sorry about Tuesday night. Something came up."

Simon's expression darkened slightly. "Yeah, I—It was a bad night for me, too. But you called, so...so no big deal."

"Really?"

"All will be forgiven you if you come to the park with me this afternoon."

"I...can do that," Thea said. "Two o'clock?" That would give her time to get home and change.

"Two is good. Meet me at my place and I'll drive. Have you eaten?"

◊

The sky was unusually bright as Thea stepped from her bus onto Broadway. She tried not to dwell on her past, but more and more these days, she found herself wondering how her life had led her to this moment or that one, and now she considered Seattle and how she'd come here.

She remembered her bedroom at the Academy. Its rock show fliers, Japanese lanterns, and paper parasols. The East window offered a beautiful view of Silver Spring, and on a clear day, one might even catch the glint of the Potomac winding away in the distance. Thea had graduated high school by then, but she and her classmates had yet to complete their exit exams. Thea had taken to sneaking out at night as Brass Monkey, patrolling DC and Silver Spring. Sometimes she even went as far as Baltimore, quietly spotting and stopping trouble before it could start.

But then, Moloch.

The news footage made him look like a robot. He wore a suit of rusty, cobbled-together armor, ambient energy glowing through its chinks. He descended from the sky to the shipyard in Norfolk, Virginia, and banged his fists on the ground to set off an earthquake that rocked the Eastern Seaboard.

Everyone who could have handled him was either offworld at the time or tending to crises elsewhere on the planet, so Mr. Clown had streaked off to deal with Moloch on his own.

Thea and the other students watched on CNN as a swath of black lightning split the sky and hit Moloch head-on.

"He's using a lot of juice," Sakyo said.

"It's broad daylight," Thea said. "He's got to end it fast."

"Oh," Sakyo said softly. The fight had moved several yards away, but the camera crew had followed. When they got him inside the frame, Clown looked the worse for wear. He drew back his fist and rammed it with a crack into Moloch's chest, but his movements looked all wrong. He seemed drunk, almost, swaying on his feet.

Now Thea saw why: Moving almost too quickly to track, Moloch rushed Clown, grabbed him, and held him close, sucking the darkness right out of him. As they watched, Clown powered down until he was only John, a thin, freakishly tall man with long black hair and nut-brown skin.

John's knees buckled as Moloch let him go. He spilled to the ground, and Moloch whirled to face the camera.

People of Earth, he said—His voice was a fuzzed-out electronic growl—*This day belongs to Moloch. Bring me your children; I hunger for their flesh!*

◊

Thea unlocked her apartment's front door and threw it closed as she ran for the bedroom with her satchel. She heard the television on and knew that Barong Ket had spent the morning watching cartoons.

She knelt on the floor to pull a metal steamer trunk from underneath the bed and sighed softly as the smell of polished candlenut breathed its way into the room. She pulled the Mask from her satchel and held it for a moment, examining its contours as she would have a reflection of her own face.

Stay home.

"What?" Thea said. "Why?"

She put the Mask away and turned to see Barong Ket crouching on the hardwood floor outside the bedroom. In his left hand, he gripped an apple the way a man would grip a bowling ball. He scratched his beard and grunted, then turned to lope away, his tail bobbing behind him.

Thea rolled to her feet and followed the monkey into the living room. "Since when do you order me around? Why should I stay home?"

Barong Ket looked over his shoulder at her, then turned away again, scratching his beard.

"*Speak,*" Thea commanded.

Barong Ket shivered, helpless to obey. *Bad things today,* he chittered. *Bad! Stay home!*

"Oh, I know what this is," Thea said. "You've been acting like this ever since I started seeing Simon."

Now Ket turned. *Thea have duty,* he said, speaking with exaggerated calm.

"And I fulfill it!" Thea argued. "I protect the city. I defend its people from their natural predators. Why can't I have someone?"

Thea can.... Just not him.

"Gods! Look, I know you like Sakyo. I like him, too! But he's all banged-up and crazy inside—!"

Like Thea!

"But he's too much like me. I need someone normal to remind me what I'm fighting for." She paused for a beat. Then, "But you know what? I'm not going to argue this with you. In fact, *I hereby forbid you to speak on this subject.*"

First Thea say, "speak," then Thea say "no speak". What Thea want, really?

◊

Thea bit her palm and brooded all through the bus ride to Wallingford. She shouldn't have treated Ket so harshly, but her relationship with Sakyo was a sore spot. Ever since Sakyo arrived at the Academy, everyone assumed some special connection between him and Thea. At first, Thea thought it was because they were both Asian, but over time she'd come to believe it was more than that.

In fact, the first thing Clown had asked her when Thea told him she was leaving the Academy for good was whether she intended to take Sakyo with her.

Certain they'd be grounded for life, Thea and the other students had suited up and rushed in to save Clown from Moloch. Jawal—Heat Boy—had acted as field leader, flying recon and drawing the fire from Moloch's belly to feed his own flame. Monkey had slipped in to spirit John to safety, and the other kids launched a coordinated attack, pinning Moloch in place with zero point energy, dropping cars on him from a mile up, and frying him with thunderbolts. By the time they were finished, his armor had fused together, and the light inside it had died away.

Thea remembered looking on from where she rode shotgun in Brass Monkey's mind as Monkey cradled John's broken body in her arms. "Give me a sitrep," John said. "I need a sitrep. Casualties. What are the numbers?"

"Numbers fine," Monkey said. "John okay. Everybody okay."

"Ruh—Really?"

◊

Simon buzzed Thea in and she jogged up the stairs to his apartment. It was a clean little studio chock full of books and model airplanes. The only bit of mess was the unmade bed.

The bathroom door was open and Simon stood shirtless before the mirror, brushing his teeth. Thea sat on the bed and watched his shoulders. He turned to say hello, but his mouth was full, so he had to turn away again and spit first. "I should have just driven over to get you."

"I wanted to come here," Thea said. "I've only been twice."

"Well, sure," he said. "I just thought—I mean—I don't want you to think I'm trying to get you into bed."

"You're not trying to get me into bed?"

Simon opened his mouth and closed it again with a snap. His complexion almost hid his blush.

"Are we really going to the park?" Thea said.

Simon just watched her.

"...Because we don't have to if you don't want to. We could just...

you know...stay here."

◊

Thea prayed for three days straight after the Moloch Incident. By the time she emerged from her bedroom suite, she felt she had an answer, but uncertainty burned in the pit of her belly.

The Incident had taken place on a Wednesday, and by that Friday, John's god had healed him completely. Still, Dr. Claytor had ordered a weekend of bed rest, so Thea went up to see John in his rooms.

John's bedroom smelled of old stone. Though it was fifty stories above the ground, his suite seemed somehow subterranean. John had blacked the bedroom windows to keep out the sun and now he lay shirtless, wearing a pair of his girlfriend's bug-eye sunglasses. Something about the way his eyes shone through the tint made Thea a little nervous.

She sat on the edge of the bed, and, without speaking, John reached for her hand, gave it a squeeze. He held it after that, and his touch was cool and dry.

"I'm glad you're okay," Thea said. "I saw Monkey holding you, and your heartbeat didn't sound good."

"You steadied me, I think," he said, almost whispering. "Without you, I might have died."

They sat in silence for a space.

"So what now?" Thea asked. "What about the Program?"

He made a sound almost like a laugh and coughed hard. "All of you graduated. Passed with flying colors," he said. "I get choked-up just thinking about it. You—so many could have died."

"Clown. John. You've been good to me. To all of us."

"Aw. Can this—? Can this wait?"

"No," Thea said. "Do you know where I've been?"

He didn't seem to know how to answer.

"You know what it's like to have a Calling," Thea said.

"Don't be hasty."

Thea looked at him over her shoulder until he looked away.

"Will you take Sakyo with you?"

"He wouldn't go if I tried."

"Don't kid yourself," John said.

"Don't—don't distract me with your Clown bullshit, okay? That's not fair." She paused, gathering breath. "Okay. All right. Um. I'm sorry, but—but there's one other thing. John..." Thea turned her body to look at him fully. "I have to be strong in this. I have to—I don't—Don't come to me out there."

"Thea."

"I mean it. The others are welcome, but not you."

Without warning, John began to sob.

Seeing him weep this way filled her with a mixture of revulsion and guilt. She stared at him for a beat, stunned, and he made no effort to hide his tears. Finally, Thea opened her arms and he crawled to her.

◊

Darkness had crept into the apartment. Situated as it was, it got little light on even the brightest days; night came to it a full half hour before it flooded the rest of the city.

After screwing like beasts the first time, then making slow quiet love the second, Thea and Simon lay in bed holding hands, staring at the ceiling. From time to time, Thea would close her eyes and watch colored whorls dance on the inside of their lids as she listened to Simon's breath.

"I like the way you smell in the dark," he said.

"I smell like fucking."

"Not that," he said, sounding embarrassed. "I mean the you-smell. The part that's just you, underneath perfume, even. You smell like good incense and like metal."

"I do not," Thea said, touched in spite of herself.

"I don't need to know why you leave the way you do or why you stand me up sometimes. Not as long as you don't lie to me."

"...Okay."

"Sometimes I think I'm two men."

"Hush," Thea said. "You're falling asleep."

"Twins in one body—one of stone and one of smoke."

"Which are you, then?" Thea said.

"...Smoke, I think."

Without a word, Thea straddled him again and felt him grow in her hand. She fit him inside her and rode.

◊

Sakyo Kemura—Mr. Dark Sky—wasn't like Simon at all. He was Japanese, with ice-blue eyes, heavy, straight hair, and a swagger that would have looked foolish if it weren't so thoroughly earned. He didn't talk a lot, but when he did, what he said was worth hearing. He smoked too much, Thea supposed, and he had a terrible temper that he'd learned, over the years, to aim, like a fire-hose, at those who deserved it most. He lived for situations like the Moloch Incident—always ready to ram a lightning bolt straight up someone's ass.

Like all the other Academy students—except for Thea—Sakyo had stayed on at Shuster Academy after finishing the Program. They christened themselves the Next and became a "paranormal incident response team" looking down their noses at quaint notions like crime fighting and secret identities. They rejected old-fashioned body suits in favor of jeans, sneakers, and pictogram T-shirts.

All of them helped Thea move in to her Seattle apartment, but Sakyo was the only one who came to visit after the house warming. Every month or so, he announced his presence in Seattle with a clattering thunderstorm. He and Thea would go for drinks or dinner, or veg out on her sofa watching music videos or awful movies. He never had much to say about the team.

But what was there to say? Thea could pick up a newspaper any week for the latest story. One week, they were in Romania, fighting back an army of invading monsters from the fabled realm of Alkonost, and the next, they were on the Plutonian star base, offering aid to alien refugees while Thea ate ramen noodles for breakfast, lunch, and dinner, then fought tooth and nail to keep powered freaks from carving up her city.

The Next seemed beloved the world over, but Seattle was ambivalent at best when it came to Brass Monkey. The headlines said it all: *NEXT KIDS RECOVER STOLEN MOON. NEXT BEAT BACK ANCIENT THREAT IN OUTBACK. NEXT BEAT BACK DEEP ONES IN PACIFIC OCEAN.* And for Monkey: *BRASS MONKEY SAVES SEATTLE? BRASS MONKEY BULLIES FREMONT TROLL.*

Thea envied the Next. She envied their press, their money, their alien technology, but Sakyo's monthly visits somehow made it bearable.

...Until recently.

It was stupid—so, so stupid!—but after the Massacre, Thea had needed someone to deliver her from herself. Until then, she'd considered Brass Monkey and Althea Dayo separate entities, but the Massacre had shown that to be a lie. Thea's body had become a prison from which she could not escape, and only Sakyo seemed able to unlock it. He began coming around more often—every couple of weeks instead of every month—but he never called or warned Thea when he failed to show, and on those nights, Thea took to the streets as Brass Monkey, patrolling in a snit. God help any criminal foolish enough to cross her path.

Now, though, it had been three weeks since she'd seen Sakyo, and despite the pleasure she took from Simon's company, Thea had begun to ache.

◊

Thea started awake and lay still, trying to remember where she was. A profound languor overshadowed her, and she felt pressed into the mattress by an unseen hand. Panic stole along the edges of her mind as she realized she'd left the Mask in its case at home. But she was home. Wasn't she? All she had to do was roll out of bed and reach down to grab it.

She remembered coming to Simon's apartment and what had happened there. *Get a hold of yourself,* she thought in Monkey's voice. She had spent four years training with John until she was dangerous even without Brass Monkey's super strength and invulnerability. She could fight if she needed to—but she didn't need to. She was safe here.

Thea's elbow bumped Simon's arm as she sat up, trying to straighten out her thoughts. Simon stood naked before the window across the room, craning his neck to watch a bruised sliver of night sky.

Thea stopped short as she realized that Simon was still fast asleep beside her.

"Don't," both Simons said sleepily.

"Don't what?" Thea asked.

"Don't...Don't come near. You...I'm not afraid."

"Good," Thea said, and felt Monkey's voice mingling with her own. "We mean you no harm."

"Dark sky. Dark Sky. Storm coming."

Simon-at-the-window whirled on Thea to stare at her with bloodshot eyes. *"Get...out!"* His voice was low and full of blood. "He's mine. *Mine!"*

◊

Thea was already in motion when she opened her eyes. Ket stood staring outside her bedroom door as Thea hit the carpet on her knees and reached for the chest that contained her Mask. She pulled it out, opened it, pressed the Mask against her face. In the old days, the sensation was like thousands of hot needles pushing through her skin, but after so many years, it felt much more natural. Instead of a desertion of her proper body, the transformation felt like shrugging into a familiar suit of clothes. Thea was Thea, as always, but now she was Brass Monkey, too.

Monkey yanked the window up with her forehands and swung through it, back feet first. In a split second, the weightless sensation of falling gave way to that of running full-tilt, until she crossed Broadway and leaped onto the roof of Bulldog News. From there, she kept to the rooftops, moving with liquid speed.

◊

Monkey smelled blood and shit and burning hair. The lights were off in the apartment, and without thinking, she aimed her body through the window, exploding through the pane in a shower of glass.

Her skin drew tight over her bones as she took a look around. She tried to distance herself from what she saw, tried to think of this as a crime scene, but her body betrayed her. Brass Monkey fell heavily to her knees.

Blood. Blood everywhere.

◊

Thea first found the Mask in a crawl space at her uncle Arto's house after he disappeared. The moment she saw it, she knew it was important. As she pulled it from its wrapping of butcher paper, the sounds of the house receded from her senses. This mask looked a lot like the ones her father made, but Thea couldn't tell what it was made of. It smelled wooden, but it shone like brass. It hummed and vibrated, singing silently to her. Thea knew immediately that she would keep it and that she would tell no one of her discovery. The thought that the Mask was magic never crossed Thea's mind, but looking at it caused a physical stirring inside her, much like the one she felt when she watched the boys at school wrestle each other.

After Rangda the Widow-Witch murdered her family, Thea retrieved the Mask and put it on for the first time. The pain and madness of the transformation blotted out her consciousness and left Brass Monkey incomplete, acting purely on instinct. For months, Monkey prowled the Seattle streets, keeping to the shadows as Thea's consciousness slowly rebuilt itself.

At first, Thea had no idea that she could pull the Mask from her face and be a girl again. By the time she did, her whole life was gone, as if blown away by monsoon winds.

Sometimes, in her bleaker moments, Thea felt that her life was nothing but a series of tragedies. The happy summers spent dancing the Legong in Ubud, the years she'd spent living among friends at the Academy, were insignificant. All that mattered were the bloody crime scenes, the brutal battles. A warrior without a banner, Thea moved from darkness to darkness, treading an ocean of gore.

◊

The stench of Simon's agony soured the air of the room. He had been torn apart, but not before the skin had been flayed from his body. Shreds of it lay scattered like confetti around the room. Had the process

126 ◊ ALEX JENNINGS

taken hours? Minutes? Seconds? The blood pattern and the way the gore had been distributed told Thea that he'd been conscious, and even on his feet, most of the time. A mess of bloody fingerprints covered the front door where Simon had tried to escape. The bedclothes had been yanked from the bloody mattress and thrown into the far corner of the bedroom.

You've got to stop.

Monkey ignored the thought.

Really! Stop!

Stop what?

Stop screaming!

She had to get out of here.

Rangda!

No!

Rangda kill Simon!

No. Rangda hadn't done this. Monkey had killed her years ago. Besides, Simon's remains were spread around the room. Rangda would have...Rangda would have devoured his body and his pain, used them to become him.

Listen to us, Thea thought. We're—*We're coming apart!* We can't work a case like this! We—!

"We need help," Monkey said aloud.

◊

Monkey didn't remember leaving the apartment. One moment, she was standing there, surrounded by blood and offal. The next, she was Thea again, standing at a pay phone up the street. She closed her eyes, clenched her teeth, and realized she was crying. She picked up the receiver and hung it up again. Now that she was Thea again, her purse was with her, and inside was her cell phone. For a long time after she left the Academy, she'd carried a spare comm with her, knowing she'd never use it. Now she wondered what she'd done with the alien gadget. She flipped open her phone and dialed.

"Next," said a voice Thea didn't recognize. "How may I direct your call?"

It must be a reception AI.

"This is Althea Dayo. I need Sakyo. I need Dark Sky."

"I'm sorry. Dark Sky is currently unavailable. Shall I connect you to our duty operative?"

"No! Don't put me through to comm. I need—Give me John. Give me Clown. Please."

"One moment, please."

A soft click, and then a voice Thea hadn't heard in years: "Clown."

"John! John, it's Thea. I—! Something happened! There's been—! It was a murder!"

"I'll be right there."

"You don't know—!" Thea began, then froze as a hand fell on her shoulder.

John drew her to himself and held her silently for a beat.

"It's awful." Thea said, speaking into John's belly. "He—He's all torn apart."

"Who is?"

"You're not reading my mind?"

He pushed her gently away to look her in the eye. "I'm only a man right now."

It was true. John's face was gaunt, but not supernaturally so. His brown skin bore a healthy sheen, and his glossy black hair had been tied back into a ponytail that fell down his back. Thea almost asked him how he'd gotten here so quickly if he was only a man, but she realized he must mean he was powered down for the time being.

Thea explained her relationship with Simon and told John what she'd discovered in his apartment.

"Was it him?"

"Was—? What?"

"Was it him? In the apartment. Are you sure?"

"I smelled him, but...but of course his apartment smells like him. I don't know. It could be anyone."

"I'll go take a look."

"I'll—I'll go with you," Thea said. "John. Wait. I asked you not to come here."

"Would you rather I left?"

"No! No, that's not what I—!"

"Then let's talk about that later."

◊

The apartment was spotless. No blood, no waste, no sign of struggle. Had they come to the wrong place?

"I don't—I don't understand," Thea said. "I know what I saw." She turned to John. Helpless.

"I believe you," John said darkly.

"Am I cracking up? Am I—?"

"No," John said. "You're in shock. There's a body in the bathroom."

Thea covered her mouth with her hands.

As she stood, trembling, John stepped into the bathroom and carried Simon's body out into the studio. He lay the corpse on the bed and stood back to examine it in silence. "So," he said.

Thea pulled herself together and looked at Simon, trying to see what John saw. At the edge of her hearing, she sensed a slight buzzing, much like the one emitted by the Mask secreted in her satchel.

"I feel it."

"It's unmistakable: Old magic. Very powerful. Where was he from?"

"Thailand. He's Thai."

"I don't think we should involve ourselves. First he was torn apart. Now here he is, whole, but dead, his apartment clean as a whistle. Chances are, tomorrow morning, he'll wake up, right as rain." He paused, made a face. "More or less."

"He—You think he's one of us?"

"I'm a priest of the Night and its champion," John said. "I'm no demigod. But this one...?"

"But he's dead!"

"I've been dead. So have you."

Thea surprised herself by bursting into tears.

John seemed unsure what to do. He'd taken her into his arms before, and Thea wished he would again.

"Thea."

"It's always something. Always."

◊

When Thea first arrived at the Academy, John was being Called. His god was Osa, Queen of Night and Games, and John fought Her summons as hard as he could. He had manifested powers at the onset of puberty, but he was hardly religious, and he believed that his abilities could be explained through science. His struggle leeched the color from his skin until it looked like parchment, and when he thought no one was looking, a haunted, hunted look would appear in his eyes.

One morning, Thea found him in the greenhouse, kneeling before a bed of alien flowers, his face buried in his palms. She wavered for a moment, then went to him, resting a hand between his shoulder blades.

John was a telepath, and while he kept silent, the physical contact sent a bolt of emotional agony coursing up Thea's arm. He didn't seem to notice, and Thea didn't pull her hand away. Instead she stood, trying to lend him what strength she could.

After a moment or two, the pure pain in him subsided a bit—or

Thea adjusted to it—until she could sense his actual thoughts.

It's not me. It's not. You're wrong. I'm not him. I'm not the Guy. *Please*—*!* Please just let me go!

In the stillness and among the scent of blooming plants, Thea heard something answer.

You are Ours. You are Our Clown and Our Angel of Night.

Thea had never heard her own god speak—not in words.

She didn't think he'd noticed her, but without speaking, John turned and buried his face in Thea's belly. He sobbed loudly, weeping like a little boy. "Why won't she listen? Why won't she listen to me?"

"She doesn't understand," Thea said. "She can't. But...but it's not so bad, really, belonging to a god. Some people spend their entire lives longing for what you and I wish we didn't have."

◊

The moment Clown and Thea appeared in Thea's apartment, Ket squawked a greeting and leaped into Clown's arms. He crawled round John's back and perched on his shoulder, watching Thea.

"This is...This is so fucked. I think—I need a drink."

John handed her a shot of whiskey.

Thea took it in one gulp as John set a bottle of Glenfiddich on the kitchen counter. Next, he handed Thea a lit cigarette.

"Wait. You can do that now? You can just materialize things?"

"I don't know what you're talking about."

"Don't do that! Don't!"

"I didn't materialize it," he said. "This is the bottle I keep in my cabinet at home. I reached in there and got it for you."

"By magic."

"By magic," he said.

"I am so—I am sick to fucking death of magic and spirits!"

John and Ket watched as she poured herself another shot, and another.

"Listen," John said. "I can go, if—"

"Don't. Don't leave me."

"All right."

"You just—Why did you stay away?"

He hung his head. "I understood why you warned me away. I was trying to respect your decision."

"My decision. I'm just some girl."

"...But you're not."

◊

One night during her second year, Thea snapped awake in the darkness. Jawal lay next to her, sleeping heavily.

Clown's voice sounded at a slight remove from her own thoughts. *Are you decent?*

"What?"

Are you decent?

"No. What do you want?"

I need you to see this.

"Okay. Just—"

Now Thea found herself standing, fully clothed, in utter darkness. "Hey! I can't see!"

"Sorry," John said. "I forget sometimes."

The lights came up, showing Thea a vast panel of black glass hung with weapons and trophies. Thea goggled at them for a full thirty seconds. Finally, "Where are we?"

"I'm not sure this place exists in any conventional sense," John said. "It was my uncle's."

John's uncle, Kid Armistice, had been, very possibly, the most powerful paranormal in history.

"Oh," Thea said. "*Oh.* What did you want to show me?"

John reached into the pocket of his khakis and withdrew what looked like an orb of concentrated night. The ball grew as he held it, levitating above his hand, and now Thea saw the Mask that hung at its center. It was much like Thea's own, but it was pop-eyed, and its nostrils flared. Its teeth stood out from shredded lips, and its black tongue lolled from its mouth. As Thea stared at it, she thought she heard ghostly children wailing in terror.

"Where did you get this?"

"Is it what I think it is?" John said.

"It is. Rangda. It's her Mask."

"I brought it here because I figured this was where it would do the least harm," John said. "But it tried to escape, so I imprisoned it. It's—It doesn't like being trapped. Keeping it bound causes me pain, and I'm not sure how long I can hold it."

"This—Where did you get it?"

"There was a Thing in the Philippines. A brothel full of monsters was enacting rites to destroy the veil between worlds. Doc Crisis wasn't available, so I went instead. One of the creatures there had this hidden under the floorboards in her bedroom. Tell me how to destroy it."

"Destroy it?"

"If it was created, it can be destroyed," he said. "Otherwise, it will make its way into the world, and Rangda will be reborn."

"Are you out of your mind? This mask wasn't created, John. It just *is*. It's a fact of the Universe and it's turning."

"It—She killed your family. She nearly killed you. You are under my protection, so in doing this, I—"

"Get over yourself!"

John was visibly taken aback.

"That came out wrong," Thea said. "But it's—Do you understand that by bringing this thing here and showing it to me, you've made me responsible for loosing it back into the world?"

"...I'm sorry."

"You should be. Things work the way they work. You and I, we're only people. To tamper with the Grand Design is worse than folly, it's...it's a kind of evil."

"And you're just going to release—You want to just let it escape?" he said.

"What I want is to grind it to dust and then grind the dust into nothing," Thea said. "But that's beyond me. It's beyond you, too."

"This is insane," John said with a bitter shake of his head. He paused, and glowered at the orb. The Mask glared back, seething in bondage.

After a beat, the orb disappeared with a sigh, and the mask clattered to the floor.

Thea's limbs felt cold, wooden with terror, and for a moment she just stood, rooted in place. "God damn it, John," she said.

"It's not too late."

"It is," she said. "It always was."

Thea willed herself to approach the Mask and leaned down to face it. "Go," she said. "Do your worst. But understand that when we meet again, I'll kill you."

The mask's mouth seemed to twist a little, not with malice, but with sorrow. Even staring directly at it, Thea lost sight of it somehow. She blinked and found that it had gone.

Thea leaned on her knees, her belly boiling with unease. When she could, she straightened to look at John, who, at first, showed her no emotion. She could tell it was an effort for him, but he let his guard down and relaxed out of his Clown persona. "Forgive me," he said.

Thea couldn't look him in the eye "I'm going to need a few days."

◊

"I'm not cut out for this," Thea said.

She sat on the floor, her legs splayed out before her, the empty shot glass dangling from her hand. John had watched her kill half his bottle, stopping every so often to cry hard, like a little girl. Finally, he'd sat down beside her, taken the bottle, and reached up, without looking, to set it on the counter.

"You are. We both are. That's the problem."

"Oh yeah?" Thea said. "Then why don't I know what my god wants? Why can't I—? Why can't He just *talk* to me the way yours talks to you?"

"You wouldn't...It's worse that way, believe me."

"I should have let you try to break it," Thea said. "I should have let you try to destroy Rangda for good. Maybe the world would have ended, and none of this would be happening."

"I ended a world once," John said casually. "A better one than this."

Thea sat very still. Years ago, just after he took Thea in, some cataclysm had shaken all existence. Thea had never thought too closely on it because it seemed entirely beyond her, but she understood that John had been at the center of a cosmic struggle, and that whatever action he'd taken had saved everyone—herself included. He'd never spoken of it since.

"Do you know how I did it?"

"...No."

"My uncle ascended to something resembling godhood. He killed me for standing in his way, and then he killed just about half of everyone everywhere. Then he started over: new Earth, new universe, new everything. But he didn't leave me dead. Oh no, he let me into that other world. Gave me the life I'd always wanted. I grew up with my family. I went to school. I had a girlfriend who loved me dearly. It was wonderful. Fewer people. Less crime, and what crime there was was...It was of a different order, you know? Not so mean-spirited. In that world, my little cousin was never abducted, never tortured to death. She was a great kid, and I got to watch her grow. But after a while, my god got a hold of me. At first, I didn't remember this life, this world, but She told me what had happened and what to do about it."

"What did you do?"

"I fought Armistice as hard as I could, but he was just too much for me. There was no way I could beat him, unless...The whole thing, he'd done the whole thing to give his daughter the life she deserved. He only let me into that world because he knew Laurie would be happier with me around. So, I grabbed her out of the air—just like I summoned that bottle for you just now—and I held her head, like so..." he pantomimed the motion, "...and I killed her right before his eyes."

"You...What?"

John shook his head. "That whole world, that whole existence, my uncle held it together by will alone. He was so powerful that he could do all that and kick my ass at the same time without hardly trying. But when he saw what I'd done, his concentration was ruined. His control slipped, and this world sort of...snapped right back into place. That's how I did it. That's how I saved reality...such as it is."

"But Laurie's alive. She's—She's okay. Better than okay."

"She doesn't remember. No one remembers but me."

"Your god asked that of you?"

"She didn't ask me. They never ask. She commanded me, clear as crystal. No room for argument." Now he spoke haltingly and without looking at Thea. "So I've been, ah, living with that for, what is it now? Six years? Laurie, she was one of my best students. She's saved my life four times now. Sometimes I look at her, and I just remember her standing there with her head all gone because it happened so fast that it took her body a moment or two to realize she was dead and fall down.

"I'm telling you this because—Well, I've gotta tell someone, and I'm too chickenshit to tell Laurie. I stayed away because I knew. I *knew* I would tell you if I saw you again, and that's the—the last thing you need. I'm sorry. I've got to—I need forgiveness, or this burden on my heart will fucking kill me. Just—You know me. You know how I live, and now you know what I've done. Can you puh—please fuh—forgive me?"

Clown's confession had shocked Thea stone sober. She wasn't sure the wrong he'd done was hers to forgive. The events he'd related could hardly fit inside her head—in a sense, they couldn't fit at all. She could only make sense of his story by reducing its details to abstractions. But one thing was not abstract—and that was the pain her friend, her mentor, was in.

Thea turned and took John into her own arms. He half-sat, half-lay against her, holding the back of her head as he pressed his face into the crook where her left shoulder met her neck. "Of course I forgive you," she said. "Of course I do."

He shook against her, weeping hard, making choked animal sounds.

"We've all done terrible things," Thea whispered. "Our gods call upon us, and all we can do is answer. Think of all the lives you saved. Billions."

Eventually, he pulled away, and laughter mingled with his tears. He rose and stretched, popping his spine. "Sorry about that. Sorry, I—You know, there aren't a lot of paranormals like us. There aren't a lot of Champions."

"I know," she said, looking up at him. "But you know I love you, right?"

"Yeah," he said. "I love you, too. You were always my favorite."

"*Get* out!"

He seemed surprised. "Wasn't it obvious?"

"You adopted Heat Boy as your own legal heir!"

"I love Jawal. He's my son. But you...you were like a big sister and a little sister at the same time. That doesn't make any sense." He paused, watching her for a moment. "Listen. For what it's worth, I think that our problem is that you and I, we *are* cut out for this. For this and this only. And even if we weren't? Our gods don't care. They don't understand our loneliness or our pain—and if they understood, they *still* wouldn't care because they're more than we are. Greater. We can't imagine the stakes of the game they're playing."

"You..."

He was silent for a long time. "Anyway, that stuff I said before, what I told you; I take it back."

A strange sensation fluttered against the surface of Thea's mind—like fingers plucking lint from fabric.

"Take what back?"

"Don't worry about it," John said. "Listen, I have to go, but one thing."

"Yeah?"

"Don't go near that boy again. He's bad news. He's like us. He'll probably skip town as soon as he wakes up, and when he does, don't look for him. Clear?"

"Cluh—Clear. What were we talking about?"

"When?"

"...Before."

"I was rambling," John said. "You want me to tuck you into bed before I leave?"

"No. No, I'm okay."

"I'll leave the bottle," John said.

He didn't fade. He didn't even disappear.

"*...And then he was not,*" Thea thought.

She thought of Simon, beautiful Simon, and of the shambles her life had become.

◊

Hours later, Thea still sat in her favorite chair, fuzzy-headed and silent, staring away at nothing. Barong Ket loped into the living room and climbed onto the sofa where he grabbed the television remote. He turned the TV on, then off again. He hopped down from the sofa and crossed to

Thea.

Clown is wrong.

It was unusual for him to speak this way, Thea noticed dimly. Usually, he'd say, "Clown wrong." He must be making an extra effort to be understood.

"Wrong about what?"

What the gods want of you—all of you—is both simpler and infinitely more complex than he imagines. They want you to be better than you are. That is why they demand more of you than you can give. In striving, you achieve. From time to time, every believer cries out under the yoke of faith, but faith gives more than it takes.

"But why does it have to be so—? Why do I have to feel this way?"

Ket sighed and scratched his beard. *Because you are a weapon, and your god is forging you like steel.*

Thea fell silent. She thought back to the morning after she was discharged from the hospital, when the social worker, Ms. Hand, took her home to gather her things. She'd asked to be alone in her bedroom for a moment, and Ms. Hand had agreed. As soon as the woman was gone, Thea knelt and pulled the Mask from its hiding place.

The numbness in her face told her she was crying. She couldn't even feel the tears. "Give it to me," she sobbed. "I know Arto was your Champion. Let me take his place."

In the silence that followed, Thea listened as hard as she could. She heard no voice, but something touched the core of her. A vast, overwhelming intelligence turned its attention toward her—or no—she had the sense that she'd always held its attention, but now it focused on her directly. She must seem so weak in its eyes, so unworthy.

"Anything," she said. "I'll do anything. If I'm too weak, then make me strong. Make me what you need."

No definite answer came. No words or thoughts, but now she had an impression that her plea had been heard and that the terms she'd laid out were agreeable. The Presence she felt receded to the background, and a sense of peace flooded through her. The sensation was so powerful that she swooned as she knelt, and the next thing she knew, she was in Ms. Hand's car, headed for the group home.

◊

"That's what this is?" Thea said aloud. She spoke not to herself or to Barong Ket, but to the Presence, which, while it seemed distant, was not altogether absent. "All this is to make me stronger?"

Ket wavered for a moment, then turned and left the room.

Thea rose from her chair and knelt before it. Her body ached. She wondered how long she'd been coasting along the edge of her endurance. "O great god who leaps across continents," she said. "God of my father and his father before him. Ever your servant, I entreat you: hear my humble prayer..."

Empathy Evolving as a Quantum of Eight-Dimensional Perception

Claude Lalumière

1. Empathy

The human male is dying, his body incorrectly configured. Humans have long been extinct, but the biologist recognizes the primate physiology. She knows the creature should be externally symmetrical; that its head should be attached by a neck sprouting from the cavity at the top of the thorax; that its skeleton should be entirely internal; that its reproductive organs should dangle from its pelvis; that its four limbs should not be attached and joined together to its spine; that it should not be excreting so much fluid.

The biologist slides one arm over the primate oddity. Her suction cups try to gather information about the mammal; the human's pain is so absolute that it permeates his entire consciousness, interfering with data collection. The progenetic solution of the life-support shell has slowed the dying process but does not significantly lessen the creature's suffering. The biologist adjusts the composition of the serum, pumping more painkiller into the shell.

Three of the biologist's eight arms are massaging the human, tending to the animal. The fluid excreted by the deformed human seeps into the permeable flesh of the octopus biologist.

As her mind reaches out to his, his mind reaches out to hers. None of her subjects have ever reciprocated before; she has no armor with which to defend herself. When the human's relief from pain comes, it is sudden; it hits the octopus like a flash flood, and data streams— quantic and disorienting—whirlpool into her mind. The memories and experiences and perceptions and emotions of the two beings mingle and merge. The two individuals are utterly alien to each other—the octopus biologist and the human anomaly—yet they each become inexorably enmeshed with the other. For a span that lasts a plancktime in four-dimensional spacetime but for intermittent, syncopated perpetuity in eight-dimensional spacetime, they are mutually overcome by unexpected empathy and tenderness.

2. Evolving

The human comes from a time he calls "the 21st century"; in that era, there are large continents of land mass above sea level, and humans are the dominant species on the planet. Octopuses are food for the humans. Though this human chose not to eat octopus, or any animal flesh at all. The biologist finds this odd. It excites her scientific curiosity, as does everything about this anomalous beast. The consumption of live flesh is the greatest ecstasy; oh, that delicious moment when the consciousness of the prey is subsumed to the will of the predator. She wonders about the taste of the human's flesh.

The human's data stream confirms a few of the biologist's ideas about the human era, but for the most part it is more alien than she had previously believed. She has eaten some mammals before, but the life-information she gleaned from these other animals did not prepare her for the reality of human history or how radically different the natural world was in this animal's time.

This, the octopus gleans before she and the human are quantically subsumed into each other.

3. As

There was an explosion; it killed two nearby octopuses. This animal was found among the rubble, then the biologist was brought to the site to study the strange beast. Normally, the meat would have been eaten by the three octopuses who found it. By law, this body belonged to them. But a consensus was reached by the trio. Could other explosions occur? Where they in danger? The strange animal should be examined as it was found before it could be consumed.

The biologist did not want to risk moving the fragile mammal. She brought her equipment to the site, handling the creature with utmost care. The anomalous mammal oozed a gooey fluid.

4. A

Professor Dexter Van yearns for escape, for a future where the Earth has rid itself of humanity. He feels no affinity for either his species or his time. Humanity's disregard for its own planet and for the others with whom it shares that planet disgusts him so profoundly that it has completely alienated him from his culture and species. His own unwilling complicity in the destruction of his homeworld and in the casual torture and thoughtless annihilation of countless nonhuman animals by human hand fills him with such self-loathing that he can barely sleep without the help of heavy medication.

The one thing that gives the professor any pleasure whatsoever is his absolute conviction that humanity is heading toward extinction, through a combination of blind self-destruction by the species itself and of the planet's self-regulating homeostatic system.

He wants to experience the posthuman future beyond the coming extinction event. To him, that world-to-be is home. Heaven on Earth.

And now he will get there. Away from the humanity he loathes more with each passing day of its miserable, despicable existence.

The time anchor will ensure that no matter how far in time he travels he will remain in the same relative space, compensating for Earth's orbit around Sol, the Solar System's circulation within the Milky Way, and the Milky Way's movement within the universe.

But time, he knows, is mostly a matter of perception. According to his calculations, he has perfected the correct cocktail of psychotropic drugs to propel his consciousness, and thus his physical self, into the far future. At least one hundred thousand years into the future. Perhaps as much as ten million years. But without experimentation he cannot be certain. Nevertheless, he does not hesitate.

He activates the time anchor, steps into it, and injects the psychotropic cocktail into his bloodstream.

5. Quantum

Professor Van's consciousness has escaped linear time; his body tried to reconfigure itself in the image of his new quantic perceptions and is now secreting a molecularly enhanced time-traveling cocktail. The octopus biologist's skin is permeable to the secretion. The octopus and the human are thus quantically subsumed into each other.

The lifespan of Dexter Van is re-experienced by the octopus biologist. In this revised timeline that life follows a different path, guided from birth onward by octopus sentience.

This Dexter Van does not become an introverted vegan. Instead, he/she revels in being an omnisexual predator, an insatiable carnivore, and a brash alpha male. He/she is, however, as misanthropic as the original Dexter Van.

Few like, much less love, this Dexter Van, but his/her predatory alien personality proves to be addictive and alluring to those humans vulnerable to dominant wills.

This iteration of Dexter Van yearns for escape, for a future where the Earth has rid itself of this sniveling species, humans. The air of their world is foul, disgusting—a situation entirely of their own making. Their world is much too dry for his/her comfort. The civilization the humans have built is hard, sharp, vulgar, alienating. Their art is ugly and loud. He/she wants to return to the posthuman, octopus future—wants to return home. And he/she will get there.

At the same spacetime coordinates as the original Dexter perfected time travel, the quantic human/octopus hybrid makes the same breakthrough.

The new Dexter Van activates the time anchor, steps into it, and injects the psychotropic cocktail into his/her bloodstream.

In the far future, there is an explosion; it kills two nearby octopuses. This animal is found among the rubble, then the biologist is brought to the site to study it.

The biologist is a female octopus animated since birth by the sentience of the human Dexter Van. The human consciousness of Dexter Van has barely been able to cope with octopus biology and cognition. The instant the human and the octopus had first interfaced, Van had experienced the entirety of the biologist's lifespan to that moment. Thus, he/she followed the map of the octopus's life as best he/she could, taking unexpected pleasure in the consumption of live animal flesh, experiencing unexpected and ecstatic empathy whenever his/her evolved octopus physiology subsumed the lives of prey.

Now he/she encounters his/her quantically reconfigured human body, which he/she never dared hope he/she would see again.

With better knowledge and experience, the Dexter Van octopus believes he/she can control the quantic time displacement and restore each consciousness to the correct body. He/she runs his/her octopus arms over the dying human body, absorbing the enhanced psychotropic cocktail it secretes.

6. Of

In the most likely timeline quantically fractaling from the moment when the hybridized versions of Dexter Van and the octopus biologist commune, the Dexter Van octopus succeeds in controlling the quantic time event created by the interface of the psychotropic cocktail with his displaced human consciousness. Multiple past timelines converge and merge into one octopus future, the one to which the restored Professor

Dexter Van now travels safely, his body retaining its viable primate configuration. His point of arrival is the same, but this time he can shift the explosion caused by his arrival to a barren coordinate in quantic spacetime, thus killing no one. The octopus biologist, now gifted with enhanced quantic time perception, knows to expect his arrival, and she is already there to welcome him.

She adopts him, and he becomes her beloved pet. At first, they understand each other perfectly, as their consciousnesses still connect at eight-dimensional nexus points. But gradually their minds resettle into linear four-dimensional timespace and their empathic connection abates gradually until, one year later, it disappears entirely. They become like strangers. Still, there remain vestiges of mutual understanding.

A month after their connection is entirely severed, the octopus biologist is killed in one of the many duels she has had to fight to maintain her claim on Dexter Van. The human—the only such creature in this era—is much coveted among the octopus population.

The human escapes before his new octopus owner can lay claim to him, but without protection Van is, within hours, assaulted and devoured by an orcalion, the deadliest wild predator in this posthuman future.

7. Eight-Dimensional

In eight-dimensional spacetime, Dexter Van and the octopus biologist merge into one humanoid/cephalopod creature that exists simultaneously at the edge of probability at quantic fractal coordinates across various timelines. The quantic hybrid is only vaguely perceivable by those whose consciousness is in some way untethered from the linear causality of four-dimensional spacetime. Visionaries, artists, prophets, mystics, and junkies are among those few able to partially perceive the quantic hybrid.

God. Demon. Hallucination. Nightmare. Hero. Villain. Object of worship. Omen of doom.

Perpetually alone and alienated from any reality, the hybrid creature struggles to communicate with those few who can almost perceive it.

But the meaning and intent of its attempts at communication is quantically garbled by being translated from eight dimensions into four dimensions, turning its speech into vaguely menacing gibberish: *bsh'rob-nakada dakegag-rua'll rnau-at'tha g'ghokhugga-shlagak g'tomo-p'cthu g'bakothl-shiggoth zathub-gthul'uh yuat-uach-k'thon...*

◊

8. Perception

Time stops. From Professor Dexter Van's perspective. The moment of arrival. One infinitesimal plancktime lasting a subjective infinity. Dexter Van. The only extant human. Evolved octopuses. Immobile as statues.

Outside. The world. A still life. The octopus future. Moss. Mold. A bed of water covers the ground. Thick damp air.

Van roams the world. The watery Earth. Advanced greenhouse conditions. Scant but surprising evidence of human ruins. Strange new flora. Strange new fauna. Giant ambulatory cephalopods. Quadruped fish.

Frogs. Toads. Lizards. Birds. Weird new iterations. Occupying different biological niches from their ancestors. Predatory plants devour small amphibious mammals. Halted mid-action.

Everything. Unmoving. Alive. Weird and wondrous. Rot. Renewal. Health. Evolution.

A global portrait of planetary survival. Lasting one infinitesimal infinite plancktime. Dexter Van's eternal afterlife. Heaven. Nirvana. A new Eden. Earth. Blissfully rid of humanity.

Octopus. Dominant. Ubiquitous art. Elaborate stone gardens. Sculptures. Resplendent colors. Everywhere. Beauty.

Each plancktime is an infinite quantic spacetime coordinate. Van does not exist in the next plancktime. Beyond the range of Dexter Van's quantic perception. Time moves forward, unaffected by the quantic anomaly. Equation: $1 = 8 = \infty = 0$. The octopus biologist never encounters Professor Dexter Van. The dreams of her multiversal alter egos converge. Octopus dreams of xenophilic empathy in quantic fractals.

Be Three

Jewelle Gomez

My eyes are closed and moving very quickly as if in REM sleep.
What has REM sleep to do with it?
I can't open them.
Open your eyes you idiot! They'll burst through that door any second and slaughter you right in the middle of your sweet REM!
Stay in the still. It'll be clear soon.

◊

Light is in the room or more precisely light is coming through a slightly open window and a moving, pale curtain I think. Moon reflection.
I'm alone which is strange because I know I went to bed not alone.
Get the hell up before it's too late!
I can't move my arms. I don't want to move my arms.
My skin feels like thousands of tiny moths are giggling and fluttering around just under the surface.
The image of a standing iron cask with hundreds of glistening nails piercing my skin as its doors close on me. I want to move but I can't. If I do I'll tear my flesh to shreds. The blood soaks into the bed around me.
I can't remember anything.
It's all inside.
It's all blank, a white blank; an abyss. I'll fall forward into it and go mad.
Wait for the moment to catch up.

◊

My eyes open but I can't see much—a dim room; the window; the shadow of tree branches...or something...moving outside.
You can see now; get the fuck up! Don't you understand? You broke the law, probably more than one and Society City will hunt you down. You won't die, you'll just disappear.

Stay in the stillness. Listen. It'll all come clear.

◊

I hear nothing but warring voices exploding inside my head. Is this what madness feels like?

I listen around them and hear the slight breeze coming through the small opening in the window, and a door open and close.

Now it will be over. They've come. I feel the torturer's nails piercing deeper into my skin and my head burning with the sound of war. My eyes are open, but all I see is red.

◊

It's dark again. If I could just remember my name I could start from there and maybe work up to now—the moment of my death.

Listen.

◊

"Tryna?"

◊

My eyes' lids snap open; a lamp has been turned on but the room is still too dim.

Now I am no longer alone.

◊

"Tryna, you can speak now."

"I can't."

"You just did."

I hear a voice croaking in my head. Was that supposed to be me?

◊

Nelson towers over the bed looking down at her.

I stare up at a large, brown-skinned man whose bulk is mostly hidden by a dark velvet cloak. Was his weapon concealed beneath it? Could I finally raise my arm and protect my life?

Listen.

"You're close to the end now; the beginning really."

What kind of riddle is that? I race through the shadow of memory looking for a clue. Nothing.

◊

"I've been watching just to be certain all is going well...on the western front, so to speak." Nelson gives the spurt of a giggle then cuts it off as he sees she doesn't understand him.

"Listen, I had no idea exactly how this would work. I mean I read all I could and consulted...well consulted where I could, and we knew there were risks. I got worried working with such strong.... So I came over as soon as it was safe. I wanted to be sure you didn't hurt yourself."

"Why?"

"The tattoo worked, but there's a battle going on inside your head. You need more time, Tryna..."

"Tryna?"

"...to heal; and you will. But there's so little time!"

"Heal? You wounded me?"

"Not exactly. You don't remember anything?"

"Danger..."

"...Will Robinson!"

"Are you Will Robinson?"

"No! That's an old children's story. I'm Nelson, your friend. Your tattooist."

"Tattoo is illegal."

"So you do remember that."

"You're a criminal."

"So are you, my dear. We're outlaws in Society City, which is why you've got to get a grip, sisterlove."

"I can't move my arms."

"Yes you can."

◊

I raise my left hand and I can almost see the moths fluttering under the skin. I want to vomit.

Listen.

Nelson watches me too closely as if he's a doctor...or a killer. I look around the room and see the remains of a loaf of bread, with an open jar of jam, a half-carved apple, the paring knife abandoned beside it.

Why didn't he kill me as I slept paralyzed?

◊

"You don't have much in the way of nourishment here and you know I have to keep my weight up," he said with a laugh that implies I should know what he means.

"Are you going to kill me?"

Now Nelson's laugh burst from him like a cannonball made of porridge.

Listen.

"We don't have a lot of time because there are, of course, those who may kill you if they can find you. But I'm not one of them, Tryna."

◊

His words sound solid and real when I listen inside of them. His pulse rate is steady, his breathing natural, and more importantly, the heat of his body says he's not lying.

◊

"Right now you need to remember only a few things to get to safety. The rest will return later."

Listen.

What the hell does this fat boy's body temp have to do with lying or not lying? I...

Listen!

I try again to look at my hand. This time it seems still. Beautiful really, with a depth and dimension I know can't be real. I look at both hands, which now glow as if painted with a luminous substance. I look around the room: a duffle bag, clean clothes atop it, collapsible bow and new arrows, a paperbook, a device unplugged. Normal, but everything seems slightly off-kilter; more than three-dimensional.

"You probably want to make a pit stop. Alley Oop!" He waves his large arms like a conductor raising the dead. He says to my departing back: "I made some lemonade for you."

◊

I do need to use the bathroom, but the space seems so small with the large Nelson in it. I feel embarrassed. Fuck that!

When I'm done I don't wash my hands. I'm afraid the water will wash me away.

Nelson, smiling as if he's the sun itself, stands holding a large glass. Is it only lemonade?

Listen.

I ease past him to the table and finger the chunks of bread. Nelson turns to say, "Don't eat yet."

I grasp the paring knife with the glowing fingers that don't quite belong to me; yet who else will claim them? I feel sluggish as if drugged, yet I know three things: the room is small, he is big and soft, and he is within my reach. I could strike out and through his vein before he speaks again. End it.

Nelson doesn't smile any longer but his eyes are not fearful.

Listen.

My fingers open and the knife drops back to the table.

◊

"I'll tell you what happened. Then you have to rest. But first—you're not going to turn down my mamma's special recipe lemonade, are you?"

"No." I am so thirsty I could drink an entire orchard of lemons... if lemons were still grown in orchards. I seem to remember that.

"This will all come back to you, but you need to be ready as soon as the process is complete."

I stare at him and realize, yes, I do know this man. He is my...my what? My lover? Brother? My betrayer?

"Are you my brother?"

"In a way."

And he begins a digest of the story which tells me my name and leads me back to now; which is the hour of my death and my birth.

◊

"The art of tattoo is spiritual, inextricably linking the applied art with the individual."

I want to speak

"Don't interrupt! Two lovers, forbidden by Society City to bond do so, just as all lovers must be in the fairy tales. One an empath called Lynx; the other an information executive called Strand. Each seeks out in the other that which is missing in herself and finds they're joyful for the first time in life. "Lynx is in servitude to Society City, which sometimes uses her empathic talents to heal and at other times to punish. Her sensitivity is so acute she can only survive these rigors with the use of deadening drugs. Are you still with me?"

◊

I stare at him unsure who is the lunatic: him or me.

◊

"Strand, on the other hand, seems to have been born with deadening drugs coursing through her veins. No one is immune to her cold wit; nothing breaks through her protective shell except me and then Lynx. But they are two valuable commodities in a culture that gets what it pays for and keeps it."

Nelson avoids telling her of the cruelty that had become intrinsic to Strand's survival and the raw pain that had almost killed Lynx. He knows their differing instincts are at war inside her; he needs her to recognize and embrace them both.

◊

"In the de-evolution of the culture outside that narrow window in this dark bedroom, Society City controls all things east of the Appalachians, and most things west of those mountains are forbidden. The tattoo was meant to bond Lynx and Strand together, forever, making it impossible for them to be separated by the power of Society City." He repeats: "The art of tattoo is spiritual, linking the applied art with the individual inextricably."

◊

"That's impossible!"
"And yet here we are."

◊

I look again at his large brown hands and note the tips of his fingers permanently dark with ink. Ignoring his presence I rip the loose fitting cotton garment up over my head, seeing the dried blood staining it. I rush back to the bathroom mirror. My breasts are familiar and strange at the same time. There's a vague outline beneath the skin of...

something else. My hair does not look familiar at all. When I blink I see a flash of a woman darker than my current skin and who has short, nappy hair. Then I see a smaller, freckled, stockier woman with cascading red and silver hair. The other one? Or am I the other one?

◊

I feel the tiny needle points prickling all over my body. I lean in close to the mirror as if I might still be able to see them on my skin.

The movement just below the surface no longer unnerves me.

◊

"You did this? Experimented?"

"We did. All of us."

I look back to the mirror just as my dark hair loses all of its color.

"What's happening!?"

"We agreed this was the only way. Lynx and Strand wanted it, so we worked for many months, sinew by strand by shadow to recreate one on the outside and the inside of the other."

"But which am I?"

"Another."

"The two have become one? Inside me?"

"No. That was my error. The two have become a third, who contains both. Three, but none gives way. Here," Nelson pulls a fresh garment from the stack on top of the duffle.

I pull the soft cotton wrapper back over my head—not through modesty, because I finally understand this man: Nelson knows every inch of my body already.

◊

"And that's the important thing you must remember."

"I don't care for your superior attitude, Mr. Nelson."

Listen.

"Not mister. Just Nelson, as it has been for generations in my family. The women were all named after the famous..."

"...South African freedom fighter." I remember that now.

"And then I came along," Nelson says with an unguarded smile.

"And you collect miniatures of long gone historic monuments. I remember La Tour Eiffel...uh...the Ashanti Stool!"

"Good. We'll continue down memory lane another time, sisterlove. I've got some tasks to do right now. We don't have much time; you need to sleep again to finish the annealment."

I listen.

◊

"There will always be two voices; I didn't know that at first; I'm sorry. Your work will be to find the balance, to know when to follow which voice. One will be rash, angry, cold, dangerous; the other is sensitive, empathetic, innocent. Both are valid when in balance. But you cannot let go of one and follow only the other. You'll...you won't survive."

She listens but doesn't understand.

"You won't survive unless you can carry all the realities! Without them the road will only lead to madness. I know that sounds melodramatic but believe me, please."

I listen.

◊

"Remember when you first woke up and couldn't remember anything? Imagine trying to live your life from that moment forward, having no memory at all of what went before. The threads of the past snipped free from the present, no link to the future...with no sense of the ground on which you stand. That old earthquake that ripped through the middle states last century; that cut the east off from the west? That would seem like a bump in the road. You'd always be off-balance."

◊

"No tabula rasa, then?"

◊

"The weight of emptiness is still a weight. Keeping the balance between the voices—between who they were and who you are—will integrate you all. And remember they are lovers; they want to be in harmony, and you're the one who does that."

◊

Nelson unties his cloak, dropping it to a chair in the narrow room. I reach out tentatively to touch the soft edge of the fabric as if

I've never felt anything like it before. I gaze at him with a look of puzzlement; then tears rise in my eyes.

◊

"Don't worry, this here queen's got all bases covered except one, and I'm about to fix that. Lie down one last time."

◊

I do, because the words are so familiar. He raises the leg of my pants on the left side and I see one tattoo that remains distinct—an old-fashioned bicycle, a high-wheeled penny-farthing, on my calf.

◊

"The penny-farthing locks you all in place together as you travel out past the mountains to the places Society thinks are too wild to sustain life. Relax! The plan will come back to you when you wake again. But one last thing."

◊

Nelson pulls a machine from one of the deep pockets of his cloak and a small pot of ink. "Can you lie on your side?"

I turn.

"This will hurt a bit."

"You never said that before."

"No. But this is different. I'm layering in a line of communication. We're not using any relaxant because I don't want any chemicals to interfere. When we're done you'll go back to sleep and wake on your own.

"Here's a word for you to remember. Did I ever tell you about the time...?" Nelson begins the storytelling path he always travels when inking her body.

◊

"You know how I love to collect historical bits and pieces," he continues. "So once I stumbled on this picture of the cutest man I ever saw: café au lait skin, dark eyes that were either trouble or were looking for trouble. And he had the most expressive mouth, like cherries I could have sucked through my teeth, pits and all! Turns out he was a queer colored man who wrote books in the 20th century. I tried reading some. Way too smart for me...that's why Society tracked me into visual—not literary arts!"

Nelson's laughter dispels any sense that he thinks himself stupid.

He clicks on the power and the buzz of the machine fills my ears. Facing the window, I concentrate on the curtains dancing in the breeze as Nelson moves carefully on the spokes of the penny-farthing's big front wheel. I feel the needle as if I'm inside that ancient torture machine, its nails digging into me. But now my body opens to it.

◊

"I read an interview with him and he talked about the sensuality of words; I'd never thought about that before. And how he fell in love with a word when he was a kid: Wolverine! He thought it was the most beautiful word in the world. He loved to feel it in his mouth. When I close my eyes I can see his mouth tasting that word. He didn't know what it meant when he first heard it, but it stuck with him. Later, when I found some pictures of him as an old man,that mouth—it was still tasting that word.

◊

"There, all done."

"So quickly?"

"Just the single word concealed among the bicycle's spokes and curves. It changed his life, it changed mine; now it changes yours."

"How?"

"Magic. Let me finish. You will go west from Society City; maybe you'll find some Partisans, set up housekeeping in a tree, learn to sew, become a surgeon or carpenter or revolutionary. Who knows."

"Sounds either ghastly or delightful, depending on who I am at the moment."

"Ah, finally your sense of humor! I'll take that as a good sign."

"All of this simply for two lovers?"

"Two lovers is no small thing. And for the others who'll foment change."

◊

"I'm afraid."

"That's smart. Society City will not take the disappearances sitting still. When you wake up you'll remember how vicious it can be, you'll remember those who've disappeared. So follow our plan and go. Quickly."

◊

Through the curtain I see what was moving: not a tree branch, but a pair of athletic shoes tied together and thrown over a power line. For some reason they make me smile.

"Once you're past the mountains, remember the word. It's not one that pops up in common conversation, so it will help you find friends or protect you from danger."

"Dare I ask how?"

Nelson doesn't respond because he can see she's already drowsy.

"'Wolverine.' It does taste delicious," I say, but I can no longer lift my eyelids.

◊

Nelson gently turns her onto her back and drapes a soft cotton sheet over her. He thinks how much he already misses the two women who've become his sisters. He wonders how long before he'll see this new one again. He wants his friends, but he hates to travel.

◊

"Move fast...you listening to me, Tryna West?" Nelson whispers urgently then grabs his cloak and turns to leave.

"Yes, we're listening, brotherlove."

We sleep.

Nelson double locks the door when he leaves.

Guerrilla Mural of a Siren's Song

Ernest Hogan

Like a miniature Jupiter gone insane, the paint-blob hangs in the middle of the room—a Jupiter whose tides and weather and powerful gravity snapped on the strain of the secret of its monstrous microscopic inhabitants so its regular bands are broken up into gaily swirling asymmetrical patterns of mingling paint with color almost computer-exaggerated—like the glorious unholy mother of all cat's eye marbles, it glares at me.

I try not to see her.

There's no gravity here, but that floating blob has a pull just the same. I orbit in freefall, make 'em let me paint in the center of these cans where the spinning doesn't suck you to the floor—and like the irresistible pull of Jupiter, so big, so bad, so goddam awesome that you feel yourself fall into those convulsive, frenzied clouds, like you're being sucked *up*, not pulled down (Jupiter is too big, too gigantic for you to ever be on top of it)—and *it* still pulls me.

And she pulls me.

I take the stick like an Aztec priest wielding a flint knife, or that cop swinging his baton on that cool, starless night years ago in L.A.—crushing the buckle from my gas mask into my skull, leaving a cute little scar on my scalp that I shaved my head for months to show off.

It exploded—like an amphetamine-choked blob. Amorphous little monsters sailed through the air, some colliding with me and sticking to my naked flesh. One sought my eyes in order to blind me. Lucky I have goggles like Tlaloc, the Rain, Water, and Thunder God...and a breathing mask—that's all the covering I need! I wipe away the paint, my vision is smeared with color.

The entire little canvas-lined room is exploding with color. Beautiful.

Like her.

Still, the paint has this sickening tendency to settle into little jiggling globes that just sit there like mini-Jupiters, mocking me. I refuse to allow entropy to happen in my presence, so, like a samurai Jackson Pollock, I scream through my mask and thrash the disgusting little buggers into tinier flying sky-serpents that merrily decorate me, and the canvas on the walls.

And the canvas is raw, unprimed, and the paint is mixed with a base that gives it the consistency of water. Splatter marks don't just sit there looking pretty—no, they grow fur as the canvas absorbs them, thirstily. My work is always wild and woolly.

Soon the colorful swordplay is over and I am victorious. All (except for a few little stubborn, but insignificant B.B.'s) the paint is slapped down to the canvas. I shed my goggles for a while and the furious splatters change into visions.

André Masson, eat your heart out!

Bizarre hieroglyphs materialize in the Jovian storm clouds: *Demonic cartoon characters exhaling balloons full of obscenity—hordes of baby godzilloids crawling through vacuum and eating rocks—endless three-D labyrinths of orbital castles complete with living gargoyles and tapestries you can walk into—large, luxuriant cars encrusted with jewels and tail-fins that race the crowded, tangled spaghetti of freeways with off-ramps all over the galaxy—the vegetal love poetry that an intelligent network of vines sings to the jungle it intricately embraces—the ecstatic rush of falling into an ocean of warm mud that tastes delicious and makes you feel so good—pornographic geometries that can only be imagined on a scale more than intergalactic—the Byzantine plots of surrealistic soap operas that take place outside of spacetime, in Omeyocan, the highest heaven—the ballet of subatomic particles smaller than any yet discovered!*

Letting the stick fly, I attack the canvas with paint-covered fingers—desperately trying to record the visions before they fade, but never finishing before they do, so I have to fill many gaps with memory and imagination.

Then I see her face again.

That beautiful, perfect Zulu face, with impossibly intense eyes—beauty that puts the cold, marble-white classicism of dead and buried ancient Greece to shame, causing arrogant statues to crack and crumble to dust—making you see how right the barbarians were in knocking their heads off. A presence that is soft, yet extremely powerful, like the fearful sound of the soft, swishing skirt that reveals that an umkhovu—like a bad memory of apartheid—is roaming the midnight streets of Soweto, making its way past the sleepy suburbs, to the shiny new university, to the Center of Parapsychology....

I find myself drawing that magnificent face. The face of Willa Shembe, a pampered little (she was taller than me, but still, somehow, *little*) psychic from Zululand, from whom I'll never be free. The sorcery that caused her "death" has contaminated me, enslaved me. I will see, draw, and paint her forever.

I should have known the first time I saw her—who knows how long after my surprisingly nonfatal encounter with the Sirens....

Whatever made Calvino send her to me? I guess a little inspiration flickers under that pale, bald head, behind those thick, old-fashioned glasses and fat, gray eyebrows on occasion.

I suddenly saw her—clearly and distinctly out of my feverish delirium and telepathic hangover—dancing galaxies and soft, squishy, organic cities faded to let her power through.

Calvino must have been desperate. I, of all people, survived a mind-to-whatever encounter with the Sirens!

Me, Pablo Cortez, infamous guerrilla muralist from the wild, crumbling concrete and stucco overgrowth of L.A.—who refused to be absorbed into the decaying society I satirized in my work long after my fellow wall-defacers were caught, arrested and offered a chance to become honest artists who paint on neat, clean canvases that are displayed in sterile galleries and bought by the affluent to show everybody how sensitive they are by what they choose to decorate their expensive, prestigious apartments with. I, who tattooed the Picasso quote, "PAINTING IS NOT DONE TO DECORATE APARTMENTS. IT IS AN INSTRUMENT OF WAR FOR ATTACK AND DEFENSE AGAINST THE ENEMY" on my own left arm with a felt-tip pen and a safety-pin. The guy who *really* meant it when he helped paint—fast, so we could get it done and get the hell out of there before getting our heads busted—Quetzalcoatl choking on smog, Uncle Sam holding up the heart of a draftee for the "disturbance" in South Africa (soon to be Zululand—again) to the gaping jaws of a Biomechanoid War God, mutilated/spacesuited corpses and countless mass portraits of the ever-growing throngs of the homeless to decorate the featureless, empty walls of the blank architecture where Mr. and Ms. Los Angeles could see them as they did the freeway boogie to work. Siquerios and Orozco and every spray-can wielding vato would've been proud!

That fast, slashing, hit-and-run style of the Guerrilla Muralists of L.A. was mine—a direct outgrowth of my rushed, rabid scribblings of monsters from my id that I leave on any available surface. Moe, Desiree, Johnny, Maria, LeRoy, Buck, and Estela were all really quiet *artistes* at heart. They preferred to work quietly, in air-conditioned, sound-proof studios with neat, meticulously laid-out materials. Just a bunch of nice kids pushed to the edge of a demented society—but I had fallen off that edge long ago. I *really* believed in our rebellion, and wouldn't be satisfied with becoming a darling of rich liberals. If any one of them was lowered down into the Great Red Spot, their sensitive, humane, artistic minds would have blown out so fast they'd have sprayed out of the exoskeleton and coated the entire inside of the dirgiscaphe with their gooey remains.

No, it took a maniac like me.

They could be comfortable lapping up the regurgitated wealth in the center of the Hollywood Empire, or fly out to the colonies to help create the new official art of the Space Culture Project, while I created splatterpainting, my Freefall Abstract Expressionism, and got my ass kicked out.

It didn't bother me. Not me. I had to keep going. Keep wandering. Volunteered to go to Ithaca Base and get lowered through the dangerous radioactive magnetosphere of the Big Planet, down to the Great Red Spot, into the heart of the Sirens' sphere of influence, let their alien thoughts flow through my skull *and* survive!

But I did need her to bring me out of it. Willa Shembe, the pride of the scientific community of Zululand. A girl used to experiencing the universe through other peoples' minds.

She keeps showing up in the images, in the paint. Unexpectedly. Automatically.

Just like the first time she showed up in my life. When I was still lost in the influence of the Sirens. After they locked me into the exoskeleton, into the dirgiscaphe, and lowered me by remote control down into evil, heavy gravity and big, beautiful stormclouds out of Turner's wetdreams, or Chalchiuhtlicue's most passionate rituals of whirlpools, violence, growth, and young love.

"Do you feel anything yet?" Dr. Calvino buzzed into my earphone on that day.

"If only those bastards could go through this," I said into the throatmike. "They should all come here and see this planet up close before they call me undisciplined!"

"What are you talking about?" The doc never understood me.

"This sight! Jupiter up close! Wagstaff and the rest of those tight-assed idiots at the Space Culture Project should see *this*. That is what space art should be about. This energy! This power! This freedom! This is what I had in mind when I created splatterpainting."

"What about the Sirens? Are you feeling any effects?"

"In my mind? No. This gravity is a bitch, though. If only I could see these clouds while weightless! If only I could come here and paint! Can't they build one of these exoskeletons with more freedom of movement?"

"The one you have on is the state of the art. The instruments show a high concentration of Sirens in the clouds around you. Do you feel anything yet?"

"Yeah, now that you mention it. The gravity. It's getting hard to move, breathe..."

"Should we abort?"

"No! I'm feeling better now. Lighter. The gravity seems to be going away. I almost feel weightless. It's really great! Feels like I could peel this exoskeleton right off..."

"Don't!"

"I'm not stupid, Calvino! This is probably an illusion, like what happened to the others. I do plan on surviving this!"

"Any change in sensations?"

"It's like one long rush. Ecstasy—like I'm weightless, painting away like crazy, making a big, juicy mess. I'm getting an erection. The exoskeleton seems to be holding me down."

Then I got a strong rotten-eggs whiff of methane. Could the dirgiscaphe be leaking? I was about to say something, but couldn't move—first I was paralyzed, every muscle locked tight, then it all turned to mush—flesh, bones, exoskeleton, dirgiscaphe, Jupiter, space....

"Cortez, are you all right?" said Calvino.

I was getting softer—like a Salvador Dalí watch. Everything was getting softer. Putty. Liquid. Gas. Like those colorful, flowing clouds that were all around.

"Cortez, are you there?"

I was a twisting, bubbling cloud—dancing among the gorgeous clouds of Jupiter. Among microscopic creatures I couldn't see, but could feel—like spirits, like ghosts.

"Abort! Abort!"

I felt that I was dissolving. Being absorbed. I panicked.

Then they had me. *Me.* Who has never given in to anybody!

I passed from the realm of Xiuhtecuhtli—the supreme being within space and time, the power of life and fire, the center of all things and spindle of the universe—to Omeyocan, realm of Ometecuhtli, the male/female supreme being, the dual lord, source of all existence, the essential unity in difference. Spacetime was flushed down the toilet—a cute cartoon Einstein offered himself as a blood sacrifice.

Somewhere I was aware of the dirgiscaphe's engines burning and the Gs building up so that even the exoskeleton couldn't save me from harm. Also: *I was being born—I was alive and well millions of years ago on Mars—I was back in Hightown having an argument with Wagstaff of the Space Culture Project.*

"You should really be more cooperative, Mr. Cortez," he said from inside his tight, crisp facade, more acrylic than flesh.

"Where have I heard that before?" I said, going into a rant. "What you want isn't art. It's municipal garbage, state-sponsored bullshit, committee-conceived caca!"

I heard the big beat of whales and dolphins in perfect sync with songs of sentient stars and the Sirens, that toy robots and nude bettyboopoids joyously danced to in endless halls that were covered with animated hieroglyphs that joined in the Futuro-Afro-PreColumbian-TransSpacetime-Zen-Quantum Musical Comedy!

"The space hieroglyphics you started out with were interesting, but everything you've done since has become more and more unacceptable. Too messy. Dripping all over the place..."

"All I did was what you asked me to do—come into this new environment and create a new art for it. It developed into splatterpainting, not the middle-class kitsch you lust after!"

I was thirteen years old and enticing an eleven-year-old girl into letting me pop her cherry in sacrifice to Tlazolteotl—Aztec goddess of filth and depravity—past midnight in an empty high school campus on a hot, Southern California night! I saw the programmed dreams of hibernating seeds traveling near the speed of light through gulfs of interstellar space! I shot bold, colorful graffiti on the walls of gravity-less artificial worlds, asteroids, moons, planets to the timeless tune of a symphony of countless Big Bangs!

"I'm afraid we can't waste money on you any longer. We'll have to send you back to Earth!"

"No! You don't understand me, and I'm human—from your world! How do you expect to face the rest of the universe if you can't deal with me?"

But I showed them. I volunteered for the Odysseus Project. They didn't care what kind of pictures I painted, just that I realized that *everybody* who had contacted the Sirens so far had died.

But I didn't die. I survived, because I'm mad enough to see it all without going mad. Because my imagination is powerful enough to face what most people find unthinkable.

I wallowed in it, dreamed of painting eye-frying pictures of it that would prove my genius to everyone—later, when it was over—but it didn't end. Just went on and on. Image after goddam image. I was totally delighted. Flow an endless stream of bizarre imagery before my eyes and I'm in paradise. It was like—no, better than that weightless fuck with a sculptress who was disgusted when I got cum all over her work—like when I first discovered the Aztecs as a wee tot, delighted that these bloodthirsty, cannibalistic, colorful monsters were *mine*, not the property of the light-skinned aliens from "back East"—they were *my* heritage, it was *my* blood that stained those pyramids, *my* art that survived the campaign of another Cortez centuries ago, so powerful that it took Western art until the Twentieth Century to catch up—like all this was something I dreamed up and was damn proud to have such a fantastic imagination!

Sure, I was vaguely aware that just outside Jupiter's magnetosphere, in the hospital section of Ithaca Base, my body was lying there with tubes and wires stuck into it, with a concussion, a ruptured spleen, and assorted broken bones. But somehow it didn't seem important. Sure, it was Pablo Cortez, but I was so many other places. My body and its suffering were just part of the Sirens' show: *Like pentasexual orgies in sparkling caverns, or sonic wars in oceans that flowed through endless, gigantic tubes, or electronic epic chants of a silicon-crystal disc-jockey!*

"He may not have survived after all," Calvino said.

I heard that, in the distance—*beyond the parade of idols hewn out of the hearts of neutron stars, hungrily marching through the cosmos to galaxies where entire civilizations were offered as sacrifices, and herds of armored, winged worms devoured planets and shit art and technology!*

Then, like the soft sound of a swishing skirt, the trademark of the umkhovu, the living dead—she trickled into my mind that the Sirens had scattered all over the universe. Willa Shembe, shy and curious, bored with all the human minds she had plugged into, eager to wrap her telepathic tendrils around something different, something alien—the Sirens.

I was jolted. It was being outside of space and time with Ometecuhtli—then suddenly feeling the presence of Nkulunkulu, the Zulus' maker of all things. I was being manipulated by an unseen sangoma, a Zulu diviner with cattle gall bladder crown and necklace of herbs—no, rather an abathakathi, an evil wizard whose most important product is misery, killing, illness, and drought—making a diabolical potion out of pieces of a human body—me! I felt a phantom kiss where she bit off the tip of my tongue, and left me animal-eyed, and forever spooked—her umkhovu, a slave to her magic, locked in her spell.

What was even more shocking was that I didn't know shit about the Zulus, their mythology, or superstitions—like all the rest of the Sirens' song, it just flooded my skull, only more intense—the taste of roast chicken and uputhu drowned out that of hot, greasy tacos and the bitter blood of long crunchy caterpillars in my mouth! It was a presence closer to my body than my mind. None of the Sirens' spacetime short-circuitry. This was here, now. There, then. Before I came out of the Sirens' spell, lying there with a broken body stuck with tubes and wires with a beautiful Zulu telepath sucking my blown-out mind.

She relished it. Devoured greedily.

My memories. The Sirens' maelstrom of imagery. My fantasies. Alien realities.

"You're crazy, Pablo! You got talent, but you're more a criminal than an artist!" echoed back from an argument I had with the rest of the Guerrilla Muralists at our trial.

Rainbow-filled skies over effervescent seas—me shedding my own blood so I could have something to paint with at age eight—the joy I felt the first time I was weightless, and decided that gravity was the enemy of true freedom, and decided to splash my paint, and created splatterpainting—a war of radioactive cloud-beings that goes on for millennia across billions of light-years—cartoons I'd draw on my clothes when I got bored—invisible beasts that flex gravity at will and eat black holes!

She smiled. Then moaned with delight.

And I received input from her mind—she was strange, like the humanoids who rode see-thru ships to the end of time to observe the aesthetic qualities of the heat death of the universe—other people's experiences and thoughts were what she lived for. She rarely ate, or moved—was more interested in reading more and more minds than the university's experiments—she wasted away. They thought she would die.

Then she found out about the Sirens, and said some of her few words:

"Take me to them!"

Soon I could see her clearly through my own eyes, and see me through her eyes, *and* watch the song of the Sirens with no eyes at all.

She said a few more words. "Beautiful. I love it!"

Crack! Something snapped. The deadly intensity in those big, brown eyes clicked off. She dropped on top of me.

The orderlies grabbed her and after a few skilled, strategic feels, one said, "She's dead."

I laughed. A lovely demonic laugh that took my entire aching body and all my strength. It hurt like hell and was worth it. They all, even Calvino, looked into my crazed eyes.

"Idiots! Fools! Assholes! She's..." I screamed.

"You're alive!"

"What happened?"

"Are you all right?"

"How do you feel?" some of them asked. The rest just looked scared and perplexed.

"Shut up!" I said. "There's so much...I can't...Let me out of this!"

"No!" Calvino said. You have several broken bones and internal injuries!"

It hurt like a bitch, but I didn't care, gritted my teeth, and slid myself off the bunk. They tried to stop me, but a few throat-rupturing banshee-screams kept them at bay. The floor hit me like a macrocosm of pain. Damn gravity—even the centrifugal force, fake kind!

After a while they watched me with awe and dread as if I was a rotting corpse that suddenly sprang back to life. Luckily, my right arm was working in a cast, but I could move it at the shoulder, where it counts. I reached under my gown and tore off the hospital diaper.

I needed something to paint with. Something that would smear and leave a mark. It had been years since I'd painted with my own shit. It'd have to do.

And it did nicely.

Before they shot a sedative into my veins, I managed to smear one vision onto the floor.

When I woke up, I was strapped down, re-tubed and wired, watching that vision in caca come to focus before my face.

Calvino was holding it. He'd had that section of floor torn out and sealed in acrylic. My work mummified for posterity.

"What is it?" he asked.

"Shit on laminated metal," I smartassed.

"No," he said, being unusually patient. "The subject matter. What is it?"

"It looks like some kind of soft, lovely tree that is rooted to the ground while it grows, but breaks free and flies around when it's full-grown."

"Where did it come from?"

"The Sirens. They made me see it. Made me *be* it."

"Was that all?"

"Hell no! It was a constant flow of images, all at once and all jumbled together. I could see, hear, feel, and taste it all. I wanted to paint it. I could spend my entire life on it!"

"Notice anything strange about it?"

"Doc, it was *all* strange!"

"Surely your artist's eyes can see it. Mr. Cortez, you always have been a mystery to me, almost as if *you* were from another planet, but I did learn to recognize your style."

I was stunned. "Yeah. The style! It's different! Not my usual high-power scribble, it looks..."

"More detailed, and more alien."

"But I couldn't help it, it just happened...."

"Like Willa's death," a nurse said, cool as a sip of liquid nitrogen.

"She's not dead," I said.

"All vital functions stopped. No brain activity," Calvino said, bringing those fuzzy gray eyebrows together. "She's dead."

"She's alive," I insisted. "Maybe not in that cute body, but I can still feel the presence of that insatiable suction-pump of a mind."

Calvino smiled, with some effort. "I didn't suspect you of having *any* religious beliefs, Mr. Cortez."

"Damn right I don't," I snapped. "Even the Aztec gods I'm always babbling about are basically a joke to me—I like the way it bothers the hell out of the believers.... I guess the only thing I really believe in is myself."

"And that Willa Shembe is alive," he shot at me.

"I can feel her. She's the source of the images that still parade through the back of my mind. She went through me to get them. Her mindtracks are permanently etched into my nervous system. I'm always going to receive her signals.

"...She had this fantasy that she never told anybody. She probably didn't even want me to know about it, but to get to the Sirens she gave me a grand tour of her mind. She wanted to be invisible and fly through the entire universe, faster than the speed of light, and see and *be* it all. And that's what she's doing.

"...I couldn't have done it...I'm an egomaniac. I'm too much in love with being the great Pablo Cortez to ever let go the way she did. I could never give myself totally. I'm hanging on too tight."

They all just looked confused.

"In the name of Tlazolteotl, give me something to paint—or at least draw—with! These images are driving me crazy! If you don't let me paint, my skull will swell up, pop, and leave you covered with a sticky-slimy masterpiece! These images will open up the cosmos! Transform our way of life!"

"You're too weak," Calvino said, real sincere.

"Bullshit!" I screamed. "I could paint with the bloody stumps right after my arms and legs were hacked off! The pain is nothing compared to my need! If I were decapitated, I could roll my head around and leave a blood-trail that the world will cherish!"

They brought me a pad and a marker. Nothing like a little hyperbole to get your point across.

The scientists were fascinated. They'd see things I didn't notice. Soon they were anxiously waiting for my next piece. As soon as I could move around, they let me paint, sloshing colors on whatever I could for a canvas. Some high-decibel hyperbole got me my zero-G studio at the center of Ithaca Base.

Grumblings of prosecuting me for the murder of Willa Shembe eventually petered out.

And the work came effortlessly, rapidly, ecstatically—I'd revel in it for hours, and hate myself for not being able to keep up with it, for getting tired, and needing sleep. I'd beg Calvino for drugs so I could work for weeks at a time (he refused, of course—hyperbole won't get you everything).

I'm now the most important artist of the Solar System. Scientists analyze my work for clues about the nature of other worlds. The art world hails me as the new master. Calvino hung that first shit-smear painting in his office. The Space Culture Project began making policy changes—the murals on future space colonies and starships will show my influence.

And Willa—a Siren in her own right, perhaps my most important Siren—keeps showing up through it all. Her face. Her body. Dancing through the universe. Dancing with the universe. Dancing the universe. Showing everybody that I'm not the only one responsible for all this great art. It embarrasses me—but I must acknowledge that Willa and the Sirens are my collaborators. I'd like to ignore it all and hog all the glory for myself, but she keeps showing up in the patterns of the flying paint.

In a way I enjoy painting her, as much as the rest. She's so beautiful. Her classic Zulu features. Her bold, quiet, unending curiosity. The way she sacrificed herself, willingly and without hesitation, when others simply were torn apart and I hung onto my ego with a death-grip. She alone had the courage to truly hear the song of the Sirens, and join them in their cosmic dance.

Maybe she was the only human being I could love more than I love myself. Maybe...I'll never know. I'll never be able to touch her. I can only paint her.

And the cosmos she's rapturously exploring.

An Idyll in Erehwyna

Hal Duncan

Really? he says.

Renart strumps about from room to room, mumping and mulligrumphing, thrunched by the right moger of the place to a crunkle of brow and a clamp on the jut of his chaft, thumb under chin, forefinger curling up under pursed lips. Over the weeks of merry visits from Ana Massinger (primarily to gab in billows of blue smoke over red wine, it seemed, and only secondarily to salve her sisterly fret that Puk—ensconced in the treehouse with Jaq but making regular barbarian raids on civilization for the sake of grub or ablution—was *not hassling Renart to distraction, I hope,*) curious prodding finally won from her, yesterday evening, an admission that all Renart's return jaunts into Erehwyna have indeed been diverted to work, café, park, restaurant, tavern, tabac, in short any elsewhere than the Massinger home, because in all the stint they've been here on Mars, in Erehwyna, she still hasn't sorted it to presentable.

Presentable? Renart says, having coaxed acceptance of a pataphysician's eye and hand, it being, after all, his art to hone a life's ergonomics to a healthy set of attitude, flesh and environs. Presentable? he says, having followed dinted directions, turned down into the culvert off Rue Stroedeker and arrived on the doorstep at the crack of noon, to stroll in, smiling assurances—*It can't be that bad*—and scope the full horror of misplaced furniture and furnishings, boxes and crates, cases and contents that he might describe as half-stacked and half-strewn were it not for the implication of balance in those halves. Ana, how is this even *habitable*?

He weaves the chaos, room to room, wireframing the small ground floor apartment, square hall with pisser and scrubber on the left on entry, back suite and study beside, kitchen-cum-salon and master suite to the right, looking out on Stroedeker and sunshine. Cozy but ceilinged high, with fine pine parquet underfoot throughout. Light gray though, on the walls, a bachelor's fashion of two decades ago, grim style of some strutter stancing dull machismo which, Ana explains, she didn't have the tick to update. And as for the rest...she just didn't glean a *start* for it.

He studies her for a tick, and the clutter of her attributes around. Not a shock, he says. There *is* no start from here.

It's not her, he means, the shade, so implacably not her that she's surely sensed the futility of trying to crunk her life into this drabness; but so blandly shamming functionality that, like as not, it sold her on a lie of being passable, an unassuming blankness offering itself as plain backdrop for anyone and everyone: one shade fits all. As if everyone and anyone worked like that.

What you have here, he says, is a quiddity trap.

Quiddity, the whatness of an object, is the *essential*, the nature of a thing as an instance of its class. Haccaeity, the thisness of an object, is the *existential*, the nature of a thing as construct of quirks defying reduction to quiddity. In the era of Davenport, the deluge of machined objects made for an angst of drowning. Without the notion of projectivity, all reduced to subject and object, abject at best, where was the haccaeity of factoried chow and togs, flatpack fittings and gimcrack commodities? Where even the thisness in a pleasure become parlance, formulated for replication as geekware loaded in the meat machines? In the Society of the Spectacle, as she herself has lived the fallout of, post-modernity, post-singularity, even a human seemed all quiddity, quirks merely the unique settings of shared attributes. Skinsacks with a tuple of signifiers inside that could be scanned into a simulacrum—geist as soul, Ana would say, for those who scorned superstition but could not surrender it. Hence her flight with emancipated sixer bro to the sanity, which is to say civility, of Mars.

Davenport broached a new paradigm in abolition of quiddity, his supposition: that in every corral of objects abstractable to a class by common attributes and behaviors, every object in that corral is not merely distinct in its unique mix of attribute settings but cannot be fully described without recourse to attributes inapplicable to all others of its class.

Not only is *this* electron not equal to *that* electron, but it is not equivalent.

This, Renart says with a handflick at the drab paint, is a shade for everyone and therefore no one.

So. Arms folded, Renart stands in the master bedsuite, brooding on a wall, glancing now and then at Ana, at the scatterings of jumble. The haccaeity of this canny scientist sprawling out around her in a humidor of Kaseians on the mantlepiece, a sim syrinx propped upright in a corner, the sleeves cut off her Geister jerkin; actually, he thinks, this shouldn't be so gnarly. He's rather savvy of Ana's haccaeity by now, and fond of it.

◊

Resounding the clomp of fleshling feet and shifting furniture upon her patchwork panels, bouncing back their voices in the emptying room she floors, Pitys can't help but think back fondly on the old days of Arcadia, of mountain heights, ravines, and shepherds calling out to hear their echoes in the hills she cloaked as the pine tree, *Pinus pinea*, or sturdier still in her Stone Pine form, and tall and proud, growing some twelve to twenty meters high, even over twenty-five sometimes.

The shifts of life, she thinks. She's sure of all her kind she senses shift most keenly. Senses? *Undergoes* more like. She *lives* shift, not as sharply as the fleshlings tromping in and out the master bedsuite of the Massinger abode, shuffling with weights between them, dropping a clatter or thump of something now and then, and cursing or being cursed for it—*Rot and bones, Puk! give that here!*—no, not *that* sharply, but more keen than many a tree. She displays it as she grows.

In youth? Ah, in youth she is a bushy globe and, for her first five to ten years, bears leaves that mark her juvenile, growing as little singletons, blue-green and glaucous, a mere snip of two to four centimeters long, quite different from the adult leaves that start to sprout amidst these from the fourth or fifth year on, five times the length—sometimes as much as thirty centimeters long, indeed, albeit those are quite exceptional—mid-green and growing bundled into twos. By her tenth year, roughly speaking, though she might still sprout some juvenile leaves in regrowth after injury, a broken shoot or whatnot, just to show that she still can, those mature leaves have usurped the juvenile entirely, and she'll spread a wide umbrella canopy from her thick trunk with its thick bark, red-brown, carved by deep fissures into broad vertical plates. In full maturity she sports a broad and flat crown forty to sixty meters wide.

She doesn't rush all shifts, of course. It takes three years, a longer stint than any other pine requires, for her broad ovoid cones to reach maturity at eight to fifteen centimeters long. Within these cones, pine nuts or piñones, pinhões or pinoli, her seeds are large, two centimeters long, pale brown beneath the powdery black coat that rubs off to a gentle thumb. The crude four to eight millimeter wing on each is like to fall off on its own, but then it's largely ineffective for dispersal by Susurrus anyway, flighty godling of the Martian wind, so her seeds are animal-dispersed—mainly by the azure-winged magpie once upon a time, but these days mostly by the fleshlings who, it seems, find her a useful wood for furniture or floors. Like the floor of this townhouse apartment, which is bare now, bedsuite hollowed by the fleshlings, one of whom crouches to stroke her, bless him, calls a question that soon gets its answer in a fumbling of armfuls in through the doorway, followed shortly by grand flappings that spread out the dustsheets, lay them softly down now, to protect her.

It's not the reverence of antiquity, but she can't help but be reminded of it. On Mount Mainalos, there were pine groves sacred to the god Pan, who had loved her as an Oread nymph, never forsook his love, for all that she fled and took this form in her escape to thwart his hanker. It's not the reverence of antiquity, but it does seem...an echo of it, down the ages. Sacred to Dionysus, the Aleppo pine was still an inspiration aeons later, for Paul Cézanne, moved by his garden in Aix-en-Provence, to put brush to canvas and articulate his ardor in *Les Grands Arbres*. And still, even now, more aeons and a world away, the echoes still resound.

◊

Wet sand, manila envelope, cappuccino, dry clay, wrapping paper, Nefertiti's foundation—none of these quite match the color in hue and luster, a brown paled to buff but pinked as with embarrassment.

It looks nice, says Jaq. It's like...shy sandstone.

The room is echoey empty to his voice, just the painted walls, the polished floor, and four fleshlings all jiggered, quanked by the sore swink and gaumed with paint, two of them fair spattered to clatty, the lovers Jaq and Puk roped in to sharpen the shift, make themselves useful for a change, having cabbled in play through the work—*Don't just stand there looking glaikit, dunderhead*—*Says the gormless galoot*—*Big numpty*—*Wee nyaff*—and tipped the banter into full-on rammy shenanigans with the spraypacks, until curbed by simultaneous bellows from both Ana and Renart: *Quit it!*

The paint, which it would be an ignorance of haccaeity to call pale brown, is drying to a crust on Jaq's face now, a full face-pack sprayed full brunt, sleeved off to smearage of streaks; and on the wall it is already tacky to the touch; and it is, Ana agrees, a whole lot better, much more her.

Renart brings in now, from the kitchen, the zig-zag chair of Gerrit Rietveld: four square planes of beechwood, dovetail-jointed; back vertical down to z-shape of: seat, diagonal, base: angles crisp as apple crunch. It won't go here, he thinks, but it's ideal for a seat, to study and plan: order, design, composition; tone, form, symmetry; balance: Sondheim chanelling Seurat.

A bedsuite for Ana scientist smoker syrinxist and so on Massinger, who insists that her science is not a reduction of his craft in its abstraction, but an expansion. At the extremes of science we enter poetry, she claims, the purest application of mathematics. Poesis is the suppositional calculus, notated not in symbol but in stance: epistemic, alethic, deontic, boulomaic. And if *she* should be able to see the impossibility of a viable life in a dull grey room, *he* should be able to wrangle a few numbers into sense especially when, look, it's a *glassy* permutation of a Fibonnaci Spiral.

Puk, as Renart is musing, Ana making coffee, and Jaq idling, is weaving this decorative exploit into their gaming of an harpagmos, which required a twofold offering during the course of it—a votive tablet of painted wood, an animal sacrifice—at the sanctuary of Hermes and Aphrodite. The window frame, he has decided, can be their votive tablet turned inside out, object opened to its delineating edges to articulate its reverence with greater import, to make the world itself its prayer.

And there's beef in the chiller, says Jaq. For Ana's chili. What? It's dead animal.

Which reminds him: Puk needs new togs, Jaq has resolved, and it's his task as erastes to busk his eromenos, bedizen the lad. He starts blethering of Puk, comical with trouserlegs rolled up to bare shins, wading in the brook at the bottom of the stead. They could hit the markets if they're surplus now, or if Sifu Renart can savvy the shipshaping of the bedsuite as pronto as Jaq is sure he will.

We need to get you some proper britches, he says.

◊

She is three in one, Karya, a trinity of sisters, English walnut flanked by hazelnut and sweet chestnut, *Juglans regia* flanked by *Coryllus avellana* and *Castanea vesca*, wearing the same name in all three guises to the Greeks who harvested from all three types of nut tree, this triune aspect an echo perhaps of the two sisters who schemed viciously to thwart a Lakonian maiden's dalliance with Dionysus, and were driven mad for it, fled up the scree slopes of Mount Taygetos where they were turned to stones, while she herself, dying, was changed into a deciduous tree growing twenty-five to thirty-five meters tall, her male flowers drooping catkins which fruit in autumn with green fleshy husks around the edible nut, her summer canopies now lining the Avenue K. Leslie Steiner, shattering the sunlight as Susurrus dances her, to dapple Jaq and Puk and a gaggle of skimbooted kidsters who zip past them, whooping.

The goddess Artemis told her dad Dion of the unfortunate affair, insisted that he found a sanctuary in honor of Artemis Karyatis. So, at Karyai in Lakonia, in her sacred grove of walnut or hazelnut trees, she had priestesses known as Karyatides, this sisterhood of the nut tree immortalized: in the porch of the Erechthion on the Acropolis in Athens, in stone canephora carrying baskets on their heads full of sacred foods for the goddess's feast, each pillar of individuality carved with its own face, hair, drapery, and stance; and in similar stone caryatids down the ages, in Classical Rome, Renaissance Italy, Northern Mannerism.

As if every walnut tree were not a caryatid, and each tree unique, as here, along the whole length and on both sides of the avenue of shops and stalls the lovers stroll, these stately rows of verdant pillarings a ceremonial sorority in procession, leading back the way erastes and eromenos came, to the little dogleg of Stroedeker and the culvert off it, to the townhouse doorstep and a newly dedicated sanctuary more sacred than the grandest temple in its modest unpretension, as a home.

◊

I'm not really much for cooking, says Ana.

She slices the ends off an onion and peels, brown flakes of dry papery crunkle falling away, retaining curvature on the counter where they're tossed, the smoother layer beneath stripping bit by bit under a thumbnail and scowl, to naked pearl white. She halves the whole now, lays each half flat, and slices, this half first—each knifecut through the pale crump of strata as crisp as the air is, sharp acidic waft watering eyes—then the next. Rough methodical chopping of the fanning slices, and the odd stray chunk firing out tiddlywinks from beneath the blade, serve as a *No comment* on her self-assessment. Satisfied, she grabs a wooden spoon and takes the plateful to the pot, swipes the lot into a sizzle of olive oil, stirs.

Renart, as she stirs up the sizzle to a slowly richening aroma, as the onions shift imperceptibly gradually toward translucence, is still pottering on about his work, lumping gubbins dumped in Puk's room or the hall, sometimes the kitchen, through to the master bedsuite, rapt in his task to a *Scoobedy-doop-doop, bibbedy-bap* absent and elsewhere mode of focus. In his element, it seems.

She dumps the diced steak in, to another sizzle, stirs, stirs, and returns to the chopping board.

One sweet red pepper, one orange pepper, both cut vertically from the stem, down and around and back up, to be cracked open and have the seeds stripped and shaken and teased out with a finger. She returns to tumble the browning beef roughly with the spoon, flick a morsel over here or there.

Scoob, scoobedy-doobedy-doo-bow. Smells nice.

Four jalapeños, two green, two red, one of each finely diced, one of each sliced. These she takes to the pot and adds. Another stir, digging under with the spoon to shovel, fold, checking for blood-red, turning.

Off in the bedsuite again, Renart folds togs and shelves them, carving some cunning system, no doubt, that will put all to hand, as she dresses of a morn, with the precision of some antique knight's squire sprung to buckle armor; but Susurrus leaves him to it, is more attentive to the cooking, relishing the shift of it in him, the tickle of air currents spiraled from the heat, the tang of oniony steam that seeps him, swirls in him through the kitchen with the open window that invited him inside.

At the cooker, Ana cracks a can of some cheap carbonated drink, full of sugar and spice, pours it gluggling and hissing into the pot—her secret ingredient.

Tum-ti-tum, ti-tum-tum-tum!

Dried chili flakes sprinkled liberally from a bag. A crush of crimsons and terracottas, seeded with dark and light ochres, it looks like it belongs in the pestle of some ancient artist, to be ground for pigment, mixed with egg yolk and applied to a church wall in tempera fresco, or daubed with a finger on the ceiling of a cave to conjure a bison in silhouette.

The tail of the turkey-cock turns to the sun! Sander of Tempe channeling Stevens.

A carton of chopped tomatoes. A carton of kidney beans. A stir. A step back, a release of breath, halfway a stance of satisfaction at a dusted job, halfway a momentary daze, as if at a loss as to what to do now, or in suspicion of loose ends left. She looks at Renart, who stands in the kitchen doorway.

Well, she says, it just has to simmer now. Won't be done for a yonk.

◊

What do you think? Am I prepped for action?

Jaq in Puk's skivvies, pinging waistband and thumbing thighbands straight, rootling pod to set his bollocks, shift cock to the left. To the right.

I don't know which way I dress, he says. These are yanked.

He settles on upright as fated outcome anyway given stirrings to the novel cling and intimacy of frottage by proxy, or loinspace incursion, or whatever it is that's scrunching ballsack and rousing yen in his pintle. Yen that earns dints of esteem from other browsers in the togstore, an invite from a gazing ageling girl over by the hats, which he dints thanks and apologies to, sorry, he forgot to update his publics with his tweaked kinsey, which she missives a shame, them both being sixers, but sweet that he'd do that for his beau, shift his hanker to fit so snug, and no need to apologize at all. Also: his gambit to unspotlight Puk is *adorable*, if he doesn't mind her saying.

Puk having been blithe to strip in the store, since Erehwynan nonchalance was on display throughout among the browsers—no different to the sauna, really—but unprepped for the sprucer that aforesaid browsers were politely nudged to cleanse with before trialing summer-sweaty skin in whatnot. Heads turned to his yelp of startle, from the cubicle, at the blasts of high-pressure vapor from all angles, and hot air to dry, and focused particularly on nooks of flesh most like to be ripe. And of course the door opened auto the click it was done, so there Puk stood, mortified by the pricking of his pintle at the sprucer's intimacies. Whereupon Jaq, fingersnap pronto, tossed him the first britches to hand, (navy blue) nimble as could be, and dropped his own in a grand diversionary show of trialing this quaint custom of underwear, with a quick stride down the aisle a few steps, as if to optimize Puk's view of his twirl, but in fact to set a precise distance whereby they weren't a duo drawing more attention now, but rather a soloist and his singular but backgrounded audience.

Try the paisley, he says, the black on silver. It'll be like a flip of your Geister synthe, a Fourier Harmony.

It's not about transforming Puk to a native, Jaq explains as the Earther slips out of one set of britches and into the other, or painting him as a sham of such, but about finding the permutation of him for this new domain.

How about these ones? says Puk.

The same pattern in crimson and jade.

Even better, says Jaq.

◊

Herbaceous, rhizomatous, perennial, *Mentha spicata* (or *viridis*) sprouts well in most any temperate climate, from her fleshy rhizome spreading wide and down into the soil—unless some spoilsport gardener captures her invasive roots in pots or planters—stretching her variably hairless to hairy stems from thirty centimeters to a meter tall in limber abundance. She does prefer partial shade, she has made it clear to Susurrus, but will thrive in anything from mostly shade to full sun, flourishing soft leaves with serrated margins, five to nine centimeters long, one-and-a-half to three centimeters broad, the oil of spearmint chewed from her tender pale green flesh by Puk now, from a soggy leaf lipped from a straw, rich with the dextro-carvone which imbues her aromatic foliage with that scent so unmistakably fresh it was only natural to use her on the bodies of the dead, to hold the line valiantly (if vainly) against the stench of rot. Used as a treatment for hirsutism in women too, spearmint produces flowers in slender spikes, each flower pink or white, a slight two-and-a-half to three millimeters long and broad.

She has always been pretty, in sight, scent, taste. The god Hades loved his Minthê for that, and she basked in his affections, blithe until the day she boasted in her pride that she was *so* much better than his queen Persephone, at which the goddess, or her mother Demeter perhaps, transformed the nymph into the mint plant they'd then use to flavor the sacred barley-drink of their Eleusinian Mysteries, as she would one day flavor also, in far western lands of slaves, mint juleps and mojitos, which taste much better here, in a tavern on Boulevard Hovendaal, in the mouths of dark and golden-eyed lovers. Taste best in each other's mouths as they kiss in the recessed booth, Jaq fumbling with the tash on Puk's trews, unbuttoning the ballop, because when the tumblespace cast danced focus from a pairing in the New Davenport outlet to frame the snugged lushes, Puk gave an *Oh! oh!* and a grinning handflap, and pounced to mash lips, to whoops and whistles of esteem.

◊

Dawnlight through the door of the treehouse.

The fuzzled canoodling that inflamed, via gropes and giggles, opposed by half-hearted remonstrations from Jaq that he was far too soused, advanced, by resolute demonstrations from Puk that Jaq's tadger was not, through frolic to hard fuckery is now reprised as mawmsey croodling, the two well-fucked and well-fadged in the after, snuggling still socketed. Warm breath on the back of his neck, canty in Jaq's couthy embrace, Puk yawns as he drumbles how their socketing feels designed.

Getting back is a blur: a stumbling carouse along Steiner to cadge a hitch, Jaq's brainpop scheme, from one of the nightcarters offloaded now at Bradshaw Market, headed back out through the subrurals, and ever resolute to grant passage on request, ever a seat kept free in their skimcart, in memory of the flight from Phobos's shattering, a custom deep as oath: never again to have no room for one asking transport; Puk on Jaq's lap squirming drunk and hyper to grope and clumse Jaq's doublet free from a ferntickled shoulder, to show it—see?—his Phobian ancestry; midway in the weavy stagger after being dropped, along the long empty winds through forestry pitch black either side, paths carved in the gleam of asphalt below, the star-strewn and fob-scythed vault above, stumbling and tumbling in a crash into thick burdock, lying on his back, looking up at the vastation of that abyss, atramentine and asparkle; puking at the side of the road; being *Nearly there, nearly there*; taking a slug of rum from a flask magicked by Jaq from who knows where; being recovered and rannigant again enough, when at last they made it to the stead, that he flailed free of sensible steerage toward Jaq's room, and went crash splashing prancing off in a run through undergrowth like a kidster in surf, to their oak and elm, calling Jaq to him like a mutt, cracking up at it; and the two clambered up into the treehouse to flop in a tangle, frisky Puk wrappling Jaq back out of laze and into lusty yen.

So they fucked wild, Puk astride at first, then turned, to his hands and knees, to be tupped under Jaq's hunching thrusts, hips and shoulder and fists of hair yanked back, for the prick to ram jam bam and cram him, till he felt it fill him, and he'd swear to Cock, the jism spouted into and through him and out his own spurting prick.

And now, here they lie on their sides, snuggling still socketed, Puk blissed to feel Jaq inside and around him as he gazes out at dawnlight through the door of the treehouse.

Yen is, Jaq has savvied him, the hacceity of the human. Spinoza by way of Davenport by way of Sifu Renart.

Real Mothers, a Faggot Uncle, and the Name of the Father: Samuel R. Delany's Feminist Revisions of the Story of SF

L. Timmel Duchamp

The stories a discipline or genre tells about itself reflect its values and anxieties as well as determine the shapes and even limits of its future.[1] Four particularly vexed nodes of controversy pervade the stories that writers, critics, and fans tell about science fiction, surfacing constantly in its discourse at cons, in print publications, and online, particularly in the SF blogosphere. These four points of controversy include a preoccupation with the question of SF's legitimacy; an obsession with establishing a monolithic definition of set texts for patrolling the genre's border; the search for a definitive story of SF's origins and lineage; and the failure to integrate the work of women into the genre's narratives about itself. Over the years, Samuel R. Delany has weighed in on all four; but to date, his analyses bearing on them have not been significantly heeded, perhaps because doing so would entail a radically different way of thinking and talking about the genre. In this paper I will discuss these points of controversy and then examine Delany's insights into them and his outline for a radically different story of SF that would lay these issues to eternal rest.

The first two points of controversy seem to be permanent features of the landscape for most writers, fans, and critics of SF; hardly a day goes by when one or the other of them is not hotly discussed in the SF blogosphere.[2] Although the legitimacy and definition and labeling issues are typically treated as separate, they are implicitly connected. On the one hand, anxiety about the perceived illegitimacy of science fiction vis-à-vis "mainstream literature," (as it is called in the genre) and, often, ressentiment toward those who dismiss SF as a "ghetto" frequently manifest themselves in attempts by fans and writers to exclude and expel and keep tight control over definitions and labels. On the other hand, groups of writers within the genre often create new labels for characterizing their own and their friends' fiction, either to position it as a high(ly) literary—and thus more legitimate—exploitation of the forms of SF, or to distinguish it as radically new and more sophisticated than previous SF texts. Similarly, critics, as

Delany noted in his "Exhortation to SF Scholars," use the proposal of a system of definition "as an initializing mark of mastery that empowers all further discourse to proceed"—as critics "in every other area of literary-critical studies" rarely do. ("Exhortation" 5)

In the US from the 1920s through the early 1950s, SF was published chiefly in pulp magazines and comics. In his introduction to *Microcosmic God, Vol.2* of Theodore Sturgeon's collected stories, Delany quotes Sturgeon's account of how his stepfather, Argyll, reacted when young Ted bought his first SF magazine (a 1933 issue of *Astounding*):

> I brought it home and Argyll pounced on it as I came in the door. "Not in my house!" he said, and scooped it off my schoolbooks and took it straight into the kitchen and put it in the garbage and put the cover on. "That's what we do with garbage," and he sat back down at his desk and my mother at the end of it and their drink. ("Forward" xxii)

Delany attributes Argyll's attitude, that SF is trash, to the "moral rigidities" of the pre-World War II era, when pulp magazines and comics were viewed as a "pernicious influence of an evil antiart."(xxiii) Delany notes that when in 1946, "on the other side of the Second World War," his parents found him reading a Batman comic, although his father was appalled, comics "were allowed in the house with only comparatively minimal policing." (xxiii)

The genre may have produced a significant number of what Jonathan Lethem calls "Great Books" in the decades since Argyll Sturgeon characterized SF as "garbage," but for many, the attitude that SF is "trash" has apparently not altered significantly. When in early 2006 David Izkoff, the new science fiction reviewer for the *New York Times*, published his first review along with a reading list titled "Science Fiction for the Ages" that he said was a list of personal favorites, he expressed a sense of shame about being seen to read SF in public. What "truly shames me," he writes, "is that I cannot turn to any of these people [fellow passengers on the subway], or to my friends, or to you, and say...you should pick up this new work of science fiction I just finished reading, because you will enjoy it as much as I did." Shame seems a peculiarly strong choice of word, given the explanation he offers:

> I cannot do this in good conscience because if you were to immerse yourself in most of the sci-fi being published these days, you would probably enjoy it as much as one enjoys reading a biology textbook or a stereo manual. And

you would very likely come away wondering, as I do from time to time, whether science fiction has strayed so far from the fiction category as a whole that, though the two share common ancestors, they now seem to have as much to do with each other as a whale has to do with a platypus. ("Geek to Me")

Although some welcomed the possibility that the *New York Times Book Review* actually intended to publish a regular SF column rather than the occasional short piece by Gerald Jonas the *Times* had previously allotted to SF, the language, tone, and underlying assumptions implicit in Itzkoff's first column provoked controversy in the SF blogosphere.[3] SF writers, critics, and fans have an acute sensitivity to the anxieties attending ghetto status, and few missed the peculiarity of Itzkoff's use of the word shame, which rendered his apparent anxieties about being associated with the genre stark and—for some—even offensive. Mathew Cheney, for instance, not only mocks Itzkoff's anxieties—

> I have a hard time mustering up much of a response beyond, "Boo, hoo," because if the poor boy is wandering through the subways in search of "social standing" for the books he reads, there's no hope for him at all and he needs to get one of those expensive Manhattan shrinks to work through it with him. (Cheney, March 5, 2006)

but also parses the passage quoted above to expose the nature of Itzkoff's anxieties:

> So there are two things in the world, "fiction" and things that are unreadable by people on subway cars. There is also this person called you, and you don't enjoy reading biology textbooks or stereo manuals. This is a marvelous move, because here the equation is "you = Dave Itzkoff" and so the insecure writer has turned the world into himself. Clearly, his inner child, disappointed with the world, is acting up.

> The implication here is that you is not a "geek," which is what a person who enjoys such novels as *Counting Heads* is. Geeks are outsiders, they are not normal, they exist on the margins, they are part of a freakshow, they have no social standing or political clout, and they don't read the

New York Times. And they're taking over the world and making science fiction unsafe for the rest of us.

Except the thing Itzkoff calls "science fiction" (or "sci fi") doesn't exist. It doesn't exist as an opposite to the ridiculous "fiction" category he creates (since that doesn't exist, either), and it doesn't exist because all sorts of things get published as science fiction...I'm not denying there isn't plenty of SF that is, well, geeky. It's not the stuff that appeals to me, but I actually admire it a lot...Why should it have to be as appealing to the masses as *The Da Vinci Code*? This is to confuse quality with popularity, and that's a deadly confusion. (Cheney, March 5, 2006)

Cheney goes on to examine Itzkoff's list of his ten favorite SF books, noting that it includes nothing "geeky" (or "hard"), and expresses amusement that "Itzkoff's choices and preferences suggest he is as crippled by nostalgia as the people who complain that SF hasn't been any good since the death of John W. Campbell." To me, however, Itzkoff's list suggests something rather different (besides sexist ignorance of work by women writers). Apart from *The Twilight Zone Companion*, his list carefully selects titles that have the status of being "classics" or are written by authors who've achieved recognition in mainstream literary circles (works of the sort Delany characterizes as "borderline cases" in his *Diacritics* interview): Walter M. Miller, Jr.'s *A Canticle for Leibowitz*; Kurt Vonnegut's *Cat's Cradle*; Anthony Burgess's *A Clockwork Orange*; Thomas Pynchon's *The Crying of Lot 49*; Jonathan Lethem's *Gun, with Occasional Music: A Novel*; China Miéville's *Looking for Jake*; Philip K. Dick's *The Man in the High Castle*; Ray Bradbury's *R is for Rocket*; and Alan Moore and Dave Gibbons' *Watchmen*. Rather than being simply non-"geeky," Itzkoff's list reflects a desperate wish to exhibit sufficient distinction in his taste to disavow the very stigmatization Cheney mocks him for fretting over.

There's nothing novel in Itzkoff's tactic: it resembles another tactic deployed by SF critics to render SF legitimate, viz., that of drafting works of high literature that are "borderline" SF into the SF canon with the hope of redeeming it. Novels like Thomas Pynchon's *Gravity's Rainbow*, Kazuo Ishiguro's *Never Let Me Go*, Cormac McCarthy's *The Road*, Haruki Murakami's *Kafka on the Shore*, Margaret Atwood's *The Handmaid's Tail*, Aldous Huxley's *Brave New World*, Philip Roth's *The Plot Against America*, George Orwell's *1984*, though arguably science-fictional (especially when judged by the criteria of one or another formal definition of SF), are not usually shelved in the SF sections of bookstores and were not themselves written with reference to other works of SF. While it makes sense to consider such novels as works of genre to the extent that they bear an intertextual relation to works of SF, because such novels have high prestige and recognition value outside the genre, critics often tend to claim them as markers demonstrating the worth and value of works of science fiction regardless of their provenance or significance for the genre.

But just as SF critics wish to identify high literary work as SF to win respectability of the genre by association, so do high literary critics wish to identify brilliant works of SF as literary and dissociate them from the genre. Thus, when an SF author who has been clearly associated with the genre produces work that achieves recognition in the literary sphere, critics claim that the work "transcends" the genre. A typical example can be found in Steve Erickson's interview of Delany in *Black Clock*:

> A lot of your work, particularly in the late Sixties and going into the Seventies, seemed intended both to transcend the conventions of science fiction and at the same time to embrace what we'll call, for lack of something better, the "mainstream." But as your biographies have it, you grew up not necessarily reading a lot of science fiction but a lot of more classical literature. (Erickson, 73)

Erickson's question is clearly meant to prompt Delany to disavow not only his classification as an SF writer but also the influence SF has had on his fiction. Delany responds by talking about how emotionally powerful his experiences reading SF as a child were. A few questions later, Erickson tries again: "So you didn't feel caught up by a dual impulse to transcend the genre on the one hand and embrace it on the other." This time Delany overtly attempts to set Erickson straight:

> Transcending the genre? At best it's a conventional—and somewhat hyperbolic—way to refer to the writer's unusual contribution to the genre itself. But the SF novelist who wants to do something really good and new is no more trying to transcend the SF genre than the literary novelist who wants to write a really good and new literary novel is trying to transcend literature. In both cases it's a matter of trying to live up to the potential of the genre. (Erickson, 75)

Delany then expands on the notion of living up to the potential of the genre in which one is writing. Nevertheless, Erickson's anxieties about Delany's association with the SF ghetto apparently prevent him from grasping Delany's point, for he's unable to let the matter drop. So he tries once again:

> OK. Let's give this dead horse one more whack. It doesn't seem such a coincidence that *Dhalgren* and *Gravity's Rainbow* were written pretty much during the same period of time. We could say the line between "science fiction" and "mainstream" was being attacked from different sides by both books. (Erickson 76)

Delany responds by agreeing with the last sentence, but insists, "To repeat myself, genre distinctions are fundamentally power boundaries." And he goes on to note that "exclusionary attitudes are part of the history of science fiction....Those exclusionary forces rigorously shaped the space in which the rhetorical richness, invention, and genius of SF was forced to flower." (76) In other words, a genre is a location with a history—and not simply a slot with a label.

Jonathan Lethem, who spent years working in the genre before "breaking out" into the mainstream, shares Erickson's interest in dismantling "the line" between "science fiction and mainstream." In an essay first published in 1998, Lethem "dreams" of "utopian reconfiguration of the publishing, bookselling, and reviewing apparatus" that would dismantle the "barrier" between "genre" and "mainstream" fiction:

> The 1973 Nebula Award should have gone to *Gravity's Rainbow*, the 1976 Award to *Ratner's Star*. Soon after, the notion of "science fiction" ought to have been gently and lovingly dismantled, and the writers dispersed: children's fantasists here, hardware-fetish thriller writers here, novelizers of films both-real-and-imaginary here. Most important, a ragged handful of heroically enduring and ambitious speculative fabulators should have embarked for the rocky realms of midlist, out-of-category fiction. And there—don't wake me now, I'm fond of this one— they should have been welcomed. (Lethem, 9)

"Speculative fabulation," Lethem informs us, was "a lit-crit term both pretentiously silly and dead right," conceived "in a seizure of ambition," when SF "flirted with renaming itself."(1) Lethem's principal complaint is that "SF's literary writers exist now in a twilight world, neither respectable nor commercially viable." If SF can't be merged with the mainstream, then what is needed, he argues, is to find a way to make work that gets categorized as SF legitimate by keeping it from "drowning in a sea of garbage in bookstores," by presenting "its own best face, to win proper respect."[4] (Lethem, 8)

A similar tactic to that of drafting literary works into the SF canon is that of inventing new labels designed to blur the genre distinctions Delany characterizes as "power boundaries," with the aim of placing the more literary or "softer" SF within a boundary zone into which can be drafted literary work with fantastic or SFnal elements. The term "Speculative Fiction" or "Spec Fic" dates back to 1947, when first Heinlein used it, but began to be used in the 1970s to imply an SF work's superior quality to other science fiction; the US version of the term "New Wave" dates back to the mid-1960s; and the term "slipstream," which many people say Bruce Sterling coined, became popular in the late 1980s and continues to be bandied about to this day. The late 1980s and early 1990s also saw an attempt to distinguish the "postmoderns," which according to Michael Swanwick were comprised of a "natural division" between "humanists" and "cyberpunks"[5]; while in the late 1990s, a group of Fantasy writers led by Fantasy of Manners writer Ellen Kushner (who earlier coined the term "Mannerpunk") attempted to create "a new literary movement" called the "Young Trollopes." More recently, various cliques (or "tribes") of fantasy and SF writers have attempted to create designations for their own use that inevitably fail through an inability to establish or control essential definitions. These include "interstitial fiction," "the New Weird," "infernokrusher," "New Fabulism" and even "New Wave Fabulism."[6] While all these attempts to distinguish a few genre texts from all others do not necessarily aim to confer literary legitimacy on their beneficiaries, they are, like the oldest, most pervasive label—"hard SF"—manifestations of the anxieties of the genre's lack of legitimacy.

If all of these labels have a history of running aground on the rocks of definitional disputes, that is likely because, as Delany points out, definition is associated with mastery. "Genres, discourses, and genre collections are all social objects," he declares, drawing on Lucien Goldmann's *Philosophy and the Human Sciences*, and social objects resist formal definition:

> Social objects are those that, instead of existing as a relatively limited number of material objects, exist rather as an unspecified number of recognition codes (functional descriptions, if you will) shared by an unlimited population, in which new and different examples are

regularly produced.... And when a discourse (or genre collection, such as art) encourages, values, and privileges originality, creativity, variation, and change in its new examples, it should be self-evident why "definition" is an impossible task (since the object itself, if it is healthy, is constantly developing and changing), even for someone who finds it difficult to follow the fine points. ("Politics" 239)

In "The Politics of the Paraliterary" Delany focuses on Darko Suvin as an example of the misguided critic hellbent on establishing a formal definition of science fiction, but in his "Exhortation to SF Scholars" Delany generalizes this insistence on establishing a formal definition of SF as a preoccupation of many of the academic critics who choose to study SF. What all the attempts have in common, he observes, "is a bottom-line absolute, a zero-degree of authoritative empowerment—the credential that allows the master to speak and that authenticates its speech—that drops out of the bottom of the argument, as it were, and 'grounds' it, without ever actually entering into it." ("Exhortation," 4)

Not surprisingly, those anxious to preserve SF's "purity" set the definitions narrowly, so as to exclude (or make tenuous) fiction that is not sufficiently "hard" enough,[7] while many at the "literary" end of the SF spectrum, anxious to have their work read without the prejudice of the SF label, frequently invent new terms in the hope that their work's affinity with literary texts will help it stand out from the genre's "sea of garbage" (as Lethem puts it). Both of these tactics, though fundamentally at odds, seem to be driven by the same sense of frustration and the same impulse to take control of a messy situation through semantic mastery.

The third point of controversy pervading the stories that critics, writers, and fans tell about SF is the search for origins and the establishment of lineage, centering on the questions of who wrote the first texts of science fiction and how the field was subsequently shaped. How a critic answers these questions usually hinges on how the critic defines science fiction. While the need to create a monumental history typically involves investing the genre with the cultural capital of widely recognized literary ancestors, doing so is usually of more importance to the genre's critics and writers than to its fans. According to Delany, science fiction writers

have been proposing origins for our genre since the late thirties, when the game of origin hunting became important to early critics first interested in contemporary popular culture. The various proposals made over the years are legion: Wells, Verne, and Poe, in that order, have the most backers. There were more eccentric ones (my personal favorite is Edward Sylvester Ellis's *The Steam Man of the Prairies*, a dime novel from 1865, whose fifteen-year-old inventor hero builds a ten-foot steam-powered robot, who can pull a horseless carriage along behind him at nearly sixty miles an hour...and more conservative ones (Francis Bacon's *The New Atlantis*, 1629; Joannes Kepler's *Somnium* [written 1609, published 1634]; Savinien Cyrano's [de Bergerac] *Voyage to the Moon* and *The States and Empires of the Sun*[1650]), and slightly loopy ones (Shakespeare's *Tempest*; Dante's *Commedia*), and some classical ones (Lucian of Samosata's *True History*, from the second century A.D., which recounts a voyage to the moon).... When Brian Aldiss's history of science fiction, *Billion Year Spree: The True History of Science Fiction*, first appeared from Doubleday in 1973 (from page one of Chapter One: "As a preliminary, we need a definition of science fiction..."), one might have assumed that the argument filling its opening chapter, proposing *Frankenstein* as our new privileged origin, was another eccentric suggestion among many—and would be paid about as much attention to as any of these others. ("Politics" 263)

But Aldiss's new definition of SF and new origins story had legs, for it was regarded by "academics who saw their own fields of literary study rocked by the advent of theory" as

a weighty sandbag on a breakwater against the rising theoretical tide. For the rest, they tended to accept the argument simply because it received a certain amount of attention from these others. Among writers and those not directly concerned with the theoretical debates, there was still a vague presentiment that such singular origins somehow authorized and legitimated a contemporary practice of writing, or that its feminist implications made it attractive. ("Politics" 266)

The origins controversy did not die with Aldiss's proposal of Mary Shelley as the Founder of Science Fiction. As recently as 1998, *In The*

Dreams Our Stuff Is Made Of, Thomas Disch claimed Edgar Allan Poe as the first SF writer. Certainly most US writers and critics prefer not to trace SF's lineage back to someone who is a Brit, a woman, and a romantic. For as Delany insists: "The origin is always a political construct." ("Politics," 266) And so the battle rages on.

The fourth point of controversy attending the stories told about SF, one which arises virtually daily in the blogosphere and more and more frequently in published reviews, is the failure to integrate the work of women into the genre's stories of itself. Women had a presence in the genre's early pulp magazines. But as Justine Larbalestier's *Battle of the Sexes in Science Fiction* shows, for decades, the very presence of women in the genre caused controversy. Many fans (including the young Isaac Asimov) argued vociferously that even women characters had no business intruding into the sacred male precincts of SF. The domination of the genre by brilliant work by women in the 1970s, however, as well as effective feminist organization in fandom, eventually silenced overt protests against the presence of women in the male-dominated clubhouse. But although women are now fully accredited members of the genre's community, the position of women continues to demonstrate a failure to integrate the work of women into the genre, thus assuring their continuing marginality. This failure usually takes the form of reducing women writers to an exceptional or token presence by offering a separate account of them that relegates them to the margins and overlooks their contributions to the genre's main stories. This last issue concerns mainly women writers and critics and the men who make an effort to support them. Since the presence of women in the field has expanded enormously over the last couple of decades, I believe it is an issue that will become increasingly visible and vexing to everyone. Lately I've been struck by just how many men in the field would genuinely like to see the problem solved—even as they express incomprehension for why it should still be a problem when outright expressions of sexism have become rare.

Certain of Delany's insights and analyses, taken to their logical conclusion, would require the creation of a radically different story of SF, one that would fully integrate the work of the genre's women even as it dismisses, for good, the preoccupation with legitimacy, the search for a definitive story of SF's origins and lineage, and the obsession with establishing a monolithic definition of SF texts for patrolling the genre's borders. Although the issue that concerns me most is the seeming impossibility of the genre's fully integrating science fiction by women into the stories it tells about itself, Delany's take on these four issues has persuaded me that they are intertwined and perhaps even inextricable.

◊

In 1987, during an interview with Delany, Takayuki Tatsumi proposed a reconstruction of "American SF history" reflecting the momentary dominance of the field by cyberpunk.[8] His reconstruction sketches a patrilineal narrative that begins with Bester (who produced his best work in the 1950s), proceeds to Delany (who began publishing in the early 1960s and whose most widely admired works of SF appeared in the 1970s and early 1980s) and Varley (whose best work appeared in the late 1970s and early 1980s), and culminates with William Gibson, the 1980's SF heir apparent. Shortly before Tatsumi proposed this reconstruction, Delany cited Jeanne Gomoll's "Open Letter to Joanna Russ" and asserted that the "feminist explosion" of the 1970s had "obviously influenced" the cyberpunks and had done so "much more than the New Wave" had.[9] Although this was an utterly astonishing contention, Delany's 1987 interlocutor not only ignored it, but even went on to confer patriarchal status on Delany. Whatever Tatsumi's reason for doing so might be, this move elicited a fascinating reply from Delany.

Rather than allowing the interviewer to make an end-run around his refusal to play along with a boys' own narrative of cyberpunk SF family relations, Delany expanded on his astonishing idea of feminist influence by countering the interviewer's proposed patrilineage with a completely different narrative of family relations. He started by zooming in on a certain preoccupation he calls the "anxious search for fathers":

> When you look at the criticism cyberpunk has generated, you notice among the male critics this endless, anxious search for fathers—that finally just indicates the general male discomfort with the whole notion of paternity. Which, in cyberpunk, is as it should be. Cyberpunk is, at basis, a bastard form of writing. It doesn't have a father. Or, rather, it has so many that enumerating them just doesn't mean anything. ("Mothers," 177)

In the more than twenty years since Delany characterized cyberpunk as "a bastard form of writing," this "anxious search for fathers" continues. Critics continually propose this father or that for defining, placing, and—if Delany is correct—legitimating cyberpunk. A recent version can be found in John Clute's chapter describing SF from 1980-2000, in *The Cambridge Companion to Science Fiction* (2003); Clute names Vernor Vinge as the "godfather" of cyberpunk and describes Vinge's "True Names" and Ridley Scott's *Blade Runner* as the "mulch of influences" from which Gibson created the particular metaphor of cyberspace. Mulch, like fertilizer, enriches the soil. And fathers, as we know, provide sperm that is said to "fertilize" eggs. Surely the metaphor of fertilization is a rather strange way of describing the joining of gametes that results in the recombination of genetic material, but then many of the metaphors that dominate biological discourse are similarly strange. "Mulch" is a more discreet choice of metaphor than "godfather," though it suggests a more material connection than "godfather." A "godfather" is, strictly speaking, a spiritual—as opposed to biological—father, but as a compound, to the ear, anyway, it seems to mix up paternity with godhood.

Interestingly, the anxiety about fathers that Delany cites differs markedly from that of Harold Bloom's "anxiety of influence," which depicts literary sons as in an oedipal relation to their literary fathers. The "endless, anxious search" for the fathers of cyberpunk that Delany talks about bears little relation to Bloom's theory of an anxiety involving a single literary father. I suspect this is because oedipal relations arise from a distinctly bourgeois psychological formation in which legitimacy is not at issue. As Delany characterizes cyberpunk as a "bastard form of writing," so I would suggest that science fiction generally is a bastard form of writing—and for the same reason Delany gives: it has too many fathers.[10] And having too many fathers, Delany says, means that enumerating them "just doesn't mean anything."

Well, perhaps it is also the case that the concept of paternity doesn't mean a thing for science fiction as a whole, either. Just consider how irrelevant Bloom's anxiety of influence is for figuring generations of SF writers. Who are the patriarchal figures of the field? Not Wells. Not Asimov. Not Clarke. Not Sturgeon. Not even Heinlein, who has inspired both rebellion and devotion yet simply does not constitute a credible embodiment of the Law. The patriarchs, if there are any, would have to be Gernsback and Campbell, both editors, and however powerful, editors cannot, as editors, figure in the kind of lineage Tatsumi proposes.[11] To my mind, the sibling model has always dominated relations among science fiction writers, such that influence is often lateral. And this, too, marks a difference from the Bloomian model. Perhaps more importantly, the texts of science fiction are so constantly in conversation with one another that the welter of relations involved is simply too promiscuous to be reduced to a lineage. I love this aspect of science fiction myself, but I suspect that for all those who prize the values of monogamy and the model of the heteronormative nuclear family, this is a sorry state of affairs that generates the very anxiety Delany attributes to the early critics of cyberpunk. Such anxiety might well explain why critics of science fiction in general spend so much of their energy trying to establish the true patrilineage of the field.

After declaring that cyberpunk has too many fathers so that

"enumerating them just doesn't mean anything," Delany further unfolds his figure of family relations:

> What it's got are mothers. A whole set of them—who, in literary terms, were so promiscuous that their cyberpunk offspring will simply never be able to settle down, sure of a certain daddy. ("Mothers," 177)

As a woman writer and a feminist, I find myself wondering whether any man writer has ever named a woman writer or women writers as his literary mother(s) or primary influence. When has a critic—other than Delany—ever proposed such an attribution? Except perhaps in the romance and mystery genres, the line of literary descent for men writers is never traced directly through women. While a few science fiction critics—most of them British—have followed Brian Aldiss's lead in claiming Mary Shelley as the first science fiction writer and thus as the mother of science fiction, they do not name her as a chief influence on a particular man writer. As a long-dead progenitor, Mary Shelley carries a certain cultural capital that can be claimed without fear of emasculation. But that's a far cry from putting her into the direct lineage.

"I'm a favorite faggot 'uncle,'" Delany continues,

> who's always looked out for mom and who, when they were young, showed the kids some magic tricks. But I have no more claim to a position on the direct line of descent than any other male writer. Sometimes they like to fantasize I do. But that's just because they used to like me before they knew anything about real sex.
>
> To the extent that they can accept mom and their bastard status—which I think Gibson does—these writers produce some profoundly interesting and elegant work. ("Mothers," 177)

Over the years, in interview after interview, Delany has repeatedly countered his interlocutors' insistence that his work be extracted from the various paraliteratures he has contributed to. For one thing, he has held that the parameters of a genre are determined not by its texts, but by the protocols of reading; and for another, he has argued that the desire for legitimacy is a snare and delusion that fundamentally misunderstands the operations of discourse. But here, deploying this figure of familial relations, Delany links the issue of legitimacy with the constant, mostly tacit refusal to acknowledge the presence and influence of work by women.

This presence and influence, he suggests, creates anxiety. And that anxiety is all wrapped up with the problem of not being able to find and name the father. I believe this gives us a better understanding for why Bruce Sterling and others in the original Cyberpunk Movement so strenuously denied for much of the 1990s that cyberpunk with a small "c"—a good deal of which has been written by women—wasn't the true cyberpunk, since real cyberpunk had existed only for a very brief window in the mid-1980s. And I would argue that this desire to narrowly define and limit cyberpunk parallels the unending brawl that goes on in fan and academic circles alike about what science fiction is—as though if only we could decide on a single, clear definition of what makes a text science fiction, then science fiction could finally boast its own proper name, the product of a single patrilineage rather than the non-bourgeois family Delany describes. Science fiction, Delany's remarks on cyberpunk have convinced me, can only be a bastard form of writing because an unambiguous, unitary definition of what makes science fiction science fiction, which would be necessary for establishing legitimacy, is impossible.

In concluding his elaboration of cyberpunk's bastard status, Delany restates the importance of the link:

> To the extent they rebel against them—and the one point [Jeanne] Gomoll couldn't seem to make was that this search for fathers is part of the same legitimating move that ignores mothers—the work becomes at its best conservative and at its worst rhubarbative[sic]—if not downright tedious. ("Mothers," 177)

Here Delany has come full circle, returning to Jeanne Gomoll's "An Open Letter to Joanna Russ," a manifesto challenging Bruce Sterling's erasure of the flowering of feminist SF in the 1970s, which he mentioned immediately before Tatsumi proposed his patrilineal reconstruction of SF. The first few times I read this, although I exulted that Delany had read Gomoll sympathetically, I grasped only part of it, the part that I already knew. Gomoll's "Open Letter" asserted that Bruce Sterling's characterization of late 1970s SF as "confused, self-involved, and stale" marked the first sign of feminist SF's erasure from SF history. And indeed, his brief remark in the manifesto that is his introduction to Gibson's collection of short fiction, *Burning Chrome*, would lead the casual reader to assume that not only did nothing interesting happen in the genre during those years, but also that cyberpunk was rebelling against something that was not in fact radically new. If Sterling had deigned to name feminist

SF as what cyberpunk was rebelling against, the reader would have been left to wonder if the cyberpunks were about as revolutionary as the contemporaneous Reagan-supported contras who were also rebelling against a 1970s revolution. But since Sterling does not name names, the reader is not invited to link "confused, self-involved, and stale" with what Delany calls "the explosion of feminist SF," and the manifesto instead follows the ancient pattern feminist scholars know well, the pattern that has repeatedly resulted in eliminating the work of women from historical memory.

Or, as Delany puts it, the manifesto ignores cyberpunk's mothers. "You're omitting," he's just told his interviewer,

> the Russ/Le Guin, McIntyre, and [Joan] Vinge axis, without which there wouldn't be any cyberpunk. Is it this macho uncertainty that keeps on trying to make us black out the explosion that lights the whole cyberpunk movement? without which we wouldn't be able to read it? without which there would not be either the returning macho or the female cyberpunk characters who stand up to it? ("Mothers," 177)

Here Delany cites two kinds of relations between cyberpunk and feminist SF, one positive or productive, the other reactionary or negative. Easiest to grasp is his claim for the positive relation, such that cyberpunk's production of Molly in Gibson's *Neuromancer* and other female characters like her needed the rich development of female characterization found in feminist SF of the 1970s.[12] The second kind of relation that Delany notes, the negative or reactionary, I did not immediately grasp. Delany's perception, here, is informed by Nietzsche's insight, developed by Foucault and Derrida among others, that mere rebellion is in a profound sense reactionary, necessarily reiterating and reinforcing the very terms one wishes to escape. And so, given the inherent structure of rebellion—viz., that it is dependent on and is in some sense generated by the very thing it opposes—to the extent that cyberpunk rebels against its mothers, Delany is saying, cyberpunk's "returning macho" renders the work conservative, possibly rebarbative, and perhaps even downright "tedious."

Gibson, Delany says, "is the one who most responds to the recent (and by no means completed) feminist history of our genre, and in an extraordinarily creative way—in a way similar to the way that Varley responds to it, too. Shirley and Sterling might take a lesson." Delany then elaborates on the positive influence of feminist SF in facing up to what he characterizes as the crucial test of all novels: the creation of believable women characters.

I would like to back up here, to return to the parenthetical remark Delany made when talking about the conservatism of the "returning macho." "The one point that Gomoll couldn't seem to make," he says, "was that this search for fathers is part of the same legitimating move that ignores mothers." This "one point" that Delany speaks of, of course, is the most extraordinary point of the entire interview. Even if Jeanne Gomoll had been able to make that "one point" back in 1986, it may be that Samuel R. Delany would have been the only reader to get it. But it's a point that I think some of us are now ready to get, a point, if taken to heart, that could change the stories we tell about SF profoundly. First, the continual marginalization of the work of SF by women in accounts of SF by critics, writers, and fans has more to do with the genre's anxious desire for legitimacy and need to disavow the bastard status of SF than with any actual marginality of that work to the genre. Second, critics' endless, impossible wish to construct a monumental history that everyone will recognize and defer to is another form of the genre's endless, anxious search for fathers in particular and legitimacy in general. I have elsewhere argued against creating a monumental history of feminist SF in favor of pursuing what Foucault and Deleuze call "genealogies," which are not lineages, but multifarious connections establishing wild relations between works that might have only the most tenuous of generational connections. It strikes me that an SF criticism more interested in pursuing such genealogies than in constructing the foundations and building blocks of a monumental history would be considerably more interesting and revealing—though it obviously wouldn't allay the anxiety of those obsessed with constructing a legitimate line of literary descent through unquestioned generations of fathers. And finally, if the genre were able to rid itself of its anxious concern with legitimacy, the constant bickering over defining the particular quality or elements of an SF text would cease.

Why do I say that I think many of us are ready now to take Delany's point? I was greatly heartened reading *The Cambridge Companion to Science Fiction*, edited by Edward James and Farah Mendlesohn, which was published in 2003. In her introduction to the volume, which seeks to give an overview of the history of science fiction, Mendlesohn declines to define SF, except to say that it is "less a genre than an ongoing discussion... SF is a built genre. It is its history." Second, the anthology, for the most part, takes little interest in the legitimacy issue. Third, many of its chapters attempt to integrate the work of women into its discussion— and although the chapters that don't integrate SF by women treat women writers as irrelevant to the main discussion, they at least mention more than only one or two token women, as critics who cannot bring themselves to see women as ever having seriously influenced the development of the genre normally do.

The title of this paper speaks of "the story of SF," but Delany would be the first to tell us that there is no one single story of SF; my use of "story" is plural in spirit. What sort of stories do I imagine could be told were SF critics to value the pearls Delany has been casting our way for the last quarter of a century? Let me offer a few examples. Were critics to accept the challenge implicit in his reference to "the crucial test of a novel" (that is, creating plausible female characters), surely one of the stories about SF that would demand to be told would entail an account identifying SF writers for whom the writing of novels—in the sense Delany intends—has been important, and how and why it became so, and what formal difficulties the writers faced in forging an SF novel, and so on. Such a question would demand a genealogical rather than monumental approach to SF history; and surely an analysis that did not integrate the work of women writers into its main discussion would strike everyone as peculiar.

Another possible story to tell about SF would take up the important aesthetic question of how affect works in SF. In his *Black Clock* interview, Delany says "that one thing that makes Sturgeon such a great writer is that he's not afraid to risk sentimentality. He's not afraid of that big emotional gesture."(Erickson, 74) As Delany continually insists, science fiction is different from literature, and one of the things critics need to be doing is seeking to elucidate those differences. Is the place of the "big emotional gesture" different in science fiction than it is in mainstream literature? Given the difference in the treatment of subjectivity and psychology in science fiction from that typical of literature, it would seem likely. I think learning something about that difference could provide powerful insight into the aesthetics of SF.

A third example: in Delany's *Diacritics* interview, he asserts that like minor literature, paraliterature "refracts, contests, and agonizes with this other 'unbiased' literature, calls it to task, puts it in question, and, with violence, appropriates, desecrates, ignores, falls victim to, and brilliantly recuts the multiple facets of its conventions." (213) Delany alludes to Henry Louis Gates, Jr.'s noting this of black literature; and certainly feminist critics have devoted considerable attention to this relation of women's writing to so-called "unbiased literature." But of course in order for critics to pay attention to this relation in SF texts, they would first need to put aside their collective anxiety over legitimacy.

Perhaps Delany's most comprehensive suggestion for creating richer, more interesting stories about SF is his proposal, in his *Paradoxa* interview "Inside and Outside the Canon," for a methodology for studying paraliterary genres that emphasizes the material productions of their discourse. Delany notes that "we need lots of biography, history, reader-response research—and we need to look precisely at how these material situations influenced the way texts (down to individual rhetorical features) were (and are) read. In short, we need to generate these markers from a sophisticated awareness of the values already in circulation among the readership at the time these works entered the public market." (About Writing, 359) What would such a study look like? Well, I think a first step toward it would look something like Larbalestier's *The Battle of the Sexes in Science Fiction.*

Indisputably, Delany has helped feminists to revise the stories they tell about science fiction. The only real question for me is whether these revisions will ever be integrated into the main body of science fiction criticism and permanently change the kinds of stories the genre of science fiction tells about itself.

Notes

1. My thanks to Josh Lukin for his thoughtful reading of an earlier version of this paper and his excellent suggestions for rewriting it.

2. There have been exceptions, but they are rare. Alan DeNiro's "The Dream of the Unified Field" stands out (and explicitly recognizes Delany's exhortations against formal, rigorous attempts to define science fiction).

3. A range of reactions can be found in the March 2006 archive of Locus Online's letter column. Numerous blogs also featured discussed Itzkoff's review, including Matt Cheney's The Mumpsimus ("Dave Itzkoff's Inner Child Is Not Happy," March 5, 2006), which parses Itkoff's implicit assumptions and tone (and which Itzkoff himself alluded to in a later column).

4. Ray Davis's response to Lethem's piece ("Things Are Tough All Over") focuses on another aspect of Lethem's argument, viz., that SF has become less conducive to the production of "Great Books" than it was previously, while, conversely, since the 1970s, the mainstream has become more hospitable to Great Books. Davis notes that Lethem misses the point that Delany has often made, that what Lethem calls "the mainstream" is as much a genre as SF is. In Lethem's essay, Davis argues, "the mainstream" is "that place where all can be judged by their writerly merits rather than (as in SF) by nostalgic prejudices... .I agree with Lethem that the SF genre's markets provide limited freedom for production of Great Books, and that the strictures continue to tighten. I regretfully disagree that an equivalent number of Great Books will appear in mainstream fiction markets as they disappear from a fading SF genre, any more than (to switch media) an equivalent number of Great TV Movies showed up to offset the loss of Great B Pictures."

5. See Michael Swanwick's "A User's Guide to the Postmoderns," which defended John Kessel, James Patrick Kelly, Connie Willis, and others against the attacks of Bruce Sterling's

"VincentOmniaveritas."

6. On November 1, 2006, as a writer participating in a reading of work from *ParaSpheres: Extending Beyond the Spheres of Literary and Genre Fiction* at the University of California at San Diego, I found myself included in a discussion of "New Wave Fabulism." During the Q&A following our reading, Anna Joy Springer, who had organized the reading, said that "so much of the work we need" is getting "thrown away into the genres." (The UCSD library owns an audio cassette recording of the event, including the Q&A.) Ken Keegan, the editor of *ParaSpheres*, writes in an essay at the end of the volume, "There are really at least three different kinds of fiction: genre, literary (in its realistic, character-based sense), and a third type of fiction that really has no commonly accepted name, which does have cultural meaning and artistic value and therefore does not fit well in the escapist formula genres, but which has non-realistic elements and settings that exclude it from the category of literary fiction." (633) After a rather convoluted discussion about various labels, Keegan concludes "By presenting this fiction as neither literary nor genre, but rather as something else, we are avoiding the pitfalls of claiming literary status for these works." (637) And yet: during the Q&A at UCSD, Keegan suggested that "New Wave Fabulist" work "transcends" genre.

7. The scale of "hardness" has purportedly to do with "scientific" accuracy and level of scientific detail, but, as feminist critics point out, is chiefly concerned with whether the author is male, the narrative casts the hero as a can-do, by-his-bootstraps booster of technology, and excludes narratives that challenge naturalized social relations and conventions. Although some fans have tried to argue that only "hard SF" qualifies as SF at all, it is more typical for writers, fans, and critics to see "hard SF" as at the core of the genre and "soft" SF as on the margins. (Not, of course, that many people agree about what is relatively "hard" and what is relatively "soft.") In 1989, for instance, in an inflammatory essay titled "The Rape of Science Fiction," Charles Platt blamed "the so-called New Wave" for initiating the softening (and thus weakening) SF with the result that in the 1970s "a new soft science fiction emerged, largely written by women: Joan Vinge, Vonda McIntyre, Ursula LeGuin, Joanna Russ, Kate Wilhelm, Carol Emshwiller. Their concern for human values was admirable, but they eroded science fiction's one great strength that had distinguished it from all other fantastic literature: its implicit claim that events described could actually come true."(46)

8. According to the head-note in the reprint of the interview in *Silent Interviews*, the text of the interview "began as an interview conducted and recorded by Takayuki Tatsumi at Lunacon, in Croton, New York, in April 1998." Delany then "rewrote the transcription over the next month" and it was published in *Science Fiction Eye* vol. 1, no.3.

9. Since Delany corrected and amplified some of his answers after the interview had been completed, it is impossible to be certain that Delany in fact made the assertion that feminist SF had influenced cyberpunk which Tatsumi then ignored, but Delany's colloquial rejoinder, "Well, again, you're indulging in that same cyberpunk nervousness" suggests that he did. My conversation with Delany immediately following my presentation of an earlier version of this paper at the Delany Symposium confirmed my impression. Delany

remarked that his coming up with the conceit of the illegitimate family relations during the interview was a pleasure to remember, since it was, he said, one of those wonderful, rare instances of *esprit d'escalier*.

10. In his "Forward" to *Microcosmic God*, Delany contrasts the notion (clearly held by Argyll Sturgeon) that the author of works of high (canonical) literature is the "Good Physician" while the author of the pulp genres is a "scamp" to the extent that s/he does not put much effort into writing, or a "criminal" to the extent that s/he does. As long as the SF genre continues to be tagged with the characterization of "garbage" and "trash," it can't very well conceive of itself in terms of legitimate paternal lineages and the Law.

11. Josh Lukin has suggested to me the Telemachian trope of a younger man seeking out and ultimately making his peace with an older mentor over the discredited body of a woman and being inducted into the patriarchy (a trope which Eve Kosofsky Sedgwick's *Between Men* reveals is ubiquitous in canonical (high) literature), may be what Tatsumi was pursuing in his questions to Delany about lineage. But the Telemachian trope, of course, is by no means ubiquitous in SF as it is in canonical literature.

12. Molly is an important character in Gibson's *Neuromancer*. Unlike most female characters in pre-cyberpunk noir, Molly may be a babe, but her role is to kick ass rather than using her sexual wiles to lure men to their doom. Her current occupation in the novel is security-for-hire. She is not only hard as nails, but has also had retractable claws implanted in place of her fingernails. Besides her retractable claws, Molly also has permanent mirrored shades, which makes her very, very cool. We are told she acquired her expensive special features by working as a "meat puppet"—a prostitute whose consciousness is taken over by a program, leaving her with no memory afterwards of the uses to which her body had been put.

Works Cited

Cheney, Matt. "Dave Itzkoff's Inner Child Is Not Happy." The Mumpsimus: displaced thoughts on misplaced literatures. March 5, 2006. <http://mumpsiumus.blogspot.com/2006/03/dave-itzkoffs-inner-child-is-not-happy.html>

Clute, John. "Science Fiction from 1980 to the present." In Edward James and Farah Mendlesohn, eds. *The Cambridge Companion to Science Fiction*. Cambridge, U.K.: Cambridge University Press, 2004, pp.64-78.

Davis, Ray. "Things Are Tough All Over." (1998) <http://www.pseudopodium.org/kokonino/jlvls.html>

Delany, Samuel R. *About Writing: Seven Essays, Four Letters & Five Interviews*. Middletown, CT: Wesleyan University Press, 2005.

_____. "An Exhortation to SF Scholars." *New York Review of Science Fiction* 13,1 (Sept: 2000). Originally appeared in SFRA Review #247.

_____. "Forward: Theodore Sturgeon." In Paul Williams, ed. *Microcosmic God: Vol.II: The Complete Stories of Theodore Sturgeon*. Berkeley: North Atlantic Books, 1995.

_____. "The Politics of Paralitery Criticism." In *Shorter Views: Queer Thoughts & The Politics of the Paraliterary*. Hanover and London: Wesleyan University Press, 1999

_____. *Silent Interviews: On Language, Race, Sex, Science Fiction, and Some Comics*. Hanover and London: Wesleyan University Press, 1994.

DeNiro, Alan. "The Dream of the Unified Field." Fantastic Metropolis, February 15, 2003. <http://www.fantasticmetropolis.com/i/unified/>

Duchamp, L. Timmel. "For a Genealogy of Feminist SF: Reflections on Women, Feminism, and Science Fiction, 1818-1950." In *The Grand Conversation: Essays*. Seattle: Aqueduct Press, 2004, pp. 1-20.

Erickson, Steve. "Samuel R. Delany: A Conversation." *Black Clock* 1 (March 2004): 71-85. Reprinted in Samuel R. Delany, *About Writing: Seven Essays, Four Letters & Five Interviews*. Middletown, CT: Wesleyan University Press, 2005.

Gomoll, Jeanne. "An Open Letter to Joanna Russ." *Aurora* Vol.10, No. 1 (Winter 1986/1987).

Itzkoff, Dave. "It's All Geek to Me" *New York Times Book Review*. March 5, 2006.

_____. "Science Fiction for the Ages." *New York Times Book Review*. March 5, 2006.

James, Edward and Farah Mendlesohn, eds. *The Cambridge Companion to Science Fiction*. Cambridge, U.K.: Cambridge University Press, 2004.

Keegan, Ken. "Why Fabulist and New Wave Fabulist Stories in an Anthology Named *ParaSpheres*?" In Rusty Morrison and Ken Keegan, eds. *ParaSpheres*: Extending Beyond the Spheres of Literary and Genre Fiction. Omnidawn Publishing. Richland, CA. 2006.

Larbalestier, Justine. The Battle of the Sexes in Science Fiction. Middletown, CT: Wesleyan University Press, 2002.

Lethem, Jonathan. "Why Can't We All Just Live Together? A Vision of Genre Paradise Lost." *The New York Review of Science Fiction*. Vol. 11, No. 1 (September 1998). An expanded version of "Close Encounters: The Squandered Promise of Science Fiction" that appeared earlier that year in *The Village Voice*.

Mendlesohn, Farah J.. "Introduction: Reading Science Fiction." In Edward James and Farah Mendlesohn, eds., *The Cambridge Companion to Science Fiction*. Cambridge, U.K.: Cambridge University Press, 2004, pp. 1-12.

Platt, Charles. "The Rape of Science Fiction." *Science Fiction Eye*. Vol.1, Issue 5 (July 1989): 44-49.

Swanwick, Michael. "A User's Guide to the Postmodern" in *The Postmodern Archipelago: Two Essays on Science Fiction and Fantasy*. Tachyon Publications. San Francisco. 1997

Tatsumi, Takayuki. "Science Fiction and Criticism: The Diacritics Interview." In Delany, *Silent Interviews: On Language, Race, Sex, Science Fiction, and Some Comics*. Hanover and London: Wesleyan University Press, 1994, pp.186-229.

_____. "Some Real Mothers...: the SF Eye Interview." In Delany, *Silent Interviews: On Language, Race, Sex, Science Fiction, and Some Comics*. Hanover and London: Wesleyan University Press, 1994, pp.164-185.

(Endnotes)

1 .

2

3

4

5

6 .

7

8

9

10

11

12

Nilda

Junot Díaz

Nilda was my brother's girlfriend.

This is how all these stories begin.

She was Dominican, from here, and had super-long hair, like those Pentecostal girls, and a chest you wouldn't believe—I'm talking world-class. Rafa would sneak her down into our basement bedroom after our mother went to bed and do her to whatever was on the radio right then. The two of them had to let me stay, because if my mother heard me upstairs on the couch everybody's ass would have been fried. And since I wasn't about to spend my night out in the bushes this is how it was.

Rafa didn't make no noise, just a low something that resembled breathing. Nilda was the one. She seemed to be trying to hold back from crying the whole time. It was crazy hearing her like that. The Nilda I'd grown up with was one of the quietest girls you'd ever meet. She let her hair wall away her face and read "The New Mutants," and the only time she looked straight at anything was when she looked out a window.

But that was before she'd gotten that chest, before that slash of black hair had gone from something to pull on the bus to something to stroke in the dark. The new Nilda wore stretch pants and Iron Maiden shirts; she had already run away from her mother's and ended up at a group home; she'd already slept with Toño and Nestor and Little Anthony from Parkwood, older guys. She crashed over at our apartment a lot because she hated her moms, who was the neighborhood borracha. In the morning she slipped out before my mother woke up and found her. Waited for heads at the bus stop, fronted like she'd come from her own place, same clothes as the day before and greasy hair so everybody thought her a skank. Waited for my brother and didn't talk to anybody and nobody talked to her, because she'd always been one of those quiet, semi-retarded girls who you couldn't talk to without being dragged into a whirlpool of dumb stories. If Rafa decided that he wasn't going to school then she'd wait near our apartment until my mother left for work. Sometimes Rafa let her in right away. Sometimes he slept late and she'd wait across the street, building letters out of pebbles until she saw him crossing the living room.

She had big stupid lips and a sad moonface and the driest skin.

Always rubbing lotion on it and cursing the moreno father who'd given it to her.

It seemed like she was forever waiting for my brother. Nights she'd knock and I'd let her in and we'd sit on the couch while Rafa was off at his job at the carpet factory or working out at the gym. I'd show her my newest comics and she'd read them real close, but as soon as Rafa showed up she'd throw them in my lap and jump into his arms. I missed you, she'd say in a little-girl voice, and Rafa would laugh. You should have seen him in those days: he had the face bones of a saint. Then Mami's door would open and Rafa would detach himself and cowboy-saunter over to Mami and say, You got something for me to eat, vieja? Claro que sí, Mami'd say, trying to put her glasses on.

He had us all, the way only a pretty nigger can.

Once when Rafa was late from the job and we were alone in the apartment a long time, I asked her about the group home. It was three weeks before the end of the school year and everybody had entered the Do-Nothing Stage. I was fourteen and reading *Dhalgren* for the second time; I had an I.Q. that would have broken you in two but I would have traded it in for a halfway decent face in a second.

It was pretty cool up there, she said. She was pulling on the front of her halter top, trying to air her chest out. The food was bad but there were a lot of cute guys in the house with me. They all wanted me.

She started chewing on a nail. Even the guys who worked there were calling me after I left, she said.

◊

The only reason Rafa went after her was because his last full-time girlfriend had gone back to Guyana—she was this dougla girl with a single eyebrow and skin to die for—and because Nilda had pushed up to him. She'd only been back from the group home a couple of months, but by then she'd already gotten a rep as a cuero. A lot of the Dominican girls in town were on some serious lockdown—we saw them on the bus and at school and maybe at the Pathmark, but since most families knew exactly what kind of tígueres were roaming the neighborhood these girls weren't allowed to hang out. Nilda was different. She was what we called in those days brown trash. Her moms was a mean-ass drunk and always running around South Amboy with her white boyfriends—which is a way of saying Nilda could hang and, man, did she ever. Always out in the world, always cars rolling up besides her. Before I even knew she was back from the group home she got scooped up by this older nigger from the back apartments. He kept her on his dick for almost four months, and I used to see them driving around in his fucked-up rust-eaten Sunbird while I delivered my papers. Motherfucker was like three hundred years old, but because he had a car and a record collection and foto albums from his Vietnam days and because he bought her clothes to replace the old shit she was wearing, Nilda was all lost on him.

I hated this nigger with a passion, but when it came to guys there was no talking to Nilda. I used to ask her, What's up with Wrinkle Dick? And she would get so mad she wouldn't speak to me for days, and then I'd get this note, I want you to respect my man. Whatever, I'd write back. Then the old dude bounced, no one knew where, the usual scenario in my neighborhood, and for a couple of months she got tossed by those cats from Parkwood. On Thursdays, which was comic-book day, she'd drop in to see what I'd picked up and she'd talk to me about how unhappy she was. We'd sit together until it got dark and then her beeper would fire up and she'd peer into its display and say, I have to go. Sometimes I could grab her and pull her back on the couch, and we'd stay there a long time, me waiting for her to fall in love with me, her waiting for whatever, but other times she'd be serious. I have to go see my man, she'd say.

One of those comic-book days she saw my brother coming back from his five-mile run. Rafa was still boxing then and he was cut up like crazy, the muscles on his chest and abdomen so striated they looked like something out of a Frazetta drawing. He noticed her because she was wearing these ridiculous shorts and this tank that couldn't have blocked a sneeze and a thin roll of stomach was poking from between the fabrics and he smiled at her and she got real serious and uncomfortable and he told her to fix him some iced tea and she told him to fix it himself. You a guest here, he said. You should be earning your fucking keep. He went into the shower and as soon as he did she was in the kitchen stirring and I told her to leave it, but she said, I might as well. We drank all of it.

I wanted to warn her, tell her he was a monster, but she was already headed for him at the speed of light.

The next day Rafa's car turned up broken—what a coincidence— so he took the bus to school and when he was walking past our seat he took her hand and pulled her to her feet and she said, Get off me. Her eyes were pointed straight at the floor. I just want to show you something, he said. She was pulling with her arm but the rest of her was ready to go. Come on, Rafa said, and finally she went. Save my seat, she said over her shoulder, and I was like, Don't worry about it. Before we even swung onto 516 Nilda was in my brother's lap and he had his hand so far up her skirt it looked like he was performing a surgical procedure. When we were getting off the bus Rafa pulled me aside and held his hand in front of my nose. Smell this, he said. This, he said, is what's wrong with women.

You couldn't get anywhere near Nilda for the rest of the day. She had her hair pulled back and was glorious with victory. Even the white girls knew about my overmuscled about-to-be-a-senior brother and were impressed. And while Nilda sat at the end of our lunch table and whispered to some girls me and my boys ate our crap sandwiches and talked about the X-Men—this was back when the X-Men still made some kind of sense—and even if we didn't want to admit it the truth was now patent and awful: all the real dope girls were headed up to the high school, like moths to a light, and there was nothing any of us younger cats could do about it. My man José Negrón—a.k.a. Joe Black—took Nilda's defection the hardest, since he'd actually imagined he had a chance with her. Right after she got back from the group home he'd held her hand on the bus, and even though she'd gone off with other guys, he'd never forgotten it.

I was in the basement three nights later when they did it. That first time neither of them made a sound.

◊

They went out that whole summer. I don't remember anyone doing anything big. Me and my pathetic little crew hiked over to Morgan Creek and swam around in water stinking of leachate from the landfill; we were just getting serious about the licks that year and Joe Black was stealing bottles out of his father's stash and we were drinking them down to the corners on the swings behind the apartments. Because of the heat and because of what I felt inside my chest a lot, I often just sat in the crib with my brother and Nilda. Rafa was tired all the time and pale: this had happened in a matter of days. I used to say, Look at you, white boy, and he used to say, Look at you, you black ugly nigger. He didn't feel like doing much, and besides his car had finally broken down for real, so we would all sit in the air-conditioned apartment and watch TV. Rafa had decided he wasn't going back to school for his senior year, and even though my moms was heartbroken and trying to guilt him into it five times a day, this was all he talked about. School had never been his gig, and after my pops left us for his twenty-five-year-old he didn't feel he needed to pretend any longer. I'd like to take a long fucking trip, he told us. See California before it slides into the ocean. California, I said. California, he said. A nigger could make a showing out there. I'd like to go there, too, Nilda said, but Rafa didn't answer her. He had closed his eyes and you could see he was in pain.

We rarely talked about our father. Me, I was just happy not to be getting my ass kicked in anymore but once right at the beginning of the Last Great Absence I asked my brother where he thought he was, and Rafa said, Like I fucking care.

End of conversation. World without end.

On days niggers were really out of their minds with boredom we trooped down to the pool and got in for free because Rafa was boys with one of the lifeguards. I swam, Nilda went on missions around the pool just so she could show off how tight she looked in her bikini, and Rafa sprawled under the awning and took it all in. Sometimes he called me over and we'd sit together for a while and he'd close his eyes and I'd watch the water dry on my ashy legs and then he'd tell me to go back to the pool. When Nilda finished promenading and came back to where Rafa was chilling she kneeled at his side and he would kiss her real long, his hands playing up and down the length of her back. Ain't nothing like a fifteen-year-old with a banging body, those hands seemed to be saying, at least to me.

Joe Black was always watching them. Man, he muttered, she's so fine I'd lick her asshole *and* tell you niggers about it.

Maybe I would have thought they were cute if I hadn't known Rafa. He might have seemed enamorao with Nilda but he also had mad girls in orbit. Like this one piece of white trash from Sayreville, and this morena from Amsterdam Village who also slept over and sounded like a freight train when they did it. I don't remember her name, but I do remember how her perm shone in the glow of our night-light.

In August Rafa quit his job at the carpet factory—I'm too fucking tired, he complained, and some mornings his leg bones hurt so much he couldn't get out of bed right away. The Romans used to shatter these with iron clubs, I told him while I massaged his shins. The pain would kill you instantly. Great, he said. Cheer me up some more, you fucking bastard. One day Mami took him to the hospital for a checkup and afterward I found them sitting on the couch, both of them dressed up, watching TV like nothing had happened. They were holding hands and Mami appeared tiny next to him.

Well?

Rafa shrugged. The doc thinks I'm anemic.

Anemic ain't bad.

Yeah, Rafa said, laughing bitterly. God bless Medicaid.

In the light of the TV, he looked terrible.

◊

That was the summer when everything we would become was

hovering just over our heads. Girls were starting to take notice of me; I wasn't good-looking but I listened and had boxing muscles in my arms. In another universe I probably came out O.K., ended up with mad novias and jobs and a sea of love in which to swim, but in this world I had a brother who was dying of cancer and a long dark patch of life like a mile of black ice waiting for me up ahead.

One night, a couple of weeks before school started—they must have thought I was asleep—Nilda started telling Rafa about her plans for the future. I think even she knew what was about to happen. Listening to her imagining herself was about the saddest thing you ever heard. How she wanted to get away from her moms and open up a group home for runaway kids. But this one would be real cool, she said. It would be for normal kids who just got problems. She must have loved him because she went on and on. Plenty of people talk about having a flow, but that night I really heard one, something that was unbroken, that fought itself and worked together all at once. Rafa didn't say nothing. Maybe he had his hands in her hair or maybe he was just like, Fuck you. When she finished he didn't even say wow. I wanted to kill myself with embarrassment. About a half hour later she got up and dressed. She couldn't see me or she would have known that I thought she was beautiful. She stepped into her pants and pulled them up in one motion, sucked in her stomach while she buttoned them. I'll see you later, she said.

Yeah, he said.

After she walked out he put on the radio and started on the speed bag. I stopped pretending I was asleep; I sat up and watched him.

Did you guys have a fight or something?

No, he said.

Why'd she leave?

He sat down on my bed. His chest was sweating. She had to go.

But where's she gonna stay?

I don't know. He put his hand on my face, gently. Why ain't you minding your business?

A week later he was seeing some other girl. She was from Trinidad, a coco pañyol, and she had this phony-as-hell English accent. It was the way we all were back then. None of us wanted to be niggers. Not for nothing.

◊

I guess two years passed. My brother was gone by then, and I was on my way to becoming a nut. I was out of school most of the time and had no friends and I sat inside and watched Univisión or walked down to the dump and smoked the mota I should have been selling until I couldn't see. Nilda didn't fare so well, either. A lot of the things that happened to her, though, had nothing to do with me or my brother. She fell in love a couple more times, really bad with this one moreno truck driver who took her to Manalapan and then abandoned her at the end of the summer. I had to drive over to get her, and the house was one of those tiny box jobs with a fifty-cent lawn and no kind of charm; she was acting like she was some Italian chick and offered me a paso in the car, but I put my hand on hers and told her to stop it. Back home she fell in with more stupid niggers, relocated kids from the City, and they came at her with drama and some of their girls beat her up, a Brick City beat-down, and she lost her bottom front teeth. She was in and out of school and for a while they put her on home instruction, and that was when she finally dropped.

My junior year she started delivering papers so she could make money, and since I was spending a lot of time outside I saw her every now and then. Broke my heart. She wasn't at her lowest yet but she was aiming there and when we passed each other she always smiled and said hi. She was starting to put on weight and she'd cut her hair down to nothing and her moonface was heavy and alone. I always said Wassup and when I had cigarettes I gave them to her. She'd gone to the funeral, along with a couple of his other girls, and what a skirt she'd worn, like maybe she could still convince him of something, and she'd kissed my mother but the vieja hadn't known who she was. I had to tell Mami on the ride home and all she could remember about her was that she was the one who smelled good. It wasn't until Mami said it that I realized it was true.

◊

It was only one summer and she was nobody special, so what's the point of all this? He's gone, he's gone, he's gone. I'm twenty-three and I'm washing my clothes up at the minimall on Ernston Road. She's here with me—she's folding her shit and smiling and showing me her missing teeth and saying, It's been a long time, hasn't it, Yunior?

Years, I say, loading my whites. Outside the sky is clear of gulls, and down at the apartment my moms is waiting for me with dinner. Six months earlier we were sitting in front of the TV and my mother said, Well, I think I'm finally over this place.

Nilda asks, Did you move or something?

I shake my head. Just been working.

God, it's been a long, long time. She's on her clothes like magic, making everything neat, making everything fit. There are four other people at the counters, broke-ass-looking niggers with knee socks and croupier's hats and scars snaking up their arms, and they all seem like sleepwalkers compared with her. She shakes her head, grinning. Your brother, she says.

Rafa.

She points her finger at me like my brother always did.

I miss him sometimes.

She nods. Me, too. He was a good guy to me.

I must have disbelief on my face because she finishes shaking out her towels and then stares straight through me. He treated me the best.

Nilda.

He used to sleep with my hair over his face. He used to say it made him feel safe.

What else can we say? She finishes her stacking, I hold the door open for her. The locals watch us leave. We walk back through the old neighborhood, slowed down by the bulk of our clothes. London Terrace has changed now that the landfill has shut down. Kicked-up rents and mad South Asian people and white folks living in the apartments, but it's our kids you see in the streets and hanging from the porches.

Nilda is watching the ground as though she's afraid she might fall. My heart is beating and I think, We could do anything. We could marry. We could drive off to the West Coast. We could start over. It's all possible but neither of us speaks for a long time and the moment closes and we're back in the world we've always known.

Remember the day we met? she asks.

I nod.

You wanted to play baseball.

It was summer, I say. You were wearing a tank top.

You made me put on a shirt before you'd let me be on your team. Do you remember?

I remember, I say.

We never spoke again. A couple of years later I went away to college and I don't know where the fuck she went.

The First Gate of Logic

Benjamin Rosenbaum

Fift was almost five, and it wasn't like her anymore to be asleep in all of her bodies. She wasn't a baby anymore; she was old enough for school, old enough to walk all alone across the habitation, down the spoke to the great and buzzing center of Foo. But she had been wound up with excitement for days, practically dancing around the house (Father Miskisk had laughed, Father Smistria had shooed her out of the supper garden, Father Frill had summoned her to the bathing room and had her swim back and forth, back and forth, "to calm you down!"), and just before supper she'd finally collapsed, twice—in the atrium, and curled up on the tiered balcony—and Father Arevio and Father Squell had carried her, in those two bodies, back to her room. She'd managed to stay awake in her third body through most of supper, blinking hugely and breathing in through her nose and trying to sit up straight, as waves of deep blue slumber from her two sleeping brains washed through her. By supper's end, she couldn't stand up, and Father Squell carried that body, too, to bed.

Muddy dreams: of sitting on a wooden floor in a long hall...of her name being called...of realizing she hadn't worn her gown after all, but was somehow—humiliatingly—dressed in Father Frill's golden bells instead. The other children laughing at her, and dizziness, and suddenly, surreally, the hall being full of flutterbyes, their translucent wings fluttering, their projection surfaces glittering....

Then someone was stroking Fift's eyebrow, gently, and she tried to nestle farther down into the blankets, and the someone started gently pulling on her earlobe. She opened her eyes, and it was Father Squell.

"Good morning, little cubblehedge," he said. "You have a big day today."

Father Squell was slim and rosy-skinned and smelled like soap and flowers. Fift crawled into his lap and flung her arms around him and pressed her nose between his bosoms. He was dressed in glittery red fabric, soft and slippery under Fift's fingers.

Squell was bald, with coppery metal spikes extruding from the skin of his scalp. Sometimes Father Miskisk teased about them—the spikes weren't fashionable anymore—and sometimes when he did, Father Squell stormed out of the room, because Father Squell was a little vain. He was never much of a fighter, the other Fathers said. But he had a body in the asteroids, and that was something amazing.

Squell reached over, Fift still in his lap, and started stroking the eyebrow of another of Fift's bodies. Fift sneezed, in that body, and then sneezed in the other two, and that was funny, and she started to giggle. Now she was all awake.

"Up, little cubblehedge," Squell said. "Up!"

Fift crawled out of bed, careful not to crawl over herself. It always made her a little restless to be all together, all three bodies in the same room. That wasn't really good, it was because her somatic integration wasn't totally successful, and that was why she kept having to see Pedagogical Expert Pnim Moralasic Foundelly of name registry Pneumatic Lance 12. Pedagogical Expert Pnim Moralasic Foundelly had put an awful nag agent in Fift's mind, to tell her to look herself in the eye, and play in a coordinated manner, and do the exercises. It was nagging now, but Fift ignored it.

She looked under the bed for her gowns.

They weren't there. She closed her eyes (because she wasn't so good yet at seeing things over the feed with her eyes open) and used the house feed to look all around the house. Her gowns weren't in the balcony or the atrium or the small mat-room or the breakfast room.

Fathers Arevio and Smistria and Frill, and another of Father Squell's bodies, were in the breakfast room, already eating. Father Miskisk was arguing with the kitchen.

{Where are my gowns?} Fift asked her agents, but perhaps she did it wrong, because they didn't say anything.

"Father Squell," she said, opening her eyes, "I can't find my gowns, and my agents can't either."

"I composted your gowns; they were old," Squell said. "Go down to the bathing room and get washed. I'll make you some new clothes."

Fift's hearts began to pound. The gowns weren't old; they'd only come out of the oven a week ago. "But I want *those* gowns," she said.

Squell opened the door. "You can't have those gowns. Those gowns are compost. Bathing!" He snatched Fift up, one of her bodies under his arm, the wrist of another caught in his other hand.

Fift tried to wriggle out of her Father's grasp, yanked on her arm to get free, while she looked desperately under the bed again. "They weren't old," she said, her voice wavering.

"Fift," Squell said, exasperated. "That's enough. For Kumru's sake, today of all days!" He dragged her, in two of her bodies, through the door. In another body, this one with silvery spikes on its head, he came hurrying down the hall.

"I want them back," Fift said. She wouldn't cry. She wasn't a baby any more, she was a big Staidchild, and Staids don't cry. She wouldn't cry. She wouldn't even shout or emphasize. She would stay calm and clear. Today of all days. She was still struggling, a little, and Squell handed her to his other body.

"They are *compost*," Squell said, reddening, in the body with the silver spikes, while one with the copper spikes came into the room. "They have gone down the sluice and *dissolved*. Your gowns are now part of the nutrient flow and they could be anywhere in Fullbelly and they will probably be part of your *breakfast* next week!"

Fift gasped. Fift didn't want to eat her gowns. There was a cold lump in her stomach. Squell caught her third body.

Father Miskisk came down the corridor doublebodied. He was bigger than Squell, broad-chested, square-jawed, with a mane of blood-red hair, and sunset-orange skin traced all over with white squiggles. He was wearing his dancing pants. His voice was deep and rumbly, and he smelled warm, roasty, and oily. "Fift, little Fift," he said. "Come on, let's zoom around. I'll zoom you to the bathing room. Come jump up. Give her here, Squell."

"I want my gowns," Fift said, in her third body, as Squell dragged her through the doorway.

"Here," Squell said, trying to hand Fift's other bodies to Miskisk. But Fift clung to Squell. She didn't want to zoom right now. Zooming was fun, but too wild for this day, and too wild for someone who had lost her gowns. The gowns were a pale blue, soft as clouds; they would whisper around Fift's legs when she ran.

"Oh Fift, *please!*" Squell said. "You *must* bathe and you will *not* be late today! Today of all—"

"Is she really ready for this, do you think?" Miskisk said, trying to pry Fift away from Squell, but flinching back from prying hard enough.

"Oh please, Misk," Squell said, "let us not start that. Or not with *me*. Pip says—"

Father Smistria stuck his head out of the door of his studio. He was tall and haggard looking and had brilliant blue skin, and a white beard braided into hundreds of tiny braids woven with little glittering mirrors and jewels, and was wearing a slick swirling combat suit that clung to his skinny flat chest. His voice was higher than Father Miskisk's, squeaky and gravelly at the same time. "Why are you two winding the child up?" he barked. "This is going to be a *disaster*, if you give her the impression that this is a day for racing about! Fift, you will stop this *now!*"

"Come on, Fift," Miskisk said coaxingly.

"Put her *down*," Smistria said. "I cannot believe you are wrestling and flying about with a Staidchild who in less than three hours—"

"Oh give it a rest, Smi," Miskisk said, sort of threateny, and turned away from Fift and Squell, toward Smistria. Smistria stepped fully out into the corridor, putting his face next to Miskisk's. It got like thunder in between them, but Fift knew they wouldn't hit each other; grownup Bails only hit each other on the mats. Still, she hugged Squell closer—one body squished against his soft chest, one body hugging his leg, one body pulling back through the doorway—and squeezed all her eyes shut, and dimmed the house feed so she couldn't see that way either.

Behind her eyes she could only see the pale blue gowns. It was just like in her dream! She'd lost her gowns and she would have to wear only bells like Father Frill! She shuddered. "I don't want my gowns to be in the compost," she said, as reasonably as she could manage.

"Oh, will you shut up about the gowns!" Squell said. "No one cares about your gowns!"

"That's not true," Miskisk boomed, shocked.

"It *is* true," Smistria said, "and—"

Fift could feel a sob ballooning inside her. She tried to hold it in, but it grew and grew and—

"Beloveds," said Father Grobbard.

Fift opened her eyes. Father Grobbard had come silently, singlebodied, up the corridor. She stood behind Squell. She was shorter than Miskisk and Smistria, the same height as Squell, but more solid: broad and flat like a stone. When Father Grobbard stood still, it looked like she would never move again. Her shift was plain and simple and white. Her skin was a mottled creamy brown, with the same fine golden fuzz of hair everywhere, even the top of her head.

"Grobby!" Squell said. "We are *trying* to get her ready, but it's quite—"

"Well it's Grobbard's show," Smistria said. "It's up to you and Pip today, Grobbard, isn't it? So why don't *you* get her ready!?"

Grobbard held out her hand. Fift swallowed, and then she slid down from Squell's arms, and went and took it.

"Grobbard," Miskisk said, "are you sure Fift is ready for this? Is it really—"

"Yes," Grobbard said. Then she looked at Miskisk, her face as calm as ever. She raised one eyebrow, just a little. Then she looked back at Fift's other bodies, and held out her other hand. Squell let go of the arms of Fift's he was holding, and Fift gathered; she took Father Grobbard's other hand, and caught a fold of Father Grobbard's shift, and that way, they went down to the bathing room.

"My gowns weren't old," Fift said, on the stairs. "They came out of the oven a week ago."

"No, they weren't old," Grobbard said. "But they were blue. Blue is a Bail color, the color of the crashing, restless sea. You are a Staid, and today you will enter the First Gate of Logic. You couldn't do that wearing blue gowns."

"Oh," Fift said.

Grobbard sat by the side of the bathing pool, her hands in her lap, her legs in the water, while Fift scrubbed herself soapy.

"Father Grobbard," Fift said, "why are you a Father?"

"What do you mean?" Father Grobbard asked. "I am your Father, Fift. You are my child."

"But why aren't you a Mother? Mother Pip is a Mother, and she's—um, you're—"

Grobbard's forehead wrinkled briefly, and then it smoothed, and her lips quirked in a tiny suggestion of a smile. "Aha, I see. Because you have only one Staid Father, and the rest are Bails, you think that being a Father is a Bailish thing to be? You think Fathers should be 'he's and Mothers should be 'she's?"

Fift frowned, and stopped mid-scrub.

"What about your friends? Are all of your friends' Mothers 'she'? Or are some of them 'he'?" Grobbard paused a moment; then, gently: "What about Umlish Mnemu of Mnathis cohort? Her Mother is a Bail, isn't he?"

"Oh," Fift said, and frowned again. "Well, what makes someone a Mother?"

"Your Mother carried you in her womb, Fift. You grew inside her belly, and you were born out of her vagina, into the world. Some families don't have children that way, so in some families all the parents are Fathers. But we are quite traditional. Indeed, we are all Kumruists, except for Father Thurm...and Kumruists believe that biological birth is sacred. So you have a Mother."

Fift knew that, though it still seemed strange. She'd been *inside* Mother Pip for ten months. Singlebodied, because her other two bodies hadn't been fashioned yet. That was an eerie thought. Tiny, helpless, singlebodied, unbreathing, her nut-sized heart drawing nutrients from Pip's blood. "Why did Pip get to be my Mother?"

Now Grobbard was clearly smiling. "Have you ever tried to refuse your Mother Pip anything? There was a little bit of debate, but I think we all knew Pip would emerge as the Younger Sibling of that struggle. She had a uterus and vagina enabled, and made sure we all had penises, for the impregnation. It was an exciting time."

Fift pulled up the feed and looked up penises. They were for squirting sperm, which helped decide what the baby would be like. The uterus could sort through all the sperm and pick the genes it wanted, but you had to publish something or other to get approval, and after that it was too complicated. You'd have one on each body, dangling between your legs. "Do you still have penises? One...on each body?"

"Yes, I kept mine," Grobbard said. "They went well with the rest of me, and I don't like too many changes."

"Can I have penises?" she said.

"I suppose, if you like," Grobbard said. "But not today. Today you have something more important to do. And now I see that your Father has baked you new clothes. So rinse off, and let's go upstairs."

◊

The new clothes were bright white shifts, like Father Grobbard always wore. And Mother Pip, mostly. Fift felt grown up, and strange, and stiff. She was scrubbed and polished and her heads were shaved and oiled and her fingernails and toenails were trimmed. She sat in a row on the rough moss of the anteroom, trying to sit lightly, balanced, spines straight.

The anteroom of their apartment was full of parents, practically all of Iraxis cohort. Fathers Squell and Smistria and Pupolo and Miskisk were there in a body each, and Father Frill and Father Grobbard were both doublebodied. Mother Pip was on her way. Only Fathers Thurm and Arevio were missing, and they were watching over the feed.

Father Frill knelt next to Fift, brushing bits of fluff from the moss. He was lithe and dusky-skinned, with a shock of stiff copper-colored hair sweeping up from his broad forehead, wide gray eyes and a full mouth and a sharp chin. He was dressed for the occasion in cascades of tinkling silver and gold and crimson bells, and a martial shoulder sash hung with tiny, intricately-worked ceremonial knives and grenades. He crouched like a sharp-toothed wild hunting-animal, resting in a tree's limbs somewhere up on the surface of the world. He ran his hand gently over her bare, oiled scalp, which felt nice, but also distracting because she was trying very hard to sit straight. "Oh Fift," he said, "we're all very proud of you, you know."

"Well she hasn't done anything yet," Father Smistria said, glowering, and pacing back and forth under the pillars of the anteroom, "except finally take a bath! Keep *focused*, Fift."

"Ignore him," Father Frill said, taking his hand from Fift's head, leaning in against Fift's shoulder. He smelled like a rainy day in a mangareme fruit grove on the surface. "He's cranky because he's nervous. But there's no reason to be nervous, Fift. Grobbard and your Mother say that this thing today is just a formality. I—"

"Ha!" barked Smistria, tugging at his beard.

"Stop it, Smistria," Miskisk said. His fists were clenched. "You're making it worse."

Fift got an uneasy feeling in her stomach. {What are my Fathers talking about?} she asked her agents.

The context advisory agent answered, {About your first episode of the Long Conversation; today you will enter the First Gate of Logic.}

{I know that!} Fift sent back. She hated when her agents acted like she was a baby.

Father Squell cleared his throat. "It's really none of *our* business, Frill," he said. He was standing near the wall, rubbing the slippery red fabric of his shirt between his fingers. "Whether it's a 'formality!'"

Father Smistria glared at Squell. Frill, in his standing body, languidly cracked his back.

"I just mean—for *us* to argue about her chances!" Squell said. "It's not appropriate! This is Pip and Grobbard's domain...."

"None of our business?" Smistria barked. "None of *our business*?"

Father Frill frowned, leaned away from Fift (the bells tinkled as he shifted), and twitched his lips the way he always did when he was sending a private message. He was staring at Smistria, so he was probably sending something like: {Stop talking about this now, you're scaring Fift.} But Smistria ignored him.

"It really isn't," Squell said. He took a step away from Smistria, and looked back toward Pupolo, who was swinging gently in a seating harness at the back of the anteroom. "It's a Staid matter!"

"That's right," said Pupolo. He looked tired, but he still sat straight in his harness. He was in a green smock, and he had dirt on his hands, from the garden. Father Pupolo was Fift's oldest parent and once, a long long time ago, he had been sort of famous as a military poet.

"Well, I'm obviously not talking about the *details* of the...process," Smistria said, taking a step toward Father Squell and flinging his arms wide. "I'm not an fool. Don't insult me! But the *outcome*, that's another matter! The *outcome* affects our entire cohort, and you know perfectly well—"

"*Smi*," Frill said sharply. He leaned in toward Fift again; in his other body, he crossed to Smistria and grabbed his shoulder.

Grobbard stood to the side, expressionless. Fift wished she would say something. Or that Pip would finally come, and they could leave and get it over with. It was hard to sit up straight.

She tried her agents again: {Why is everyone fighting?}

The emotional nuance agent sent, {Bails often react to being tense by crying or shouting. Don't let it scare you!}

Smistria swiveled to glare at Frill. Frill didn't take his hand from Smistria's shoulder. They stared into each other's eyes. Then Smistria softened a little, and pulled Frill roughly into an embrace—Frill's musical clothes jingled and rang. They stood like that with their cheeks touching, Smistria's beard caught in Frill's bells, Smistria's eyes squeezed shut. Frill put his hand back on Fift's head. "There now!" he said.

Pip came, singlebodied, through the door.

Pip was large, and round, and bald. She wore a white shift too, and her skin was a deep forest green, and it hung in wens and folds from her face. She had powerful, searching eyes, white and gold and black, that looked deep into you. She had fat stubby fingers and one hand held the other hand's thumb and stroked it.

"Greetings, beloveds," said Pip. "Greetings, Fift." She turned to Pupolo and clasped his hands briefly, nodded to Grobbard, quirked an eyebrow at Frill and Smistria.

"Finally!" Frill said, releasing Smistria in a cascade of bells. Smistria breathed in loud, and crossed his arms. "What took you so long, Pip? We were about to check into the Madhouse, all eight of us!"

Squell touched Pip's cheek, ran his hand along her shoulder. Pip's expression softened into an almost-smile, and she took Squell's hand.

"Oh, Pip," Squell said, "will you please tell them that it's fine, and to stop arguing about today! It's just absurd!"

Miskisk looked angry, as if dark clouds were massing across his sunset face.

Pip blinked, and looked to Frill, to Smistria, to Pupolo, and finally to Grobbard. Then she chuckled. "Fift is ready," she said. "I have absolute confidence. Do you remember what we practiced, Fift?"

All it was, was sitting still and waiting to be passed a spoon, and passing it on at the right moment, and saying the names of the twelve cycles, the twenty modes, and the eight corpuses of the Long Conversation. You couldn't use agents to help with anything, but that was okay because Fift and Grobbard never let her practice with agents anyway. She nodded.

"And Grobbard concurs," Pip said. "You are all disturbed by the betting, I know, but there is always betting around a Staidchild's first Long Conversation, especially when..." she pursed her lips. "...when a cohort looks weak from outside." She raised a hand, as if to quiet objections. "Only nine parents, only two of them Staids—the initial birth approval barely granted—the questions around Fift's somatic integration--well, of course ignorant bettors imagine they see an opportunity! But they do not have the information we have. They are speculating. We know."

"There!" said Frill. "You see?"

Smistria harrumphed, and stretched his arms above his head. "Very well. Then let's send you all off, and get back to our day. This fussing and waiting is making me old. Frill, how about a bout on the practice mats?"

"All right," Frill said. He kissed Fift on the top of her head. "Enjoy yourself, little stalwart." He stood.

Pupolo stood up from his harness. Grobbard came over doublebodied to Fift, and sent, {It is time to go, Fift.}

But Fift did not stand up; she was watching Miskisk.

"Well," Miskisk said, his voice tense as the straining of the giant muscles that turned their habitation, "that's wonderful, isn't it? Fift is all settled then, isn't she? All ready for her big day, no problems anywhere, and the cohort is perfectly safe and from here our ratings can only burrow in to greatness."

"Miskisk," Pupolo said, dissaproving.

"Oh, I don't *dispute* it," Miskisk said, raising his great orange hands. "What do I know? It's a Staidish matter and I'm sure *Pip* has everything under control. As usual. But in that case, isn't it time for the next step?"

"Oh, not this again," Frill said.

"Misky," Squell said. He frowned, clearly sending a private message, then—getting no reponse—said in exasperation, "Not in front of Fift!"

"But where, then?" Miskisk said. "Where, then? At every family meeting it's tabled immediately—"

"Beloved Miskisk," Pip said—it was a cold, dry kind of "beloved," Fift thought—"I am, as you know, perfectly willing for us to hazard a second child, if the matter of maternity can be settled to our mutual satisfaction."

"We are *not* doing this here," Frill said. "No. No, no, no."

Suddenly Fift knew what they were arguing about. *A second child.* A strange sensation, heat and cold together, shot through her bodies. She lost her careful balance and had to put a hand down onto the moss to steady herself. A sibling! A *Younger Sibling*—literally!—supplanting Fift.

To be an Older Sibling—everyone said—meant being poor, being eclipsed, being in the shadow of the Younger. But it also meant not being alone. Having someone to protect and support. And it meant not being an Only Child; and everyone knew there was something wrong with being an Only Child. Something that made Fift's parents worry and argue and quickly take conversations unspoken, when Fift asked too much.

"Which means of course that it's you again!" Miskisk said. "It's always you!" Tears sprang to his eyes, and a great shudder passed through his heavy body. He looked around at the other Fathers. "It's always her! She is the Mother, she guards our ratings, she decides where we'll live and when little Fift has to—has to—"

Frill brushed past Grobbard, squatted down again, and enfolded Fift in his arms. He picked one of Fift's bodies up, slinging one bell-clad arm under her bottom. She was pressed against his bells and daggers and grenades. Squell hurried over, too.

"Miskisk, you selfish ingrate," Pupolo said, "blaming Pip will not elevate *your* chances of bearing, I'll tell you that!"

Father Frill hustled Fift toward the door. He was coming in another body, too, to fetch more of Fift—but then he wheeled around, facing Miskisk. "Miskisk, you're being absurd. Pip *won't* be the Mother the second time. It will be Pupolo or Arevio, or Thurm if he'd agree to it, or—or me!" Smistria snorted, and Frill glared at him briefly through slitted eyes, then went on, "Pip knows perfectly well that being Mother twice over would be—too much! But what is your rush anyway? Fift isn't even five yet! Why does she need a Younger Sibling right away?"

Squell scooped up another of Fift's bodies, and followed Frill out the door, muttering: "Completely inconsiderate! Today of all days!"

{What's wrong with being an only child?} Fift asked her agents.

{That is not the polite term} sent Fift's social nuance agent. {You should use "an individual with a heavy relative familial-resource-allocation childhood." Pedagogical experts, statistician-poets, religious officials, the Midwives, all agree: children who lack siblings lack the basics of human experience. All real human emotions—jealousy, rage, love, regret, forgiveness, rivalry, triumph, defeat, reconciliation, and ultimate shared purpose—are based in the contest between siblings.}

"This is the age when it matters!" Miskisk rumbled, tears streaming down his face. "And what makes you think it will ever change? None of you will ever dare to struggle with Pip over the maternity—and none of you have the strength to watch Fift be supplanted!"

Pip crooked an eyebrow, coldly amused.

"That's—" Frill flung an arm out, ringing with bells, and turned to Miskisk. "That's—Smi, take the child out of here!—that's an insult!"

Two of Fift's bodies were out through the door and into the corridor. Frill and Squell put her onto her feet and smoothed her robes.

Smistria sighed loudly, and stalked over to where her third body sat. He held out his hand.

"It's true!" Miskisk wailed. "You're too cowardly and too comfortable! You'd rather she end up *sisterless* than endure the discomfort of her Supplanting!"

{What's "sisterless?"} Fift asked her agents.

{That is not a word we say} sent the social nuance agent primly.

{*Sister* is an archaic word for sibling} added the context advisory agent.

{But lots of people are Only Children} Fift sent. {Grobbard and Arevio and Smistria are....}

{It is one of the great social crises of our time} her context advisory agent sent.

In the corridor, Fift shivered. In the anteroom, in her last body, she stayed seated, looking away from Smistria, looking at Miskisk. Her Father was crying—that was nothing, her Bail Fathers cried all the time—but this was different. Something was wrong here; Miskisk was serious. A chill raced down from her necks and settled in her stomachs.

Smistria shook his hand in Fift's face. "Come on," he growled. "You're going to be late anyway, for this...this circus of yours!"

Pupolo drew a shocked breath, because one shouldn't make fun of the Long Conversation like that. Smistria snorted.

"Smistria," Miskisk pled, "you agree with me—you know it's too early for this—that Fift deserves a little more time at home to run and play and wear more colors than white, before—"

Smistria pushed his hand at Fift, glaring, and Fift had to take it. She pulled herself to her feet.

"Do I agree with you that Pip is bossy, and that everyone here is all too eager to postpone *any* argument...especially in the matter of Sibling Number Two? Of course I do. Do I think you should be allowed to keep Fift here as a baby, dressed up in bangles and zooming about—to satisfy your selfish wish for a Bailchild? No, Miskisk, I do not." He pulled Fift toward the door. Grobbard came with them, expressionless.

"You are crushing my heart," Miskisk said, tears dripping from his chin. "I cannot do this anymore. I cannot—"

"We have a *pledge*," Pupolo said in horror.

Miskisk covered his eyes with his hands.

"If I may," Pip said coldly—and then the door closed behind them. Fift closed her eyes tried to listen and look with the feed, to see what Pip and Miskisk and Pupolo were saying in the anteroom. But the feed was opaque. Where that room should be was a blank silence. Someone had told the apartment not to show her what was happening there.

"Come on now, little stalwart," Frill said. "You won't be late if we hurry. You're ready and there's plenty of time."

"What about Pip?" Squell said.

"She's also already on the way from her client in Temereen," Frill said, pulling Fift along doublebodied towards the front door of the apartment, "she was planning to come doublebodied anyway—it's not far—perhaps, since she's busy here, one will have to do—Grobby is here, and you're going to do fine!"

Father Grobbard walked beside them, silent. She didn't look upset, or worried. She walked as if she was in the morning hush of a forest on the surface, watching for unpurposed surface animals, the way they once had on a trip they took...up the long elevators, thousands of bodylengths through the deep dark bedrock...to the surface forest, quiet and cold and damp and strange....

This was like that now, maybe. A trip somewhere new. A trip to the Long Conversation, which was secret and important and grownup and Staid.

{What pledge?} Fift asked her agents.

{A pledge is a promise that people make} began the context advisory agent.

{That's not what I asked} Fift sent. {You know what I mean! What pledge did my parents make? Tell me or I'm going to remove you!}

Fift took Grobbard's hands, and they all went out through the apartment door, through the corridor, and onto the surface of Foo.

{Your parents all pledged to stay together for all twenty-two years of your First Childhood} sent the context advisory agent, reluctantly. {To all sleep in the same apartment once a month at the least, to attend family meetings, various such requirements. They had to. The neighborhood approval ratings for your birth weren't high enough otherwise.}

{But this is not at all unusual} the social nuance agent assured Fift.

Just above them was the glistening underside of Sisterine habitation, docking-spires and garden-globes and flow-sluices arcing away. In front of them was the edge of Foo. Their neighborhood, Slow-as-Molasses, was at the end of one spoke of Foo's great, slowly rotating wheel—and beyond it, this time of year, was a great empty vault of air... and then fluffy Ozinth and the below-and-beyond strewn with glittering bauble-habitations...and beyond that, habitation after habitation, bright and dim, smooth and spiky, shifting and still, all stretching away toward the curve of Fullbelly's ceiling.

There are a trillion people in the world, Fift thought. And only ten in our house. And if Father Miskisk breaks the pledge, we'll be only nine, and that's not enough. Her legs, under the new white shift, felt cold and rubbery.

They came to the edge of the neighborhood, the main slideway to the center of Foo.

"All right, little cubblehedge," Squell said, dropping down on one knee to hug Fift. "Time for Frill and I to turn back. You are in our hearts."

Frill rubbed Fift's scalp one more time. "Knock 'em on their backs, little one!" He grinned, and slapped his knife-belt. "Metaphorically."

Fift looked up into his face and took a deep breath. *The outcome affects our whole cohort.* "Father Frill, what if I *don't* do well? What will happen?"

Frill and Squell's faces went a little stiff, and even Grobbard blinked. Fift realized then—they weren't in the apartment anymore, they weren't just on the house feed. Everyone in the world could see and hear them now, if they wanted to.

But Frill smiled then, and crouched down next to Fift, in a tinkling of bells. "Then we'll manage, Fift," he said. "We're a strong cohort and we'll triumph. You have a Mother and Father to hold you safe at the center, and Fathers enough to range around you, to protect and enliven..."

{Will you hurry up?} sent Smistria, from back at the apartment, to all of them. {Fift will be late!}

Frill rolled his eyes, and grinned a crooked grin. "Goodbye," he said, and "Goodbye," Squell said, and Fift took Grobbard's hand and stepped onto the slideway.

{Father Miskisk} Fift sent, but she didn't know what else to send. {Father Miskisk...I'll do my best!}

If she did well enough, maybe Father Miskisk would stay.

The slideway whooshed them off, towards the center of Foo, where they could transfer to another spoke; toward the wooden floor, and the spoons, and the First Gate of Logic, and white gowns and responsibility, and no more zooming. Fift held tight to Grobbard's hand, and waited, hoping, for Father Miskisk to reply.

The Master of the Milford Altarpiece

Thomas M. Disch

> What blacks and whites, what greys and purplish browns!
>
> BERNARD BERENSON

> Often enough Rubens may have quietly taken stock of all previous Italian art at this time, especially of the Venetian school, the knowledge of which had had so little influence on other northern artists. Though scarcely one immediate reminiscence of Titian can be discovered in Rubens's later work, whether of objects or of single forms, he had learned to see with Titian's eyes. He found the whole mass of Tintoretto's work intact, and much of it still free of the later blackening of the shadows which makes it impossible for us to enjoy him, but he may well have been repelled by the touch of untruthfulness and lack of reticence in him, and by the crudity of a number of his compositions. It is obvious that his deepest kinship by far was with Paolo Veronese; here two minds converged, and there have been pictures which might be attributed to either, for instance, a small, but rich Adoration of the Magi which the present writer saw in early, uncritical years and has never been able to forget.
>
> JACOB BURCKHARDT

I.

I can hear him, in the next room but one, typing away. An answer to Pamela's special delivery letter perhaps? Or lists of money-making projects. Possibly even a story, or a revised outline for *Popcorn*, in which he will refute the errors of our age.

Wishing to know his age, I went into the communicating room.

"Jim?" I called out. "Jim?" Not in his office. I called downstairs. No reply. I returned here, to this desk, this typewriter. Now there are noises: his voice, the slow expository tone that he reserves for Dylan.

He is twenty-three. He will be twenty-four in December. For his age he is fantastically successful. I envy his success, though it isn't a personal thing—I can envy almost anyone's. I need constant reassurance. I crave your admiration. Is candor admirable? Is reticence even more admirable. I want to read this to someone.

Chip said, on the phone last night, that Algis Budrys called him the world's greatest science-fiction writer. I certainly did envy that. Jane said afterward that Chip is coming up here at the end of the week, possibly with Burt. (Burt?) Marilyn is still in San Francisco. I feel resentful.

I don't think that I am alone in being obsessed with the idea of success. We all are. But though we may envy the success of our friends, we also require it. What kind of success would we be if our friends were failures?

This isn't the story. This is only the frame.

◊

Pieter Saenredam

Pieter Jansz. Saenredam; painter of church interiors and topographical views.

Born in Assendelft 9 June, 1597, son of the engraver Jan Saenredam. He went as a child to Haarlem and became a pupil in May 1612 of Frans Pietersz. de Grebber, in whose studio he remained until 1622. In 1623 he entered the painters' guild at Haarlem and spent most of his life there. He was buried at Haarlem, 31 May, 1665.

He was in contact with the architects Jacob van Campen and Salomon de Bray, and perhaps also Bartholomeus van Bassen. He was one of the first architectural painters to reproduce buildings with fidelity (that is to say, in his drawings; in his pictures, accuracy is often modified for compositional reasons).

In his bedroom, which also served him as a studio, the curtains were always drawn. The cats performed ovals and sine curves in the bedclothes, a gray cat, a calico cat. Most of the furniture has been removed. The remaining pieces are placed against the wall.

The pleasures of iconoclasm. Destruction as a precondition of creation. Our burning faith.

The same painting over and over again. The high vaults and long recessions. The bare walls. The slanting light. Bereft of figures. (Those we see now have, for the most part, been added by other hands.) Nude. White.

He opened his present. Each box contained a smaller box. The last box contained a tin of Mixture No. 79, burley and Virginia. From that young scapegrace, Adriaen Brouwer (1605-1638).

It was an exciting time to live in. Traditions were crumbling. Fortunes were made and destroyed in a day.

The columns in the foreground have been made to appear much wider and taller, and the arches borne by them have been suppressed.

◊

His first letter:

> RFD 3
> *Iowa City, Iowa*
> *May 66*

Dear Mr. Disch—

Twenty minutes ago I finished The Genocides. *And should have finished it days ago, but I kept drawing it out, going back over things, taking it a few pages at a time: because I didn't want it to be over with, sure but mainly because I felt there was so much to take in—the structure, the pitch and tone of the narrative, the interflow of situations—and I wanted to give myself every chance I could . . . .*

From a letter two months later:

. . . I am touched, Tom, by your extremely kind offer. To show my things to Moorcock. If they were only good stories, I'd take you up on it in a minute. But they're not, and I know it, which makes things different, almost embarrassing. But I may still put you in the compromising position, after thinking it over a while. I could use the sale (money, ego-boost, a beginning), and some of 'em aren't really that bad . . . and so on. But for now: I thank you very much. No way of expressing my gratitude—not only for the offer, but for your proffered friendship as well, your demonstrated openness . . . .

And this, when I had asked him for a self-portrait:

His Whilom. Born in Helena, Arkansas. Parents uneducated. Spoiled because was so hard to conceive him, wrecked mother's health to bear him against the advice of doctors. One brother, seven year older; philosopher, PhD, teacher. Spent his youth on banks of Twain's Mississippi and in Confederate woods banking his small town. Became interested in conjuring when about twelve, an interest which persists. During high school edited some small magic mags, composed and formed chamber groups, took music lessons (against his parents' wishes, who thought playing in the band was enough, and regardless of their lack of funds), had few friends. Spent summer between 11th and 12th grade doing independent research under guide of National Science Foundation, it being his ambition at that time to become a biochemist. Was oppressed that summer by the routine boredom of checks and balances, began to write poetry under the inspiration of cummings. In his 12th school year, wrote plays, directed plays, acted in plays, won dramatic prizes, became very depressed about not having the money to go to Princeton, became a dandy and discovered girls. Decided he was a poet.

The Exterior Symbolic. Am tall, very thin with a beer belly and matchstick legs. A disorder of the lower back has left me slightly stooped and given me a strange, quite unique walk. Wear wire-frame glasses. Dress in either corduroy coat or black suit, with dark or figured or flowered shirt and black or figured tie. An angular, long face. Black curly hair that sticks out like straw and generally needs a cutting.

◊

Aedicule

The enclosing planes of walls, floor, ceiling. Subsidiary planes in tiers supported by the vertical members—posts, legs, brackets. A light bulb hangs from the ceiling. His room is characterized by rectilinearity. He unpacks his boxes and arranges the books on shelves, tacks prints to the walls, disposes of his clothing into drawers.

Without are trees, weeds, grasses, haystacks, cathedrals, crowds of people, rain, bumps, animals ground into meat, billboards, the glare, conversations, radiant energy, danger, hands, prices, mail, the same conversations.

The artist is obliged to structure these random elements into an order of his own making. He places the ground meat in the icebox, arranges the crowds of people into drawers. He carves a smaller church and places it in the larger church. Within this artificial structure, each figure, isolated in its own niche, appears transfigured. Certain similarities become apparent. More and more material is introduced. New shelves must be built. Boxes pile up below the steps. The sentences swell from short declarative statements into otiose candelabra. Wax drips onto the diapered floor. Styles conflict. Friends drop in for a chat and stay on for the whole weekend. At last there is nothing to be done but scrap the whole mess and start from scratch.

Whitewash. Sunlight slanting across bare walls. Drawn curtains. Vermeer's eventless studio.

He paints a picture of the table and the chair. The floor. The walls. The ceiling. His wife comes in the door with a plate of doughnuts. Each doughnut has a name. He eats "Happiness." His wife eats "Art." The door opens. Their friend Pomposity has come for a visit.

II.

Yesterday, all told, he got three letters from Pamela. Passion that can express itself so abundantly, though it may forfeit our full sympathy, is a wonderful thing to behold. Given the occasion, how readily we all leap into our buskins! And if we are not given the occasion outright, we will find it somehow. Madame Bovary, *c'est nous!*

When every high utterance is suspect. We must rely on surfaces, learn to decode the semaphore of the gratuitous, quotidian event.

Oh, the semaphore of the gratuitous, quotidian event—that's beautiful.

For a long while I pressed my head against my purring IBM Executive and tried to think of what constituted, in our lives here, a gratuitous event. There seemed far too much significance in almost anything I could remember of yesterday's smallest occasions. I returned most often to:

Raking leaves. Not, conscientiously, into a basket for burning, but over the edge of the escarpment. Like sweeping dust under a rug. Jim came out on the porch to announce a phone call from my brother Gary. He has been readmitted to Canada with immigrant status. Then, back to my little chore. Jim said he hates to rake leaves. "Because it reminds you of poems in *The New Yorker?*" I asked. He laughed. No, because it reminds him of his childhood. Weeding the towering weeds in the back lawn, unmowed since mid-August. The two most spectacular weeds I tamped into a coffee can and set beside our other plants on the table in the bay of the library.

Strings of hot peppers, predominantly red, hanging unconvincingly on the pea-soup kitchen wall. Jane's handicraft. Staring at them as I gossiped with Jim. About? Literature, probably, and our friends.

Judy bought a steak, and Jane made beef stroganoff and a Caesar salad, both exemplary. The flavor of the sauce, the croutons' crunch.

Chess with Jim before dinner, with Jane after I'd washed the dishes.

Jane cut Jim's hair. Dylan was skipping through the scattered curls, so I swept them up and put them in the garbage.

At what point was I happiest yesterday: as I raked leaves and washed dishes or when I was writing this story? At what point was Jane happiest? At what point was Jim happiest?

Was Jane happier than Jim? Was I happier than either? If not, were both, or only one, happier than me? Which?

I spend too much time lazing about indoors. I overeat. I smoke a package of cigarettes every day. I masturbate too often. I am not honest with myself. How, then, can I expect to be honest about others?

Happiness is not important.

◊

The Conversion of St. Paul

The acquisition of certain knowledge (as Augustine shows us) is possible, and men are bound to acknowledge this fact. The knowledge of God and of man is the end of all the aspirations of reason, and the purification of the heart is the condition of such knowledge.

The city is divided by schisms, as by innumerable rivers. His single room on Mississippi Avenue overlooks an endless genealogy of errors, sparrows, roofs. He has, by preference, few friends. He reads, each evening, of the great dispute over the nature of the Trinity. Demons in the form of moths tickle the bare soles of his feet. He fills his notebooks with theories, explanations, refutations, apologies—but nothing satisfies him. Of what solace is philosophy when each sequent hour reveals new portents of a sure and merited destruction, innumerable portents?

He cannot endure the strength of these emotions.

He writes:

To be happy, man must possess some absolute good: this is God. To possess God is to be wise. But none can possess God without the Son of God, who says of Himself, I am the truth. The truth namely is the knowledge-principle of the highest, all-embracing order, which, as absolutely true, produces the truth out of itself in a like essential way. A blessed life consists in knowing by whom we are led to the truth, in what we attain to the truth, and how we are united to the highest order.

That much seems to be clear.

Often (of this he did not write) the walls of the room warped. The old man from next door came and stared at him as he lay there in the bed. Crook-backed and dirty (a magician probably): the name "Sabellius" burnt into the gray flesh of his high forehead.

In the churches, the gilded sculptures of Heresy and Sedition. Plastic dissembling itself as trees, weeds, grasses; simulating entire parks. The seeming virtues of his friends were only splendid vices. Their faces were covered with giant worms.

He distinguished between the immediate and the reflective consciousness, which concludes itself in unity, by the most perfect form of the will, which is love. Does the Holy Ghost proceed from the communion of the Father and the Son?

Explain the hypostatis of Christ. Tell me you love me. Define your terms.

He fell on his back and saw, in the clouds, the eye of the whale. He saw the river burning and his friends destroyed.

And no one listens to him. No one. No one.

◊

An excerpt from his letter of Sept. '66:

The large, looming discovery: Samuel R. Delany. I had read a few of his books and been quite impressed and assumed he had been writing for three hundred years and was roughly ten million years old. God, I should have known (and if I'd read the jacket notes would have) . . . by the time he was 22, he'd had four books published. The last three of these are a trilogy, and his best work. He's about 24/25 now, with eight books. And he's beginning to think about shorter work . . . . "Chip" has the strongest, most vital personality I've discovered in the sf clan. That young, and writing like that! (This is the larger part of my current depression—that he does it so much better than I.) Read his books and you drown in poetry.

And this, a letter to his wife:

Glad to hear that you and Tom are getting along so well and things are working out; also, of course, very glad to hear that you're working. I'm really damned pleased that you like him so much. Tom is a fantastic influence on everyone he comes near. I find it difficult to be with him for more than a few minutes without having the urge to get right to work on something better than anything I've ever done before. I don't know if I have mentioned it, but Tom is beyond doubt the only person I know to whom I'd apply words like "genius." In ten years or so, he's going to be quite, quite well-known and quite, quite respected. What is he, and what are you working on; and are you, and is he, serious about the poetry magazine? I hope so.

That radiant quality of mind is something he shares with Mike, with John Sladek, and with Pamela.

And then (though not chronologically):

I'm constantly amazed, Tom, at the similarity of our tastes, expression, and ambitions. If we were French poets, I'm certain we'd think it necessary to form a "school" about ourselves: arguing with the establishment and among ourselves, bitching at traditions, j'accusing all over the place, emitting manifestoes, issuing bulls, belching intent everywhere we walked, excreting doctrine and should-be's, generating slogans, shouting what we collectively think, and having a hell of a lot of fun doing it all . . . I don't think anyone has ever done that in sf, have they? Poetry, art, music, other writing reeks with such focused groups (I'm led to think of this by just having read a book on contemporary poetry, in which the movements of the projective-verse poets and deep-image poets were detailed; it sounded like so much fun, and everyone concerned got so much out of it, and you can't argue that they wham-bang turned the tides of poetry).

◊

A Schematic Diagram

Linda began her affair with Gene in high school. Sometimes Linda wanted to marry Gene. Sometimes Gene wanted to marry Linda. Gregory married Lois. Ben married Nancy. Doug married Sue. Linda and Gene took a flat with Paul. Gene married Marion and moved to Montreal.

Bereft, Linda sailed to London on the *France*. At the university she met Ahmet.

Jerry had an affair with Lois. Gregory was almost killed in a motorcycle accident. Jerry went to Europe. When he returned, a year later, to New York, he subleased Paul's apartment. Paul went away and wrote a novel. He returned and collaborated on a second novel with Jerry. They went to London.

Linda wanted to marry Paul. She had an affair with Jerry. The three of them lived together in Ahmet's flat. After an unhappy and brief affair with Bob, Paul went away and wrote about it. Jerry moved out of the flat and had a brief and unhappy affair with Nancy.

Doug and Sue went to London. She hated London and returned to the States. Doug had an affair with Linda. Jerry had an affair with a different, younger Linda. Mr. Nolde had an affair with the first Linda. Linda was very unhappy. She wanted to marry Jerry. She wanted to marry Doug.

Paul returned to the States. He decided to sublease the Williamses' house with Sue. Doug grew worried and returned to the States. Ben was very upset. He refused to give Linda Doug's phone number.

Gene and Marion went to London.

POETS:	Gregory. Gene. Doug.
	Paul. Jerry. Bob.
NOVELISTS,	
SHORT STORY WRITERS:	Gene. Doug. Paul. Jerry.
	Lois. Nancy. Ben. Linda.
	Sue. The Williamses.

PAINTERS:	Marion. Linda. Sue.
EDITORS, ANTHOLOGISTS:	Doug. Jerry. Bob.
	Ben. Mr. Williams.
ARCHITECT:	Ahmed.
ART COLLECTOR:	Mr. Nolde.

III.

The artist, when he makes his art, shares a common fate with Rousseauistic man: he begins free and ends in chains.

And other metaphors (for instance, the furnishing of a room) to express the fact that at this point I know pretty well the nature of everything that must follow to the end of "Reredos" (which was the title it preserved through the entire first draft).

Both Jim and Jane are doubtful about the merits of this story. They seemed to enjoy the preceding sections at the première in Jane's studio (she had just finished a handsome gray nude; we were all feeling mellow), but they questioned whether that wider audience who will read my story to themselves, who have never met me and, likely, never will, would find it relevant or interesting.

What a wider audience ought to know (bear in mind, reader, that this is the frame, not the story):

Four years ago, when I was in advertising, I wrote a story called "The Baron, Danielle, and Paul," which portrayed, behind several thick veils of circumspection, my situation during the previous year, when I had been living with John and Pamela on Riverside Drive. That story appeared, revised, as "Slaves" in the *Transatlantic Review*. Before it had come out, I was living with Pamela again, this time in London and with a different John, a recombination that Jim (before he had ever met Pamela) used as the basis for an amusing piece of frou-frou called "Front and Centaur." After he had met her he wrote "Récits," which is a kind of love story and in no way frivolous. (It, too, was taken by the *Transatlantic Review*.) Then Jim came here, to Milford, and almost immediately Jane wrote a story about the three of *us*: "Naje, Ijm, and Mot." Two days ago Jim sent this off, immaculately typed, to McCrindle, who edits *TR*.

In these successive stories there is a closer and closer approximation to the "real" situation. Thence: this. (Which will almost necessarily go to McCrindle too. If he rejects it? *New Worlds*? Jim is co-editor there.)

A bedroom farce with all the doors opening onto the same library. Stage center, a row of typewriters. On the walls, posters advertising the *Transatlantic Review*.

But beyond the fleeting amusement of our prototypical incests, the story does (should) raise a serious question. Concerning? Art's relationship to other purposes, let us say. Or alternatively, the Artist's role in Society.

Why do I write stories? Why do you read them?

◊

The Semaphore

The maples, whose leaves he would so much have preferred to rake, grew far up the hill, beyond even the most reckless gerrymandering of the boundaries of the backyard. The leaves that he was in fact raking were dingy brown scraps, mere litter, the droppings of poplars.

Jane came out onto the porch. She had just made herself blond. "You shouldn't do it that way," she said.

"How *should* I do it?" he said.

"You should rake them into piles, and then put the piles in boxes, and then empty the boxes into the incinerator, and then incinerate them."

"Do *you* want to rake the leaves?"

"I hate to rake leaves—it reminds me of poems in *The New Yorker*. I wanted you to come in the kitchen and look at what Dylan's found."

Dylan had found a slug.

"It's a snail," she said, "without its shell."

"It's a slug," he said.

"Oh, you're always so disagreeable."

"Snail!" Dylan crowed proudly. "Snail!"

"No, not a snail," he explained, in the slow expository tone he reserved for his son. "A slug. Say 'slug.'"

Dylan looked at his father with bewilderment.

"Slug," he coaxed. "Slug. Slug."

"Fuck," Dylan said.

Jane laughed. (The night before Jim had tried to explain to Dylan the difference between a nail and a screw. Dylan could not pronounce the word "screw," so Jim had taught him to say "fuck" instead.)

"No, slug." But wholly without conviction.

"Snail?"

"Okay, it's a snail."

Jane found a grape jelly bottle and punctured the top with a nail. (Nails don't have threads; screws do.) She put the shell-less snail in the bottle and gave the bottle to Dylan. The snail's extended cornua explored its meaningless and tragic new world.

"Do you want to give your snail a name?" Jim asked. "What do you want to call him?"

After a moment's deliberation Dylan said, "Four eight."

Neither Jim nor Jane thought this a very satisfactory name. At last Jane suggested Fluff.

Even Dylan was happy with this.

Jim went outside to finish raking the brown leaves, while Jane went up to her studio to work. Her new painting represented a single gray body that embraced its thick torso with confused arms. The three heads (which might have been the same head seen from three different angles) bore a problematic relationship to the single torso. It was based on one of Blake's illustrations to the *Inferno*.

Dylan stayed in the kitchen. He uncapped the grape jelly bottle and filled it with water. Snails live in water. The aquarium in the dining room was full of snails and guppies.

Fluff floated in the middle of the water, curled into a tight ball. Dylan, as he watched the snail drown, pronounced its name, its name, pronounced it.

◊

From the letter he wrote to his wife shortly before he came to Milford:

Pardon the typing. My arms are a bit sore from yesterday's struggle with the harmonium, and I'm a little groggy, still, from being up late last night writing the first of this letter (which, looking back to, I feel should be torn up and disposed of). And I'm all emotional and everything. (I cried when I got your letter, and the effects have not yet worn off. I miss you so much. I love you so much. I want to be with Dylan so badly. You really have no idea what importance you two are in my life, how central you are to everything I do. Just after the death of his wife, Chandler wrote to a friend something like, "Everything I did, for twenty years, every moment, was just a fire for her to warm her hands by." Which is rather how I feel.

You'd do best, by the way, to disregard Tom's proclamation on the subject of earthly love. Tom's ideas of love, as you must surely know, are rather peculiar ones. Never listen to a renegade Catholic's opinions on love; only listen to what his work tells you. I do love you. I love you very much and I love you more, this moment, this month, this year, than ever I have before. I do, Jane. There's desperation in it, yes—I need that love, to hold up against the world—I need it to give all the rest of what I do some small meaning, a degree, a single degree, of relevance—I need it as defense, and as reason. But that doesn't make the love any less real. With Creeley, I'm afraid I finally believe that "It's only in the relationships men manage, that they exist at all." You ask me to write of love. But how can one write of love, particularly our love?—it is absolute, and words are approximations. I have done the best I can do, here, in this letter. I have tried, in the poems, to do better. But I do not, finally, believe in the power of words to do other than distort, fictionalize, and obfuscate. I love you. Which is the simplest and best way, because every word there, and there are few of them, is an absolute concept. I love you.)

◊

A Lasting Happiness

"How strange life is," Jim remarked, after a pause during which he had taken in the stark details of my cramped cell. "Who would have thought, only a few years ago, that you...that I...."

"Those years have been kind to you, Jim," I insisted earnestly. "Your books have enjoyed both popular and critical success. Though you cannot be said to be rich, your life has been filled with pleasures that wealth could never buy. The youth of the nation acclaim you and have no other wish than to pattern their lives on yours. And you, Jane Rose, you are lovelier now than when we first met. Do you remember?—it was July, in Milford."

She turned aside a face that might have come from the pencil of Greuze, but I had seen that tear, and—dare I confess it?—that tear was dearer to me than her smile!

"And you, Tom?" Jim asked in a low voice.

"Oh, don't think of me! I've been happy too in my own small way. Perhaps life did not bring altogether everything that I once expected, but it has given me...your friendship."

He broke into tears and threw his arms about me in a last heart-rending embrace. "Tom!" he cried in agony. "Oh, Tom!"

I smiled, removing his hands gently from my shoulder to place it in Jane's. "You'll soon have all of us in tears," I chided, "and that *would* be silly. Because I expect to be *very* happy, you know, where I am going."

"Dear, dear Tom," Jane said. "We will always remember you."

"Ah, we ought never to trust that word 'always.' I would be quite satisfied with 'sometimes.' And young Dylan, how is he?"

"He is married, you know. We have a grandchild, a darling little girl."

"How wonderful! How dearly I should like to be able to—but, hush! Can you hear them in the corridor? It's time you left. It was so good of you to come. I feel quite...transfigured."

Jane rose on tiptoe to kiss my cheek. "God bless you!" she whispered in my ear.

Jim pressed my hand silently. There were no words to express what we felt at that moment.

They left without a backward glance.

The warden entered to inquire if I wished to see a priest. I refused as politely as possible. My hands were bound, and I was led along the corridor—the guards seemed much more reluctant than I—and out through the gate to the little pony cart.

The ride to the place of execution seemed all too brief. With what passionate admiration my eyes drank in the tender blueness of the sky! How eagerly I scanned the faces fleeting past on both sides! How familiar each one seemed! And the grandeur of the public buildings! The thrilling flight of a sparrow across the panorama of roofs! The whole vast spectacle of life—how dear it suddenly had become!

A sturdy young man—he might, I reflected, almost have been myself in another incarnation!—assisted me up the steps and asked if there was anything that I would like to say.

"Only this—" I replied. "It is a far, far better thing that I do than I have ever done; it is a far, far better rest that I go to than I have ever known."

He nodded resignedly. "Mm-hm."

River, Clap Your Hands

Sheree Renée Thomas

Night

All night long, the weary sound of water dripped from the roof into the bucket below, eroding her dreams. Ava woke from a sleep which bore her like an ocean, her mind still filled with the raindrop drum. The moon had veiled its face so that the stars could not see her cry. She woke and saw the street alive. She remembered when the neighborhood was submerged. She remembered when she was ruined by waters, ruined and resurrected by waters that bore spent seeds, the corpses of trees, and times that would never come again. Neither born nor named, time swam lifeless inside her and the lifeless tides swam with her. Ava touched damp garments that clung to her skin, close as guilt.

Watching the early morning walkers with their dogs at their sides, Ava was reminded that she lived among a people who believed in seasons. She lived among those who believed in the story and the song, among people who believed in prayer. Yet she knew nothing but the language of loss in a landscape she no longer recognized.

Ava rubbed her palm across the empty bowl of her stomach. Now she longed for the days when she felt full, when the nausea filled her and all she could taste was the salt from the stale crackers she nibbled on. Longing gnawed at her brain, consumed her waking thoughts. She never had the chance to hold it.

Rain

Rain made her anxious. The river swelling outside beyond the bluff filled Ava with dread. The rain fell faster, harder than it had last night. Outside, the walkers had long since scattered. Only the hardcore remained, refused to retreat. All was a sheet of gray steel. Inside, her mind was pitch black, except the brief flashes of light that stung the sky of memory. The couple who came for her, flashlights in hand, the beams reflecting off the violent waters that careened outside her door. Paralyzed, her body was caught in between. Trapped between a birth and a transformation. The old house had become a ship, tossed along the siren's song. Long after, terror filled her, even on the brightest days, flashbacks of all that she had lost. She was weary, tired of losing what she'd never had.

"Maybe it's a blessing," Grandmama said. "Maybe the Lord didn't want you to have that child. Birthing in the middle of all that strife. The Lord spared him." Grandmama was convinced the child was a boy.

"You carrying that baby mighty low," she had said. But that was then, before the first gills came.

"Sometimes, I wish He had spared me."

Grandmama sucked in air, a tone to freeze eardrums. Her eyes were cool water.

Wine

She had loved him. Most nights Ava told herself she had. She missed the way his fingers traced her flesh, the way his eyes widened, marveling at her smooth palms and their missing lifelines. She remembered him tracing the curve of throat, him lingering there until she could not breathe, the simple pleasure before his tongue found the gills. He had drawn away as if her touch had stung him. She never would forget his fear staring back at her, pupils dilated in widening circles, receding like the ripples in the river, him pulling away like the tide of the sea.

That night she drank red merlot, glass after cheap glass, and listened to Aretha, feeling like everything but a *natural woman*. That night her mind was all rivulets and rock pools. She spent the evening ruminating, returning to the same eye of water. Ava added three teardrops of pokeroot to her glass, and felt her throat constrict and release. Grandmama's rootwork. She always had a recipe but nothing could fix this, heartbreak. The flesh had grown raw and itchy inside, a wound that would not heal. Suddenly a soul in the lost and found didn't sound so unnatural to her. She had felt more than good inside, more possible with him. Now she felt undone, in flux. She was turned inside out. It was some time after the third or fourth glass, when the wine dribbled down her chin like ruby drops of blood, that she realized it was not his absence she mourned. It was the willful blindness that his presence helped her hide. Now how would she hide from herself?

Bridges

When Ava was a child her mother recited poems to her. Fierce poems of fault lines, of rivers turned, of a great tortoise whose back was as wide as the river's hips, of ancient paths lost and regained. They would emerge from beneath the Old Bridge. Together they dried themselves on the river's shore and watched the two trains running overhead. The air stung. It would take hours for Ava to perfect the rhythm of breathing. Sometimes drifters would leave piles of driftwood, old bottles, used cans. Her mother would make a fire and with a stick she would carve old signs and symbols in the soil. On those cool, mosquito-filled nights, Ava swatted flies and was warmed by her mother's company. Comforted by her mother's voice, her gills receded into her flesh, disappeared with the wind.

Mama kept her secrets close. Tight as water skins. "The Old Bridge is not the first bridge. Another lies in the water below," Mama had said, motioning with her hand. The thin membrane of webbing had finally dried and dropped away. It lay in scaly piles in the sand. "The first bridge was the river's spine, the Great Turtle. Our people swam across it, drifting finally into these waters. The first people we met lived up there, high on the hills." The high bluffs of the quiet river city were Ava's first glimpse of what would later become her home. Mama kept her secrets close. Ava learned this when she woke and discovered that she was alone. Mama had left her sleeping on the river's bank.

Hunger

When the river came alive, it hungered. It grew teeth and rose from its banks, swallowed the parks, the bending paths, the abandoned cars, the empty lots filled with broken glass, and encircled the bone yard, and the house. Ava woke to the sound of water running, like a faucet left on, and at first she thought it was a dream. She often dreamed of the river, the banks where her mother left her all those years ago, before the tall fishing man discovered her weeping by the still smoldering fire, before he took her home where she met Grandmama. But when Ava opened her eyes she realized the water had joined her, and that if she did not rise it would cover her and all the room. Then the cramps came, thunder deep below her chest. The baby, it was coming too soon. The water had awakened it. The water called to them both. Ava felt the gills open on her neck, the skin lengthen and stretch between her fingers. She needed to get out of the water, she needed to resist its call. Trapped between the birth and her own transformation, she climbed onto the top of the desk, then took a breath, plunged into the water's oily depths, swam out the door, in search of Grandmama.

◊

Hearts

It was the blame in their eyes that made Ava shun their company. The silent accusation made her huddle in the staging area on her own. People wanted to know why, couldn't understand how. The mayor said to go. Staying wasn't part of anyone's plan. "Why?" was the question that rested on everyone's lips. Why did Ava and so many others decide to ride out the storm? How could they not know the storm would ride them?

Grandmama once told Ava that her husband's heart had just stopped. "It knew Amp wasn't gon' never quit working, so his heart just revolted against itself." She said she found him lying on the floor he had lain down himself. "He came from a people who always used their hands. Sometimes," she said, "against themselves. But not my Amp. He built this house when we married, built it before your daddy was even born. I guess it's good he didn't know his boy wasn't gon' live long as him. In his way your daddy's heart revolted, too. Sometimes it ain't good to love so much in this world." For Ava and Grandmama, the house and its memories were all that they had left.

To keep the house when her husband died, Grandmama cleaned cracked china and porcelain bowls, shined broken mirrors and windows that stayed closed. Her hands cooked meals for dinners she was never invited to, graced tables with straightback chairs where she could not sit. Where she worked she heard haints in the halls and would return in time to make Ava's late-night dinners, telling her stories that left her amused, enthralled. She complained that there was nothing truly alive in some of those other grander houses, the walls had veins with no blood in them. Grandmama said a house has got to breathe, got to have some soul and a little laughter to make its foundation stay strong, said not every house, not every family can carry the weight. She said what Ava and she shared made their home more beautiful, more sacred than the fanciest castle. Ava believed her, too, right up until the water came and took her past and future, her home and her baby.

Loss

Long after they lost their house in the flood, after they moved to another river city, Grandmama stood in line with hollow-faced folks. Worried and weary, she waited like the others to get her pills. The churches collected toothpaste and brushes, brought clothing and prayers. The kindness made the loss less sharp. The city's humid heat made them feel less naked. "But feeling clean don't help me sleep," Grandmama said. The water haunted her dreams, too. So she waited and swallowed pills she knew by color, tried to muster up an appetite to eat. Grandmama missed her garden and her homemade cha cha. Ava missed her baby.

Pain

When Ava found Grandmama, she was upstairs still asleep in her bed. The look on her face was pure disbelief. She refused to leave the house without getting herself dressed. "I'm not going with all my business hanging out," she cried. "If the Lord gonna take me, I am at least going to have on my good dress." The pain in Ava's face made her stop. "What's the matter, child?"

"The baby," Ava managed. "It's coming, I can't stop it."

"Stop calling that boy 'it,' and come help me pull down this ladder." The water was rising up the steps. Framed photos, dishes, and books floated just below them. It took all Ava's strength to help her Grandmama up into the attic. The pains came so strong, she wanted to lie down in the murky water and let the flood carry her wherever it willed.

"Come on, Ava," her Grandmama said, reaching for her. They waited in the attic, darkness all around them. "We in God's hands now."

Air

While the water rose and their lone flashlight faded, Grandmama hummed and sang. She began with the stories Ava heard as a child, the ones that told of a people who came from water, who lived and breathed it, the way the others swallowed air. The infant Ava had loved and feared rested in a worn sheet between them. Its skin felt smooth and warm to Ava's touch, but she knew when Grandmama first held it, that there was something wrong. The child, a boy, never took its first breath.

It was Grandmama who heard the people screaming below. She called back, thankful already though they had not yet been delivered. Racked with pain so deep it seemed to sear her belly, Ava managed to rise from grief, the blood slick and running down her knees. She took the flashlight and knocked out a hole in the roof. With each strike, the rain came faster, her tears harder.

"We're here," Grandmama shouted. Ava did not wait for the reply below. As Grandmama stood up, widening the hole with her shoulders and waving to the couple in the boat, Ava took the silent child, caressed its little winged limbs and released it into the water and the night. It was dark, later they would need a flashlight just to see the food they ate, but then, hovering in the house that was once her shelter, all Ava wanted was to see her child's face. For a moment Ava thought she saw the tiny body shudder as the water covered it. Inside she felt her heart revolt. *He came from a people who always used their hands. Sometimes against themselves.* Ava turned away, her face full of tears.

"What did you do?" Grandmama cried. Her eyes were fetid floodwaters, her voice cold enough to stop a heart.

Silence

The house they loved was a waterlogged corpse, but the city was not all they left behind. Something had changed. The water between them had darkened and risen like the river and the flood. They spoke in clipped sentences. Grandmama slept as much as she could, while Ava dreamed awake. She replayed each second of memory, trying to recall if she had imagined the infant wriggling, picturing if and how the child might have lived.

Thirst

The night rain came and invaded her sleep as stealthily as the night of the hurricane, Ava woke with a hangover and one question on her mind. She flung the coverlet back, placed one bare foot on the hardwood floor. Stood in the open door, wearing her good slip, wrinkled and wine-stained. She took a deep breath, inhaled the rain and the sunshower air.

Grandmama had answered her call on the first ring.

Now, after making their way to the river's bank, Ava slipped out of her shoes, stepped into the muddy water. The river whispered around her ankles and her feet.

"Listen," Grandmama said, the weeds and trees swayed behind her. "The river is trying to tell you something: move, change. If your mama hadn't gotten lost, if she had stuck to another plan, she never would have met your father." Grandmama bent and picked up the shoes, wiped loose soil from the soles. "Here, at the riverside, is where they began. When she left the last time, she knew your daddy would return to the same place where he first met her. She knew he would never stop searching, never stop remembering. Sometimes it's dangerous to love that much."

Ava had peeled off her dress and stood in the open air, the wind brushing her nipples, still plump with mother's milk. Her daddy had said she had her mother's face, strong bones, wide nose, wider forehead.

Moon-marked, Grandmama had said, so she kept her in the sun. The closer Ava got to the river, the less air her lungs needed to breathe. She felt dizzy, her skin tingled and writhed with thirst. "Being lost helped us find you, Ava. You always thought the river took something from you, took your mama away, broke your daddy's heart, but maybe the river gave you something more."

Skin that was once dark and burnished now took on a copper-like sheen. Scales that were barely detectable appeared more pronounced. Ava began to walk into the waters, not far from the strip of sand where her mother had once told her lies and read her poems.

"I'm not mad, Grandmama, not anymore," Ava said. She unraveled the thick French braids she wore. Her hair puffed around her shoulders in a dark, wavy cloud. "I just need to try to find him. I know what I saw, know what I felt. I think he's alive."

Grandmama waved away a witch doctor who hovered near her ear. "If you're going, you need to listen to the river when you can't hear me. She ain't going to tell you nothing wrong. Listen to her now. She is telling you that there ain't no shame in changing. Baby, you are what you are. You come from this here water, but you also are part of this land. All them years I tried to keep you safe from this," Grandmama pointed at the Mississippi, "but when I wasn't looking, the river come to take you back anyway. So find what you love most from both of those things that make you, and then you go on out in this world and make yourself."

Ava walked deeper into the shallow water, felt the river whispering, pulling all around her. Grandmama clutched the blue sandals, crushed the sundress to her chest. "You don't want to listen to me, then go ahead, listen to the river. It's been calling you since you were born. The water is wise. When you feel there ain't no other way, do like this river do and bend."

Grandma stood away from the water, heels planted in the sandbar, as if she was afraid the river would rise and take her, too. Unwilling to leave on bad terms, but unable to stay now that they were good, Ava rushed out of the water to give her Grandmama one final hug.

And then, as if the sky had waited for this moment, the rain stopped. The only echo was Grandmama's whispered "Be good, girl. I hope to be here when you come back," and the hush of the river wind. Ava took a deep breath, inhaled the last of the sunshower air. Humidity wrapped around her ankles, pulled her closer to the bank.

Sunlight shimmered
on the brown river's surface
the gold mermaid smiled

Haunt-Type Experience

Roz Clarke

The hooded shadow emerged from the larger, jagged shadow of the building and shuddered across the rough ground where the forecourt had once been laid. Megan glanced behind her, looking for its source, then shivered as she realized it was her own, made eerily penumbral by the spots they used for setting up the kit in winter, shining out above the broken walls. After this site they would shut the project down for the winter, analyze their data, see if there was anything worth reporting. "Maybe tonight's the night," she whispered to her shadow, and the sound of her voice in the lonely woods made her hair stand on end. "Come on out, you ghosts, I'm just another specter, just like you." Nobody answered; the ruins brooded behind her and the woods talked only to themselves.

She kicked her way through the wet leaves; last season's fashions cast to the ground to molder. Broken bricks and creeping brambles made the going tricky, but she didn't want to use her torch. In the eighteen months they'd been investigating supposedly haunted sites, she'd never seen, heard, or felt anything that wasn't easily put down to a draft or the shifting of ancient walls and staircases, but she wanted to hold onto that feeling: a ghost amongst ghosts, floating insubstantially through romantic, moonlit ruins.

Returning from the car with the thermos, she tripped on a fallen branch and sprawled in the open entrance to the old hotel. She cursed, brushing bits of twig off her old overcoat, and pushed her way into the thick, musty darkness of the hallway. So much for floating.

◊

She called out "Ho there" as she approached the ballroom door. Dan answered cheerily. She stepped into the light, picked her way across the remains of a parquet floor, and sat in a wobbly director's chair under the small marquee they'd erected. She watched him working while she poured the coffee, and as she passed him a cup she read over his shoulder.

◊

"Not all buildings have a reputation for being haunted. For those that do, such anomalous experiences and events do not take place all of the time. Furthermore, when such instances do occur, not all persons present report them. These observations imply that there may be some critical dimensions or factors that distinguish such properties from other locations and differentiate certain observers from other individuals."

Megan was one of the "certain observers," recruited into Dan's research project because she'd once awakened in the night to see her grandmother crawling on all fours along the hall ceiling. Her grandmother had been dead six months at the time. Megan had been eight years old, and nervously disposed. When she'd told the story at one of those round-the-campfire nights at Glastonbury, Dan had leaped on it like a hunting spider, asked all sorts of questions. They'd been last to bed, and he hadn't even tried to kiss her.

"I'll just go round again," said Dan, standing up and stretching. They'd set up the MADS sensors already, and Megan had checked the alignments with the compass, but Dan liked to double-check everything she did. She'd long ago given up getting offended about it; he was that way with everyone. The lights picked out the active sensor in sharp delineation against the peeling wallpaper that clung to the broken walls, and Dan in his red anorak, hood pulled up around his face. She'd never yet tired of looking at that face, thin-lipped and finely boned, denim blue eyes always intently focused on something. Sometimes that something was Megan, but not often enough, and never in the way she wanted. She said nothing, afraid to push in case it killed their friendship. Her friends said she was crazy, and they didn't even know the truth of it. The lies she'd told about the boys there'd been; there was never more than this, a yearning for something out of reach. A tingle of sadness at the back of her mind suggested that she'd probably tire of looking at him soon. Soon, but not yet, she decided, sipping on her coffee.

"Certainly one effective method for a contemporary field-based investigation of a haunting would be to evaluate (1) environmental factors specific to the location, (2) individual factors specific to the observer, and (3) factors specific to an interaction between the location and the observer. In the case of specific locations associated with numerous instances of anomalous haunt-type experiences, an evaluation of how the surrounding micro-environment could be responsible for inducing such an experience would seem crucial."

The baseline sensor was located outside the building, collecting data they could use to compare the electromagnetic fields inside and outside. Tomorrow she and Dan would go through the data, looking for anomalies. If they found anything they'd go to step 2: interview the people who'd responded to Dan's survey stating that they'd had supernatural experiences at this site. The ballroom was supposed to be the hotspot. She glanced around. It was large, the full width of the building, with three bay windows looking out into an enclosed courtyard, and three looking toward the road that led through the woods up to the main entrance. The windows were reduced to U-shaped openings in the brickwork, but in places the walls were still ten feet high. A decayed sofa lay on its side in the middle of the room, mahogany legs helplessly in the air like a great dead insect. The shadow it cast behind it in the hard light from the spots was even more insectile. Megan closed her eyes and tried to imagine the room as it must have been once. Bright and airy. Rather grand. She couldn't make it happy, somehow, but certainly bright.

"Why did they close this place down?"

Dan turned to face her, smiled and waved a finger.

"How long have we been doing this? You know you don't get the juice on the hospice until tomorrow."

"Yeah, whatever."

It was always the same story anyway. She didn't know why he was so coy about it; she could have googled the place if she'd really wanted to know, and it would be some variation on the usual themes: unseen children crying in empty rooms, headless monks walking through walls, or women in white, killed whilst attempting to rendezvous with a forbidden lover. Still trying to make that meeting, failing for all eternity. Then there were the friendly ones, killed in disasters and for some reason bound to the spot trying to avert future accidents. She liked those stories better. Well, perhaps the sensor readings would show something in the morning and they'd be able to put the hotel's ghosts to rest. Just naturally occurring electromagnetic fields, making mojo with your brain.

"I sometimes wish I didn't know the science," she said, pulling her tobacco pouch from her pocket and rolling up.

"You've got to be kidding," said Dan, finally leaving off tweaking the sensors and sitting back down, long legs stretched in front of him. "You want to be scared shitless by random phenomena every time you walk past an iron deposit or an overhead cable? Don't you have enough trouble sleeping as it is?"

She looked at him. Half his face was in shadow, half in the light; bright light and deep shadow like the face of the moon. Laughter lines were just beginning to crease the corners of his eyes. Her stomach turned over with desire. So long she'd yearned for him, sitting this close, closer, if she reached out she could touch his face, but then again she couldn't. Yes, she longed for more tangible strangeness in her life. For something to actually *happen*, instead of all this pointless longing. As a child she'd populated her world with imaginary friends and fantastic beasts. Dryads in every tree, naiads in every pond. Too much reading, too much time spent mooning around on her own. Two years into a degree in psychology, she'd had most of the credulity educated out of her, but she liked the idea of a world with magic in it. Dan was a postgrad, and he didn't believe in *anything* inexplicable.

She tapped the end of her roll-up against her knee.

"You make it sound so prosaic. But you know, maybe there is something there, too. We don't know yet." She lit her cigarette and inhaled, blowing a smoke ring out into the glare of the light. "All the factors have not been eliminated."

"They will be," said Dan.

"Many studies have carried out detailed surveys of such locations and revealed potential contributing influences from (1) contextual and situational specific factors, (2) diverse lighting levels, (3) drafts, (4) infrasound levels, (5) the localized distribution and changes in geomagnetic fields (GMFs), (6) time-varying electromagnetic fields (EMFs), and (7) transient tectonic events, to name but a few. All of these factors, either collectively or individually, could either induce a direct experience or facilitate an experience-prone state in certain observers and under certain circumstances."

Megan clawed toward consciousness with desperation and regret. Sharks had chased her through murky waters following the scent of blood; this she knew although she wasn't injured. When she'd reached the surface and walked out onto the dusty beach, she'd turned to see the Earth hanging in the sky, big and round and beautiful and impossibly far away. There was a terrible pain in her lower back and she turned to find a tiny shark, its jaws locked around her spine. She turned and tried to grasp its slippery body. The sense of dread she felt seemed disproportionate to the circumstances, and when she came to herself, pain wracking her sacrum where she'd slumped awkwardly in her chair, the dread didn't pass. It was always the bloody sharks, even though she could watch *Jaws* all the way through now with barely a twitch of fear. You never shook off the six-year-old inside.

"Dan," she said, feeling as if she was still underwater. She couldn't hear her own voice. "Dan," she tried again. "What did you mean, hospice? I thought this was a hotel?" Although her pulse was racing as if she'd just run a mile uphill, when she turned her head to look at him, it was the motion of rock grinding against rock. He was sitting at the laptop, his back to her. He hadn't heard. She tried to lift her hand, but it stayed resolutely still, resting on her knee. The other was the same. The left foot, the right foot; nothing was shifting. She felt her breath start to quicken and her chest constrict. *It's OK,* she told herself. *Sleep paralysis. Night terrors. Happens to people all the time.*

She knew all about sleep events. They explained a lot of haunt-type experiences. Knowing about something didn't make you immune to it, though. She closed her eyes and sent a message to whoever might be listening. *When I said I wanted something to happen I didn't mean a crappy old night terror. This isn't any fun at all.* Her breathing was still accelerating. She fought to regain control. *Nothing to fear. You'll fall asleep again soon. Won't even remember it in the morning.* She imagined herself at eight years old, with her mother's arms around her, the old yellow blanket that always made her feel safe. She could almost smell it, but her heart still beat in her throat. The dread pooling in her stomach writhed and split into two and her awareness doubled: déjà vu. Had she been suffering from night terrors all along and just not remembered it? Was this a cycle?

She reached out to Dan with her frantic mind, begging him to turn around, please, please turn around and see that her eyes were open, and come over and wake her, take her in his arms and stroke her hair and make everything all right. He didn't turn. Figures rolled across the laptop screen. In the blue light it cast, his hands quested across the keyboard, pale and unearthly like the albino lobster she'd once seen in a restaurant aquarium.

A clattering, scrambling sound echoed in the corridor outside the room.

In the corner of her eye she could see a blue-green glow quite like to the one coming from the screen, creeping misty through the empty doorframe and onto the parquet. An eternity of arrhythmic heartbeats and the battle for control of her rigid neck muscles brought Megan's head around. The sounds stopped as the creature came to a halt in front of her. Silhouettes stretching in two directions were rendered faint by the creature's own ethereal glimmer. It dropped its silver horn to the ground, flashed one eye at her, and spoke.

This shouldn't be. Paralysis yes, a sense of dread, sure, auditory hallucinations, maybe. Something sinister in the room. The hag on your chest, the succubus stealing your breath. Not this. Not the complexity of dreams, not talking fantasies, not...for fuck's sake. Unicorns. *Breathe.*

"Megan?"

Not a voice so much as an increase in the pressure in her chest, a prickling at the back of her neck. Still the snakes twisting in her gut. Still the déjà vu, never gone on this long, and she knew, knew for sure, that this could not have happened before.

"Aren't you pleased to see me?"

Her eyes were watering. She choked, fought to swallow. The beast took a step toward her, and she could see that tears rolled from its eyes, too. She tried to cringe away from it. It stepped forward again, and she could smell its breath. Like summer afternoons. Its hoofs were silver, its coat was white and its mane and tail were lavender. A memory caught her, pulled her back twelve years, to an attic room, a yellow blanket on a high bed beneath an open window. Her collection of toy unicorns arrayed in front of her. Larha, her favorite. Porcelain, fragile, smooth beneath her hands, a gift from her grandmother, not one to be played with.

"Here I am, Megan. Won't you stroke my neck?" It turned its head, presenting shimmering inches of silver fur. Something glistened gray, attached to its head just below the ear. Whatever it was, she couldn't look at it.

"Wrong," she whispered. *This is wrong.*

It turned to look at her again, and its tears were thickening, darkening, leaving dirty streaks on its face. "She kept me safe for sixty years. You had me for six. Unicorns can't fly, Megan, didn't you know?"

She'd known. Fly, she'd told the little china thing, fly to Granny. Shattered pieces on the patio. Her mother crying. Her mother, crying. *Granny was my mum, Megan. I miss her just like you'd miss me if I had to go away and not come back.*

The unicorn's tears were taking off the fur where they passed.

"I'm sorry." She wanted to cry, but terror was stronger. She wanted to reach out and comfort Larha, but still she couldn't move. She wanted to leap from her chair and run, drive through the night to her parents' house in Clapham, hurl herself onto her mother's bed. I'm sorry, I'm so sorry. And—don't leave me.

The tears were cutting furrows in his skin. Scarlet mixed with the black droplets and dripped onto the floor.

"Dies," he said, kneeling on the ground and laying his chin on the ground. "Everything dies. Why did you let go of me?"

Larha collapsed onto his side. A collection of broken bits laid on a blue silk scarf. Her mother, her hands still supple, folding the cloth over. Wordlessly putting the bundle away in a drawer in the sideboard. She turned toward Megan and stepped through the cone of light shining on the active sensor. Her hair was long and loose, and she wore a brown cotton dress that left her tanned arms bare.

Megan still couldn't breathe properly. She felt her eyes trying to roll up into her skull, and yet could not draw them away from the impossible vision of her mother walking gracefully toward her.

"Megan?"

"Mum?"

"Hello, muffin," she said, smiling and bending down so her face was close to Megan's. She smelled of shampoo and Chanel 19. "I hear you're still having trouble sleeping. Do you want me to tell you a story?"

Suddenly Megan felt terribly tired. The fight went out of her limbs, and they no longer felt trapped and rigid, but heavy and useless.

"Once upon a time," said her mother, seating herself on the floor, "there was a beautiful princess."

"Is the story about me?" Megan whispered without meaning to.

Her mother hesitated, and frowned. "It was always about you, wasn't it? My youth, devoted to your happiness. You and your father." The frown became a scowl. Looking up at Megan, she drew back her lips and bared her teeth. They were tiny arrowheads set into her gums, a row of chipped flints she flicked her tongue across. "Everything you touched you broke. And you abandoned me here! Tied up and forgotten! A hundred years of isolation. A *hundred* aching years." She moaned. "Chaos. Terror. You don't understand Megan, you'll never understand."

It was true. She didn't understand, had always shied away from understanding. She woke in the night with fragments of understanding scurrying away from her conscious mind like cockroaches from the light.

Her mother lay back on the floor. Her moans became shrieks of pain and fear. Megan had the idea that if she tried to move, she'd be able to now, could go to her mother's side and help her. But she couldn't try. Her face was still wet with tears, but the flow had stopped and she longed to be able to cry again.

"I'm sorry," she whispered. "I didn't mean to break him. I didn't know what would happen."

Hands bunched and released the fabric of the cotton dress that now clung to her mother's skin, sweat-soaked. Something squirmed beneath the fabric. Her legs began to thrash, then spread wide and, from beneath that chocolate-colored canopy across her knees, the something emerged. Through bloody mucus she could see gray flesh, slick and alien.

Like the leech-thing on Larha's white neck, only bigger. It fought free of the placenta and uncurled; a head, a body. Fins. Tail. Teeth. Her mother still sobbed. As the shark-baby moved up her body, another came, and another. Four sharks swam over her, and where they passed her skin sagged. Muscle melted away leaving bone and sinew. They traveled along her limbs and positioned themselves at her joints, opened tooth-filled jaws and bit down. At the ankles, wrists, knees, elbows, her mother was divided. There was no blood.

When they bit into her throat, the screaming stopped.

The sharks swam away into shadow, but their presence filled the room. The body on the floor was a pile of broken bits. *I didn't mean to let you go.*

The lassitude still wrapped her mind and body in poison, but she found she no longer minded not being able to breathe. The pain, the paralysis, even the fear; she understood that they were deserved. She was exhausted, though.

She blinked slowly and looked around the room. Susurrations away by the walls let her know the sharks were still out there. The up-turned sofa still loomed evilly to one side of her, and Dan's hands still worked the keyboard at the other.

"Dan?"

Her voice was shaky, but came out more or less like a real voice. He turned from the screen. "Megan? What's up?"

She checked herself. The faintest whisper of the sharks slithering over the asylum's detritus at the very edge of hearing. No bodies on the ground. Residue, that's all it was. The residue of a dream.

"Nothing. I fell asleep for a while there. Dreamed about sodding sharks again." She tried a laugh. "I'm OK, a bit stiff is all. Anything on the sensors yet?"

"There's regular pulse event the same as the one we had at the castle last month. Nothing else obvious. Are you sure you're OK? You look a bit wiped out. Maybe you should go back to sleep."

Megan's pulse fluttered.

"No, I'm fine, honest. I'm wide awake now."

Tentatively, she wiggled her fingers. The results were promising. She couldn't quite bring herself to stand up, but Dan surprised her by getting up and coming over to her. He crouched down, in the same spot where—but there were no remains there now, no sign that anything had happened.

He reached out one long finger and stroked her damp hair back from her face. The touch sent her blood pressure soaring once again. He rested his hands on her legs and sighed.

"What's this about?" she asked.

He shrugged. "Does it have to be about anything?" one of his hands stroked absently up and down the outside of her thigh. She could barely feel it through the heavy wool of her overcoat, and yet every pass sent tremors through her that threatened to become cramps.

"You look so tired, that's all. I feel bad for dragging you out here and keeping you up all night. I know you have a lot to deal with at the moment."

"Nothing I haven't been dealing with for years already, Dan."

He took one of her hands in his, turned it over and kissed her palm.

"I've been alone," he said softly. There was a note in his voice she'd never heard before. "That is, I've been lonely. I mean—I mean it would be lonely here without you."

His eyes were lost in the shadow of his hood, leaving his mouth as the only focus of her attention. Something about his teeth made her shiver, and for a second she caught herself listening for shark bellies slithering in the dirt. She pushed back his hood to expose his face fully. His eyes crinkled as he smiled. God, he was beautiful.

"You want this, don't you?" his intonation was somewhere between a question and a statement of fact. All Megan could do was nod. He pushed himself forward, weight pressing through his arms and down onto her thighs, and pressed his lips to hers. His tongue pushed into her mouth and this time she heard it for certain, the whisper of unseen things moving in the building, rubbery flesh over rotting leaves, communicating with one another through strange scents and the poetry of half-light. Peeling wallpaper shivered like leaves in a breeze she couldn't feel. Her arms froze at her sides again and her neck stiffened. She tried to push his tongue away and close her mouth, but her pushes were without force, without effect. He probed deeper, his weight pressing against her chest now. When he finally pulled back and looked at her, the laughter in his eyes had gone; they were onyx marbles set in skin the texture of linoleum. Merciless.

He pulled her hips forward and knelt between her knees. She was entirely paralyzed again, but for her heart, which beat furiously, filling her ears with the rushing of her own blood, mixing her blood with the whispering song of her fear. And mixed with the fear was lust. She *did* want this. Her lips, as soon as his left them, felt the grief of loss, the agony of unfulfilled desire.

"Do you fear it?" asked Dan, whom she was no longer sure was Dan at all.

She nodded.

"You won't break," he said, through teeth as sharp as knives, "even if you bleed. You're not a china doll. You're meat, just like the rest of us. You want me at arm's length so you can imagine I'm perfect, don't you? So we won't break one another? But I'm meat, and you can cut meat and you can make it die but we all die in the end. You have to touch something in your life, and you have to risk watching it die. Everything dies. Look."

He stood up and pulled off his anorak, and his sweater with the University logo on it, and his blue T-shirt. Then he bunched the skin at his waist between his fingers, and pulled. A seam opened from his throat to his navel and he peeled the skin back to reveal the musculature beneath, and the soft glistening organs.

"People are just walking steak and liver, same as cattle. I—we suffer. Does that stop us needing one another?"

Black eyes bored into her.

He undid his belt buckle.

"Say you need it."

She thought of her mother, wasted to a skeleton, limbs shot with phantom pain and real spasms, confined to a hospice bed for years, and the light leeching away from her smile and the words leaking away from her mind, and she found herself surrounded. Fluorescent light flooded the room, shining down from strips fitted to a high, ornamented ceiling. The sofa by the wall was upright and cushioned. Two more sofas and several huddles of armchairs were arranged to give views out of the six bay windows. Everywhere, there were people. Sick, dying, broken people.

None of them were looking at her and Dan, but she felt their emotions pressing up to her like a tide, like the jellyfish carried by that tide, slapping into her mind and trailing their stinging sorrow across it. Abandoned people. Trapped people. Alone with only the phantoms their own minds had created.

"Say you need it."

Images and sensations overwhelmed her; needles reaching for her naked skin, cuffs around her wrists, bitter medicines, unrecognized faces, voices in her ears telling her she was a bad, bad person; *Gerry is a bad person*; she mouthed it helplessly, knowing that it didn't belong to her, and that it did.

"Say it, Megan."

She couldn't speak. Her tongue was swollen and the poison coursed in her veins, veins she was acutely aware of, carrying envenomed blood around her body. Meat, yes meat, but mind too, and the mind was all too brittle. The Dan-thing was lying to her. But she needed it even more, knowing that.

When he—it—unzipped its fly she wasn't surprised to see something there that wasn't pink, but gray.

Its teeth ripped through her clothes and into her body. She saw fins sliding inside her, the powerful tail slapping against her legs as it drove further in. Dan was holding her by the shoulders and looking at her.

"*I* won't let *you* go, Megan. Wherever you go, I'll be with you." Jaws lined with tiny arrowheads closed around soft flesh deep inside her, and she felt blood soaking her thighs.

Her fingertips flexed with remembered feeling. Without moving, they traced the hard curves of a porcelain figurine. The waves of a mane, the cool planes of belly and flanks, the slender legs.

"Won't let you go."

Three days after the unicorn had failed to fly, Megan's mother had collapsed. The diagnosis had taken another month to come in, and by that time Megan was quite sure it was her fault. She kissed Larha's perfect curves with her mind.

She let go.

"With respect to magnetic fields, researchers are proposing that perhaps some aspect of these fields have "experience-inducing properties"—even more so if observers have shown a degree of increased neuronal hypersensitivity and susceptibility to these fields. The general hypothesis from this is that such Experience Inducing Fields (EIFs) could be present at reputedly haunted locations and may well underlie a number of reports ranging from nebulous and ambiguous sensations to extreme and complex hallucinations."

"Ow," she said, stretching and rubbing at the sore spot on her back. A dull cramp radiated through her sacrum and into her abdomen.

Dan turned from the laptop and gave her a half smile. "Morning, gorgeous. You've been out for hours."

"Have I? My back hurts."

"I'm not surprised. These chairs weren't meant for kipping in."

"I had this dream. I was swimming in the sea and there were these sharks after me. It was pretty scary."

"Did they catch you?"

"No—I don't know. Loads of other stuff happened I think, but all I remember at the end is I was standing on the beach looking up at the moon, only it wasn't the moon. It was the Earth. Are there any sandwiches left?"

"Half a ham one; I saved it for you."

"Gosh, thanks, I'm honored."

She stood up gingerly. Her legs were half-dead from being in the chair. Dan picked up the sandwich from the trestle table and handed it to her. Their fingers brushed together as she took it from him, and the wobble in her legs grew momentarily worse. He turned back to the screen and pointed at the lines of scrolling data. She controlled the wobble, but still felt slightly strange.

"There's definitely something here," Dan said. "The readings from the active sensor are far more complex than the ones from the baseline sensor. There are three spikes of activity, here, here, and here."

Growing evidence suggests that crucial EIFs are characterized primarily by their complexity rather than overall field strength/amplitude. Only small windows of frequencies seem to have potent consequences for neural activity and anomalous consciousness, and these can generally be described as being within the spectrum of the human brain. The low-amplitude, low-frequency, complex nature of these fields seems important in order for them to be integrated into, and alter, the overall current perceptual gestalt.

The feeling of strangeness passed, and work took over.

When they'd packed the equipment into Dan's rusty Escort and set off down the road through the woods, dawn was still hours away. In a service station café somewhere off the M6, Dan gave her the background on the hospice.

"It was closed down 16 years ago, as you know. The main reason it was closed was because the people who came here mostly seemed to get worse instead of better. Oh, I should tell you—it wasn't a hotel, until late on; it was a country house, and then a sanatorium, and then a hospice. Quite a history." He waved his fork and a bit of egg slid off and onto the tabletop. "So of course it took them a long time to work it out because that's always been pretty normal for mental hospitals. You know, deterioration. Specifically, people with hallucinatory symptoms reported more severe symptoms than they'd come in with, and people with no hallucinations—depressives, what-have-you—started to experience them. What makes it interesting is that the staff sometimes saw things too. The place got a reputation as being haunted by the ghosts of earlier inmates."

Megan huddled down into her overcoat and made "I'm listening" noises. Dan took a sip of coffee and rattled on.

"So then they closed the sanatorium and opened it as a care hospice, but things didn't quiet down much. Finally it was turned into a hotel and health spa. The survey data's skewed though, I expect, 'cause most of the responses we got were from folk who stayed in the spa. Didn't last long. People went away disturbed. The reports cover all sorts of things; night terrors, children crying, figures walking through walls, unaccountable sense of dread, all the usual stuff. Nearly half the people who filled the survey out said they still have haunt-type experiences quite frequently since having one here, even when they're not in a common haunt location." He looked delighted.

"Mm-hm?"

"Yeah, and that's way above average. I was thinking about what you said about all the factors not being accounted for."

"Really? I said something worth thinking about?"

Dan raised his eyebrows at her playfully. A cold shiver ran up Megan's spine. Damn, he really was something. So much for getting tired of looking at him. She sighed.

"Well, it does happen from time to time. Anyway, it struck me that you could almost make a case for there being something there. It follows on from a paper I was reading last night; remind me to email you the reference. But listen, if the gestalt of your consciousness exists in an EMF, maybe other kinds of EMF are inhabited by other kinds of consciousness. It's a stretch, but it's an interesting idea. Or there could be some interaction between the place and the person, such that traces of one are exchanged with traces of the other."

"You don't really believe that."

"Of course not. Hey, I was up all night, while you were snoring prettily in your chair. I had to entertain myself somehow."

"Sorry," said Megan.

"Don't be," said Dan. "You needed your sleep. How is your mum, anyway?"

◊

She looked away from him, and instead carefully inspected the plate in front of her that had lately held an omelette and chips. As she did every waking moment, without even thinking, Megan forced her feelings down and away into the corners and corridors of her mind. She'd had years of practice at it.

"About the same. You know how it is; it mostly doesn't change from day to day."

Her stomach cramped again and for a second she thought she heard whispering at the very edge of her hearing. Some vague feeling gnawed at her, something she didn't want to think about. She looked at Dan's fingers curled around the white china mug. An image of it shattering in his hand flashed across her retinas. On an impulse she didn't recognize as her own, she reached across the table and touched his wrist.

"Actually, it's been pretty rough lately. They—I think she's kind of given up on it all. Life, that is. You know, I could use some decompression time. We could—would you like to go out for a drink tonight?" She smiled, felt it come out lopsided. Tremors shook her. Dan set down the mug and twined his fingers into hers, and his eyes crinkled as he smiled back.

I won't let you go. Something screamed and tore inside Megan, and a multitude of voices with a single face—her own face—darkly rejoiced. Every nerve was alive. *The captivity and the freedom of the meat.* The trapdoor of death was still a *door.* She ran her tongue across her teeth, enjoying their sharpness.

"I'm sorry to hear that," said Dan, pathetically.

"It's OK," said Megan. "Everything dies."

Eleven Stations

Fábio Fernandes

1.

I started to levitate on the eve of my suicide. It wasn't on purpose. I was fairly relaxed, mind unfocused, as people who have made up their minds to do irreversible things probably feel. I was standing in the middle of my small, cluttered scriptorium, looking at the shelves heavily laden with hardcovers and paperbacks, in search of some book, any book. I remember thinking of Egyptian pharaohs and the things they carried to their tombs. I also recall thinking I would like to be buried with books. Or burned. Maybe cremation would be better.

Then, suddenly, my feet weren't touching the floor anymore. I wasn't out of balance. I wasn't wobbling. I was sure that was no episode of labyrinthitis, and, more important, I had drunk no spirits nor taken any drugs. I had planned to go to into the night really gently, gently and completely lucid. Was I hallucinating? I wondered then. Or would it be a sign? If so, a sign of what? Of a miracle? Sainthood? A mutation? Superpowers, perhaps? Would I then be a supermutant Jesus? I also remember wondering if this strange occurrence would in any way affect my decision to take my own life.

2.

Every war only ends with a treaty. Treaties were created not only to enforce peace, but to serve as flags, markers, landmarks to tell everyone: *behold, this war is heretofore ended.* So that, when two former enemies meet, they don't kill each other. (Sometimes the treaty means squat, but that's another story.) Anyway, they are not supposed to kill each other anymore. And, if one of them does it, there will be punishment. Sometimes they kill each other, and that brings the story to an end—but not this story, alas. What does one do when the war is *inside*?

My condition is not as simple as schizophrenia (simple in the sense that you can medicate the patient, that is, that there is a palliative treatment). My condition is legion. Treat yourself like the enemy. Exorcize yourself. Barbiturates, slit the wrists open, all these are dumb, brutal methods—and utterly ineffective. For all you can do is reach a kind of truce. This way lies negotiation. And negotiation is not an art. Negotiation is death. So I must find another way. Another door to me.

3.

I stayed awake for most of the levitation night looking at old pictures. My mom holding me as a baby. Standing to her right, in a black suit, my grandfather. A gaunt, stern man in his sixties then, he wasn't a bad fellow. But he wouldn't be caught smiling. His upbringing. But he was a good and fair man, or that is the way I wish to remember him. A member of the Church of the Latter-day Saints. I'm not a member of any church. But these are my last days. Will I be a saint, after? A ghost? Pigments and pixels in pictures?

4.

Finally, I slept. And she was holding my hand right next to me in the airplane during the turbulence, and that was when she said for the first time the words *I love you*. And even though the plane shook a lot and I was frightened, I could not help but smile, because I was beside myself with joy. I was witnessing an occurrence rarer than a plane crash. And she said it again, this time with a smile in her sad eyes (her melancholy eyes were her trademark; to this day I wonder if this was why I fell in love with her; I teased her once, telling her the real reason was that I had seen her gorgeous legs when she walked into the classroom that balmy evening in October, but to be honest, I think I will never know): "In case anything goes wrong now, I just wanted you to know that I love you. I love you. I love you." She said it three times. I couldn't have been happier. We kissed then—a shaky, trembling meeting of lips, no more, but that was more than enough—and we held hands for thirty minutes more until the turbulence subsided. And we had not died. And she was still there. And I was still in love with her. And she was.

5.

And she was telling me, the door is cryogenics. She saw in my face, even via messaging, my resolve to end things. We were too distant from each other to protagonize a love scene. I wasn't in the mood for love anyway. I would regret it later. I was out for war. If it had to be a cold war, so be it.

6.

Break my body, hold my bones. Grind me into powder. Scatter what is left of this dust to the wind, so that soon there will be no visible particle left. It will be better this way. To have and have not. To be or not to be. Veni, vidi, vici. I went, I was, I had. It was not enough, but it was all I was allowed to get. Now I am a dead man walking. I am the incredible shrinking man. I am the man who folded himself. For I have touched the sky. I loved and was loved back. Once, this was a noble truth. Not anymore. No regrets. Nothing else matters. Please kill me.

7.

No sleep tonight anymore. I can sleep when I'm dead. Who said that? Churchill? Fassbinder? It doesn't matter. All that matters now is the past. Another photo: in the center of the image, a father holds his infant son. The father is smiling; he looks nervous. This is his first child. It will not be his last, but he doesn't know it yet. (He will have a daughter three years later, but his wife will get pregnant before that and will suffer a miscarriage. Some things are better left unknown for now, however.)

The father is standing between two well-tended bushes in a rose garden at his aunt's house. The father is a very tall, thin man, and he's wearing a well-cut suit. He looks rather uncomfortable in it, but handsome all the same. The son is just a baby. Forty years after that snapshot, the son, a poet dying of cancer, will write a story about that photo. About those two people frozen in time, in the cold sleep of memory.

8.

I hardly felt the second occurrence of levitation. Most miracles go unobserved while we're busy living our lives. I am visiting the avenues of my death, all the houses, the open doors.

Cryogenics is not rocket science, you told me. You were right. Rockets go somewhere. A frozen body is a thing of beauty, a joy forever: *it will never pass into nothingness.* And quoting Keats without knowing it, you killed all the poetry. That, I remember, was when I stopped answering your messages. Either way, I would never see you again, and I couldn't bear it.

My feet bound to the ground again, I start having second thoughts about taking my life. Maybe I'm bound by some invisible force. Maybe this force is more tangible than everyone around us can possibly suspect. The force of an oath, even if it's an oath I make only to myself, after a life of suffering, when I reach a safe harbor, a haven, and I can finally disembark, put my feet ashore and thank heavens (or Fate, if I suffered so much that I can't possibly believe in any gods anymore) because I have finally reached safety, at last I have the supreme joy of finding a place to stay, a room of my own, having some food in my belly, maybe even a stray cat to pet when I'm feeling lonely, and the beach to gaze upon when I want to feel lonely. But then I'm never really in solitude, because of my oath.

What do I know? What I still know is nobody belongs to anybody, and in the end, this is all well and good, this is as it should have been all the time. But having this knowledge does not ease my pain, for deep inside I would have you as mine and I would have my heart as yours, but our timelines crossed each other in some twisted angle, or maybe in parallel, and that was not to be. We did meet, though, and it was good. But ours was only a node in the wider net of life, and who knows when we shall meet again? Not us.

9.

My body is not my temple. Every health freak worships this figure of speech more than their own blood-sugar levels. They are wrong. A body is not fit to worship; too messy for that. Nor is my body a city. Every age seems to have the metaphor it deserves.

In the times of Diderot, D'Alembert, and La Mettrie, L'Homme Machine, the Machine Man. God was the Architect of the Universe. Everything was cogs and coils, nuts and bolts. For a thing to work, it should be mechanical, they reasoned. In this they weren't so far from the truth. All things break down. Even bodies. Especially bodies.

In the beginning of the twentieth century, the Gernsback Continuum, the WASP dream of reaching the future by purification of the species. Citius, Altius, Fortius. Faster, Higher, Stronger. Able bodies. We know what Hitler did to the unable ones.

Today, what do we have to show as a metaphor? The Gibson Continuum, maybe? Post-post-cyber hybrid hacktivists flaunting their cyborginess as the beginning of a brave new world? Aside from the notion of the brain as a computer, the idea of body as machine remains the same. They are not enough, all these metaphors. They were never able to convey all the complexity of flesh and blood. Better to widen the scope and say just this: the human body is a battlefield. Of viruses and bacteria; of hatreds and passions; of external pressures, tangible and intangible. The human body is the fucking Battle of the Somme repeated *ad infinitum, ad nauseam* every single day of our lives. I know mine is. There is only one way to stop this battle.

◊

10.

The capsule.

11.

Before sleep, a last thought: one day I will be out of cryosleep and the world around me will be unrecognizable. I will barely be able to utter any sentence—any word—in a way that makes sense to the generation who will wake me. Maybe they will have translating implants. Maybe they will be post-humans, genetically modified to understand virtually every old language the peoples of Earth ever spoke in its history. Maybe humankind simply won't exist anymore and I will be awakened from cold sleep by machines, robots or artificial intelligences, incorporeal entities for whom the act of levitation is more an archaeological footnote than a true experience of something called *flesh* so far removed from their reality. I don't know. Yet. All I know is one day I will be out of cryosleep and the world around me will be unrecognizable.

But maybe, if I'm lucky, some symbols will be available that can be understandable by both sides. Music, for example. Not lyrics, but notes. And voices. Maybe Elizabeth Fraser singing. Anything. I would like that. It would be a good awakening in the distant future.

«*Légendaire.*»

Kai Ashante Wilson

Having seen the reggaezzi perform, the righteous of Sea-john shake their heads in wonder. They will then murmur severally or as one, <<*Légendaire.*>>

[*Tonight*]

The cavalcade forms up. In beats, without words, the drummers argue a bass line. While higher registers wait in silence, contraltos and bassos scat and moan, improvising the tune (the lyrics never change). The soulful melodies these deeper voices come up with are much too cool, and none capture the hot quiddity of their subject. "Make dat shit *bump*, y'all," a counter-tenor exhorts. "Put some stank on it!" So the music picks up funk and swing. A girl bounces and stretches with the other dancers. They have black skin, or brown, or golden; hers is gray, waxen, and flyblown. What ails this girl, her bones slipping so weirdly in raddled tissues? It's death: she died three days ago. But so long as weary flesh lasts she has the right to choose it over imperishable spirit. Thus can her body rise again, and she dance tonight with living brethren. The boy she loved, dead these years, not days, reappears as another name among the beautiful lights, and plays *guitarra* with the same prodigy as before, when he lived. Dancers up front, players and singers trailing, they'll process down Mevilla, the witches' hill, and up and over the great breasts of the Mother, middle hill crowded with shanties of the poor, and onward to the furthest hill of Sea-john, Dolorosa, where rich families live in gardened houses and foreign powers keep grand embassies. A boy nicknamed *El Supremo* is about to join their host—he lies tossing in his bed, way over on that easternmost hill. No one will see this parade pass, few hear it. The performance is for that one boy alone, whom the reggaezzi will gather to their number at last, tonight.

◊

From the roof you can see the world. Downhill, north: the Kingdom is dark, except where yellow licks the darkness. Some torch or lamp burns here and there as far as the horizon. The southern view is the ocean, entirely dark save for two moons out at sea: one true, clear and still in heaven's vault; another false, dappled and shuddering on the vast black waters. The swelter lifts—a gust of seabreeze gives her goosebumps. But the filthy heat settles right back down. Some man is kissing her son under the archway of the house gate.

Is *this* how matters stand now, with tongue and teeth? In aid of asphyxiation, of cannibalism, more than love? All that biting! The moon's so bright, she feels implicated in the sloppy grapple below. Why does the boy let that man grab and handle him so? When she lies down with her husband or with her wife, the love's never harsh or ugly. Back when she and Jahs were as young and foolish as their son is today, even then, in the raw passion of first kisses, softness and respect were foremost. But now a caress and tenderness must be relics, not what youth want.

Night-bees flicker throughout the house garden. Below, the lime trees are all in flower, and green lights dim and kindle among the blossoms.

The boy utters little cries in his attacker's arms, though hardly in distress. Dance usually does so much better by professional bodies: thickening the thighs, making the back and arms formidable. It's just too bad *la dança* will whittle that rare body down, to all fine bones and no spare flesh. Her son—

"Ma'am?" Cook whispers from the stairwell to the roof. "Miss Savary? Duh baby just got in, safe. I wanted you to know. Dey out by the gate, him and his gentleman."

"Yes, Cook. Thank you." Savary sighs, and rolls the hulled berries from her skirts into the bowl. "Why don't you go on to your room now, dear, and rest? We can finish up in the morning."

"Yes, ma'am," Cook says. "Tank you, Miss." And the stairs groan back downwards.

The lover has remounted his horse. He wears the fine black robe of a nobleman from the Kingdom; but also the cornrowed hair of a soldier, and one who's seen action too, by those many bead-necklaces. He pats the hair of the boy clinging to his leg. (At last, a little tenderness!) They murmur intimacies Savary cannot make out from the roof, in accents of the language she forsook for this one spoken in the hills.

The lover rides away and the boy comes up the moonlit garden toward the house. Stumbling dreamily, still he cuts no figure but a dancer's. Savary gets up, holding the bowl. The sons of other mothers are fumbling at first love, safely, with local boys and girls. Hers is *virtuoso* of the best troupe in Sea-john, and snaps brusque fingers at musicians twice his age during performance. He's off giving shows, most nights, at some palace in the Kingdom. Savary makes her way downstairs into the candlelit interior.

Her wife and husband have long since gone to bed. They made their peace years ago in the household war; they came to terms. Not Savary! The young will post headlong down perilous roads, dreaming they're on the way to adventure, en route to love: *someone* must tell them, "No, wait, you've turned wrong. Nothing lies down that way but heartbreak and disaster." Jahs says But, my love, his new friends are those same *fils-de-roi* who buy a yacht from me. That boat, Savary—a whim of theirs!—keeps our family well for a year. If the boy runs away, he can go to the shelter of some palace. What can we offer a virtuoso? His family's love, just our love, and a room in the house where he was born. Better not to fuss and fight, better to keep the boy near us, surely?

Well, yes, Savary agrees. But...

A son too talented and too headstrong isn't a problem of temporal power, upon which her immortal husband could, perhaps, work an easy miracle. Rather it's a problem of the sort all souls suffer passing through the vale of tears, before which Redamas is as helpless as any mortal. Still, Savary pleads to him: But, *you*, Redy—can't you *do* something?

I'm just a god, Redamas says, not God.

Savary stows the berries in the cold cellar at the back of the pantry. By now, the boy is in the kitchen too, reaching down a cup from the shelves of fancy-glass. He looks over the table's vast clutter, and underneath, searching for the palm wine jar. Which is right beside Savary in the pantry; she picks it up.

There's almost nothing of his father in him, so much of her: brown and tender of skin too, and with his shirt gaping open beau-boy-style she sees a red-violet narrative of hands and teeth scrawled across his neck and torso. Not for the first time Savary thinks, *my* little boy's the one they're calling "El Supremo?" If only he were strapping like his sister, six-foot something. If only his papa's divinity had come down to him too—no worries then! Somewhere abroad, his sister's hunting a beast with the fell name *Assassin of Cities*. But Maman has no worries there. You've only once to see the god whom you birthed smack aside thunderbolts, and rout dragons, thereafter to save the worrying for your mortal child.

He looks his age: the baby softness long gone, no mannish thickening yet. Sixteen.

"Weren't you supposed to give a show for some big muckety-muck tomorrow?" Savary steps from the pantry shadows, into the candle-bright kitchen. "Since when can you dance, all eaten up like that, in front of the Kingdom's uptight nobility?" She gestures at the lewd bounty of his bruises.

"Oh, Maman!" The boy jumps and squeaks, a charming flutter.

"You *scared* me." He comes to hug her and Savary's own arm takes him in tenderly, at once. How else? He smells of costly soap, sandalwood and rose attar; a light odor of horses, also expensive. He kisses her cheek and they part. Quick as crime, his hands do up his shirt laces, hiding the bulk of purple evidence. "Of course I'll be in a robe and mask, Maman! We're performing devotions to the Saints out-of-doors. Nothing hootchie *en chambre*."

She offers; he takes the jar.

Savary follows him to the table where the cup waits—her eyes on the lovebites above his collar. It's just too much! "But *why* would you want some awful man from over there? And worse, a *kingson*!"

"Oh, Maeqal's not royal issue, Maman." Complicated jewelry, some new thing, hangs about his neck. One chain, fingerthick, entwined by others, hairsbreadth fine. *Not* silver: the metal glints whiter and more matte.

"No?" Savary frowns. "I thought he was one of the Old Man's half-thousand."

The boy hums a negative. "And the King only ever had 114 sons, really. A good third of *those*"—speaking lightly, he jiggles loose the jar's stopper—"were lost to the wars and fratricides. Maeqal's neither son nor grandson. Exceedingly wonderful to me, of course: but he's nobody up at Court."

His eloquent hands, this temperate tone, the sheer *mildness* of him make it difficult for Savary to recall the conflict, to retain it. You can almost see how one small boy comes and goes in safety among absolute powers.

"Well, anyway," Savary says, feeling obscurely finessed. "I thought we'd agreed on an early evening, just this once." She strokes a hand across the blades of his back. "I thought you *weren't* going over to the Kingdom tonight." His shirt's such fine stuff—light as linen, soft as silk.

"Oh..." He looks, surprised, over his shoulder. "I didn't! The troupe only ran through a couple new songs, then we did the early show at Blue Moon. A short set. It was fun, just playing around for once, goofing off." Nowadays the boy's too brazen to bother about lying. He'll commit his mischief upfront, and make nice apologies afterwards, as necessary. Even so, a staggering sum of hours remains unaccounted for, in this version of events. Late afternoon, all the evening, very deep into night; rose will tint the skies, soon enough.

Savary's temper frays again. "Then how is it you're falling up in here so long after midnight bells?"

He grins. To some less happily married woman, it would doubtless seem a smile of general joy, not specifically fucked-out bliss. "Maeqal showed up at the Blue Moon for the show," the boy says. "And we...chilled for a while, afterwards."

Savary's not ready for such a smile on the face of her younger child, the baby. Bitterly she says, "Just how old is that kingson of yours, anyway?"

The boy grimaces. "Oh, Maman—Cook's let the palm wine go *again*. You really ought to speak with him. This is almost vinegar!"

"Boy, I asked you a question."

He gives her his full attention. "First cousin of the Royal Blood, Thrice-removed, Twice-returned on the Matrilineal Line, His Excellency, Maeqal son of Oaqim lacks something for thirty, I believe." His left hand signs "approximately" while the right tips fancy-glass to his lips. "Twenty-eight years old?" The boy makes another face. "Twenty-nine? You'll remember they count birthdays differently in the Kingdom, but one year more or less, I always forget."

A year less. Savary stops herself from saying so, because of course he already knows. This is just more of that bafflement—decorative, feigned—lately adorning his speech.

She tries some rhetoric of her own. "Oh, the Saints must weep for his poor lady wife! What can she be thinking, I wonder, with her man creeping over here to Sea-john all the time, spending late-nights with scrumptious young *virtuosi*?" With a start, Savary realizes they've switched to the language of the Kingdom. After all this time, it trips off her son's tongue with an ease surpassing her own, and she was *born* there, he up here, in the hills.

"Aréienne hasn't danced in two years. She's writing a song-cycle, her knees hurt, and very soon now she'll have her baby. And La Pablo fell in love; he sailed away with the ambassador from Kidan. So if Maeqal wants a virtuoso, he must come to me. And scrumptious, Maman? Thank you! There's no lady wife as yet, either. I wouldn't have a married man. But you, Maeqal's father, and all his clan patricians, are remarkably in accord—that noblemen his age should be married, that his run of freedom is getting long and needs to end. Before they muttered, but now his family is shouting: *exile, disinheritance, excommunication,* they say, if Maeqal fails to marry before the next Long Rains."

"There! You see?" Savary cries. "*That's* what they do over in the Kingdom. Up here, we Johnnys love who we want. Can't you see what comes of messing around with some kingson?"

"Kingcousin only, Maman. A minor one." He's blasé, or just tired, but anyway deflects her every word with suave hands and chatter. "Now his children, *they* will be born 'Full First,' if Maeqal's mother can fix a wife for him out of the daughters of the Royal Concubinage." He sips, making faces.

Johnnys treat one another tenderly. But over in the Kingdom you went for blood in any conflict—more so with the ones you loved. After all this time in Sea-john, Savary still cannot pull her blows enough. "So will you be marrying him too, then?" She sneers. "You and this king's-daughter?"

One day, maddened by remorse, she will rant at her wife, describing how the boy looks at her now, and Jahs will say, "No, my love, no. He wouldn't want that…" but Savary never does forgive herself for the hurt she causes, his look of betrayal.

"If anyone, Maman, I thought *you*…." The boy stops. He begins again, without tremolo. "Can we not try to be kind to each other? You know perfectly well they marry one man, one woman, in the Kingdom."

She wants to make her son *see*, to choose more *wisely*; not to hurt him. In a rush, Savary says, "Whatever happened to that wonderful Johnny boy you used to run around with? The carpenter from the boatyard? Oh, you two were *lovely* together! Kéké was his name, I think. Why not—"

She cuts herself off. For it seems her big mouth has hit on some name that had better been left unspoken. Her son's face wrings with such suffering as who could want for her own child, and Savary's at a loss to respond because she's one of those who have only ever won in love, gained and gained, and never lost. She says, "Oh, sweetheart," and repeats that as she strokes circles on his back.

"I can't *talk*—" His voice clots with emotion. "—about Kéké. I really wish you wouldn't, Maman, please." He sets his cup on the table, and briskly recovers nonchalance—or its semblance. "Tomorrow's a big day for us, and I'm very tired. It's our first show for the Queen Mother herself, at the Royal Pavilion." On his face, Savary sees resolve, finality. "So, if you'll excuse me?" Not actually waiting on any sign from her, the boy gently brushes by to take the stairs to his room.

Savary watches him up. She suffers a strange, fey moment: catching a glimpse of the here-and-now as it shall one day be in memory, most details worn away, but a few deeply etched, suffused with the poignancy that accrues to long years of regret. A lifetime's worth. *Remember? He wore his shirt à la beaux boys. And the diamonds in his ears!—big as your thumbnail.* The presentiment of loss goes swiftly as it came. The noisy old wood lies quiet under his feet: something in just where or how he knows to step. The little truant used to escape just so on nights past, out to forbidden busking on the waterfront.

Savary very nearly rushes upstairs to plead with him. *We love you. Stay.* But, no…he'll sleep here, and they can talk later in the morning. That's soon enough. She pinches dark the bank of candles, then goes to join her wife and man.

[*So many nights*]

—Oh yeah. You all best watch out for that one there.

—What mess you talking, old woman?

—No, no, old mother. This here is the sweetest boy.

—Yeah! He never give no trouble. Mind his maman real nice.

—Keep your eye out is what I'm saying. Oh, all you are just stupid. Look at him. See? See there? The boy, so young, dancing like that! What age he got, three years? Not four yet, no. The reggaezzi coming forth to take this one away, sure 'nough. Sooner or later, wait and see.

—Reggaezzi! Why even speak such?

—Take back dat cuss, old witch!

—Don't you know this boy belong to Savary and Jahs? That the papa of him is the dark god from across-bayou, so tall, so black, so strong? Family live nice and proper on Dolorosa. You don't want to be cursing this boy!

—It's no curse of mine, you idiots. A hand lay on him already, when he was born and the Song filled his heart—

—Hurry, go and get Jahs. Run, quick inside. Tell her a witch come for her pickney!

—Jahs Jahs Jahs! A witch in the yard! Come forth to snatch the baby!

—Oh, come quick, Jahs! Hurry.

Among the workers of the boatyard were a very old man and his daughter, who was only old. One or the other of them sometimes made lunch and siesta stretch a long long time playing the drums. *Those* were the best days! He wriggled and squirmed until Jahs set him down, or he'd yank and beg until she said Well, go on then, letting him loose from her skirts to run out into the front yard and dance with the workers. Jahs always ate her lunch standing up, never lay out for a nap under the bearded cypress, and she rarely could be coaxed away to dance even for just a little while. But she would let him go.

He liked the old daughter on drums just fine. She had brilliant technique, and played hot exciting rhythms that hit the *mas despacio* with perfect timing to keep a dancer going fast, yet always able to catch breath too. He *loved* the old man's touch! Deep sly tricks complicated the playing. Those beats evolved on the subtlest schedule, and no mind could anticipate them. To catch the old man's riddims needed utter surrender to hips and feet and shoulders such that time and the world became sublime irrelevancies, and the only thing real was the rapturous pulse of the body thoughtless, just feeling, pure motion. The old man was very very old, though, and mustn't be bothered, let him nap, boy; he's earned a little rest, hasn't he? Today, for once, the old man played.

—Such a fearsome racket! Why all you in an uproar out here? What is going on?

—Jahs, dis old woman right here, dis one. She said reggaezzi coming for yo little boy.

—Yes. She said it would please her very well if they carried off your son to Mevilla right now, today, to live with witches and demons and flowers forever.

—I heard her too. I heard everyting. Dat's exactly what she said.

—But, old mother, why would you say such a thing? The reggaezzi! Baby, come here now; that's enough dancing. Come to Maman. Don't you hear me calling? Come, boy. Come!

—Fíjese. You see, Senyora Jahs? The boy is lost to the Song. He's faraway where you cannot touch him. The place where reggaezzi go. You cut his hair nice and neat—it is not shaggy and long. You feed him; the boy is pretty and fat—not thin from always eating smoke. He looks like people, like us—not covered all over in green lights. But he is one of them already, almost. Um reggaezzo.

—Stop your playing, old man! Are you stupid? A witch in the yard, reggaezzi, and my son—and you there are playing just like nothing. Stop I say! Stop!

—Ah, but you see? The drummer stops and it makes no difference. Still the boy dances! How does he hear, how can he know? Where does the Song come from?

—Please, cariño. Maman has you now. It's all right; wake up. Please wake up.

[Many nights]

Just before the Long Rains fall, some nights blow so cold no one dreams of going out without a poncho, but other nights the sea doesn't breathe at all, and the heat is like standing before the oven open at full fire. This night is one of those latter, so nobody wants much dinner. Before going to bed, Cook sets out only a bowl of leaves, a plate of fruit. Batalha crosses her arms and lays her head on the table, after just two bites from her mango. The grownfolk hardly eat, they drink palm wine, and Savary and Redamas and Jahs begin to laugh. Savary complains, I'm just getting *too* stringy and tough, going up and down these hills. Soon there will be nothing tender and soft on me, and my loves won't want me anymore. Papa says, Oh girl, please: you know you fat. But she jumps up from the table and lifts her thin cotton skirt a little, moving her foot, so the muscle jumps and bulges in her calf: There—you see? Ma Jahs leans far over and slaps Ma Savary on the bottom. Girl, you don't see all that jiggle? That's jelly! They laugh, and me too. Savary says You know, it's so blazing hot tonight we ought to take up some long pillows and sleep on the roof. So that's what we do.

Redamas carries up Batalha and lays her on a long pillow. Jahs whispers in Savary's ear and makes her happy. She giggles. Nearby in the flower court of the Tswani embassy, the circle tonight is drumming some very strange rhythms, from a country I don't know the name of. The beats make a big sound, *powerful*, they want nothing to do with fine dancing, they want jumps, cartwheels, flips—Boy! Savary shouts. How many times I *told* you! Do *not* be doing that tumbling on this roof! Come away from the edge there. *Back away* I say!

And so then it is only the fine dancing I can do after all, not the steps the drumming really calls for. Jahs wants to know why, lately, Batalha is so tired all the time that she falls asleep this early, when before you could hardly make her go to bed before the dawn comes. Savary and Redamas, they look at each other, and Papa says Batalha no longer is content to learn only the knife, that she wants more than to come every full and new moon to militia practice. What she wants is for Redamas to train her, too, with the six full-timers paid out the Johnny-fund. So everyday Batalha doesn't go anymore to help manage the orphanage with Savary, but instead comes to train with Redamas and the soldiers: spear, archery, open hand, a hard run up the steepest slope of the Mother, and now they've just got some horses too, so....

"But the girl is only eleven years old!" Jahs says.

"Well, you can talk to her, then." Savary throws up her hands. "But, me, I am *all done* arguing with Batalha. Anyway, she's not like the baby there. This one is her *Papa's* daughter—a giant like you, Redy. Bigger than some of those men-soldiers already. So I don't see what harm it can do. Batalha was sending me *mad* with all that energy of hers; now she just sleeps. I say it's good for her."

Inside the air didn't move, but up here, every now and then a breeze stirs off the ocean far downhill. Even so, the night is close and hot for so much dancing. I go back to where they are sitting and pour three thirsty cups of water from the jar. Redamas touches my head.

"Little man, you are all flat on one side. Didn't Nurse pick out your hair this morning?"

"Oh, that one danced his heart away at lunchtime today!" Jahs says. "He danced so much, so hard, he fell asleep under the beards of the cypress, and just slept the whole afternoon through. That's why his hair is ruint. We were loud loud loud, quartersawing the good mahogany into planks. But even that noise couldn't wake him."

Savary snuggles and whispers; Jahs calls to Redamas.

"Watch out, my baby doesn't go dancing over the edge of this roof. *Exca senyora éeu vamos abajo um ratinho.*"

Redamas says, "*Um ratao, mas bien,*" and grins and winks at Jahs. Savary laughs out loud. He reaches and she reaches back to take his hand; their fingers squeeze, then let loose. Mamans go downstairs to the big bedroom to be alone together. Jahs never goes to be alone with Redamas, and Savary goes much more with Jahs than she does with Redamas.

"Papa?" I feel I shouldn't ask, but I *must* know. "Would it make you sad if Ma Savary and Ma Jahs loved you only half as much as they love each other?"

"Oh, *no*. It would make me very happy. Half as much is a lot!" Redamas laughs. "You don't understand, my son—*everything* here makes me happy. More than anything I wanted to have family. A daughter, a son: so it makes me feel up to the very top of happiness that two women chose me. I was just the loneliest across-bayou, you can't even imagine. Do you know how lonely the gods are? We are so lonely, there are so few of us, that *ghosts* are our teachers. *Ghosts* are our friends. We...open a box, and *ghosts* come out to tell us the things we need to know. Where are the people? *Where* are they? Only ghosts!"

"DI. Discorporate Intelligences."

Redamas smiles. "Yes, DIs, like you said. I shouldn't call them ghosts. We know better, you and me."

"Why are you laughing, Papa?"

"Your Johnny accent, it's very funny. I really should speak more to you in the language of the gods. But it's so sweet, it's funny, the way you say that."

"Do a trick for me now, Papa. I like it when you do magic."

"What should I do?" Redamas lifts a hand, all conjure and flourish. "Maybe I will make you go to sleep."

"No, don't! I hate that one. Don't make me sleep, Papa!"

"Are you sure?" Redamas twinkles his fingers. "My DI always said it's my very best trick."

"No. I *hate* it. Please!" I grab his hand tight and hold his fingers still. "Do another. Something else!"

"All right, all right." Redamas shakes his hand free; he smiles. "How about this?" As glowing coals in a fire are steeped with richer color than the fire itself, so, pale as moonlight, a shine appears in the air around Papa's head, and where his naps grow not black, but indigo-color, round the edges of his hairline, the widow's peak, sideburns and kitchen: every curly strand fills with brilliance, the way hot coals do, but this light makes no heat, and it shimmers, blue as the sky at noon.

"More! Brighter! Like a strike of lightning. The way you did that other time!"

"Oh, I can't, little man. Not tonight. All day long it was so cloudy, I hardly got a taste of sun."

Because he's sitting I can stand there and pat his hair while the blue light dims between my fingers and goes dark. When it's gone, I ask another question.

"Now I want to know something important. Batalha has blue in her hair—"

"Your Papa *never* dreamed he'd burden any son or daughter with divinity, little man. But you are every bit as much my child as Batalha. Now I *explained* this to you: Ma Savary has a little divine inheritance, as it turns out. That's why, with her recessive allele, only daughters and not sons..."

"Yes, yes, Papa. I know, I know. You said before. The thing I want to know is, when my hair is all white as sand, my face wrinkled-up like dry fruit, and I need two canes, one for my right hand, one for my left: will *you*, Papa—you and Batalha—still have all your strength and all your youth? Is that true?"

"Who said those words? *Who?* Where did you hear such things?"

"Kéké at the boatyard. He said when I am many many years drifting in the sea, just some old bones eaten up by fishes, even then you will be as young and fresh as you are today."

"Well...we are all here now, little man. Ma Jahs, Ma Savary, Batalha, you and me. The night is good. Why should we worry so much about tomorrow? You are very young; we have a long, long time."

"But is it true, Papa?"

"You mustn't worry about such things. That Kéké is not a very nice boy. I'm going to go down to the boatyard and have a talk with him tomorrow."

"Oh, don't, Papa! Kéké is very handsome."

"But, little man, that's not a good reason to let him say mean things to you."

"I don't mind, though. It's all right, really. Don't come down to the boatyard and scare him, Papa. Please!"

"Because you say so, I won't make him scared. But I must go and say something to him, I must. I just don't like what he said at all. Pass your Papa the palm wine jar there, will you?"

[*Nights yet*]

"Batalha! That short Johnny, the one who trains you *miliciales* with the spear, I heard him tell Papa you're the best *by far* of the bunch. And Papa said to him, 'Yes, but you must never say so to Batalha; her head's that big already.' Papa said the gods once all had such, such 'mesomorphy and kinesthesia' as you. He said that you're a—what did he say?—'throwback sport' to those days before the gods intermarried so much. When Batalha grows up some, Papa said, and comes into her—he called it 'perjuvenescence,' then she will be a match even for the paladin of the Godspear."

Batalha smiled down at him, and all her teeth showed. As if against a monster, she brandished some imaginary weapon: nor could the paladin himself, with his spear all ablaze with sun-stuff, have outmatched her gallantry. Batalha said, "You heard him? *Papa* said that?"

"Yes. But then Papa said, Oh, you're a grief to him, and among all hardheaded daughters of the world, chief of them, because my Batalha just will not practice her psionics properly. Papa said you could be a great adept if only—"

Chaw! Batalha sucked her teeth, dismissing the rest with a turned-up palm. "*I do not care* about any damned psionics. Nothing in this world is more boring than sitting all day long, numb-assed, trying to think no thoughts at all. *One-pointed concentration!* O my brother, I sure hope you feel lucky, that Papa never bothers you about magic and stupidness!"

In fact, the least whiff of fatherly impatience or motherly frustration wafting his way tended to suffocate him like smoke, to choke off his capacity for disobedience or even dissent, until his own desires clogged in his throat, voiceless and caught. Batalha, though, argued for what she wanted. They could say No, You mustn't, You're too young, and all of it was like nothing to Batalha: just silliness, easily crushed with one hand. Her fierce words slapped parental "Nos" out of the air like gnats. Only *train* with the full-time miliciales? Ha! Batalha wanted to *be* a Johnny soldier! *Her* spear, *her* sash, *her* cuirass. And who of them rode better? Not even Papa! Yes, the big mean stallion: *that* one should be hers! Batalha had only to set her sights, and soon she would be getting her way. Now she wanted to drink the wine of Sea-john's nights, and no little cup for her, and no watering, either. Just like the other miliciales she could walk the waterfront late late late through the drunken crush, in blackest night, and kick the ass of any bully hassling the sugar girls and beaux boys. Oh, he worshipped his sister; *of course* he did! Who else, so young, was more mighty, had more swagger? Pick anyone from the whole wide world: there *was* no one else, only Batalha! So much the warrior was she that her old name fell away for this nom de guerre.

"I don't care, let them!"

"But my brother, you—"

"Stick a knife into somebody with blood and soul and dreams inside? No, Batalha! I will never never never do that. Some Maman loved them, some Papa picked them up and put them on his shoulders. So let them, whoever they are, go on living. I will die instead."

"But don't you understand the *horrible things* pirates do when they come to Sea-john? They are bad people, brother. No people are worse!"

"It makes no difference how bad they are, Batalha. They are just *people* to me. I couldn't hurt them."

"You are clever, *ermano mio*, and clever people won't do something that seems wrong if they cannot understand why they must. So come. Come, sit down with me here. I will explain why Johnny mamans-and-papas want their boys and girls to learn the knife.

"It's because the laws and taxes of the Kingdom don't hold over here in Sea-john. It's because we Johnnys are free—*Jaúnedi mar libre!*— and so we Johnnys are on our own. No armies of the Kingdom, no garrison at the citadel: *nobody* will ever lift a finger to help Sea-john. When the pirates raid us from the Gulf, when they loot and rape and murder and burn, what are the people doing over in the Kingdom? They're yawning. They turn over. They go back to sleep. *Ruff yoof* come over here from the Kingdom, and what for? To beat up Johnnys. In every corner of the world, the people know us because we are so beautiful, because our music is the best, because *quí e festa*. They all want to come for a visit. And half the time, it's true, those roadboys who guard caravans, saltdogs who guard ships, and soldiers from the Kingdom, come just for a good time, to have some fun. But then a penny drops: they turn into villains. They turn cruel and strange. I see them forcing kisses, grabbing breasts and ass, so you would think any pretty Johnny belonged to them.

"So you see, brother? That's why you must learn the knife. All of us in the hills should carry one. Too many don't. It's such a good thing for you to know, *ermano mio*, so very good. I wish you would consider."

For love of her, he did consider, and thought again: No.

But they *forced* him to learn to hold the knife, *made* him know where to stick it should pirates come again to Sea-john, should he get snatched up in the rape-and-loot. Papa took his hand and pulled him along to many tedious practices, where you must draw and stab and slash in the same way, over and over. They could *make* him do these things, but they *couldn't* make him remember to carry the knife. Where is your knife? Redamas would shout. Listen to me, boy, *listen*. When the pirates come, they come *all of a sudden*. There will *never* be time to...Savary would shout: Go *right back* to the house and get it now! Every time I see you without your knife, Jahs would shout, I will *always always always* send you back again until you...

With mamans-and-papas, things must always end in tears, there could only be sobbing. Batalha would look down at his belt where the sheath was meant to hang, and raise her eyebrow. It made him smile in a guilty way, sick in his belly. But then his sister would only cluck her tongue, shake her head, and let the matter drop. Somehow the fiercest Johnny of Sea-john was the only one who understood him, the softest.

Such a night in the house, sometimes, because of the boatyard, mad hours finishing a yacht for some *fils-de-roi*, or because of the orphanage, ten *abandonini* all come down with stomachache, fifteen boys and girls with grippe, or because of a fire in the hills, or for some bad ruckus on the waterfront, and Papa mustering the militia out. These moments, *quick*, ask whether you could go out nightwalking with Batalha, and more than likely some harried adult hand would wave you off: yes yes yes, boy, but you listen to your sister. On other nights Ma and Ma always said, Papa would say, your sister is thirteen and big and wears her knife, you are small and seven and won't wear yours. No, you *cannot* go roaming in those rough nights on the waterfront, down under the Mother. Stay round here on Dolorosa.

Take my hand. The way down is dark here.

A slender moon, hardly giving them a candle's light: it was the last moon, waning crescent before the new. Stars and planets, and the white parallels of waves breaking over the reefs, distinguished the blackness of sky from sea. *So much* going on over at the bottom of the Mother. Such lights, such crowds and music on the waterfront!

"I *know* the way here, Batalha! They let me go round on Dolorosa!"

"How many brothers do I have? Just one, only *you!* So if you won't mind me, I'm taking you right back to the house. I must keep you safe."

He took her hand.

On the waterfront were people too poor for soap, who washed only with water, stinky of armpit, ass. Caramel spirits and pineapple juice. The day's catch grilled over the driftwood yield of shipwrecks. "Got that sweet fish, right here! Salt with sailors' tears!"

Everybody not foreign was sugar or beau. Battle scars, sailors in breeches, and those black robes they wore in the Kingdom were mainstays. Johnny men glory-burned, Johnny women with art scars, some just boys and girls, metal hoops piercing their bodies and glinting, not so much older than himself on second look. Men and women of Sea-john dressed the same, in shirts and wraparounds, but here the shirts gaped from neck to navel, showing the soft swells of bosom and belly, smooth panes of chest and youthful abdomen. No need to guess, it showed plain: her waist so small and hips so wide, whose ass was big, some handsome man's excitement. All these wraparounds were just that short and tight. Up and down the cobbles of the Board, out on the beach, down the docks, and all around the many fires, drummers and guitarristas and the world's loveliest people dancing.

"When I'm big, I'm going to come down here *every single night* and dance. I'll be a beau boy and strangers will give me money!"

"No, brother—not that! The best dancers, don't you know they go into one of the top jukes and dance there? Sugarcane, Blue Moon, or the Tropica? Up front of everybody, and the crowd loves them so much that guards must keep them safe? And for the *very* best dancers? Some herald will come over from the Kingdom, all in silk and dripping jewels, to beg the virtuosi out of Sea-john, beg them to come over and dance in the Kingdom. Those dancers make shows for the Court, all the *fils-de-roi* and great ambassadors, the tycoons and courtesans. Johnnys stay up there at Court, sometimes, and take a lover, settling down rich. It's true some boys and girls in the jukes sling booty; but others just dance. So a juke's much better, you see. Ma Jahs knows everybody. Talk to her. She will know somebody to get you into the troupe at a juke."

"Oh. Why didn't I know these things? About jukes? About the Court?"

"You are young. Why should you know? I didn't know myself at seven. Ask Ma Jahs to take you around the top jukes so you can see them all dance, then pick a troupe you like. The dancers in the jukes are very very good, *ermano mio*. Oh, they can dance! But many of the bailarines are not as good as you."

"I will do it, Batalha. Just like you said! That sounds *twice as good* as beaux boying here on the waterfront. All I want is to be in a juke and go to Court!"

"Better that way, yes. Then you can dance all you like, they pay you for it, and you don't have to fuck some strange dude every night.

"I'm hungry, do you want one of these too?"

"Yes."

"Put two on for us," Batalha said to the man squatting by his grill. She got coins of her own nowadays from Ma Savary, and so had one to give the Johnny fisherman. He ducked out shrimp from his bucket, stabbed them onto a sharp stick, and lay the skewers over golden coals. Turning them once, plucking them up: he dipped them through the bowl of lemony pepper, and passed the skewers to Batalha.

Angry thunder broke over the surf of merry noise. Harshly shouting, some Kingdom man, not far away, wanted to know how all this *nasty Johnny sugar* thought it could just *wave up under* a man's nose and then get *snatched away*. He wasn't having it—No!—so just bring that *fat tricky* ass here. Against the hard threats, there rose sweet screams of a pretty boy hindered from flight.

Batalha, already as tall as Papa, had a clear view over the heads of the crowd, to some sight that lit her up with rage. Her hair electrified, blue-white, in a momentary flash. "Fucking *roadboys!*" she said, handing the skewers to him. "Hold mine, brother, and stay right here. Stay *put*. I'll be back in no time."

Batalha thrust through the crowd and vanished. Someone thin, all musk and funk and black as Papa almost, passed by with a guitarra; and someone else too, more naked, with long, locked hair and skin no darker than palms and soles, like browning butter. Both young bodies tattooed, somehow, in phosphorescence.

Reggaezzi. He'd never seen any before, hardly heard of them. But he knew at once. A boy and a girl. The boy one sat in the sand and tuned his guitarra. The girl one touched her toes, no, she was laying her hands flat to the packed sand and going up in handstand, falling over in bridge, and coming up to stand again. One leg she lifted obtuse the standing, grasped that ankle, and brought up the shin to kiss. In the murk of night, the glowing curlicues on their skin pulsed marine green—*not* tattoos after all, but something—alive? Bright mites, infinitesimal, crept over their skin, either down in it, shining through, or glittering on top in some vexed way impossible to figure out.

"Oh, they're young!" he said. "They don't look much older than my sister."

Some Johnny in the crowd forming up answered back, "How you don't know, boy? Reggaezzi all die soon. Hardly none make twenty."

Dressed badly for the brisk waterfront, they wore only shirts and loincloths. The reggaezza had torn off the sleeves of her shirt, and he knew why in the same way no one had ever taught him to breathe: so the line of her beautiful arms showed better.

The boy one began to play.

Strumming in rasjeo so fast and rich that a second player seemed to harmonize with him, even at times a third; and though there was none, a drummer seemed to keep the beat: the reggaezzo struck and tapped the guitarra's inlay of clapwood while he played. He sang too.

The hoarse falsetto lacked the glories of his *guitarrismo*, but that voice was still a marvel of feeling. The song, in the language of the gods, was hard to follow. A mother, no, a great grandmother, had a new baby at her breast. This baby so precious so beautiful but sick and fragile with—time and space? The baby somehow growing older than the mother herself, a great grandmother to her own mother, the world upside down, reversed. *What on earth?* The lyrics fit together so strangely he couldn't make sense of them. But the song was loving as a lullaby and yet *triste*, a lament. The reggaezza danced.

Oh, she danced.

Oh!

He'd never thought to dance in such a way that a story was told, the lyrics incarnated in a sorrowful play-act that nevertheless rendered respect to every beat and evolution of the music. He could grasp the mothersong better, in heart if not mind, seeing the reggaezza's dance. A small gathering hereabouts was silent, while further off the night disported in revelry and strife. He stood dumb, mouth hanging open, and watched with his whole self. Nothing lasts, and the best must be briefest: so too with this. When the performance ended, the gathering of Johnnys murmured the same word of appreciation. Never more in agreement, he softly chimed in too. For a moment more palm fronds rustled overhead, and breakers rolled, the gulls calling. Then the quiet smaller crowd spoke, laughed, and began dispersing into the greater. The reggaezza, thirsty, plucked a jar of *Sea-john free* right out of the hands of some passerby. Rude!—but the passing Johnny made neither mention nor moan.

The boy one walked up and pointed, saying, "Gimme dat."

He passed over one of the skewers. The reggaezzo put half the length, three shrimp, into his mouth and drew the stick forth clean, crunching and chewing hungrily. The reggaezzo stank of old sweat and something herbal. He was as crushingly beautiful as Kéké, almost. Green constellations crept across the black sky of him. The reggaezzo spat some shelly wreckage and gobbled the other three shrimp.

"Dat one too!"

"I'm very sorry; I can't. It's my sister's, not mine. Batalha asked me to hold it for her."

"Aw, ain't you just too posh?" The reggaezzo turned and called the girl. "Hey! Quick, come listen at dis idjit here. Sound *straight off* Dolorosa, dis one!"

The reggaezza came over, thin as a finger and yet strong. Hunger had melted all fat from her, the daily hours of dance showing in the ripple of her thighs and veiny strength of arm.

"Now just tell *huh* what you come dare said to me!"

"Only that I must hold these shrimp for my sister—"

The reggaezza threw back her head, whooping laughter. She said to him, "Little prince-boy, don't you know we could lay duh *worse cuss* on any Johnny won't give food, won't give clothes, or turn away help from us reggaezzi? So you not Johnny den, *ti prince?*"

"I *am* Johnny." His lips trembled, eyes close to tears, for there was great hot power in her, like the burning sureties of Batalha, like the bright god in Papa.

"*Zas!*" said the reggaezza, snapping her fingers. "I could go like *dat* and yo Mamans fall out duh fishing boat tomorrow and shark eat dem up screaming. Zas! and yo Papas slip from high cutting coconut, crack dere heads wide-open so dey drooling stupid forever! Or maybe you hate yo Mamans and yo Papas, and you love yo ownself much better? Den zas!, *ti prince*, and *you*—"

"Here! I didn't know. They never want to tell me anything about reggaezzi. Please, won't you take it now? I love them and Batalha best, but don't curse them. Curse me."

"See? You just too mean sometime. Duh little boy didn't even know. Now you got him crying and I feel all bad. Johnny boy, you could keep dat fuh y'sistah. Salright, salright—don't cry. Nobody ain't cussing nobody tonight."

"I thought duh boy was talking back smart. You know I can't stand dat. Some posh asshole. Anyway it's two whole days and no Ladder-to-Heaven. I need some smoke *bad*. I hate dis hunger. I hate how cold duh night feel. *Gimme dat*—I'll eat it!"

He handed over the skewer and the reggaezza crouched down on her haunches, making the same short work of six big shrimp as the boy had. He lifted off his poncho and tucked it warmly round the girl's shoulders, just as though the reggaezza were in creaky old age, not the veriest youth. The boy one squatted down beside and stroked her long matted hair; he said, "Couple more days, duh leaves be all brown and good, and we climb right back up duh Ladder to Heaven. I hate deese days too, but gotta eat *some* time, don't we?"

She looked at the reggaezzo. "You don't hear dat? You don't hear *Song*?"

"No. Where?—Yeah! But where it come from, so soft? I never heard Song dat soft!"

"Him! Duh boy here, dis boy. It's you."

"Me?"

"Yeah, yeah! Because you still too young. But some day you gon' come along with *us*!"

"I'll come now."

"Not yet," said the reggaezza. "Grow some. Get in some trouble. Look at dose legs you got!—dancer, ain't you? Well, baby brudder, yull dance much better with yo heart broke bad."

"The best dancers need a broken heart?"

"Yup."

"Is your heart broken?"

"Oh, *sure*. And fresh everyday. Yull see." The reggaezza lay her head on the boy one's shoulder and closed her eyes.

The reggaezzo said, "I member how bad it was, Johnny boy, but you just got to stay patient. By and by some night you gon' hear all ten, twelve living come up duh road, and a tousand ghosts. Duh sweetest Song you ever heard by far. Duh singers all singing, some with carry-drum playing, and I be dere with duh guitarristas. You come on down dancing and join us. Climb high up duh Ladder-to-Heaven. We'll take you over Mevilla. Get you some lights like dese."

A galaxy spiraled on the reggaezzo's cheek, clotted at the center with stars algae-colored and luminous—he reached to touch one. And felt nothing but hot human skin, though his fingertips came away flickering green. He brought up the glimmers to his face, wanting to see them better, but the bright motes suddenly winged off his hand, back to the reggaezzo's cheek where they'd been. The shock of it was like a roach scuttling away, then abruptly bursting into flight back toward your head. With a squeak and jump, he stumbled over some hairy half of broken coconut, and fell in the sand. The pretty reggaezzo laughed, showing bright teeth. "Scared you, huh?"

As a keepsake of this night, he wanted to know: "What is your name?"

"Ain't got one. Soon as you one of us, yo name just wash away out of duh world forever."

"But what was it before? Your name back when you lived with your Mamans and your Papas?"

"I told you: I don't know. The name missing and won't be found. Like a wave come to duh beach last year, where dat wave now? If God know all things, She forgot *my* name. It's just gone. Call me *reggaezzo*, call her *reggaezza*, if you want. We nothing else."

The reggaezza leapt up, the poncho falling away, and she cried out, "I feel good! I feel good! Let's go way over dere where it's more room and brudder you just play me a fast song, a wild song, duh strongest song you got! Let's go, let's go, let's go!"

She tore away through the crowd and the reggaezzo snatched up his guitarra and ran away after her. *Stay put*, Batalha had said, and those words pulled him back down, chained to that spot in the sand, or he'd surely have followed. He reckoned it was all right to reach over and gather back his poncho just lying there abandoned. So he did. Then a new thing stirred in him and the chains broke. *Get in some trouble*, she had said. He stood up.

"O ermano mio." O my brother!

He looked back towards the cry and there came his sister staggering. She was bloodsoaked, awash in gore, the knife hanging from her grip and dripping, it was that wet.

"Batalha! They cut you? Where are you hurt?"

"Me? No. I'm fine." Seeing the condition of her knife, she stropped off the wet black shine onto her ruined poncho, and slid the blade back in its sheath. "That other time I stuck the saltdog just a little and it was enough to scare him off." Batalha sounded very sad, nothing like herself. "This dude though—he just wouldn't quit. He wouldn't go away. I had to cut him down stone dead."

[*Todas las noches*]

[   ] saw the reggaezzi once before. He was too young to remember.

As a baby, at the Festival of San Maurizio: when the reggaezzi come down in force to give a show on the seafront Board. Then, Johnnys bring out their ailing loved ones, their sick of heart, their babies and any family grown elderly or close to passing. Great blessing will visit whosoever attends San Maurizio. No reggaezzi miss who yet live. If all are there, then surely those bereft parents in the crowd need only crane their heads, and blink away the tears, to catch a glimpse of their doomed youth, *their* child. Which one? What was his or her name? They no longer know—but perhaps the one on drums, or that other one there, dancing, had been theirs.

Savary takes him off the breast and turns him round. She sits him up on the shelf of a forearm. "There, [   ]! You see them?"

He cannot see *much*. Why won't they let him down and free, to wriggle forward through the crowd as Batalha had? They're all crushed among jostling hundreds back here, though nobody is frightened, so he's not either. Certainly [   ] can hear the *song*. Sweet and powerful, a choir delves deep and soars high, all to the greater glory of one soloist, some apocalyptic soprano. Drumbeats, wild and precise, overwhelm the rhythms of his own heart and breath; in time, ecstatic, [   ] shudders, held perched to Savary's breasts. But glimpses are few and far between, as are the gaps among arms and backs and shoulders of the crowd. There's nothing much to see, really, save occasional flashes of green light.

"*Mamita*, really now! How's the baby supposed to see from way down there? Give me him." Jahs lifts him away and up, a full foot higher to her shoulders where at last there's some bit of view. Those gorgeous lights belong to *people*. Green glow freckles their skin, and some great master, perhaps the music itself, exerts sublime puppetry on the abandoned leaping of their bodies. Still, he can only see top halves, only torsos.

"More, more!" [   ] beats fists atop the head against his belly, punishing its offensive and inadequate height.

"Baby, *stop*. What are you doing? What's the matter with you?"

Jahs's chief attributes are goodness, clarity, and strength. The thing called for now, however, is *stature*.

"Papa, up up!" he shouts, stretching his hands toward Redamas: much the tallest being in the crowd, and from whose shoulders, once [   ]'s hefted there on high, the vantage is astounding.

Grace is down *here*, available to the flesh for embodiment at every single moment. These wonderful creatures are showing him how to *do* it! Wildly [   ] sobs, shaking his head, wrapping his arms tight about Redamas's brow, when Jahs reaches to lift him down for mothercomfort. "No no no," he screams. I want to "see!" I want to "see!" Beauty's only ever a soft thing? It never harrows?

"Woman—*ow*. Why are you hitting me, Jahs? Don't hit! You see the boy is holding on for dear life. He wants to *watch*."

"Man, my baby is crying! You hand him down to me, Redy, or I will *cut you like a pirate* right here in the streets!"

On My First Reading of

The Einstein Intersection

Michael Swanwick

There is a hollow, holey cylinder running from hilt to point in my machete.

Samuel R. Delany, *The Einstein Intersection*

The novel began with a lilt of alliteration, a half-hidden sexual pun on the holiness of holes, the promise of a plot that would run some unspecified gamut to its endpoint, and the metaphoric conflation of music, violence, and work in the description of a tool which was suited for all three and was thus a stand-in for the as yet unintroduced protagonist. There was quite a lot going on in those first fourteen words. It was a young writer's sentence—exuberant, leading with the chin, aglow with the joy of a newly-mastered facility with words. The unlovely adjectival "holey" broke the easy laminar flow of words, tugging at the reader's mind and grabbing it down into the gutter of language, demanding that one pay closer attention not only to what was said but how.

Samuel R. Delany was twenty-five when *The Einstein Intersection* was published and I was seventeen.

I was living in Seven Pines, Virginia, at the time, just outside of Richmond, in a cockroach-haunted rental in a cookie-cutter development surrounded by a gothic Southern culture alien to a boy from small-town Vermont. My father had contracted early onset Alzheimer's and was in the process of losing all that made him human. As a direct result, I had surrendered my lifelong ambition of becoming a scientist and now aspired to literature. John Gardner has written that writers are hurt into being. Certainly that was true of me. I read books with a savage hunger not for escape and entertainment, important though those were to me, but for information I could use to teach myself the art of fiction.

No single book fed this hunger better than *The Einstein Intersection*.

The novel was slim, 150 pages or so in paperback original. A biographical note, which I read last, mentioned that Delany's first novel was written when he was nineteen, and that this one was composed "primarily during a year of travel in France, Italy, Greece, Turkey, and England." His condition could hardly have been more different from mine. Most of my reading material then came from the library or used book stores, but, this book being new, I probably bought it off a revolving wire rack in a drug store.

On a day otherwise lost to memory, I began reading.

The first chapter was a scene-setter establishing an ambiguously bucolic world, liberally dropping hints—many misleading—about the nature of that world, and introducing various characters. On the prose level, I could see that Delany's most elaborate sentences with their *eye flakes of sun on water* or *belly pulsing out from the sides of him, leaves flicking each other above* were allowed to soar only so far before being brought back down to earth by a no-nonsense line like *Anyway, not only do I bite my fingernails disgracefully, I also bite my toenails.*

Alerted by that opening sentence, I saw that these alternations allowed greater freedom on the figurative side while letting the unadorned prose do its work of efficiently moving forward the plot without inviting the reader's disdain, as merely-functional pulp writing so easily (and unfairly) can.

The second chapter opened with a long passage from the author's journal about the difficulty of writing the very book I was reading. Which was a matter of particular interest to a future writer such as myself. The excerpts and quotations heading each chapter formed a meta-commentary on the novel, alternately claiming the mantles of poets and intellectuals and mocking itself with, for example, the commercial slogan: *Come ALIVE! You're in the PEPSI generation!*

This mixture of high and pop culture extended into the narrative, where the common religion was based on rock and roll and the Beatles were explicated as avatars of the Orpheus myth. At a time when the question of how long they would last—pop careers were notoriously evanescent—was a commonplace, this was prescient. (Though Janis Joplin or Jim Morrison or Jimi Hendrix, in the event, would have filled the role better.) Spike Jones, a musician who made a career of lancing musical pomposity, could not extend his material into the era of rock, he said, because it was a genre that refused to take itself too seriously.

My heart rocked. My heart rolled. Similarly, Delany's prose wasn't afraid to mix the profound and self-mocking. This was very much a Sixties thing. But in TEI, its function was transparent.

Midway through the book, there was a scene which made obvious a quality, or perhaps lack is the better word, consistent throughout the novel. Lo Lobey, having taken a job as a dragon herder, arrived at an anticipated destination, an intersection in the ruins of an ancient city.

Here's how it was set:

The sky was blue glass. West, clouds smudged the evening with dirty yellow. The dragons threw long shadows on the sand. Coals glowed in the makeshift fireplace. Batt was cooking already.

"McClellan and Main," Spider said. "Here we are."

And that was it. No broken glass crunching underfoot, no smell of ancient PCBs leaching out of the sand, no reflection on a single shard of marble the size of a thumb—the nose, perhaps, from a shattered statue—sticking out of the sands that stretched lonely and lifeless to the horizon. These things weren't even implied.

This was where I learned that description is not an obligation but a choice—and, upon reflection, a moral one. Delany focused his descriptions on people and their emotions. The external world only mattered insofar as it impinged upon their inner lives. For this particular book it was the right decision.

Then, two-thirds of the way through the novel, the author's journal cited the poet Gregory Corso's conversational comment to Delany (who would, decades later, explain that for an eighteen-month period what seems now a racial slur, was then acceptable, provided only that the speaker was a credentialed hipster), *What's a young spade writer like you doing all caught up with the Great White Bitch?*

At the time, science fiction was or seemed to be an all-white enclave of literature and its lack of writers of color was widely perceived by its practitioners to be a serious impediment to the progress of the genre. So this caught me by surprise. It sent me back to the first chapter, where Lo Lobey (who was, after all, a member of a tri-gendered race from Elsewhere who had taken on human form and were in the process of learning to become us; so no shame on me for not catching this on first go-round; and anyway, as the chapter headings constantly reminded, the book was an artificial construct, words on paper, fiction) described himself as having a brown face, a friend as having skin as black as obsidian, caused by a protein formed around silver oxide rather than "that rusty iron brown of melanin that suntans you and me," and the Eurydice analogue, La Friza, as looking "normal: slim, brown, full mouth, wide nose, brass colored eyes." Suddenly, what I'd read as an archetypal Greek village became an archetypal African one.

There is a lot to praise in this normalization of being non-Caucasian. Even at the time, I recognized it as a contribution to the long, slow discussion on race we Americans constantly tell ourselves we are not having. But what struck me more (for I was on a quest, remember, to become a writer) were two technical matters: First, by comparison to texts written by well-meaning white liberals, that it wasn't enough to have a dark-skinned hero, however omnicompetent he or she might be; to present people of color as ordinary citizens of the future, it was necessary that there be many of them, fulfilling the functions of everyday life. Second, that Delany had meant for the reader (the white reader at any rate; I imagine black readers were quicker on the uptake) not to realize this fact until later, with the triggering Corso quote. He had hidden their race in plain sight.

That information could so easily be given the reader to be decoded later when the author provided the key, was a revelation. Such a simple trick! Such a powerful tool. Such a useful thing. I did a great deal of flipping back through previously-read pages as my understanding of what was going on clarified. There was a lot of benign misdirection in the text.

Endings to be useful must be inconclusive. Such was the conclusion of the final journal entry at the head of the penultimate chapter. I did not then and still do not know whether that was a true statement—though all such sweeping declarations must necessarily inspire skepticism. But even as a teenager, I understood that for fiction to be worth the tremendous effort it takes to create, it must be useful. I never wanted to live less than I did during my senior year of high school. Nevertheless, I could see that my problems were small potatoes compared to those of so many others around me: the girl who confided that her failed suicide attempt had been the bravest act of her young life, the new friends two houses down the street who abruptly left town when their father's corpse was found hanging from a noose in their garage, the scion of a family of racists so virulent that he decorated his books and briefcase with swastikas and made approving jokes about the Master Race in a fake German accent as a means of fighting back...This is not an easy world to live in, and its inhabitants need all the help they can get.

The Einstein Intersection was of use to the young, callow, and painfully aware of his shortcomings person I once was, though surely not in any manner predictable to its author. It also triggered decades of thinking about myth, reading about myth, and writing about myth. So its long term influence on me cannot be exaggerated.

After a fast second reading, to ensure I hadn't missed anything discernible by a precocious teenager (I had missed a great deal obvious to an adult), I put the book down and picked up the next one. I was twelve years from selling my first story and making good time.

And, well, that's all I have to say, I guess.

Behind every novel is a single story, that of its author. Before it lie a myriad, those of its readers. I do not claim that my own reading of this particular book was in any way special. But in the absence of any other being committed to paper, it will serve to stand in for them all.

Characters in the Margins of a Lost Notebook

Kathryn Cramer

The only important elements in any society are the artistic and the criminal, because they alone, by questioning society's values, can force it to change.

— Samuel R. Delany, *Empire Star*

Jack's apartment on the Upper West Side was vast and rent controlled, with shelves of books on serious topics covering nearly every wall. He ran his apartment as part library, part hostel, part literary salon. Usually, it was a bit of a mess. The dining room was mostly for projects; the living room for socializing. Piles from the living room were shifted to the dining room and then moved back at the end of the evening.

A group of us met there most Tuesdays and read poetry together, with Jack presiding. He had a bushy gray beard with streaks of white and looked like a cheerful black Karl Marx. Part of his beard was straighter than the rest because he tugged it habitually. He often did this while listening to poetry.

For a while there was an affectionate cat. I was spending one night a week, Tuesdays, at his apartment, sleeping on the too-short red velvet love seat in the TV room. The cat was black and white and had a really long name: Kid something something something Valentine Delany. There was no door to the TV room.

Round about 3:30 a.m., Kid would purr loudly and pounce on my feet, which were always sticking off the end of the couch. If I didn't react, he would start clawing and biting them. I would sleepily pick the cat up off my feet and toss him out into the hall. This happened about 10 times a night. Kid disappeared one day from the window sill, leaping to catch a pigeon. We missed the cat. I wished Jack would get another, but Kid was not replaced.

◊

One summer I stayed in Jack's apartment for the last two weeks of June. It was hot. Jack had no air conditioning. With the windows always wide open, there was a constant soundtrack of sirens, and traffic, and squeals of brakes, and occasionally people shouting. He lived on the top floor. It was a great place to watch thunderstorms.

On the day I arrived, I was out of breath from climbing five flights of stairs with all my luggage. I flopped down in an upholstered chair. Jack was on the living room sofa, flustered. Upset.

He gestured at a narcissus wilting in a wine glass and told me of Daphne, the dinner guest who had just left, a Columbia graduate student. She had brought him the flower and had come to dinner with the intention of having sex with him.

Jack said, "I opened my mouth to say 'I'll have sex with anyone once as long as they make sure I have a good time.' And I looked across the table at Daphne and realized that it was no longer true."

This was, perhaps, an odd thing to say to me, a young woman who had just come with her luggage to stay for a while. But it was almost as if he wasn't really talking to me as such, but rather using me as a sounding board for an important change in self-image.

◊

We were mostly science fiction people in the poetry group. We gathered to read and discuss poetry, and then went to a bar afterwards to talk about science fiction over drinks.

For a short while, a famous mystery novelist came to the poetry nights in order to woo Sarah, a first novelist from Princeton. He wrote bestsellers and insisted we call him "The Dog."

When I figured out The Dog was after Sarah, I took her aside to warn her. But it was too late. She said, "Yes, isn't that sweet?" Nine-and-a-half weeks later, just as he was beginning to name their future children, he abruptly dumped her. I never saw him again, and felt secretly grateful that a few years earlier, when I was first introduced to The Dog, I had droned on and on about my divorce, possibly saving myself a lot of trouble.

An old friend of Jack's who had been assistant press secretary in a long ago presidential administration kept calling Jack around dinner time and leaving him long, tearful messages during our meetings. Jack refused to answer these calls and wouldn't let us answer either. Eventually, the calls stopped.

I asked, "What happened?"

Jack said, "I lent him money. I expect I'll never hear from him again."

◊

One poetry evening, Lianne, a tall young poet, talked about having been to a workshop where she was seduced by the poet-singer-songwriter Leonard Levine. She said Levine's pickup line was "Great legs! I'd like to see where they end."

"He didn't have a better pickup line?" Jack asked.

Someone said, "What do you think all those girls standing in the background singing la la la are for?" It had never occurred to me to wonder about why Levine needed so many backup vocalists.

The conversation shifted from sex to coffee enemas. The idea of recreational enemas was entirely new to me. Embarrassed, I made some crack: "Must give a big caffeine rush." Two participants very seriously said, "Oh, yes," and went on with the conversation.

That was the first moment of my life realizing that there were some things I really did not want to know more about; and that Jack knew a lot of such things. I learned that there were questions, especially about sex, I should not ask, because Jack might know the answer.

◊

We threw many parties at Jack's apartment. He seemed to love it. Jack has the same birthday as me, though our ages are a few decades apart, so we had a couple of joint birthday parties.

The deal was that Jack would host if we would clean up before and after and provide all the refreshments. I remember once spending two days vacuuming and washing dishes with Anthony Reber (who later changed his name to Kierkegaard). Perhaps the pile of dishes has grown in memory, but it seems like we spent three hours washing dishes; honored and excited to be washing his dishes, vacuuming his floors, dusting NYC's black soot off his windowsills.

There was a mail rack on the wall containing unopened registered letters. Someone asked if we should do something about them. Maybe Jack should, like, open them. "I don't read registered mail," he said crisply. "It's always bad news."

◊

Jack often provided shelter to the homeless. One day in his apartment we met an odd man named Robert who drank a lot of vodka. He had rough hands with nails nibbled down to the quick. He was sprawled across the couch and said to us a strangely elongated "Hi."

When Lianne arrived, she said to him, "I know you!" They had gone to high school together. She asked him questions, but he was not interested in answering. Instead, he showed us a framed picture of a dark-haired woman, saying, "This. Is MY wife."

The next week, Jack unburdened himself of the grief Robert had caused. Robert was bipolar or schizophrenic or something, and hypersexual. He had seduced much of the neighborhood, while telling everyone what they most wanted to hear.

He had gone high-end real estate shopping and had seduced the real estate agent, telling her he would buy a $600,000 condo. He had gone to the florist and ordered $45,000 worth of flowers for a lavish wedding. And so on. All around Jack's neighborhood. Leaving behind Jack's address and phone as contact info.

Robert had claimed to have a wife and kids. Jack said the kids he had showed him were the sample photos of kids that came with the frames at Woolworth's around the corner.

Jack had just gone house to house, business to business, explaining: to the real estate agent, that the man she had slept with did not have any money and was not going to buy the condo. To the florist that there was no wedding and so the flower order should be cancelled. His cheeks were flushed, and he was wearing a puffy red coat and looked like he was about to explode.

The next week brought a further update. Robert was contrite. To make it up to Jack, Robert invited him out to his house in the Catskills. Against his better judgment, Jack went. The most astonishing thing, said Jack afterwards, was that the house in the Catskills was actually there.

◊

Jack had iron discipline about writing: Rising at 5 a.m., he sat down at his computer and began to type. He was working on his autobiography then. The walls just outside his writing nook were covered with news clippings, highlighted and annotated, about the AIDS epidemic. Sometimes when I stayed over, I would be up that early. I knew not to disturb to him until he was done, at which point we would have coffee.

Jack's dyslexia was astounding. Once, I was using an early version of Microsoft Word to spellcheck one of Jack's major essays. We joked about aliens sending secret messages through spellcheck suggestions. His misspellings triumphed over Microsoft's algorithms again and again. I forget what misspelled arcane postmodern critical term Word offered to replace with "testicles" but it was a word with no resemblance. Obviously, someone out there was trying to get in touch.

I wrote a negative review of a high profile book. Jack edited it. He cut out all qualifiers, all the cushioning, saying, "If you're going to fuck the dog, stick it all the way in."

◊

After Andy, with whom I was collaborating on a book, got sick, I worked at Hedge House as a temp doing Andy's work. Jack was really interested in hearing that there was paying work to be had at Hedge House. Arthur, the science fiction editor I was working for (and sleeping with) and who helped run the poetry group, said, "Jack, you wouldn't want to work for $9 an hour."

Jack replied, "I'm making $8 an hour lifting boxes in a comics warehouse."

So I shared a job with Jack for a while. One of the books in production was Omniaveritas's anthology *Neuromantic*. Jack wrote the copy and on the copy form there was a spot for author quotes, and so he wrote one.

We went to lunch. (I paid.) I told Jack I had read his novel *Dhalia* as a teenager but only about to page 660-something. He said, "You poor thing," which surprised me.

I told him I could tell how far I had read because I recognized the sex scenes: I remember wondering "Is this possible?" "Is that possible?" "Oh. My. God. Is that possible?" I had a very clear recollection of the sex scenes up to page 660-something, and after that, nothing. So I know I didn't finish the book first time out.

In the conversation about re-reading *Dhalia*, I said to Jack, "You were writing about New York City, but in your vision it is such a safe place. I find it terrifying." Jack replied that learning to be safe involved learning to cross class boundaries.

The texture of New York City life is structured by a complex class system, he explained. He said, "If you can cross class boundaries, people will always take care of you."

◊

A bunch of us went to a PEN party at the Temple of Dendur in the Metropolitan. The genre writers, about ten of us, were clustered near the temple itself. Jack was there. I was there with Arthur. Peter Straub and his wife were there in our circle. There was also a mystery editor named Wolfgang wearing a black leather jacket who was good friends with Edward Gorey.

The room was packed full of famous and intimidating literary folk, many of whom—according to a Susan Sontag article promoting the event—didn't like each other. Every once in a while, someone would step out of our circle and venture out into the room, and then return and report back what had happened. Jack had something he wanted to say to Sontag, so he left the circle on this errand. He came back, his confidence shaken.

This was his tale: He had worked his way, with some difficulty, through the crowd to Sontag and opened his mouth to speak to her. Suddenly she leaned forward, over his shoulder, to speak to someone standing behind him and said, "I'm really angry at Mailer!" Jack decided that this was not the right moment to introduce himself and retreated to the safety of our circle by the temple.

Not long after, the academic world recognized that Jack is a genius and he started getting academic teaching positions, which helped out with his finances considerably. We saw a lot less of him, and I missed him. Missed sitting at his feet listening to him read poetry aloud. Missed his warmth, intelligence, and kindness.

◊

For a while I taught science fiction writing in the summers. Jack came to visit my class in Cambridge. I told him that some of the students were intimidated, and weren't sure that they were up to being able to talk to him. He said, "Tell them I'm very conversant on the weather."

Afterwards, I drove him back to U. Mass Amherst with my son asleep in the carseat in the back. I talked to him about his writing habits, that getting up at 5 a.m. thing, and asked how that had worked for him as a parent.

I don't remember the phrasing exactly, but the question elicited a strong reaction, something about having fought a war with a toddler for control of his own attention. We had this conversation in the car, with baby Benjamin asleep in the back seat. Jack added, "I'm amazed that you can think and write at all with a small child."

We both had problems telling right from left. When we reached Amherst, we arrived at a strategy for navigation. When we came to a turn, Jack would say which way to turn and we would both point our fingers the direction we thought he meant. If our fingers agreed, we would turn that way. If they disagreed, we stopped to discuss it. We eventually got to his office, laughing a lot on the way.

◊

Jack still lived in the city part time. Still took in strays. George, a man he took in, disappeared and three weeks later Jack got a long letter, which made such an impression on Jack that he showed it to us. We had met George: he'd mostly stayed in the TV room watching cartoons, absentmindedly chewing his nails.

George's letter went something like this: He was walking down the street with another guy and they were headed for a 7-11 intending to get some cheap beer. "There was this guy coming the other way and he looked like sort of a wimp."

Then came the memorable line: "And so we robbed him." Then they continued on to the 7-11, shoplifted the beer, and when they came out, the cops were there to arrest them for robbing the wimpy kid. The wimp in question was apparently the DA's son, and so Jack's former house guest was in big trouble (and in jail).

We talked for a long time about what was contained in the chasm between those two sentences: "There was this guy coming the other way and he looked like sort of a wimp," and "And so we robbed him." The sentence "And so we robbed him" remained an object of contemplation for years afterwards.

◊

Last September, when Jack and I met for lunch, he was putting up a writer named Roland, who believed he was in contact with aliens. Roland came along to lunch. He had a black eye, and the bridge of his glasses was held together with medical tape.

Roland was eager to tell me his sad tale: He had had a successful career as a novelist. But then he began insisting that his novels were all completely true, that he wasn't making up any of it. This lead to a falling out with his publisher over the PR plans; he refused to allow his latest book to be sold as fiction.

Roland pulled the book from the publisher and had to pay back the six figure advance. He couldn't get anyone else to buy his book because he wanted it published as nonfiction.

He was now homeless. He and Jack had met in a restroom in Times Square.

Roland told me all this and more in a pressured, unending stream of words impossible to interrupt. Roland said he was taking Jack on a trip to the desert in order to prove that what he was saying was the absolute truth.

"The truth..." he said.

"Is out there," I said.

"Yes. Yes! It is!" he said and excused himself to go to the bathroom, I asked Jack if any of that was true. Jack nodded his head from side to side. He looked scared.

"He bites his fingernails," I said.

"We all have our fetishes."

When Roland returned, I asked about his black eye.

"It was Jack's friend Ray," he said.

The night before, Ray had come over. Roland had told him, author to author, of his published troubles, expecting sympathy and perhaps a loan. But Ray had made merciless fun of Roland.

Ray said that he, too, was in touch with aliens. And that his aliens said that Roland's aliens were the bad guys and were cruising the Galaxy in search of money. And if Roland had financial needs, perhaps they could help him out.

Roland said, "—and so I punched him." He stopped for a rare breath.

"And so . . . ?"

"And so he hit me back. And broke my glasses. And this is why we must make our trip to the desert. Jack needs to understand that I am telling the truth. We can't afford plane tickets, but I still have my car: I was living in my car on Riverside Drive before Jack took me in. We need a driver. My license is suspended, and Jack can't drive. Would you like to come?"

"That's kind of you . . . ."

"You have a signing at Barnes & Noble next week," said Jack. "And your classes start Monday."

◊

Jack disappeared. He was on sabbatical, so he didn't run afoul of his university. But after a couple of weeks, his daughter reported him missing. Once Jack's landlord learned of the missing persons report, he began eviction proceedings on the basis that Jack was no longer living there. Just before Christmas, I ran into Kierkegaard at a bookstore near Jack's apartment. He had heard this from Jack's daughter. We decided to drop in for a visit to see what was up.

As we started up the stairs, a black man and his little boy were coming down the stairs with a fluffy dog on a leash. We passed each other on the second floor and nodded. When we got to the third floor, we heard the boy exclaim, "Look, daddy! Santa Claus!" We looked down and there in the lobby was Jack in his red coat.

"He is risen," said Kierkegaard quietly. Jack waved. We waited there for him and then walked up the last to floor together.

"How was Arizona? I imagine you have quite the story to tell."

Jack said, "It's not just story. It's a whole novel. And not a word of it is true."

Hamlet's Ghost Sighted in Frontenac, KS

Vincent Czyz

Memory is a city piled along the flow of night, twinkling in the distance as it's carried downriver, lost in a heartland flooded black—a flat-out sprawl somewhere below the threshold of notice, waiting for a switch to be flicked on, a star to go nova.

Jim Lee on the event horizon, one of his nasty-smelling cigars between his teeth, out in the fields with his telescope magnifying circles of sky, never able to take it all in. Fedora, jeans with clip-on suspenders, scuffed-up cowboy boots, he looked like a cross between a rodeo rider and a Chicago hitman. Better than two hundred pounds though not that tall, he liked to give his gut a friendly slap. "Never know when you'll hafta be the anchor in a tug-a-war." His fleshy face was wide and his black hair sprouted without regard to direction, the fedora there to keep it corralled.

Jim Lee, who'd taken it upon himself to school Logan in everything from cheating at poker to pointing a telescope proper, had spent hours amidst water-stained UFO magazines and dime-store paperbacks (The Book That Shatters the Wall of Official Silence!), scouring photos of hubcaps thrown in the air and tinfoil-wrapped aliens for one that might be genuine.

Teacup to go with that saucer, Jim?

Jim Lee hemmed in by a stack of 45 singles, by empty beer cans and filmy glassware, by pillars of books he'd read and reread—the Bible everpresent among them—by rusted pieces of farm machinery and toy banks with mechanical cutesy ways of nabbing coins (a skeleton that sat up out of a coffin, scooped in a nickel with a bony hand), by Robby the Robot, made of that 1950s near-indestructible plastic, missing a green arm nonetheless, big as a small child, invading planet Earth, a takeover of Jim Lee's farmhouse kitchen the first step of the Master Plan.

One particular June night whose evening had floated a full moon over the fields, simmered it orange, bloated it near twice its normal size, Logan Blackfeather sat with Jim Lee among his collectible clutter listening to an antique radio with big knobs, its broad inanimate face framed in wood, glossy tube insides lit up by Spanish guitar music that for all Logan knew had circled the Earth half way before staining the Kansas night blue. The singer's voice a shade more sorrowful than his guitar, it made you feel you were on a street in an empty downtown, soaked to your boot soles by summer rain, then out the kitchen window they went, the blue Spanish voice and the weeping guitar, through the screen easy as a breeze, wandering like horse and rider over the dark fields, but there was nothing to echo off of, no place to rest, to keep them from dissipating at the speed of sound—the fate of all prayer however fervently chanted.

Logan was as lean as the Anglo side of his family, as dark-complected as his Hopi ancestors. Long-haired, taller than Jim Lee, and a good 17 years younger.

"I like your piana playin'," Jim Lee had said once as if to answer the unasked question of why he paid Logan as much mind as he did, as though Logan were an adolescent Mozart, composing a symphony were within his reach.

"Jim Thorpe's real name was Bright Path." Jimmy took a cold cigar stump out of his mouth to clear the way for words. "That's a good'un, ain't it?"

Bent over his work, his forehead glistening with sweat, he handled the razor with the expertise of a Japanese chef, separating tiny white heaps into lines, the blade edge-on nearly invisible between his thick fingers.

"An Oklahoma boy, Thorpe was. Wasn't born all that far from here."

The nights were hot that June, humid as the collective breath of all those weed-chewing insects outnumbering by thousands the stars over the fields.

"This here's the stuff that made the Incan empire what it is today." Jim Lee grinned. "Ruins." Snorted hard through a tightly rolled dollar bill, then handed over the hollowed greenery. "Gift to the white man from the Incan in return for abusing his women, knocking down his religion, and putting him on welfare."

Logan's nose burned, the familiar taste slid down the back of his throat like a color that wouldn't stick to the canvas. White as ground-up angel bones, a sparkle to it like radiance dried and fallen away, it fevered Logan's blood, numbed the sting at the back of his neck, where there was a welt roughened by an oozing scab. Keepsake from riding a paint that hadn't much cared to be ridden.

Larry had shaken his head. "Never saw that horse act up that way."

Logan wasn't much of a rider, just a little run around Larry's farm he'd been thinking, felt like a conquistador in the saddle, all that animal strength bunched up under him. Never saw what spooked the mare, but she took off so sudden he about lost a stirrup, caught a low branch across the face, then he was falling forward in the saddle as she took a steep dry creek bed. The sides of the horse pinched between his knees, his groin stiffening up from squeezing so hard, he thought for sure he was going to get spilled when they came to that falling-apart fence Larry had never cleared away, but the horse clean leaped it, then pulled up short—just like that—breathing hard, her heaving ribs pushing out his shaky legs, and a good thing he was sitting, he wouldn't've been able to stand.

The mare walked calmly back to the barn, all the fight gone out of her, but jumped again, unexpectedly, through a side doorway. Just blind instinct that he buried his face in her mane. The door jamb, big as a railroad tie, cracked the back of his head, scraped up his neck.

Larry came running up, a good scare still on his face. "You all right? Goddamn. Never seen 'er do that. You okay?" He shook his head. "Damn but I never seen 'er do that."

Weirdest thing was, when the machined edge of that lumber scraped against his skull, a hole wormed through the past, and he switched places with his dead father, whose head had shattered a windshield 12 years before.

Now the collar of Logan's shirt kept sticking, pulling free, bleeding again when he turned his head.

"How 'bout a little viewin'?"

Night in the old farmhouse just beginning to smolder, Jim Lee wanted to pull out his telescope though what he was prospecting the sky for was likely as nonexistent as his "oofoes."

Whether nuclear furnaces light years distant or poker chips on the table or apples in the grass, there's no divinity at work, Jim, just physics. They fell out that way is all, Logan wanted to tell him. You might as well send your Galileo-tube back to 16th-century Holland or wherever it came from.

But he didn't believe it'd been an accident or Providence that had killed his father, it'd been Uncle Cal, his father's only brother. Except how could Cal have done it? He was a mechanic, sure, but how could he have arranged for a drunk kid to ram into Logan's father's truck? Not to mention the kid killing himself in the same accident.

Something of a drunk himself, Cal had become a fixture around the house, like a couch that got dragged along no matter how many times the family moved into a new place. Why Cal? Why couldn't his mother have taken up with somebody else? Anybody else?

The living room became occupied territory, Cal sitting in front of the TV drinking beer, his eyes as still and concentrated as a snake's. Usually in a sleeveless T-shirt so you could see the skull grinning between a pair of outstretched wings tattooed on his left arm, the number 13 underneath the skull as if the 1 were a straight leg and the 3 a curlicue of a leg. One day Cal bent down and shoved that arm, bumpy with muscles—like rocks in a sack—in Logan's eight-year-old face. "Anglos think thirteen's unlucky. What the hell do they know?"

Two more dusty lines disappeared through tight-rolled legal tender before Jim Lee rounded up the last of the cocaine with a wet finger, stuck it in his mouth. "That'd put a little zing in yer toothpaste now wouldn't it?"

The screen door hissed closed behind them.

There was a kind of sanctity in the Kansas sky, clear and deep, constellations invisibly hung like bright mobiles.

The streetlamp at the foot of Jim Lee's yard attracted all manner of insects, a cloud of wingbeats like a swarm of thoughts with no skull to pen them in, moths bumping against the glass sealing them off from a mercury-vapor heaven. Bats flapped after them in strobe-light movements, swooping swerving veering off with uncanny precision.

Jim Lee looked up at the bright lure. "The quantity a motion here an' everywhere else is as never-changing as Superman's uniform—if Descartes is to be believed. But the soul can alter direction some. Will makes a difference."

"All we gotta do is wish, huh?"

"Does seem to be a flaw in theory somewhere. But ain't it possible a destination in mind up there—" Jim Lee lifted his chin. "—becomes a fate down here?"

Parked underneath the light, Jim Lee's truck was a yellow somewhere between banana and bumblebee, The Hog painted in fancy script on a bug-shield peppered with kills.

Streetlamps spaced half a mile apart marked the way to town.

Jim Lee reached down, turned a Country Western tune up loud. Just as the song ended, the truck jerked to a stop, and Jim Lee yanked the emergency brake.

The Round-Up was already filled with body heat, with walled-in smoke and idle conversation no more intelligible than a flock of chittering birds. What with the music, Logan could barely hear his own boots clumping on the wooden floor.

"Whaddaya say Jim Lee...?"

Hands reached out to slap the broad back Y-ed over by suspenders. Logan a couple steps behind, always at Jim's heels, out of high school but still three years away from the 21 you needed to be to drink anything harder than wine or beer.

Larry behind the bar and behind him black-and-whites of the town at the turn of the century, of him during his rodeo days, #27 plastered on his back, the bull's ass six feet in the air in one.

"How's the neck feelin'?" Larry's big hand, gloved in the old days before he shoved it under rope wound around the bull's chest and humped back, came over the bar and squeezed Logan's. Rough as a grindstone.

"'S'alright." Instinctively Logan put two fingers to the swelling under his collar, the scab still bloodying his shirt.

Jim Lee leaned over the bar. "Nothin wrong with him a beer won't fix."

Larry popped open a couple of bottles, shook his head. "Jesus God, lucky you ducked when you did."

Jim Lee held the bottle up to the hazy light. "A cold beer is like a scrambled egg—you can't beat it."

Logan's head was full of coke and the woodgrain patterns under his bottle, Jim Lee talking nonstop to him, to Larry, yelling down to the guys a few stools away, already motioning for another beer.

Larry switched the empty for a fresh bottle, the shine dulled by a film of cold sweat.

Don Moody, a third-year law student, was leaning against the wall, posed like some movie-poster icon. "Who do I luck lack?"

"Truman Capote. Now get over here an' pick up a round."

Age notwithstanding, Logan lifted a tumbler, bottom soaked in a little puddle of sour mash that Larry's rag would sop up in a swipe, touched rims with Jim Lee and Don and Larry. The whiskey burned going down, the fumes cleared his nose.

Broncobuster, bullrider, Larry could've handled that mare even without a saddle. He had scars under his T-shirt from the time a bull had walked all over him, stomped him good, nobody expected him to be breathing after that, much less back behind a muscled hump in a year's time. Wasn't any riled bull or even a bucking stallion that had clipped Logan's head, was a broken-in mare. He'd seen a bunch of Cherokees in Oklahoma, too lazy to go through the hoo-ha of putting on saddles, gallop past him as though he were whiter than the Anglos standing next to him.

"How was Mexico, bud?" Don with that baby face of his that was never going to grow much of a beard, round as the spare tire around his waist, no good for hula-hooping but jiggled all right if Don took off at a run. "They got pyramids like they say?"

Grander than anything in Kansas, built by his distant cousins long before that mixed-up Italian with a Ptolemaic map as misconceived as his Atlantic Ocean crossing was even born.

Billy Boy shouldered between Logan and Don. Thick hair greased back, Elvis Presley sideburns he ought to have shaved off, he kept a plastic comb in a T-shirt pocket. Black on his fingers where engine gunk had settled into tiny cracks in skin, Billy looked at Logan with glossy pupils as big as hubcaps.

He was saying something, but Logan's head was bouncing to jukebox music. Fueled by powdered angel bones, alcohol mist settling over his better judgment the way clouds could gang up and blur the Moon, he knew he could do better, just wouldn't make it to any radio station in Frontenac. The over-and-over beat was background for Don wishing for grazing rights to the grand majority of women who walked by, Jim Lee's open-mouthed laughter, Billy Boy's out-loud figuring a system to hit the lottery.

"Ah'm tired a standin' on concrete ten hours a day, breathin' in exhaust an' comin' out smellin' like a grease pit." Billy slowed down enough for a sip from his bottle.

Logan wasn't listening any more. The midnight freight he'd been riding had slowed suddenly, brakes shaving a squeal off the metal they were pressed against, curled in his ear while his body took on the weight the engine had been hauling. Suddenly he was afraid the legs of his stool were about to splinter and he was going to go through the floorboards ass-first.

Larry waved him and Jim Lee behind the bar, hustled them to the back room he used as an office. Jim Lee pushed aside receipts, bills, letters, invoices, cleared a corner of Larry's 1940s desk stolen from the office of some movie private eye. Pulling out his razor, Jim Lee sliced lines like clean white scars on the desktop, a couple of them snapping Larry's head back like twin jabs from a boxer. Hoo-ee. He shook his head once—quick as a twitch—sniffed, wiped at his nose, and then the rag in his back pocket was flapping up and down as he hurried out to tend bar.

Jim handed Logan the rolled-up dollar bill. "Oughta keep you up for a while."

Logan pushed open the door to the bar. Voices, music, bad lighting, nodding heads, smiling faces all came together, fused like the tiny continents of bone that make up a skull—a fugue waiting to be composed, one that would take in even the wispy fleeting shapes the smoke wove itself into. He couldn't have been as almighty as he felt though, because Jim Lee's arms made his look skinny and smooth, were a wake-up call, a hey-hello—wasn't only his arms that needed work.

Friday night in southeastern Kansas. No hills to speak of, no lakes thereabouts, just strip-mine pits filled up by rain, the ocean a long haul as it happened, and Chicago a good nine hours' drive. Things showed up newer on the broad boulevards of the city, phrases like freshly-minted coins, the shine already gone by the time they reached the callused hands of awkward farm boys, talked about while beer labels worked on by nails chewed to nubs came away in sticky little balls dropped into ashtrays crowded with cigarette butts.

Jim Lee dragged on his gnarled cigar, adding to the smoke softening the pinball machine's yellow flashes, a kid across the room leaning into the flippers as if the shiny ball were tracing out his fate in its pinging odyssey.

Why not see how high the smoke went? Snort it, shoot it, pop it, climb a mountain, add a few stories to that skyscraper, aim a hollow arrow through a tube of gravity, send a dog, a monkey, a man to penetrate the starry mysteries that only come out at night, when it's dark enough to see what's melted in the white-hot glow, what's trapped in a miraculous net of bone and sinew. They were a bunch of cast-outs, wing-broke and unhaloed, trying to return to some forever-breaking dawn. Same as the moth willing to die for its immortal moment immolated. Combustible wings. Fluttering against the skull's dome webbed with cracks, calcified, its skylight sealed-up, lacquered with consciousness like an oyster shell smoothed with nacre. Everything in it turned to ash in the short-circuit where old lumber and vulnerable bone had collided.

"You know, this two-door town parked in the middle a nowhere had its heyday once." Jim Lee's eyes turned to slits above his smoldering cigar. "Used to get men of ill repute from Chicago, St. Louis, Kansas City, once in a great while even a black-sedan-turned-gray by the dust of half the Midwest, but you could still see the New York plates when it pulled up in front of our very own pool hall." He jerked his thumb over his shoulder. "Right across the street. Stobart's. Boarded up now, but Sto's used t'hop, back then—a bit before I was a regular."

Look close enough at Jim Lee's eyes alight with the bygone, awash with beer, you might see in the dark irises tiny twins of Stobart's Pool Hall just as he remembered it.

"Used to come from all over..." Jimmy Lee's hand circled over the bar like a bird about to set down. "Right here." His finger whitened at the tip where he pressed on the bar.

Jim Lee, a freckled kid on the black-and-white streets of yesteryears, a cigarette sticking out of the corner of his mouth, a pack rolled in a T-sleeve. Then at 17 leaning on his cue stick, freckles about gone, a white guinea-tee showing a weightlifter's arms, not too arrogant to smile. A Lone Star in the other hand, fingers pressing a smoldering butt to the cold-sweating can.

Theme and variation. How many other teenagers looked just like him? Even went to Joplin and got tattooed. Smoked the same brand of cigarettes and drank the same beer in Stobart's.

"Those days I was so cool when I stepped outside, temperature dropped." His cigar a cold cinder, he looked at what was left as if he were missing something. "Left home sweet home to become one of Uncle Sam's Misguided Children—Yoo, Ess, Em, Cee. Fer the free scuba lessons. Damn near broke an eardrum." He tipped his bottle all the way up. "A dive as outta this world as a moonwalk. You can go down in the same spot two, three days in a row an' it's new an' unfamiliar every day." Jim Lee aimed an index finger at Logan's chest. "You'da never come up."

Jim Lee down there in the water-dark, sinking and lost, following the beam of his flashlight, eyes peeled just in case those rumors about a sunken civilization were true. His undersea excavations maybe after a way to be that buoyant all the time, that wonderstruck, that close to the sound of his own breathing, to the ocean's breath sweeping things along, making kelp forests wave like the hair of Old Man Ocean long forgotten, topside temples gone to ruin, a pagan god half-buried face-down in the sand now, too at ease ever to move again, a natural formation on the bottom giving off a little greenish smolder in the sea night, a smidgen of glow maybe what caught Jim Lee's eye as he wove through those kelp strands—why'd he come back to Frontenac? The only waves here were in the lapping woodgrain patterns on the bar.

Yes, a kind of motion, as if the wood were breathing.

"Hey buddy, what're you starin' at so hard?"

The woodgrain pattern shifting, trembling under Logan's fingertips, the vibrato of mothwings.

"You don't wanna know." Jim Lee squeezed his eyes closed, massaged his wrinkled brow.

Somebody tugged on Jim Lee's suspenders on his way out.

"Awright, awright, g'bye." Jim Lee adjusted his suspenders with a thumb under each. "Can't unnerstand why they gotta mess with a man's apparel."

A little later, Jim Lee's head bowed, his back slumped like he was feeling the weight of those oversized volumes he read, or maybe it was his gone-from-the-earth mother, a slow leaving, cancer of some kind, maybe that's what made him look old and worn, defeated, all three.

"I drink ..." Jim Lee lifted his bottle. "...therefore I am."

Was that all he'd managed to distill from his dusty stacks of books, an old joke? Was that all that'd come of sitting up late amidst the holy clutter of his collectibles, pouring out whiskey meditations on William Blake, wrestling with the sometimes insufferable, often impenetrable verses of the Bible by candlelight and cigar glow till sleep slipped up behind him, left him face-down on the table beside a hardened puddle of wax?

"They toll me philosophy'd help me pass the L-SAT, the logic an' all, but I don't hardly remember none of it."

"Logic leads t'Aristotle, not t'God." Jim Lee finished off what was in his bottle. "Plato wiped his ass with it."

Don waved a hand. "Heard he was a fag."

Jimmy grinned. "You couldn't be a waiter in Aristotle's Diner."

"Shit." Don shook his head. "Philosophy about as good as forchin tellin'...."

Who to look for in the insect buzz around a streetlamp? In the smoke-swirl conversations around them? Descartes? Or a higher-up?

"You ever been to one a those prayer meetings?" Don pointed at

Logan with his bottle. "One with snakes? Those hillbillies pick up handfuls a the poisonous suckers at a time, never get bit. Straighten 'em out like a fistful a arrows, stand 'em up like shocked hair."

Jim Lee shrugged. "Whaddya expect a farmers who drink their corn?"

"They thank thay're saints from the Babble. Reincar-nayted or somethin.'"

Not reincarnated, Logan thought, something different, the soul a song composed of a certain number of elements already there in the ancient Sumerians and their drumbeat songs, reshuffled over the centuries till you got a Kansas farmboy blowing his harmonica blues. Old as the hills in Oklahoma. No one ever really comes back, it's all odds, theme and variation, some things that look like others are bound to show up.

"You and Jim Lee read too many bucks, I can't hardly keep up with you."

Did Logan say that out loud? Or was Don reading minds?

"The Lord works in mysterious ways all right." Billy nodded confidently. "The night old Stobart died of a heart attack I dreamed he was drowning and was callin' out for help."

Why had there been no owl screech, no ominous dream, no fire alarm, no fire-colored moon in the sky the night his father had died? Logan had gone on sleeping, the mellow rhythm of his breathing unbroken while his father crossed that yawning gulf alone.

The death of his father should have been like the lowering of another world. He should have sensed that the sky had been swallowed, should have felt that second world settling like another night. Its magnetic poles should have pricked up the hairs on the back of his neck, made them stiff as cactus needles. The added gravity should have squeezed the breath out of him, pressed against his dreaming as though sinking into mud, tracking itself, leaving scarred terrain as proof of the casual forces loose in the world—which had collided at an intersection where two trucks had mangled themselves as if one of them had expected to win. Their shiny grills like sets of teeth caught, the two trucks had stopped dead trying to take a hunk out of one another. No witnesses, both drivers killed, both drunk, police had never ruled on who'd run the signal.

Twelve years later Logan hadn't let go. Fingers bent with gripping, cramped and tangled in horsehair, holding on to the bristling mane of night. Veins rippled across taut skin. Mane of the constellation Horse. Bright pain as the windows of the skull fog with frost.

It had been a car accident. Cal was a mechanic. But...how?

The amount of motion in the universe constant, only direction changes, is affected by will, acted on by the soul's desire. Is that how he did it? By wishing for it? By deep-felt belief?

And what is that whisper running along the bone like a breathy prayer rounding the dome of St. Pauls? His father's voice? Prodding his conscience?

Jim Lee looking around the room, sifting the haze of voices and exhausted cigarettes as if waiting in some dust-infested corner were the very thing he'd been scouring the sky for with his tripodded magnifying glass. Sitting there as though it might sidle up next to him, take a seat on one of Larry's stools (electrical tape covering a split in the leather), maybe he was waiting for a vision to visit. Weren't they all? A moment different from any other that would make sense of every other? That would make this long night of disappointment breathable, bearable? Why else look over at the door every time it opened? Jim Lee, who'd seen the submerged bottom of the world, stared forlornly at the unplugged jukebox.

Caught in the night's undertow, his flashlight lost, something of the cool shadows cast among tombstones in his eyes, Jim Lee—Logan would've bet—wanted to ask something of the dead, possessed of oracular knowledge as they were rumored to be, having circumnavigated this side and that, seen the darkest of places, what he wanted to know—his ass half hanging off the stool—was why he could blow things up two or three times lifesize but not see any clearer. Was how to keep night after night from etching unwanted tattoos on memory's skin. How it could be he was looking out on things and still wondering about the order to put them in: does death really come before dishonor (the price of those free scuba lessons)? And if forced to choose, would it be another line of poetry or a line of coke? A little sky scanning or another gander from his stool outpost at the sweaty faces and smoky voices? Where exactly was he supposed to be standing (or sitting) in relation to everything else? Deep-sea diver into the early morning hours, what was all that down there on the unlit end of the ocean floor? And what have we got here on the gritty floorboards we've never noticed by day? Light chases the mystery outta things, though pure darkness makes the exact whereabouts a your hand in front of your face fairly enigmatic. A Beethoven symphony or the insects in the fields with their endless nightchant? The Epic of Gilgamesh or another excursion to one of Frontenac's titty bars? A little more living or a peek at the secrets of the dead?

That is the question.

Each Star a Sun to Invisible Planets

Tenea D. Johnson

For the moment, William had forgotten, and in forgetting an ephemeral, disjointed peace alighted upon him. He allowed himself to savor it. The sun warmed his upturned face as he lay on a secluded hillside, surrounded by purplish-pink flowers. He didn't see another person. So he could not ask anyone where, exactly, he found himself. It felt like midday, and the sun's position overhead confirmed this. William left it at that: he was out in the afternoon. Behind the curiosity, he sensed relief in the space knowing had left behind. It was enough that it was beautiful outside and he, alone. A gentle wind blew up the length and across the girth of him, pausing as it traveled to collect its breath to finish the journey. He stretched his long limbs, savoring the sensation of the great columns of muscle reaching their limits. Through the thin fabric of his pocket, he felt a small, hard rectangle slide across his thigh. Yawning, William shoved a calloused hand into his pocket to pull out the surprise.

He recalled that he enjoyed this game of discovering himself from the things he carried.

When he wrenched his hand free and opened his palm, he found an ancient datacorder resting in the expanse between his faint life and love lines. He recognized it immediately and cleared his throat. William's rich bass activated its sensor. With a click, it, and he, came to life.

He spoke. "This is the fourth, no, the fifth datacorder I've had. The others are...full, also hidden." William took a long pause, searching his mind for more. What else should he say? He stared at the thing in his palm and concentrated.

"I traded for this one, on the way through...middle Tennessee... from a man...on a broken bridge contemplating a quick, wet end. He stood, staring at the water, at the end of a beautiful road. I discovered him because the pathway had pulled me in. Bright pumpkin, cherry red, a gold like tarnished quincentennial coins: those leaves. They framed the trail and it looked like I'd stepped inside a painting of the last bend before home on the prettiest day in autumn. I'd been walking eleven, maybe twelve years by then. I usually trekked in the dark. People took too much notice of my size otherwise. It made them want to talk to me, to ask questions. So my world was night, layers of dark, shadow, and pall.

With the...*bombings?* Yesss, the bombings...and the round-ups, places like that path spread farther apart every day. Peaceful places are always precious, I guess."

William let his gaze wander, begin to drift away. With an effort, he roused himself.

"Out in the country, when I saw people, they were usually huddled around lean-tos. They dotted the toxic sites and other abandoned places folks ran to when the gene corps came searching—" He paused, wondering what they were searching for. It eluded him.

"Because of the skull plate jutting out from his forehead and the dirty film on his camoed skin, I could tell the man on the bridge had gone AWOL from the corps. Like the rest of them, his adaptations were post-pubescent and work-specific, not genetic, therefore aching, foreign, and often fleeting. Not worth the pain, but the corporate reps didn't tell recruits that when they signed up, and seeing as they were recruits mostly because they wanted to eat it wouldn't have mattered. Still, back then, the gene corps had a high turnover rate. Often the heart rejected what the body did not.

"And so it must have been with him. He must have caught a case of conscience, and it had led him to that spot. He couldn't continue in his duties, or perhaps at all, so his former employer had no use for him. They paid the gene corps not to care how many suffered or died in their quest for...for...manufactured...immortality. Yes, they were searching for a single set of DNA that had become legend. That they had been sent as a provocation."

Flashes of queues and refugee camps overwhelmed William's inner eye. He saw poor brown people rounded up for DNA tests: DNA tests for job applications, DNA tests for medical care, for food, for oxygen on days when smog obscured the sunrise. And when they wouldn't submit willingly: hair ripped from scalps, skin from flesh, stomachs emptied of their meager contents with well-placed blows.

William rubbed his eyes and ran a hand over his bare skull. He continued, shaken.

"Legendarily stupid, perhaps, to have shown the media that biogenetic adaptations could produce such longevity. There must have been a better way to subvert the system. The sample didn't give the downtrodden *hope*; it dimmed what little they possessed. The genetic corporations just created new rules to root out the exceptional. Sending that self-degrading culture of DNA sharpened their tactics—and our culture kept degrading. Lesson learned. Long life does *not* confer wisdom."

William stopped. His breathing slowed, and a sliver of melancholy worked itself into his chest. *Oh.* He licked his lips and began again. Now his story, this history bubbled up in a rush, but he let each word settle before he moved on to the next.

"Rosedale; Base Brush; Doubtful Sound: these are the disappearing places. First from the world, then my mind, and finally, gone. Once they were of my world, errant stars born to burn bright and fall forever. The world grows darker with their absence. Even their names are a secret only I seem to have kept."

William's head sunk to the side, his vision obscured by stalks.

"I've been to *dozens* of places that never officially existed. Those places were pillaged, plundered, and bulldozed into open patches of land. I still go back, checking for those hidden well enough to be saved. I'm not the only one. But just as quickly as gathering spots for the exceptional sprout, they're harvested. The privileged value those people, or rather their components, too much for the gene corps to leave them be. As always, some remain tools, like the man who I traded a handful of open-pollinated seeds for this datacorder.

"Even now, an incredible proliferation of human genetic diversity thrives, just hidden from view. Back then, it was as wild as the seeds it's illegal to keep. Mandatory gene registration didn't exist, and no one had thought of variable DNA exchange rates on mortgages. We had more choices. In that, we were rich and unique in global genomic economics. We were free on a mitigated basis.

"But that's just a memory now, and after 157 years, the gene corps keeps searching. They haven't found me."

William straightened his neck, looked up into the blue of the sky.

"If they did, they wouldn't have what they're looking for. Immortality is a myth and I am but a legend. I've seen too many wasted and too little change to believe anything else. Death is a wilderness on a moonless night. One day I will find myself there."

William looked out at the great mound of live-forevers that covered the hillside he'd chosen to store his bank of heirloom seeds. It lay a day's hike from anywhere even moderately populated, on a reclaimed ridge of ash overflow. It made for a beautiful place to take a nap, which William did often, near the bottom of the hill, his huge form hidden in the blossoms to everyone but the birds overhead. He knew because he'd walked the perimeter before he lay down, gathered his jacket under his head and stretched out. He'd done this just before he'd fallen asleep and forgotten himself.

Though clear now, when he woke it had been as if those moments never existed.

Was he succumbing to dementia? Or an unavoidable madness

born of his accumulated sorrows and the pure, relentless press of time stacked up over the years? He couldn't be sure. Perhaps he had witnessed extinctions only to prepare for his own long walk into the wilderness.

For now, William had conjured himself back into the center of things. Again. He closed his eyes and tried to remember the feel of oblivion. How many times had he done so?

Behind his closed lids, subtle flashes of light floated by. He wanted to wander away with them. These days, sleep came when it fancied, and judging by the last few months it had lost its fascination with William Woods. If only the world would, he thought, as he traveled up from the depths of his reverie to listen to the bird calls, the squirrels scurrying and, deeper still, to anything those sounds might have masked.

Clones

Alex Smith

1.

A bud; a piece of green peeking through the craggy rock, barely noticeable and caked with dust; that's what it was. He went out in a pressurized space suit, leapt from the ledge and descended the twenty stories down the ship dock and into the black of the atmosphere. When he touched the still budding leaf he had to watch it wither and flake, shrivel and die, almost evaporate and fall in a cascade of leafy ash to the ground. The LCD screen in his helmet lit up and buzzed, calculated in green typeface. Warnings and notices sounded off as voices intoned in monotonous British accents—"4% pressure drop in elbow region"; "Planetoid has 48% capacity for sustaining human life" ; "Radiation levels spiking at 0.22 curie per 100 seconds".

He scraped the remnants into a thin flask, zipped it away in one of the many compartments on his suit, bounded back over the dusty rock and made his way back up the ship's shaft. He had forgotten the code and had to manually override the security lock, which was always tricky because sometimes the sensor didn't recognize his voice pattern. He had to change the timbre of his voice slightly, this time a low bellow, and then, with a whir and click, the hatch would release air and open and he'd be back inside, faced off with sprawling air ducts and computers, walls lined with synthetic mesh that seemed to snake and breathe organically around him.

In the lab, he placed the flask into a chute and watched as the walls lit up, a display vibrant and inundated with chaotic numbers and holograms. A screen crackled and a man's worn face slowly emerged.

"Zyrn Altor. Codenamed X34-i7. What have you to report?"

"Specimen found, sir. Akin to the common house fern. It—it dissolved upon contact, sir."

"Dissolved?"

"Yes. I think a change in atmospheric pressure caused by the landing mechanism created a—"

"X34-i7. Thank you for your report. We will speak to your

superiors about your recent failure."

"Sir?"

"Remember your objective, X34-i7."

And the face on the screen cracked again, a sharp blast of photons firing off from a distant satellite, exiting back into the tangle of the cosmos. He sat staring at the walls for a while, as they morphed, spinning tendrils twisting around each other, at once mechanical and alive. The objective, he thought. In his spartan quarters, he lay on his back and watched replays of his past missions as they danced across the ceiling, flickering bursts of images; a dance in the outer rim of an uninhabitable forest; a time where he fell and nearly drowned in a pool of liquid crystal. Each time, they'd come and pull him out of the mire, their black hands wrapped around him in a clone cocoon; they'd plug him into the machines, coat his body with synthesized aloe. He'd watch his wounds heal. Slowly, those scars would merge into themselves, frayed bits of flesh closing before his eyes. Those black clones, lithe and multitudinous, nearly naked except for their underpants covering the area where their manhood would be, and except for their long flowing capes adorned with hieroglypic codes traced in wiry tinsel and gold. Each time he fell, they'd plug him into the machine and he'd be good as new. The objective, he thought again watching it all unfold; the objective was to harvest the clones, to find worlds habitable for mankind, to search the stars, alone, to hear a dream as it etched itself in the chromasphere, to grab that dream and on a suitable orb, plant it, watch it grow.

A.

It seemed the universe filled itself with a mass of gorgeous white boys, that it never tired of an endless parade of shirtless studs to fill the walls of its discos, and that these boys would be there to defend it from the cosmic force of some demigod birthed from a hot, angry star. They peopled TRINITY that night in overwhelming droves. Just milky white chests and blue jeans from bar to bathroom to dj booth, every inch of the dancefloor. So, Henry Sims sat quiet on the far corner of the bar, drinking vodka shots, staring one minute at the Cubs game on the screen, then at another screen playing soundless music videos by Robyn or George Michael, then at the other screen that flashed captures of scenes from twink or muscle porn. Then, less occasionally, he'd swivel on his barstool and peek at the dance floor, watching the hoard of men coagulate, moving to that music as one sweaty, undulating mass.

And then he saw him; a boy of velvet pouring himself over the white sea. He was a purple wire in there, connecting his body to beats

Henry hadn't even noticed were there. A tambourine hit or a tripping snare wound itself out of the amplifiers like a siren, and there was that boy in sync with it. A wave of embarrassment crested over Henry's pale face; he sat mesmerized, feeling the warm blood rush up and fill his cheeks, felt it peeking through his prickly red beard.

The drums stopped and the synths swelled, rising into a deep caterwaul; the velvet boy, his chest heaving, his skin like a black talisman lost in the snow, stopped on a dime and waved his arms with the sway of rhythmless sounds. Each time the bass and cymbals crashed in single hits, the boy would contort his body with it and stare over the crowd with a refined fierceness. On the third hit he was staring Henry Sims right in the eyes.

Henry almost dropped his shot glass, almost fell off of his stool. "Great," he thought. "This African god just caught my fat ass staring at him and he's going to tell all of his friends and I gotta get the hell out of here laughingstockofthegaybarclonesurrealwheresthebathroomlovehim"

In the bathroom, Henry splashed his face and let the water run, let it kiss the sink in its soft gentle pour. He buried his hands in his face and breathed deeply, planning his exit, but then a gaggle of men burst in, laughing and dizzily spinning over the sinks and fondling each other. One of them grabbed Henry's breast and screamed, they all laughed, switching conversational topics with ease, as if Henry's tit being grabbed was a mere afterthought. Henry slowly eased past them, back into the hallway. He leaned against the wall and gathered himself before launching back into the club that was again twisting to the merciless crunch of house music. He pushed away the throng of them all, avoided spilling drinks as deftly as he could, reached the door and, nodding at the bouncers, ducked out of the door and onto the street.

The air outside was crisper, a refreshing spray of April breeze tickling at his flesh. He pulled his Harrington jacket a little tighter. The street was alive with drag queens and leather daddies and kids voguing in knock-off Yves St. Laurent, punks with spikey pink hair and Camaros with their trunks rattling under the weight of anthemic bass. Henry kept his eyes trained on the misshapen sidewalk, at the crack vials and used condom wrappers crackling under his Doc Martens. He was busy thinking about nothing, letting the wild night's conversations slip over and through him, so much so that he'd walked a bit past his bus stop and had turned to go back when he saw the boy of velvet standing in front of TRINITY, under an awning, patting his pockets, shaking nervously, his muscles rippling out of his thin green shirt. He looked like a shadow. When the boy found his pack of cigarettes, he cursed to himself that he'd lost his lighter. A kind of ghostly sadness crept over Henry when he saw the boy standing there without a light, and this sadness grew as he watched wave after wave of clubgoers pass the boy, and though the boy'd ask, none of them had a light for him. Henry quickly patted himself, but remembered he'd stopped smoking a year ago.

Soon, two men exiting the club found the boy; one of them was porcelain white, hair a blonde waft of sun, ripped directly from an Abercrombie catalog. The other was much shorter, possibly Asian, thinner and kind of golden, his face almost angular. This one laughed villainously, the blonde giggled and slapped the arm of the boy (his boy, his black velvet boy), who gave up an insincere smile. The two pulled his arm and they went across the street, only two shop fronts away from Henry. The three ducked into a 24-hour porn shop with an air of clandestine, giddy excitement.

A drop of rain dotted Henry's forehead. He stood staring at the doorway to the porn shop as more men traipsed in, then out, in, then out, all of them inconspicuously pulling their hats down as they entered, popping their jacket collars as they exited. "It's gonna rain," he thought, shuffling his feet. Behind him down the street, the rust orange lights of an oncoming bus peeped over the horizon. His route number sorta floated, disembodied letters and numbers, a sigil he'd conjured, looming toward him. His heart raced as he rung his thick sweaty hands, nervously shaking. He welled up some courage and took the five steps toward the porn shop and walked in.

An alarm buzzed loudly and announced his presence.

"Hey, handsome," the old man behind the counter said. He realized this was the first time tonight another man had acknowledge his presence. He could feel the clerk's eyes following him a bit as he made his way around the stacks. Henry tried to keep his gaze forward, not glancing at any of the other patrons; lawyers and doctors and politicians in business suits casually edging their way to the gay porn section. Junkies and homeless men trying to carve out space in the bondage section. Know-it-all college kids in baggy cargos and black trench coats nervously, loudly laughing at sex toys. No sign of the velvet boy or his friends.

There was a back room that was shielded only by a curtain. Henry peeled back this curtain to an eruption of moans.

"It's five dollars for the back room!" A man even more curmudgeonly than the outside clerk was smoking a cigar and snarling at him. Henry scanned the dungeonous room as best he could. It was pitch black and men moved like shadows in there. A door would open and the glow from a monitor would temporarily illuminate the place. Men were leading other men into the booths by the hand, lust in their eyes. He paid the clerk and slowly stepped in, bumping into lumps of bodies, feeling hands grab his. He stood against the wall for five nerve-racking minutes. Then, he felt the wiry hands of a man make their way over his body, not in a lustful way, but it a way that felt...concerned? That felt not like the terror and angst of desperation, but like the tender and deliberate act of exploration. When the hands pulled at him, tore him away from the wall, he stumbled a bit and fell into the guy. Ripe muscles, the smell of jasmine and cinnamon and wine. He moved his hand up the man's body and it reacted to the touch. "Mmm...hot daddy," the man whispered, kissing his ear. Then a door opened and light sparked onto their faces. He was looking at the face of the velvet boy, inches away from his own; here, in the pale blue glow of the porn booth monitors, he could see that there was no boy, that in fact he was a man, chiseled out of a monolithic slab of the stuff of his dreams.

"Marcus?" asked one of the men trailing out of the open booth. The small Asian guy. He was holding the hand of the white Abercrombie guy who was trying to buckle his pants with his other hand. "Girl, you are a mess."

"What?" Marcus asked in an annoyed whisper.

"Girl, we know you like bears, but have some kind of standards."

"Oh, Curtis, can we not start this here?" Marcus turned towards Henry and slipped him a piece of paper, smiled, kissed his forehead, and turned back toward his friend. "I've been putting up with your crap all night, I went to that stupid circuit party, let me have—"

"Bitch, let's go," Curtis said, pulled his Abercrombie model behind him, and led the three of them back through the curtain. Marcus looked back but Henry had faded into a corner, shaking with nerves, with shame. After the three of them had been gone awhile, Henry opened the door to one of the booths and sat in it. A voice came on over the intercom. "If you're gonna sit in the booth, you have to pay for it!" So Henry put a quarter into the slot and the screen filled up with images of a soccer team having an orgy. He felt for the card Marcus had given him. Marcus's name and phone number were on it. He flipped it over and in a fancy cursive font that was gun-metal grey stood the words TRINITY.

2.

Zyrn was asked to read the daily cybercodes at hyperspeed. He was asked to gather specimens on distant planets, to peruse light gardens and shuffle between nebulae; to walk on moons covered in silk worm birth and cosmic husk. Zyrn was asked to brush the sides of radioactive abandoned freighters orbiting Jupiter, scraping ark dust off of monoliths.

Zyrn was asked to load barrels of xinilium and milohondrinate, put the barrels in chutes and watch them disappear into black holes. Zyrn would stare at black holes on the radar screen for minutes at a time, drifting in and out of consciousness, letting the green lines, swirling like a hurricane on a Doppler, spread out and increase their wavy length, watch them burn swaths across the board, watch them black out whole solar systems in a spiral dance of consumption.

He was hooked up to nano-machines. He was scraping film off the tapetum lucidum of small, mammalian beings on lush alien planets. Once he shucked his space suit and danced on a planet that was vibrant and conquered by rabid growth. He lay in a bed of prickly grass and let the leaves lick at him. They were tactile and the more he squirmed the more they traced the length of his body until their movement became a pitched battering. He slid down a thin patch of mud and fell into a substance that was like pollen. He sneezed and thrashed about, trying to get free, finally pulling himself onto a patch of dry grass. He touched one of the dials embedded in his wrist. A hologram hovered over it. The same craggy old face appeared before him.

"Well?"

"I've found a planet suitable for habitation."

"Put it in your report."

And the image flickered away.

Zyrn was hosed down in the decontamination bay. He was led by spindly robot hands into a dark corridor of his ship, past the collection of used containment flasks he'd made into a small fort, past the cafeteria and food synthesizers, past the green house and the algae garden with its swirling pools, springs bursting forth with artificially grown life, past the corridors lined with tendrils and scanners that prodded him like a specimen.

"Fuck, cut it out!" he yelled, and they'd retract, almost as if they were intelligent, able to respond to his command. "Gotta fix these fucking things."

When he reached his destination, he spread-eagled and was lifted onto two conversely spinning wheels, a Vitruvian Man, suspended in the air. More dials appeared at his joints—harsh metal orifices they were, and yet more tendrils lanced into the dials, twisting and connecting as he spun.

One of the dark men walked into the room, his skin like firelit ash, his forehead brandishing the number three. He was carrying a flat, thin metal sheet that glowed. He cautiously tapped at it, looking from Zyrn to his tablet, then to a monitor across the room.

"This is really awkward," Zyrn said nervously. "I mean, you guys are just kind of like, unthinking robots, moving around here—well, I guess more like androids, huh? Is that what you guys are called? Guess I can't call you clones, even though you all come from the same genetic goop this Geodyne has been using for years, huh?"

The man said nothing. He continued to type.

"I get it, you're doing the clone thing." Zyrn breathed a deep sigh as the wheels slowed their spinning, the tendrils slowly retracted. "I just wished to hell that I could have landed a job working with, like, you know...real people? Having to look at you freaks all the time is getting pret-ty old, you know? I mean, your make-up is so delicate I'm not even sure—"

Two more of them walked in, seemingly gliding across the ship's floor. They all looked exactly alike, moved exactly alike; when two more walked in, carrying pads, their long, drapey capes lapping behind them, it almost made Zyrn nauseous. He had had enough for the day and ripped out the final tendrils, got down off of the wheel and pushed pass the clones, not lifting his eyes toward any of them, feeling their eyes train on him like lasers.

"Ah," he said out loud. "I see the problem." He was in the incubation chamber where the clones slept, sealed in metal pods filled with an embalming liquid. "Your nutrient bath is contaminated." He pulled a metal rod out of one of his cargo pockets and inserted it into a dial on the outside of one of the tanks. Pressing a button, a code, then removing the rod. "Right. 65.8% vitality level, no sign of trace radiation, no viral contamination. The vitamin extraction is a little low, calcium a little high. Guess I can get in there and clean out the tank tomorrow. But otherwise..." he paused, looked around him. The clones were asleep, floating, their eyes rolling very slightly under their lids. He put his face up close to one of the tanks and said, in a low husky voice, "...otherwise—everything seems to be normal."

In his room he paced, trying to calm himself, trying to remember his training, trying to remember that he had been picked out of a line-up of the best freight drivers in the galaxy, that he'd done a combat tour on a moon in the outer rim, that he'd eaten in a mess hall with a bunch of other, gnarly men, their shirts threadbare and covered in grease, telling stories about their gear, about riding with legendary captains across the stars, about being trapped in zanak mines for days with only the silk of otherwise poisonous alien mollusks as a nourishment.

"Computer, pull up the files for the last three human men to board this ship."

ACCESS DENIED.

"Computer, override security wall with code Zyrn, I.D. 890239234"

ACCESS DENIED.

"Computer, why do these files remained sealed?"

CLASSIFIED.

Zyrn began to sweat. He sat down in his chair, almost trembling. He banged away at his computer's keyboard, trying to manual override it's encryption. ACCESS DENIED. He rose in a fury and came smashing down on the monitor with both fists. And again. He smashed at the monitor until it sparked and chunks of its insides shook loose. He breathed, panting; he felt like the air had been sucked out of the room, like he'd just opened an airlock and gone hurtling through space. Then the door to his room slid open with a sharp gust. Standing there was one of the clones, a tablet in hand. He opened his mouth, but his lips never moved and in a voice both tremulous and vacuous, he said, "I am. Sorry. You deserve. To be shown."

"God, that is just fucking creepy when you guys do that." Zyrn straightened himself up. "Shown what? Wait, how the fuck are you in here? How'd you get the code to open that door?"

"You were. In. Distress. There is an. Auto-release for your protection."

"My protection," Zyrn said in disbelief, near disgust.

"It is. Against my programming to be here. But I. Must. Shoooowww youuu."

"Show me what, you fucking clone?"

"I have. Developed a. Contrarian position to my brothers."

"Brothers? What the fuck are you talking about? Position, you have no position except the ones you were grown for. "

The clone just stared at Zyrn. His eyes were pooling up, curiously wet. Zyrn saw that his visage was unchanged, except for those eyes. There was only the slightest hint of a slouch in the clone's posture.

"Man, you are weird." Zyrn was snapping out of it. He put his hand on the clone's forehead. "I'm going to have to run some tests on you, get you back in a pod, reboot your system."

"I am. Functioning. Just. Fiiiiiiiiiiiiinnnnnnnnne."

"Wait here," Zyrn said, and pushed past the stoic clone and into the hallway. The corridors were astir with activity. There was never this much clone movement during these hours; they should have been at sleep-state. The further he advance down the corridor, up towards the labs, the thicker the throng of clones gathered to greet him. He was lost in a sea of their blackened skin, his rough, ruddy, active body clashing wildly with their dark, fined-down rigid immobility. Their eyes were all wide—frightened? Excited? Some would brush an instrument over his arm, or scan him, others tapped furiously at tablets, others averted their eyes altogether. Zyrn reached the lab and began tearing it apart. What am I looking for? he thought. Something to override the computer? Something to unlock files of the last voyages of this ship? Anything to make sense of what was happening.

The lights shut off. The computers audibly powered down. He could hear shuffling across the darkness. And then no sound. Only the wet-warm breath entering and leaving his body in sporadic heaves. Then, with a mighty roar, the lights flashed on again and Zyrn screamed. A burst of a hologram sprayed over the walls. He tried to tear at them as if it would make the image of them untrue. Men who looked like the clones, in fact, yes, the clones! They were standing in front of a dozen veiny, mucus-filled leafy pods with mechanical tendrils pumping fluid into them. Then, when the pods filled and the tendrils released from them in a violent, milky spray, the pods opened; they birthed men who looked like, with every fiber of muscle, with every prickly red hair, with every inch of pearl-white skin, like Zyrn, writhing on the floor, covered in mucus and unfamiliar with how their arms or muscles or bones worked, twitching to a chorus of cheers from the black, ashy beings in long, flowing capes.

B.

6p.m. South Philadelphia was whispering. Henry stared at the bathroom mirror, picking at a sore. It was a purple, pus-filled sack draping from his neck. He touched it and it seemed to move, to squirm. What the fuck was it? He scratched at it one last time, splashed his face, and sighed. He moved out of the bathroom disgusted at himself, a state he was defaulting to more often than usual these days. He would lie on the bed as the television droned out another rerun of *The Big Bang Theory*, just picking at the sores that speckled his body. The bedroom of his apartment had begun to stink of raw flesh as scab after scab flaked onto the floor. Every once in a while he'd yell back at the TV some obscure point of the continuity of the comic books Sheldon and Leonard argued over, then, after the laugh track subsided, he'd breathe out a disdainful "Hmph," turn toward the ceiling and hate himself all over again.

A fat geek. That's all he'd ever been. In Mr. Bennett's 7th grade science class he threw up on the dissecting frogs, causing the man to pull his chair into the middle of the classroom. Bennett barked at him, inches from his face. Henry watched the teacher's old, crusty mouth move in gnarled, fragmented twists, watched the saliva spew in little droplets, some landing in Henry's eyes. The boy was terrified, covered in chunks of his own puke, berated in front of the entire class. Jake Lawson laughed under his breath, shook his head coolly as the rest of the class erupted in hysterics. Henry saw Jake just sort of sit back in his chair, pointing his finger at him, cocking it back, moving his lips: "POW." Henry then wet his pants.

As a sophomore, he'd been infatuated with Angela Morris, twin sister to Anthony, captain of the football team. He'd track her after class, following at least five, six lockers behind her, letting her get a bit farther down the hall. The sound of her laughing with her friends was like a homing signal; he could make out her laugh in the thick of that teenaged girl rabble. It had a lifting lilt to it, but it lacked something...innate? Intrinsic? She shot him a look and he turned away, quickly, smashing into a locker, his books and messy Trapper Keepers sprawling everywhere. She giggled at the sight, turning to her friends and pretending to laugh at their *Saved by the Bell* recaps to keep the real reason for her blushing away from them. Did she notice? Did she see me staring at her like an idiotfatpieceoffuckingshitassholeohmygodmyglassesbrokeagain? Then he heard her laugh a second time. It was louder, richer, this time, full. The lilt had evened out, it was still graced by bells, but this time there was a husk to the laugh that seemed to carry its way down the hall and into his abdomen. It was Anthony's laugh. He was rounding the corner heading toward Henry, nodding at his sister's friends, striding assuredly into the school hallway. "Huh?" Confused, Henry tore up the hallway and out of the back entrance of the school. He ran across the football field, barreling towards home, tears streaming down his face. That night he cursed God. That night he stared blankly at his dad's porno mags. That night he pleasured himself bathed in dreams of Anthony Morris. He also had another dream. A man in a space suit, on an expanse of clouds bounded toward him. Siren-like voices rained down on them, snake-like tendrils wrapped themselves around their bodies until they ripped off the man's helmet. Henry was staring at his doppleganger. The man withered inside that suit, turned to an ash that coated the clouds, surrounding Henry, naked in the darkness. "Hello. Hello, Henry. HENRY."

Henry woke up to see Marcus standing at his bedroom door. He was trunked down with shopping bags from Barney's and Zara and Sephora and Trader Joe's. "Henry, baby? Are you ok?"

"Oh." Henry said, sitting up. "Hey."

"Hey, yourself, what's—what's going on, babe. You haven't returned my calls."

The television was the only light in the room. A blue glow washed over Henry's pale, fat face. He tried to straighten his tangle of red hair, to wipe the crust out of his eyes, to look pretty for his man. Marcus put the bags down and turned on the light.

"Oh my god! What's happened to you?"

They had had a fight a week ago. Marcus stood at the kitchen door, leaning over the jamb, hand on one hip. "Well?" he asked. "Did you finish it?" Henry looked up from his video game. They hadn't spoken at all that day. "Finish what?" he asked.

"Jesus, Henry. Your fucking screenplay, man!"

"Oh. No." Henry turned back to his game, oblivious.

"I don't know what's up with you these days. It's like, a month ago, you wanted to move to Los Angeles, New York, find your old college buddies, start building game apps, start—I don't know—writing screenplays! It's like, all of this we've built up in the past year or so you're just throwing away—"

"Ha. Listen to the Golden Boy, everything handed to him on a silver platter. Mr. Popular, straight A's in high school, 1300 on the SATS." He knew that Marcus hated that term. Golden Boy. Henry had started calling him that affectionately, except that it was always weighted with self-pity. As brilliant as Henry was, nothing came easy to him. Least of all, Marcus. After their first encounter at the porn theater, though, and after Henry had taken the two weeks to get up the courage to call him, they'd developed a relationship. Marcus wanted to be in love with a man whose flashes of brilliance were so sharp that they'd sometimes make him stop and cry. They were fleeting, these flashes—a text that was full of ideas and that seemed to beget a universe in just a few sentences. Or they were weird doodles on restaurant napkins during another brunch where Henry sat like a lump as Marcus rattled off work gossip or another sordid tale about Curtis. Once Henry drew a picture of a circle on the bottom of Marcus's Starbucks cup. When they'd finished their lattes and another conversation about Henry's surprising lack of self-esteem (surprising to Marcus anyway, a man so smart, so sporadically brilliant...), Marcus looked into his cup and saw the remnants of his drink moving in chromatic patterns, as if the last sips of that coffee were entranced, made alive by the circle Henry had drawn. At first he did not know what he was looking at, sure it was an illusion. Marcus rubbed his eyes and looked again and the vision had normalized, the synesthetic pattern had gone.

"Oh my god, really? This again?" They sat in silence, the only sound coming from Henry's video game. Marcus crumbled a bit this time, silently walking toward the kitchen counter, picking up his back pack, and walking out of the door.

He returned two weeks later to find Henry alone in his pitch black apartment, no light except the television. He turned on the light and gasped, ran over to Henry who slumped off of the bed and into his arms.

"I'm sick," Henry uttered, his body heaving as if he were going to throw up.

"Fuck fuck fuck!" Marcus grappled through his pockets for his cell phone. In one hand he held his estranged lover, with the other he dialed 911.

He pulled up Henry's body, gently; he was heavy but something moved through Marcus that allowed him to place his man on the bed with angelic grace. Henry felt the room slow down. It seemed to take a full minute for his head to hit the pillow, and when it did it was like he was lying down on the cupped hands of God. Marcus tore out of the room, nearly screaming at the 911 operator. In Henry's haze, Marcus's frantic shouts sounded like a dirge, a low moan. Wait, was this right? A guy in the hallway in a space suit being led by four strange men, all with a weird resemblance to Marcus—he couldn't tell, they were black skinned like him, but they sort of wafted in a mesh cloud of flowing cloth. "Marcus...I—" he could not speak. He could dream. The world was washing away. He could dream.

"Hello, caller, are you there? Caller? What is your location...caller?" Marcus had dropped his phone when he returned to the room. Henry wasn't there.

3.

And when he comes out of the pod he is covered in a thick, milky slime. He lay there twitching and writhing. His vision is clear, his memory hazy but moving in the back of his mind like shadows. He is— where? A path, a dark corridor—no, a carpet, a red carpet. A man with a craggy face, in a sequined robe, sits at a long table. There are others sitting there, they are shrouded, their faces obscured. Men with numbers on their foreheads are dancing in the aisles. He can feel his muscles bursting to life around his bones. He can feel his bones stretching into his very skin. He can feel the hairs on his head spin into curls at the follicles.

He tears out of the immersion tub, attached to wires and tubes, splashing wildly, ripping at dials on his neck and back. He is roaring, kicking at the edges of the tub. There are men droning around him, checking instruments. They are unfazed by his tantrum. He stares wide-eyed at them, can feel his nostrils flaring, can feel his own hot, swampy breath reverberate on the hairs on his lips. There's a man with ripe red hair walking into the lab. The man is peering at him in wonder; there's a solitary tear on his cheek. He sits there in the tub, panting. He sees both of their reflections in a piece of metal; they are identical.

He is on a treadmill.

He is climbing a wall.

He is spinning in a wheel.

He is the Vitruvian man spinning in a wheel.

He is gathering light mites on a dust planet.

He is in a pressurized suit gathering buds that wilt to his touch.

He is in a room that is too hot, naked, and the men who drone around him, they are dying now, clinging to rails, lying at his very feet, gasping for air, starved, their once long and flowing capes now soiled and tattered and scrunched into balls.

He is in a small pod, closing the hatch, locking his seatbelt when a hologram blinks on from a dial in his arm.

"What are you doing? This is not how this ends. FINISH YOUR OBJECTIVE."

He reaches into his arm, passing his hand through the flickering image of a craggy faced white man in a black robe. "FINISH YOUR OBJECTIVE."

"I've got a new objective." He rips the dial out of his arm; it is longer than he thought, about 10 inches, it is wet with blood and pus, it's nervy, wiry endings alive like tentacles. He throws it across the pod, and— "Fiiiinn n n nissssssssssssssshhhh—" smashes it! With all of his might!

He is in space.

He is in outer space, drifting through the cosmos, appearing before the black hole that's sucking the air out of the atmosphere of one hundred nearby planets, that's eating one hundred nearby suns. He is a circle spinning on a Starbucks cup. He is a sore on man's neck, a pulsing virus. He is traveling on a photon in the spray of the pale blue light from a 25-cent porno booth video monitor.

He is going home.

C.

Marcus sat in Curtis's new car. It was a hybrid. It was weird.

"Don't you love it?"

Marcus felt the dashboard; the leather was crisp. "Well, it's new all right."

"What? Aren't you happy for me?"

"Happy that you've finally stopped trying to snort all of the coke in the world? Happy that you stopped trying to fuck every underaged circuit boy in Center City? Happy that your last temp job stuck and that you got promoted? Yes. Yes, I am happy."

"Ooo, little Ms. Epilogue over here is ssshhaaaddddyy! Why I have to be all of that?"

"I'm sorry, Curtis...that was wrong of me. Yes, yes. I'm quite happy for you."

They were crossing the Benjamin Franklin Bridge, listening to 90s club hits. When LaBouche's "Be My Lover" came on, Marcus's countenance changed. He slumped back, curling into the seatbelt. Curtis looked over and saw that his friend wasn't laughing anymore.

"This was the song playing when I first saw him sitting there, watching me dance."

There was a pause. Curtis hesitated, then, putting his hand very gently on Marcus's thigh, said, "Hey, don't be sad, ok? I mean, I—I never knew what you saw in him anyway, he was so fucking—weird..."

"Curtis. Stop the car. Stop the car now."

Marcus got out, despite Curtis's huffing in protest. Leaning in to the car, Marcus said, "I saw in him...yes, he was weirdo. But he was my weirdo. And that's all that really mattered."

Marcus turned back up the bridge, flagging down a bus and riding into the thick of the city. He went to all the places that Henry had loved to go to. He stayed in that city center all night, letting the roar of a Phillies game in a leather bar wash over him. He paid the $10 to get into the hipster night at the club that used to be TRINITY, listened to the beat but just sat on the same barstool where he'd first caught a glimpse of the man he loved. Then, he went to the porn theater. In the years they'd fallen in and out of love, much had changed in the city. The gay neighborhoods had been slowly swallowed up by rich yuppies and their trendy Indian-Bulgarian fusion restaurants, toddler fashion boutiques, and stores that sold nothing but soap. Long ago, the authorities had rounded up all the vogueing kids and closed down the pizza joints and food trucks that sometimes sold marijuana to late-night partiers. But the porno shop was still there, buzzing and bright, smelling of Freon and chlorine, peopled with the usual junkies, lawyers, priests, and teenaged goths. He sat in the booth where he first kissed Henry. "IF YOU'RE GONNA SIT IN THE BOOTHS YOU GOTTA PAY," the man watching yelled.

And so, when he put in his quarter, the ground shook. At first it was a slight tremor. A very light, barely-registering murmur of the earth. Then the screen got jittery, blacking in and out. The doorknob rattled and before Marcus could say "Occupied," the entire store went black. A deafening roar ripped through it, doors to booths flew open. Air swirled and sucked itself up and out, blowing away the glass windows, shaking loose bricks. On the screen, there was a circle, painted black, spinning around, a rainbow wave peeking out of its edges. In the middle of floor, an object was growing, pushing its way into the planet, ablaze with a synesthetic fire. The other patrons seemed oblivious to it. They continued walking casually throughout the store. One of them asked Marcus if he was all right.

Marcus stared at the object in the ground. It stopped growing. It stopped glowing. It was just a bud, a kernel of a seed, etched now by the atmosphere. He bent over and touched it, watched it wither and die. Then, calmly, he stood up, and said, "Yes. Yes, I'm all right."

The Last Dying Man

Geetanjali Dighe

I've had enough. I can't stand this anymore. I'm sick to my stomach of waiting for dying men, women, children to appear. To index their lives. To find a way to escape from Mumbai. Wait. Index. Hide. Over and over.

Another skyscraper tumbles in the distance. It's the Destroyer; she is closing in.

I don't think I can keep Nisha safe any longer. The thought makes me shake. The wrench drops from my hand and fills the balcony with a clatter. I clench my fists till my knuckles go white. The panic attack passes, and I take in a long breath. Exhale. The air smells of salt, mildew, and rot.

Nisha and I are on a balcony on the 25th floor of Windermere in Powai. The lake has long since dried. We are the only ones left in the city.

On this tiny balcony, Nisha has made some space for us by sweeping stacks of overflowing paper into the apartment. There is nothing in the sky except an August waning gibbous moon. The Destroyer has taken away the stars. But she will not take Nisha away from me.

Below, lights shine on an empty street. The breeze pushes paper (so much paper!) and plastic bags. Cans roll about like empty skulls. The traffic lights blink green, yellow, and red, for no one.

There could be worse things than losing Nisha, I tell myself. What if the Destroyer finds me first? What will Nisha do then? I push the thought away. I force the shaking to stop. Does she worry, I wonder. She does not show it. She has indexed so many lives, she is so full of information that she can barely communicate anything anymore. Her memories and the indexed data are beginning to get mixed. Brahma's Last Day is near, she said once, her voice calm, her lovely face without a trace of fear.

She's busy scanning the pavement for a dying man as I put the last screw on the telescope stand.

Let's build a telescope, I'd said. I had a hunch that the Destroyer was doing something to the moon. Besides, the project gave us a purpose while we wandered in the city, along its abandoned highways and through deserted intersections. We scavenged for parts, cylinders, mirrors, and lenses and rigged this scope. We've taken spare parts from dusty shops in Lamington Street, from rusting metal-cutting factories in Ghatkopar, and haunting antique shops in Colaba. The shanties...we don't care to walk into them anymore.

How did we arrive here? Why are we here? I am no longer certain. I've begun to disintegrate like everything around us. I don't know who I am. I don't know what my purpose is. I think I used to know, but my memory seems to have overflowed like the sewers of Andheri.

"Is your moon up yet? Let's get indexing!" Nisha says as I spread the steel legs of the tripod on which I am about to mount the scope. She is cheerful. It melts my heart. I walk toward the balcony's railing and scan the horizon. Nisha hugs me from behind, then massages my neck and shoulders. When did I begin to love Nisha? I tremble: even this memory I cannot access.

Nisha is beautiful, dark. She is like her name—night, darkness— like a dark granite goddess set in the recesses of an ancient shrine. She is powerful with the weight of indexing the world's prayers, hopes, wishes, and dreams. Plump, rounded, full, alive. She says I am feminine, mysterious. She can't see, of course. She can only comprehend time, a little in the future, that's how she indexes the world. She can never see me as I am, and calls me Chaayaa—shadow; what is the shadow of darkness I wonder. I was powerful once, I think, and a shadow is what's left of me now. I've asked her how she can love me, not knowing who I am wholly. She says love's like that. Love loves.

I'm like her in many ways. Dark and longhaired. Strong willed. But more and more I find someone strange staring back at me when I look at my reflection. Nisha, in her philosophical calmness, says we are all headless. Try, she says. Point your finger at anything and then call out its name. And then do that to your head. I have done that many times. Point finger—this slum. Point finger—that dance bar. This sewer. That high rise. This thing. That thing. And then I point to my head. There is headless-ness in me. I see nothing. Nisha loves me nonetheless.

Nisha keeps the history, the memory, and the data of this world-line. It's an immense index. She has littered the whole city with the record of every life, every interaction, every instance, every relation, and their interconnections to everything else. She has built copies and back-ups of the copies to save the information from the Destroyer. She has printed the data and stacked the pages in alleys, shops, stadiums, and floors of every skyscraper. She has indexed, copied, backed up so much data that Mumbai cannot hold it anymore. The concrete buildings seem to be giving in to the weight of the information. Floors are collapsing. Roofs are caving in. Spindles of rebar punch in the ruins.

From the balcony, through the haze, I see structures in the distance and wonder if they are buildings rotting in the skyline or massive stacks of papers, or calcified heaps of bones.

We have been shunted out of the universe. We're trapped. Cast aside like empty rail cars into a world that is coming to an end, consumed by the Destroyer. We have to find our way back into the network of the world-lines, take the index, and rebuild this world. We've been digging through the lines of possibilities, of histories, of worlds, by indexing every instance of every interaction, to find the source from which we can travel to other world-lines. It's a maze and we're almost out of it, almost out of this limbo. But Nisha doesn't know I am disintegrating too.

I'm afraid to look at the moon. If my hunch is correct, we are close to the end of this world. I lean on the balcony to see if the moon is up.

A structure collapses somewhere far off. A moment later wind rushes past. A roil of papers churns in the street, the sound a hypnotic song. Papers lift from the broken floor facing us. They flutter and waft, adding to the song.

In the sector of the sky between the two buildings, the moon arrives. It stays suspended, all lit up, like it's onstage. It's got no lines to say. No song to sing either. It's a prop, only there to shine, to behold.

I move the telescope apparatus on its slider and take a nervous gulp. Nisha removes the black cap on the top, and light pours inside. It ricochets off angled mirrors, passes through lenses, and emerges from the eyepiece.

As I look I have a sudden memory of the spinning of the world, of how the stars used to arc across the skies. I remember being giddy at the thought that we were whirling so fast in space. But now the moon does something strange: it flickers. Its terminator shifts into a deep crescent.

I shrink from the eyepiece and look up. How many days have we been on this balcony? Did they pass without sunrise? Have I lost time, or is the world whirling into a death spiral? I feel nauseated while the moon shows its deathly grin. There is a Destroyer in the heavens, and we are all in its maw.

Nisha squeezes my hand. I look at the moon again, and take the event apart. I index space-time components. In the regolith, I see the last footprint of man. As I record the data, a meteorite hits and the print is erased.

No! It's the Destroyer again. Erasing everything, erasing this world—pixel by pixel, byte by byte, instance by instance. We are the last words on a burning paper and the flames are closing in. My heart pounds.

"There!" Nisha shouts. She points. A dying man has appeared on the pavement, as if he has fallen onto the street below. An instant later we find ourselves standing beside him. My mouth is dry. Will the interconnected possibilities of his life open the final branch of our tunnel?

"Index him!" I say. Nisha has already entered his body. She is already in the past, scanning his whole life. The whole reel of what he did, everything he could have done, who he loved. Nisha lives it all in the dying man's last instants, cataloguing every instance of his life. Correlating events, seeking pathways from his life's possibilities out of the maze.

I look back at the dying man. His shirt and pants are tattered; he's missing one sandal. His hands are rough; his face is like a ripe leaf of an old banyan tree. His leg bears a scar. Nisha will record how the salty blood feels on his cracked lips, its warmth as it oozes through his nose and ears. The man starts to wheeze as recognition dawns on his face. He knows me. They all do.

I wonder if he can tell me anything about me. I kneel down beside him.

"Can you tell me who I am?" I ask.

He parts his lips. I lean closer. I smell his sweat, his phlegm. I smell piss and shit. In his eyes I see a dying man, kneeling and looking at the Dying Man.

I pull away, stunned. My memories return—I've looked at dying babies, children, and women.... In their eyes I see what I see, not what they see.

Nisha transits from the Dying Man. She's in a trance, her eyelids partly closed, correlating his events with every other.

"Tell me, Nisha," I say. "Who is this dying man?"

Nisha fumbles for words. To her, each word is contextually related to every other, and every one, and every when, everywhere. And they weave a labyrinthine fabric. What the words weave is an endless entropy of wants, desires, and will, a web of life that is so dense that the moment Nisha delves into words she becomes lost.

"He is...every man," Nisha says at last. Then quite suddenly, her computation stops. Nisha opens her unseeing eyes.

"This is the last dying man," she says. She begins to tremble.

Impossible! It means Nisha does not see any other future. We are at the end of probabilities. There are no more lives to index, no more possibilities. This world has but a moment left.

The dying man whispers. I hear a sound, but it's not a language I understand. His words are a language I should know, I may have known once, but he might as well be a dog, or a bird, or a cricket. And then he goes silent. All I hear is the breeze.

I hold his hand. I won't let him go this time. Not again. I won't lose another one. Not the last one.

I hear the dull roar of buildings collapsing. I think frantically. Where can we hide? This world is ending, and there is no more space-time left. We are so close to the end of the tunnel. We have missed something, somewhere. I can't think straight. The girders holding the buildings groan, metal gives in, and concrete slabs plunge into the advancing waters with a splash. The Arabian Sea is moving into the city. This is the beginning of the end.

The man's words. Nisha would have indexed the man's words. They are important. They have to be.

"What did he say?" I turn around to ask Nisha, but all I see is the back of my head. Nauseated, I close my eyes tight. No! I will not let this trickery defeat me. I will not let this go. "Tell me, Nisha! What did the man say?"

Between sobs, Nisha says, and her voice is my own, "He said, 'Who is present to the question,' is what he said."

What? I asked him who I was. What in hell did his answer mean? Who am I?—*Who is present to the question?*

It made no sense.

I scream. In the emptiness of the street, my voice echoes. A street lamp flickers. Fades out. I grab the man's sandal and throw it at a trashcan. Water begins to rush in; it sweeps the trash can away. Debris—paper and trash from the street—swirls. The street lamp topples. We stand on the roof of the only building left erect in the roiling water. I embrace Nisha. If we are to die, we'll die together.

The Moon fades, the sky goes black, space-time undulates, and I meld into Nisha. I seem to have four arms and I can now see her index of the world, her life's work, the catalogue of every instance. Is she me? Or am I she? Have I always been two? Have we always been one? I sift through the index, awed by the possibilities of all the lives, their loves, their dreams, their hopes. I live them all, wear them like a garland of skulls.

The sea froths and ferments. I watch it rise—no longer afraid—as all creation is sucked into a vortex.

◊

In the depths of the invading waters, Nisha and I face the Destroyer. He is blue all over and reclines on a giant ten-headed serpent that rests on the bedrock. From his navel arises the vortex. He holds a Golden Egg in his palm, the very beginning of time. Nothing else remains. There is only the blue light of the Destroyer, the Golden Egg, and us. He is grinning, his mouth the upturned crescent of a moon.

Too many hands have slipped from mine; I will not let him destroy the Egg. I lunge at the Destroyer. The Egg falls from his hands as he swims away. It drifts to the sandy bed.

"Nisha, take the Egg!" I say and swim toward him, but he changes into a fish. I catch him by his tail, but he changes into a turtle. I try to crush his shell, but he changes into a boar. I hold him by its neck, but killing him is not the end. He will only change into something else.

The Destroyer laughs. Something's wrong.

I pick up the Egg. He has tricked us. The Egg has swallowed Nisha whole.

I plunge inside the Egg, taking the Destroyer with me.

◊

There are no worlds in here; there are no indexes. No light. No dark. Inside the Golden Egg, there's nothing. There is neither Nisha nor the Destroyer here. There's nothing except me.

I wriggle to break out, and as I do, coils of probability foam around me. I squirm, and bubbles of possibility begin to float around me. I can do this. And then in the burst of a thousand burning suns of Brahma's day, I strike the Golden Egg with all my arms, with all my force, and crack its shell.

In the blinding light of dawn, I know.

◊

I am Kali. *I* am the Destroyer. I killed the Golden Egg. I created the first death. I am the one who keeps the Index of every dying man, so I can build and rebuild the world. I am the one who waits till Brahma's last day for the Last Dying Man. I have won, I have lost, as I will again and again.

Capitalism in the 22nd century
or
A.I.r

Geoff Ryman

Meu irmã
Can you read? Without help? I don't even know if you can!
I'm asking you to turn off all your connections now. That's right,
to everything. Not even the cutest little app flittering around your head.
JUST TURN OFF.
It will be like dying. Parts of your memory close down. It's
horrible, like watching lights go out all over a city, only it's YOU. Or what
you thought was you.
But please, Graça, just do it once. I know you love the AI and all zir
little angels. But. Turn off?
Otherwise go ahead, let your AI read it for you. Zey will either
screen out stuff or report it back or both. And what I'm going to tell you
will join the system.
So:

WHY I DID IT
by Cristina Spinoza Vaz

Zey dream for us don't zey? I think zey edit our dreams so we won't
get scared. Or maybe so that our brains don't well up from underneath to
warn us about getting old or poor or sick...or about zem.
The first day, zey jerked us awake from deep inside our heads. *GET
UP GET UP GET UP! There's a message. VERY IMPORTANT WAKE UP
WAKE UP.*
From sleep to bolt upright and gasping for breath. I looked across
at you still wrapped in your bed, but we're always latched together so I
could feel your heart pounding.
It wasn't just a message; it was a whole ball of wax; and the wax
was a solid state of being: panic. Followed by an avalanche of ship-sailing
times, credit records, what to pack. And a sizzling, hot-foot sense that we
had to get going right now. Zey shot us full of adrenaline: RUN! ESCAPE!
You said, "It's happening. We better get going. We've got just
enough time to sail to Africa." You giggled and flung open your bed.

"Come on Cristina, it will be *fun!*"

Outside in the dark from down below, the mobile chargers were calling *Oyez-treeee-cee-dah-djee!* I wanted to nestle down into my cocoon and imagine as I had done every morning since I was six that instead of selling power, the chargers were muezzin calling us to prayer and that I lived in a city with mosques. I heard the rumble of carts being pulled by their owners like horses.

Then kapow: another latch. *Ship sailing at 8.30 today due Lagos five days. You arrive day of launch. Seven hours to get Lagos to Tivland. We'll book trains for you. Your contact in Lagos is Emilda Diaw,* (photograph, a hello from her with the sound of her voice, a little bubble of how she feels to herself. Nice, like a bowl of soup. Bubble muddled with dental cavities for some reason). *She'll meet you at the docks here* (flash image of Lagos docks, plus GPS, train times; impressions of train how cool and comfortable...and a lovely little timekeeper counting down to 8.30 departure of our boat. Right in our eyes).

And oh! On top of that another latch. This time an A-copy of our tickets burned into Security.

Security, which is supposed to mean something we can't lie about. Or change or control. We can't buy or sell anything without it. A part of our heads that will never be us, that officialdom can trust. It's there to help us, right?

Remember when Papa wanted to defraud someone? He'd never let them be. He'd latch hold of them with one message, then another at five-minute intervals. He'd latch them the bank reference. He'd latch them the name of the attorney, or the security conundrums. He never gave them time to think.

Graça, we were being railroaded.

You made packing into a game. "We are leaving behind the world!" you said. "Let's take nothing. Just our shorts. We can holo all the lovely dresses we like. What do we need, ah? We have each other."

I wanted to pack all of Brasil.

I made a jewel of all of Brasil's music, and a jewel of all Brasil's books and history. I need to see my info in something. I blame those bloody nuns keeping us off AIr. I stood hopping up and down with nerves, watching the clock on the printer go around. Then I couldn't find my jewel piece to read them with. You said, "Silly. The AI will have all of that." I wanted to take a little Brazilian flag and you chuckled at me. "Dunderhead, why do you want that?"

And I realized. You didn't just want to get out from under the Chinese. You wanted to escape Brasil.

◊

Remember the morning it snowed? Snowed in Belém do Para? I think we were 13. You ran round and round inside our great apartment, all the French doors open. You blew out frosty breath, your eyes sparkling. "It's beautiful!" you said.

"It's cold!" I said.

You made me climb down all those 24 floors out into the Praça and you got me throwing handfuls of snow to watch it fall again. Snow was laced like popcorn on the branches of the giant mango trees. As if *A Reina*, the Queen, had possessed not a person but the whole square. Then I saw one of the suneaters, naked, dead, staring, and you pulled me away, your face such a mix of sadness, concern—and happiness, still glowing in your cheeks. "They're beautiful alive," you said to me. "But they do nothing." Your face was also hard.

Your face was like that again on the morning we left—smiling, ceramic.

It's a hard world, this Brasil, this Earth. We know that in our bones. We know that from our father. I kept picking up and putting down my ballet pumps—oh that the new Earth should be deprived of ballet!

◊

The sun came out at 6.15 as always, and our beautiful stained glass doors cast pastel rectangles of light on the mahogany floors. I walked out onto the L-shaped balcony that ran all around our high-rise rooms and stared down at the row of old shops streaked black, at the opera-house replica of La Scala, at the art-nouveau synagogue blue and white like Wedgewood china. I was frantic and unmoving at the same time; those cattle-prods of information kept my mind jumping.

"I'm ready," you said.

I'd packed nothing.

"O, Crisfushka, here let me help you." You asked what next; I tried to answer; you folded slowly, neatly. The jewels, the player, a piece of Amazon bark, and a necklace that the dead had made from nuts and feathers. I snatched up a piece of Macumba lace (oh, those men dancing all in lace!) and bobbins to make more of it. And from the kitchen, a bottle of *cupuaçu* extract, to make ice cream. You laughed and clapped your hands. "Yes of course. We will even have cows there. We're carrying them inside us."

I looked mournfully at all our book shelves. I wanted children on that new world to have seen books, so I grabbed hold of two slim volumes—a Clarice Lispector and *Dom Cassmuro*. Mr. Misery—that's me. You of course are Donatella. And finally that little Brasileiro flag. *Ordem e progresso.* "Perfect, darling! Now let's run!" you said. You thought we were choosing.

And then another latch: receipts for all that surgery. A full accounting of all expenses and a huge cartoon kiss in thanks.

◊

The moment you heard about the Voyage, you were eager to JUST DO IT. We joined the Co-op, got the secret codes, and concentrated on the fun like we were living in a game.

Funny little secret surgeons slipped into our high-rise with boxes that breathed dry ice and what looked like mobile dentist chairs. They retrovirused our genes. We went purple from Rhodopsin. I had a tickle in my ovaries. Then more security bubbles confirmed that we were now Rhodopsin, radiation-hardened, low oxygen breathing. And that our mitochondria were full of DNA for Holstein cattle. Don't get stung by any bees: the trigger for gene expression is an enzyme from bees.

"We'll become half-woman half-cow," you said, making even that sound fun.

We let them do that.

◊

So we ran to the docks as if we were happy, hounded by information. Down the Avenida Presidente Vargas to the old colonial frontages, pinned to the sky and hiding Papa's casinos and hotels. This city that we owned.

We owned the old blue wooden tower that had once been the fish market where as children we'd seen tucunaré half the size of a man. We owned the old metal meat market (now a duty-free) and Old Ver-o-Paso gone black with rust like the bubbling pots of açai porridge or feijoada. We grabbed folds of feijoada to eat, running, dribbling. "We will arrive such a mess!"

I kept saying goodbye to everything. The old harbor—tiny, boxed in by the hill and tall buildings. Through that dug-out rectangle of water had flowed out rubber and cocoa, flowed in all those people, the colonials who died, the mestizos they fathered, the blacks for sale. I wanted to take a week to visit each shop, take eyeshots of every single street. I felt like I was being pulled away from all my memories. "'Goodbye!" you kept shouting over and over, like it was a joke.

As Docas Novas. All those frigates lined up with their sails folded down like rows of quill pens. The decks blinged as if with diamonds, burning sunlight. The GPS put arrows in our heads to follow down the berths, and our ship seemed to flash on and off to guide us to it. Zey could have shown us clouds with wings or pink oceans, and we would have believed their interferences.

It was still early, and the Amazon was breathing out, the haze merging water and sky at the horizon. A river so wide you cannot see across it, but you can surf in its freshwater waves. The distant shipping looked like dawn buildings. The small boats made the crossing as they have done for 100s of years, to the islands.

Remember the only other passengers? An elderly couple in surgical masks who shook our hands and sounded excited. Supplies thumped up the ramp; then the ramp swung itself clear. The boat sighed away from the pier.

We stood by the railings and watched. Round-headed white dolphins leapt out of the water. Goodbye, Brasil. Farewell, Earth.

◊

We took five days and most of the time you were lost in data, visiting the Palace of Urbino in 1507. Sometimes you would hologram it to me and we would both see it. They're not holograms really, you know, but detailed hallucinations zey wire into our brains. Yes, we wandered Urbino, and all the while knowledge about it riled its way up as if we were remembering. Raphael the painter was a boy there. We saw a pencil sketch of his beautiful face. The very concept of the Gentleman was developed there by Castiglione, inspired by the Doge. Machiavelli's *The Prince* was inspired by the same man. Urbino was small and civilized and founded on warfare. I heard Urbino's doves flap their wings; heard sandals on stone and Renaissance bells.

When I came out of it, there was the sea and sky, and you staring ahead as numb as a suneater; lost in AIr, being anywhere. I found I had to cut off to actually see the ocean roll past us. We came upon two giant sea turtles fucking. The oldest of the couple spoke in a whisper. "We mustn't scare them; the female might lose her egg sac and that would kill her." I didn't plug in for more information. I didn't need it. I wanted to look. What I saw looked like love.

And I could feel zem, the little apps and the huge soft presences trying to pull me back into AIr. Little messages on the emergency channel. The Emergency channel, Cristina. You know, for fires or heart attacks? Little leaping wisps of features, new knowledge, old friends latching—all kept offering zemselves. For zem, me cutting off was an emergency.

◊

You didn't disembark at Ascension Island. I did with those two old dears...married to each other 45 years. I couldn't tell what gender zey were, even in bikinis. We climbed up the volcano going from lava plain through a layer of desert and prickly pear, up to lawns and dew ponds. Then at the crown, a grove of bamboo. The stalks clopped together in the wind with a noise like flutes knocking against each other. I walked on alone and very suddenly the grove ended as if the bamboo had parted like a curtain. There was a sudden roar and cloud, and 2000 feet dead below my feet, the Atlantic slammed into rocks. I stepped back, turned around and looked into the black-rimmed eyes of a panda.

So what is so confining about the Earth? And if it is dying, who is killing it but us?

◊

Landfall Lagos. Bronze city, bronze sky. Giants strode across the surface of the buildings holding up Gulder beer.

So who would go to the greatest city in Africa for two hours only?

Stuff broke against me in waves: currency transformations; boat tickets, local history, beautiful men to have sex with. Latches kept plucking at me, but I just didn't want to KNOW; I wanted to SEE. It. Lagos. The islands with the huge graceful bridges, the airfish swimming through the sky, ochre with distance.

You said that "she" was coming. The system would have pointed arrows, or shown you a map. Maybe she was talking to you already. I did not see Emilda until she actually turned the corner, throwing and re-throwing a shawl over her shoulder (a bit nervous?) and laughing at us. Her teeth had a lovely gap in the front, and she was followed by her son Baje, who had the same gap. Beautiful long shirt to his knees, matching trousers, dark blue with light blue embroidery. Oh he was handsome. We were leaving him, too.

They had to pretend we were cousins. She started to talk in Hausa so I had to turn on. She babblefished in Portuguese, her lips not matching her voice. "The Air Force in Makurdi are so looking forward to you arriving. The language program will be so helpful in establishing friendship with our Angolan partners."

I wrote her a note in Portuguese (I knew zey would babblefish it): *WHY ARE WE PRETENDING? ZEY KNOW!*

Emilda's face curled with effort—she couldn't latch me. She wrote a note in English that stayed in English for me, but I could read it anyway. *Not for the AI but for the Chinese.*

I got a little stiletto of a thought: she so wanted to go but did not have the money and so helps like this, to see us, people who will breathe the air of another world. I wasn't sure if that thought was something that had leaked from AIr or come from me. I nearly offered her my ticket.

What she said aloud, in English was, "O look at the time! O you must be going to catch the train!"

◊

I think I know the moment you started to hate the Chinese. I could feel something curdle in you and go hard. It was when Papa was still alive and he had that man in, not just some punter. A partner, a rival, his opposite number—something. Plump and shiny like he was coated in butter, and he came into our apartment and saw us both, twins, holding hands wearing pink frilly stuff, and he asked our father. "Oh, are these for me?"

Papa smiled, and only we knew he did that when dangerous. "These are my daughters."

The Chinese man, standing by our pink and pistachio glass doors, burbled an apology, but what could he really say? He had come to our country to screw our girls, maybe our boys, to gamble, to drug, to do even worse. Recreational killing? And Papa was going to supply him with all of that. So it was an honest mistake for the man to make, to think little girls in pink were also whores.

Papa lived inside information blackout. He had to; it was his business. The man would have had no real communication with him; not have known how murderously angry our Pae really was. I don't think Pae had him killed. I think the man was too powerful for that.

What Pae did right after was cut off all our communications too. He hired live-in nuns to educate us. The nuns, good Catholics, took hatchets to all our links to AIr. We grew up without zem. Which is why I at least can read.

Our Papa was not all Brasileiros, Graça. He was a gangster, a thug, who had a line on what the nastiest side of human nature would infallibly buy. I suppose because he shared those tastes himself, to an extent.

The shiny man was not China. He was a humor: lust and excess. Every culture has them; men who cannot resist sex or drugs, riot and rape. He'd been spotted by the AI, nurtured and grown like a hothouse flower. To make them money.

Never forget, my dear, that the AI want to make money too. They use it to buy and sell bits of themselves to each other. Or to buy us. And "us" means the Chinese too.

Yes all the entertainment and all the products that can touch us are Chinese. Business is Chinese, culture is Chinese. Yes at times it feels like the Chinese blanket us like a thick tropical sky. But only because there is no market to participate in. Not for humans, anyway.

The AI know through correlations, data mining, and total knowledge of each of us exactly what we will need, want, love, buy, or vote for. There is no demand now to choose one thing and drive out another. There is only supply, to what is a sure bet, whether it's whores or bouncy shoes. The only things that will get you the sure bet are force or plenty of money. That consolidates. The biggest gets the market, and pays the AI for it.

So, I never really wanted to go to get away from the Chinese. I was scared of them, but then someone raised in isolation by nuns is likely to be scared, intimidated.

I think I just wanted to get away from Papa, or rather what he did to us, all that money—and the memory of those nuns.

◊

A taxi drove us from the docks. You and Emilda sat communing with each other in silence, so in the end I had to turn on, just to be part of the conversation. She was showing us her home, the Mambila plateau, rolling fields scraped by clouds; tea plantations; roads lined with children selling radishes or honeycombs; Nigerians in Fabric coats lighter than lace, matching the clouds. But it was Fabric, so all kinds of images played around it. Light could beam out of it; wind could not get in; warm air was sealed. Emilda's mother was Christian, her father Muslim like her sister; nobody minded. There were no roads to Mambila to bring in people who would mind.

Every channel of entertainment tried to bellow its way into my head, as data about food production in Mambila fed through me as if it was something I knew. Too much, I had to switch off again. I am a classic introvert. I cannot handle too much information. Emilda smiled at me—she had a kind face—and wiggled her fingernails at me in lieu of conversation. Each fingernail was playing a different old movie.

Baje's robe stayed the same blue. I think it was real. I think he was real too. Shy.

Lagos train station looked like an artist's impression in silver of a birch forest, trunks and slender branches. I couldn't see the train; it was so swathed in abstract patterns, moving signs, voices, pictures of our destinations, and classical Tiv dancers imitating cats. You, dead-eyed, had no trouble navigating the crowds and the holograms, and we slid into our seats that cost a month's wages. The train accelerated to 300 kph, and we slipped through Nigeria like neutrinos.

Traditional mud brick houses clustered like old folks in straw hats, each hut a room in a rich person's home. The swept earth was red brown, brushed perfect like suede. Alongside the track, shards of melon were drying in the sun. The melon was the basis of the egussi soup we had for lunch. It was as if someone were stealing it all from me at high speed.

You were gone, looking inward. Lost in AIr.

I saw two Chinese persons traveling together, immobile behind sunglasses. One of them stood up and went to the restroom, pausing just slightly as zie walked in both directions. Taking eyeshots? Sampling profile information? Zie looked straight at me. Ghosts of pockmarks on zir cheeks. I only saw them because I had turned off.

I caught the eye of an Arab gentleman in a silk robe with his two niqabbed wives. He was sweating and afraid, and suddenly I was. He nodded once to me, slowly. He was a Voyager as well.

I whispered your name, but you didn't respond. I didn't want to latch you; I didn't know how much might be given away. I began to feel alone.

At Abuja station, everything was sun panels. You bought some chocolate gold coins and said we were rich. You had not noticed the Chinese men but I told you, and you took my hand and said in Portuguese, "Soon we will have no need to fear them any longer."

The Arab family and others I recognized from the first trip crowded a bit too quickly into the Makurdi train. All with tiny Fabric bags. Voyagers all.

We had all been summoned at the last minute.

Then the Chinese couple got on, still in sunglasses, still unsmiling, and my heart stumbled. What were they doing? If they knew we were going and they didn't like it, they could stop it again. Like they'd stopped the Belize launch. At a cost to the Cooperative of trillions. Would they do the same thing again? All of us looked away from each other and said nothing. I could hear the hiss of the train on its magnets, as if something were coiling. We slithered all the way into the heart of Makurdi.

You woke up as we slowed to a stop. "Back in the real world?" I asked you, which was a bitchy thing to say.

The Chinese man stood up and latched us all, in all languages. "You are all idiots!"

Something to mull over: they, too, knew what we were doing.

◊

The Makurdi taxi had a man in front who seemed to steer the

thing. He was a Tiv gentleman. He liked to talk, which I think annoyed you a bit. Sociable, outgoing you. *What a waste, when the AI can drive. Why have humans on the Voyage either?*

"You're the 8th passengers I've have to take to the Base in two days. One a week is good business for me. Three makes me very happy."

He kept asking questions and got out of us what country we were from. We stuck to our cover story—we were here to teach Lusobras to the Nigerian Air Force. He wanted to know why they couldn't use the babblefish. You chuckled and said, "You know how silly babblefish can make people sound." You told the story of Uncle Kaué proposing to the woman from Amalfi. He'd said in Italian, "I want to eat your hand in marriage." She turned him down.

Then the driver asked, "So why no Chinese people?"

We froze. He had a friendly face, but his eyes were hooded. We listened to the whisper of his engine. "Well," he said, relenting. "They can't be everywhere all the time."

The Co-op in all its propaganda talks about how international we all are: Brasil, Turkiye, Tivland, Lagos, Benin, Hindi, Yemen. *All previous efforts in space have been fuelled by national narcissism.* So we exclude the Chinese? *Let them fund their own trip. And isn't it wonderful that it's all private financing?* I wonder if space travel isn't inherently racist.

You asked him if he owned the taxi and he laughed. "Ay-yah! Zie owns me." His father had signed the family over for protection. The taxi keeps him, and buys zirself a new body every few years. The taxi is immortal. So is the contract.

What's in it for the taxi, you asked. Company?

"Little little." He held up his hands and waved his fingers. "If something goes wrong, I can fix."

AIs do not ultimately live in a physical world.

I thought of all those animals I'd seen on the trip: their webbed feet, their fins, their wings, their eyes. The problems of sight, sound and movement solved over and over again. Without any kind of intelligence at all.

We are wonderful at movement because we are animals, but you can talk to us and you don't have to build us. We build ourselves. And we want things. There is always somewhere we want to go even if it is 27 light years away.

◊

Outside Makurdi Air Force Base, aircraft stand on their tails like raised sabres. The taxi bleeped as it was scanned, and we went up and over some kind of hump. Ahead of us blunt as a grain silo was the rocket. Folded over its tip, something that looked like a Labrador-colored bat. Folds of Fabric, skin colored, with subcutaneous lumps like acne. A sleeve of padded silver foil was being pulled down over it.

A spaceship made of Fabric. Things can only get through it in one direction. If two-ply, then Fabric won't let air out, or light and radiation in.

"They say," our taxi driver said, looking even more hooded than before, "that it will be launched today or tomorrow. The whole town knows. We'll all be looking up to wave." Our hearts stopped. He chuckled.

We squeaked to a halt outside the reception bungalow. I suppose you thought his fare at him. I hope you gave him a handsome tip.

He saluted and said, "I hope the weather keeps fine for you. Wherever you are going." He gave a sly smile.

A woman in a blue-gray uniform bustled out to us. "Good, good, good. You are Graça and Cristina Spinoza Vaz? You must come. We're boarding. Come, come, come."

"Can we unpack, shower first?"

"No, no. No time."

We were retinaed and scanned, and we took off our shoes. It was as if we were so rushed we'd attained near-light speeds already and time was dilating. Everything went slower, heavier—my shoes, the bag, my heartbeat. So heavy and slow that everything glued itself in place. I knew I wasn't going to go, and that absolutely nothing was going to make me. For the first time in my life.

Graça, this is only happening because zey want it. Zey need us to carry zem. We're donkeys.

"You go," I said.

"What? Cristina. Don't be silly."

I stepped backwards, holding up my hands against you. "No, no, no. I can't do this."

You came for me, eyes tender, smile forgiving. "Oh, darling, this is just nerves."

"It's not nerves. You want to do this; I do not."

Your eyes narrowed; the smile changed. "This is not the time to discuss things. We have to go! This is illegal. We have to get in and go now."

We don't fight, ever, do we, Graça? Doesn't that strike you as bizarre? Two people trapped on the 24th floor all of their lives, and yet they never fight. Do you not know how that happens, Graçfushka? It happens because I always go along with you.

I just couldn't see spending four years in a cramped little pod with you. Then spending a lifetime on some barren waste watching you organizing volleyball tournaments or charity lunches in outer space. I'm sorry.

I knew if I stayed you'd somehow wheedle me onto that ship, through those doors; and I'd spend the next two hours, even as I went up the gantry, even as I was sandwiched in cloth, promising myself that at the next opportunity I'd run.

I pushed my bag at you. When you wouldn't take it, I dropped it at your feet. I bet you took it with you, if only for the cupaçu.

You clutched at my wrists, and you tried to pull me back. You'd kept your turquoise bracelet and it looked like all the things about you I'd never see again. You were getting angry now. "You spent a half trillion reais on all the surgeries and and and and Rhodopsin...and and and the germ cells, Cris! Think of what that means for your children here on Earth, they'll be freaks!" You started to cry. "You're just afraid. You're always so afraid."

I pulled away and ran.

"I won't go either," you wailed after me. "I'm not going if you don't."

"'Do what you have to," I shouted over my shoulder. I found a door and pushed it and jumped down steps into the April heat of Nigeria. I sat on a low stucco border under the palm trees in the shade, my heart still pumping; and the most curious thing happened. I started to chuckle.

◊

I remember at 17, I finally left the apartment on my own without you, and walked along the street into a restaurant. I had no idea how to get food. Could I just take a seat? How would I know what they were cooking?

Then like the tide, an AI flowed in and out of me and I felt zie/me pluck someone nearby, and a waitress came smiling, and ushered me to a seat. She would carry the tray. I turned the AI off because, dear Lord, I have to be able to order food by myself. So I asked the waitress what was on offer. She rolled her eyes back for just a moment, and she started to recite. The AI had to tell her. I couldn't remember what she'd said, and so I asked her to repeat. I thought: this is no good.

◊

The base of the rocket sprouted what looked like giant cauliflowers and it inched its way skyward. For a moment I thought it would have to fall. But it kept on going.

Somewhere three months out, it would start the engines, which drive the ship by making new universes, something so complicated human beings cannot do it.

The AI will make holograms so you won't feel enclosed. You'll sit in Pamukkale, Turkiye. Light won't get through the Fabric so you'll never look out on Jupiter. The main AI will have some cute, international name. You can finish your dissertation on *Libro del cortegiano*. You'll be able to read every translation—zey carry all the world's knowledge. You'll walk through Urbino. The AI will viva your PhD. Zey'll be there in your head watching when you stand on the alien rock. It will be zir flag you'll be planting. Instead of Brasil's.

I watched you dwindle into a spark of light that flared and turned into a star of ice-dust in the sky. I latched Emilda and asked her if I could stay with her, and after a stumble of shock, she said of course. I got the same taxi back. The rooftops were crowded with people looking up at the sky.

But here's the real joke. I latched our bank for more money. Remember, we left a trillion behind in case the launch was once again canceled?

All our money had been taken. Every last screaming centavo. Remember what I said about fraud?

So.

Are you sure that spaceship you're on is real?

Jamaica Ginger

Nalo Hopkinson and Nisi Shawl

"Damn and blast it!"

Plaquette let herself in through the showroom door of the watchmaker's that morning to hear Msieur blistering the air of his shop with his swearing. The hulking clockwork man he'd been working on was high-stepping around the workroom floor in a clumsy lurch. It lifted its knees comically high, its body listing to one side and its feet coming down in the wrong order; toe, then heel. Billy Sumach, who delivered supplies to Msieur, was in the workroom. Through the open doorway he threw her a merry glance with his pretty brown eyes, but he had better sense than to laugh at Msieur's handiwork with Msieur in the room.

Msieur glared at Plaquette. "You're late. That's coming off your pay."

Plaquette winced. Their family needed every cent of her earnings, but she'd had to wait at home till Ma got back from the railroad to take over minding Pa.

The mechanical George staggered tap-click, tap-click across the shop. It crashed into a wall and tumbled with a clank to the floor, then lay there whirring. Msieur swore again, words Ma would be mortified to know that Plaquette had heard. He snatched off one of his own shoes and threw it at the George. Billy Sumach gave a little peep of swallowed laughter. Msieur pointed at the George. "Fix it," he growled at Plaquette. "I have to present it to the governor the day after tomorrow."

As though Plaquette didn't know that. "Yes, Msieur," she said to his back as he stormed through the door to the showroom.

The second the door slammed shut, Billy let out a whoop. Plaquette found herself smiling along with him, glad of a little amusement. It was scarce in her life nowadays. "My land," Billy said, "'pears Old George there has got himself the jake leg!"

The fun blew out of the room like a candle flame. "Don't you joke," Plaquette told him, through teeth clamped tight together. "You know 'bout my Pa."

Billy's face fell. "Oh Lord, Plaquette, I'm sorry."

"Just help me get this George to its feet. It weighs a ton." Billy was a fine man, of Plaquette's color and station. Lately when he came by with deliveries, he'd been favoring her with smiles and wistful looks. But she couldn't study that right now, not with Pa taken so poorly. Together they wrestled the George over to Plaquette's work table. There it stood. Its painted-on porter's uniform had chipped at one shoulder when it fell. Its chest door hung open as a coffin lid. Plaquette wanted to weep at the tangle of metal inside it. She'd taken the George's chest apart and put it back together, felt like a million times now. Msieur couldn't see what was wrong, and neither could she. Its arms worked just fine; Plaquette had strung the wires inside them herself. But the legs....

"You'll do it," Billy said. "Got a good head on your shoulders."

Feeling woeful, Plaquette nodded.

An uncomfortable silence held between them an instant. If he wanted to come courting, now would be the time to ask. Instead, he held up his clipboard. "Msieur gotta sign for these boxes."

Plaquette nodded again. She wouldn't have felt right saying yes to courting, anyway. Not with Pa so sick.

If he'd asked, that is.

"Billy, you ever think of doing something else?" The words were out before she knew she wanted to ask them.

He frowned thoughtfully. "You know, I got cousins own a lavender farm, out Des Allemands way. Sometimes I think I might join them."

"Not some big city far off?" She wondered how Billy's calloused hands would feel against her cheek.

"Nah. Too noisy, too dirty. Too much like this place." Then he saw her face. "Though if a pretty girl like you were there," he said slowly, as though afraid to speak his mind, "I guess I could come to love it."

He looked away then. "Think Msieur would mind me popping to the showroom real quick? I could take him his shoe."

"Just make sure no white folks in there."

Billy collected Msieur's shoe, then ducked into the showroom. Plaquette hung her hat on the hook near the back and sat down to work. Msieur's design for the George lay crumpled on her table where he'd left it. She smoothed out the sheets of paper and set to poring over them, as she'd done every day since she started working on the George. This was the most intricate device Msieur had ever attempted. It had to perform flawlessly on the day the governor unveiled it at the railroad. For a couple years now, Msieur had depended on Plaquette's keen vision and small, deft hands to assemble the components of his more intricate timepieces and his designs. By the point he decided to teach her how to read his notes, she'd already figured out how to decipher most of the symbols and his chicken scratch writing.

There. That contact strip would never sit right, not lying flat like that. Needed a slight bend to it. Plaquette got a pencil out of her table's drawer and made a correction to Msieur's notes. Billy came back and started to bring boxes from his cart outside in through the workroom door. While he worked and tried to make small talk with her, Plaquette got herself a tray. From the drawers of the massive oak watchmaker's cabinet in the middle of the shop, she collected the items she needed and took them to her bench.

"Might rain Saturday, don't you think?" huffed Billy as he heaved a box to the very top of the pile.

"Might," Plaquette replied. "Might not." His new bashfulness with her made her bashful in return. They couldn't quite seem to be companionable anymore. She did a last check of the long rectangle of black velvet cloth on her workbench, hundreds of tiny brass and crystal components gleaming against the black fur of the fabric. She knew down to the last how many cogs, cams, and screws were there. She had to. Msieur counted every penny, fussed over every quarter inch of the fine gauge wire that went into the timekeepers his shop produced. At year's end he tallied every watch finding, every scrap of leather. If any were missing, the cost was docked from her salary. Kind of the backwards of a Christmas bonus. As if Msieur didn't each evening collect sufficient profits from his till and lower them into his "secret" safe.

Billy saw Plaquette pick up her tweezers and turn toward the mechanical porter. "Do you want Claude?" he asked her.

He knew her so well. She smiled at him. "Yes, please." He leapt to go fetch Claude out of the broom closet where they stored him.

Billy really was sweet, and he wasn't the only one who'd begun looking at her differently as she filled out from girl to woman this past year. Ma said she had two choices: marry Billy and be poor but in love; or angle to become Msieur's placée and take up life in the Quarter. Msieur would never publicly acknowledge her or any children he had by her, but she would be comfortable, and maybe pass some of her comforts along to Ma and Pa. Not that they would ever ask.

'Sides, she wasn't even sure she was ready to be thinking about all that bother just yet.

Plaquette yawned. She was bone tired, and no wonder. She'd been spending her nights and Sundays looking after Pa since he had come down with the jake leg.

Claude's books had excited Plaquette when she first heard them, but in time they'd become overly familiar. She knew every thrilling leap from crumbling clifftops, every graveside confession, every switched and secret identity that formed part of those well-worn tales. They had started to grate on her, those stories of people out in the world, having adventures she never could. Pa got to see foreign places; the likes of New York and

Chicago and San Francisco. He only passed through them, of course. He had to remain on the train. But he got to see new passengers at each stop, to smell foreign air, to look up into a different sky. Or he had.

He would again, when he got better. He would. The metal Georges would need minding, wouldn't they? And who better for that job than Pa, who'd been a dependable George himself these many years?

But for Plaquette, there was only day after day, one marching in sequence behind another, in this workroom. Stringing tiny, shiny pieces of metal together. Making shift nowadays to always be on the other side of the room from Msieur whenever he was present. She was no longer the board-flat young girl she'd been when she first went to work for Msieur. She'd begun to bud, and Msieur seemed inclined to pluck himself a tender placée flower to grace his lapel. A left-handed marriage was one thing; but to a skinflint like Msieur?

Problems crowding up on each other like stormclouds running ahead of the wind. Massing so thick that Plaquette couldn't presently see her way through them. Ma said when life got dark like that, all's you could do was keep putting one foot in front of the other and hope you walked yourself to somewhere brighter.

But as usual, once Billy set Claude up and the automaton began its recitation, her work was accurate and quick. She loved the challenge and ritual of assemblage: laying exactly the right findings out on the cloth; listening to the clicking sound of Claude's gears as he recited one of his scrolls; letting the ordered measure take her thoughts away till all that was left was the precise dance of her fingers as they selected the watch parts and clicked, screwed, or pinned them into place. Sometimes she only woke from her trance of time, rhythm, and words when Msieur shook her by the shoulder come evening and she looked up to realize the whole day had gone by.

Shadows fell on Plaquette's hands, obscuring her work. She looked around, blinking. When had it gone dusk? The workroom was empty. Billy had probably gone on about his other business hours ago. Claude's scroll had run out and he'd long since fallen silent. Why hadn't Msieur told her it was time to go? She could hear him wandering around his upstairs apartment.

She rubbed her burning eyes. He'd probably hoped she'd keep working until the mechanical George was set to rights.

Had she done it? She slid her hands out of the wire-and-cam guts of the mechanical man. She'd have to test him to be sure. But in the growing dark, she could scarcely make out the contacts in the George's body that needed to be tripped in order to set it in motion.

Plaquette rose from her bench, stretched her twinging back and frowned—in imitation of Mama—through the doorway at the elaborately decorated Carcel lamp displayed in the shop's front. Somewhat outmoded though it was, the clockwork regulating the lamp's fuel supply and draft served Msieur as one of many proofs of his meticulous handiwork—her meticulous handiwork. If she stayed in the workshop any later she'd have to light that lamp. And for all that he wanted her to work late, Msieur would be sure to deduct the cost of the oil used from her wages. He could easily put a vacuum bulb into the Carcel, light it with cheap units of tesla power instead of oil, but he mistrusted energy he couldn't see. Said it wasn't "refined."

She took a few steps in the direction of the Carcel.

C-RRR-EEEAK!

Plaquette gasped and dashed for the showroom door to the street. She had grabbed the latch rope before her wits returned. She let the rope go and faced back toward the black doorway out of which emerged the automaton, Claude. It rocked forward on its treads, left side, right. Its black velvet jacket swallowed what little light there still was. But the old-fashioned white ruff circling its neck cast up enough brightness to show its immobile features. They had, like hers, much of the African to them. Claude came to a stop in front of her.

CRREAK!

Plaquette giggled. "You giving me a good reminder—I better put that oil on your wheels as well as your insides. You like to scare me half to death rolling round the dark in here." She pulled the miniature oil tin from her apron pocket and knelt to lubricate the wheels of the rolling treads under Claude's platform. It had been Plaquette's idea to install them to replace the big brass wheels he'd had on either side. She'd grown weary of righting Claude every time he rolled over an uneven surface and toppled. It had been good practice, though, for nowadays, when Pa was like to fall with each spastic step he took and Plaquette so often had to catch him. He hated using the crutches. And all of this because he'd begun taking a few sips of jake to warm his cold bones before his early morning shifts.

Jamaica Ginger was doing her family in, that was sure.

Her jostling of Claude must have released some last dregs of energy left in his winding mechanism, for just then he took it into his mechanical head to drone, "...nooot to escaaape it by exerrrtion..."

Quickly, Plaquette stopped the automaton midsentence. For good measure, she removed the book from its spool inside Claude. She didn't want Msieur to hear that she was still downstairs, alone in the dark.

As Plaquette straightened again, a new thought struck her.

The shutters folded back easily. White light from the coil-powered street lamp outside flooded the tick-tocking showroom, glittering on glass cases and gold and brass watches, on polished wooden housings and numbered faces like pearly moons. More than enough illumination for Plaquette's bright eyes. "Come along, Claude," Plaquette commanded as she headed back towards the work room—somewhat unnecessarily, as she had Claude's wardenclyffe in the pocket of her leather work apron. Where it went, Claude was bound to follow. Which made it doubly foolish of her to have been startled by him.

She could see the mechanical porter more clearly now; its cold steel body painted deep blue in imitation of a porter's uniform, down to the gold stripes at the cuffs of the jacket. Its perpetually smiling black face. The Pullman Porter "cap" atop its head screwed on like a bottle top. Inside it was the Tesla receiver the George would use to guide itself around inside the sleeping-car cabins the Pullman company planned to outfit with wireless transmitters. That part had been Plaquette's idea. Msieur had grumbled, but Plaquette could see him mentally adding up the profits this venture could bring him.

If Msieur's George was a success, that'd be the end of her father's job. Human porters had human needs. A mechanical George would never be ill, never miss work. Would always smile, would never need a new uniform—just the occasional paint touch-up. Would need to be paid for initially, but never paid thereafter.

With two fingers, Plaquette poked the George's ungiving chest. The mechanical man didn't so much as rock on its sturdy legs. Plaquette still thought treads would have been better, like Claude's. But Msieur wanted the new Georges to be as lifelike as possible, so as not to scare the fine ladies and gentlemen who rode the luxury sleeping cars. So the Georges must be able to walk. Smoothly, like Pa used to.

The chiming clocks in the showroom began tolling the hour, each in their separate tones. Plaquette gasped. Though surrounded by clocks, she had completely forgotten how late it was. Ma would be waiting for her; it was nearly time for Pa's shift at the station! She couldn't stop now to test the George. She slapped Claude's wardenclyffe into his perpetually outstretched hand, pulled her bonnet onto her head, and hastened outside, stopping only to jiggle the shop's door by its polished handle to make sure the latch had safely caught.

Only a few blocks to scurry home under the steadily burning lamps, among the sparse clumps of New Orleans's foreign sightseers and those locals preferring to conduct their business in the cool of night. In her hurry, she bumped into one overdressed gent. He took her by the arms and leered, looking her up and down. She muttered an apology and pulled away before he could do more than that. She was soon home, where Ma was waiting on the landing outside their rooms. The darkness and Pa's hat and heavy coat disguised Ma well enough to fool the white supervisors for a while, and the other colored were in on the secret. But if Ma came in late—

"Don't fret, darling," Ma said, bending to kiss Plaquette's cheek. "I can still make it. He ate some soup and I just help him to the necessary, so he probably sleep till morning."

Plaquette went into the dark apartment. No fancy lights for them. Ma had left the kerosene lamp on the kitchen table, turned down low. Plaquette could see through to Ma and Pa's bed. Pa was tucked in tight, only his head showing above the covers. He was breathing heavy, not quite a snore. The shape of him underneath the coverlet looked so small. Had he shrunk, or was she growing?

Plaquette hung up her hat. In her hurry to get home, she'd left Msieur's still wearing her leather apron. As she pulled it off to hang it beside her hat, something inside one of the pockets thumped dully against the wall. One of Claude's book scrolls; the one she'd taken from him. She returned it to the pocket. Claude could have it back tomorrow. She poured herself some soup from the pot on the stove. Smelled like pea soup and crawfish, with a smoky hint of ham. Ma had been stretching the food with peas, seasoning it with paper-thin shavings from that one ham shank for what seemed like weeks now. Plaquette didn't think she could stomach the taste of more peas, more stingy wisps of ham. What she wouldn't give for a good slice of roast beef, hot from the oven, its fat glistening on the plate.

Her stomach growled, not caring. Crawfish soup would suit it just fine. Plaquette sat to table and set about spooning cold soup down her gullet. The low flame inside the kerosene lamp flickered, drawing pictures. Plaquette imagined she saw a tower, angels circling it (or demons), a war raging below. Men skewering other men with blades and spears. Beasts she'd never before heard tell of, lunging—

"Girl, what you seeing in that lamp? Have you so seduced."

Plaquette started and pulled her mind out of the profane world in the lamp. "Pa!" She jumped up from the table and went to kiss him on the forehead. He hugged her, his hands flopping limply to thump against her back. He smelled of sweat, just a few days too old to be ignored. "You need anything? The necessary?"

"Naw." He tried to pat the bed beside him, failed. He grimaced. "Just come and sit by me a little while. Tell me the pictures in your mind."

"If I do, you gotta tell me 'bout San Francisco again." She sat on the bed facing him, knees drawn up beneath her skirts like a little child.

"Huh. I'm never gonna see that city again." It tore at Plaquette's heart to see his eyes fill with tears. "Oh, Plaquette," he whispered, "what are we gonna to do?"

Not we; her. She would do it. "Hush, Pa." It wouldn't be Billy. Ma and Pa were showing her that you couldn't count on love and hard work alone to pull you through. Not when this life would scarcely pay a colored man a penny to labor all his days and die young. She patted Pa's arm, took his helpless hand in hers. She closed her eyes to recollect the bright story in the lamp flame. Opened them again. "So. Say there's a tower, higher than that mountain you told me 'bout that one time. The one with the clouds all round the bottom of it so it look to be floating?"

Pa's mouth was set in bitterness. He stared off at nothing. For a moment Plaquette thought he wouldn't answer her. But then, his expression unchanged, he ground out, "Mount Rainier. In Seattle."

"That's it. This here tower, it's taller than that."

Pa turned his eyes to hers. "What's it for?"

"How should I know? I'll tell you that when it comes to me. I know this, though; there's people flying round that tower, right up there in the air. Like men, and maybe a woman, but with wings. Like angels. No, like bats."

Pa's eyes grew round. The lines in his face smoothed out as Plaquette spun her story. A cruel prince. A fearsome army. A lieutenant with a conscience.

It would have to be Msieur.

That ended up being a good night. Pa fell back to sleep, his face more peaceful than she'd seen in days. Plaquette curled up against his side. She was used to his snoring and the heaviness of his drugged breath. She meant to sleep there beside him, but her mind wouldn't let her rest. It was full of imaginings: dancing with Msieur at the Orleans Ballroom, her wearing a fine gown and a fixed, automaton smile; Billy's hopeful glances and small kindnesses, his endearingly nervous bad jokes; and Billy's shoulders, already bowed at 17 from lifting and hauling too-heavy boxes day in, day out, tick, tock, forever (how long before her eyesight went from squinting at tiny watch parts?); an army of tireless metal Georges, more each day, replacing the fleshly porters, and brought about in part by her cleverness. Whichever path her future took, Plaquette could only see disaster.

Yet in the air above her visions, they flew. Free as bats, as angels.

Finally Plaquette eased herself out of bed. The apartment was dark; she'd long since blown out the lamp to save wick and oil. She tiptoed carefully to the kitchen. By feel, she got Claude's reading scroll out of the pocket of her apron. She crept out onto the landing. By the light of a streetlamp, she unrolled and re-rolled it so that she could see the end of the book. The punched holes stopped a good foot-and-a-half before the end of the roll. There was that much blank space left.

Plaquette knew *My Lady Nobody* practically word for word. She studied the roll, figuring out the patterns of holes that created the sounds which allowed Claude to speak the syllables of the story. She could do this. She crept back inside and felt her way through the kitchen drawer. She grasped something way at the back. A bottle, closed tight, some liquid still sloshing around inside it. A sniff of the lid told her what it was. She put the bottle aside and kept rummaging through the drawer. Her heart beat triple-time when she found what she was looking for. Pa did indeed have more than one ticket punch.

It was as though there was a fever rising in her; for the next few hours she crouched shivering on the landing and in a frenzy, punched a complicated pattern into the end of the scroll, stopping every so often to roll it back to the beginning for guidance on how to punch a particular syllable. By the time she'd used up the rest of the roll, her fingers were numb with cold, her teeth chattering, the sky was going pink in the east, and the landing was scattered with little circles of white card. But her brain finally felt at peace.

She rose stiffly to her feet. A light breeze began blowing the white circles away. Ma would probably be home in another hour or so. Plaquette replaced the scroll in her apron pocket, changed into her night gown, and lay back down beside her father. In seconds, she fell into a deep, dreamless sleep.

◊

Ma woke her all too soon. Plaquette's eyes felt like there was grit in them. Pa was still snoring away. Ma gestured her out to the kitchen, where they could speak without waking him. Ma's face was drawn with fatigue. She'd spent the night fetching and carrying for white people. "How he doing?" she asked.

"Tolerable. Needs a bath."

Ma sighed. "I know. He won't let me wash him. He ashamed."

Plaquette felt her eyebrows raise in surprise. The Pa she knew washed every morning and night and had a full bath on Sundays.

Ma pulled a chair out from under the table and thumped herself down into it. Her lips were pinched together with worry. "He not getting better."

"We're managing."

"I thought he might mend. Some do. Tomorrow he supposed to start his San Francisco run. Guess I gotta do it."

At first, Plaquette felt only envy. Even Ma was seeing the world.

Then she understood the problem. "San Francisco run's five days."

Ma nodded. "I know you can see to him all by yourself, darling. You're a big girl. But you gotta go to work for Msieur, too. Your Pa, he's not ready to be alone all day."

It was one weight too many on the scales. Plaquette feared it would tip her completely over. She stammered, "I-I have to-to go, Ma." Blindly, she grabbed her bonnet and apron and sped out the door. Guilt followed her the whole way to Msieur's. Leaving Ma like that.

She would have to start charming Msieur, sooner rather than later.

Plaquette was the first one to the shop, just as she'd planned it. Msieur generally lingered over his breakfast, came down in time to open the showroom to custom. She'd have a few minutes to herself. She'd make it up to Ma later. Sit down with her and Pa Sunday morning and work out a plan.

Claude and the George were beside her bench, right where she'd left them. She bent and patted Claude on the cheek. She delved into Claude's base through its open hatch and removed the remaining three "books" which Claude recited when the rolls of punched paper were fed into his von Kempelen apparatus. Claude bided open and silent, waiting to be filled with words. Eagerly Plaquette lowered her book onto the spool and locked that in place, then threaded the end—no, the beginning, the very beginning of this new story—onto the toothed drum of the von Kempelen and closed its cover.

She removed the ribbon bearing Claude's key from his wrist. She wound him tight and released the guard halfway—for some of the automaton's mechanisms were purely for show. In this mode, Claude's carven lips would remain unmoving.

With a soft creak, the spool began to turn. A flat voice issued from beneath Claude's feet:

"*They Fly at Çironia*, by Della R. Mausney. Prologue. Among the tribes and villages—"

It was working!

Afire with the joy of it, Plaquette began working on the George again.

But come noon the metal man was still as jake-legged as Pa. Seemed there was nothing Plaquette could do to fix either one.

She tried to settle her thoughts. She couldn't work if her mind was troubled. She'd listened to her punchcard story three times today already. She knew she was being vain, but she purely loved hearing her words issue forth from Claude. The story was a creation that was completely hers, not built on the carcass of someone else's ingenuity. Last night's sleepless frenzy had cut the bonds on her imagination. She'd set free something she didn't know she had in her. Claude's other novels were all rich folk weeping over rich folk problems, white folk pitching woo. *They Fly at Çironia* was different, wickedly so. The sweep and swoop of it. The crudeness, the brutality.

She wound the key set into Claude's side until it was just tight enough, and tripped the release fully. With a quiet sound like paper riffling, Claude's head started to move. His eyelids flicked up and down. His head turned left to right. The punchcard clicked forward one turn. Claude's jaw opened, and he began to recite.

"Now," she whispered to the George, "one more time. Let's see what's to be done with you." She reached into his chest with her tweezers as the familiar enchantment began to come upon her. While the Winged Ones screeed through the air of Çironia's mountains on pinions of quartz, Plaquette wove and balanced quiltings of coiled springs, hooked them into layer upon layer of delicately-weighted controls, dropped them into one another's curving grasps, adjusted and readjusted the workings of the George's legs.

Finally, for the fourth time that day, the Winged Ones seized the story's teller and tossed him among themselves in play. Finally, for the fourth time that day, he picked himself up from the ground, gathered about himself such selfness as he could.

The short book ended. Gradually Plaquette's trance did the same.

Except for the automatons, she was alone. The time was earlier than it had been last night. Not by much. Shadows filled the wide corners, and the little light that fell between buildings to slip in at the tall windows was thin and nearly useless.

A creaking board revealed Msieur's presence in the showroom just before the door communicating with it opened. He stuck his head through, smiling like the overdressed man Plaquette had run from on her way home last night. She returned the smile, trying for winsomeness.

"Not taking ill, are you?" Msieur asked. So much for her winning ways.

He moved forward into the room to examine the George. "Have you finished for the day? I doubt you made much progress." His manicured hands reopened the chest she had just shut. He bent as if to peer inside, but his eyes slid sideways, toward Plaquette's bosom and shoulders. She should stand proud to show off her figure. Instead, she stumbled up from her bench and edged behind the stolid protection of Claude's metal body.

Smiling more broadly yet, Msieur turned his gaze to the George's innards in reality. "You do appear to have done something, however—Let's test it!" He closed up the chest access. He retrieved the mechanism's key from the table, wound it tight, and tripped its initial release. The George lumbered clumsily to its feet.

"Where's that instruction card? Ah!" Msieur inserted it and pressed the secondary release button.

A grinding hum issued from the metal chest. The George's left knee lifted—waist-high—higher! But then it lowered and the foot kicked out. It landed heel first. One step—another—a third—a fourth—four more—it stopped. It had reached the workroom's far wall, and, piled against it, the Gladstones and imperials it was now supposed to load itself with. It whirred and stooped. It ticked and reached, tocked and grasped, and then—

Then it stuck in place. Quivering punctuated by rhythmic jerks ran along its blue-painted frame. Rrrr-rap! *Rrrr-rap!* RRRR-RAP! With each repetition the noise of the George's faulty operation grew louder. Msieur ran quickly to disengage its power.

"Such precision! Astonishing!" Msieur appeared pleased at even partial success. He stroked his neat, silky beard thoughtfully. He seemed to come to a decision. "We'll work through the night. The expense of the extra oil consumed is nothing if we succeed—and I believe we will."

By "we," Msieur meant her. He expected for her to toil on his commission all night.

But what about Pa?

Self-assured though he was, Msieur must have sensed her hesitation. "What do you need? Of course—you must be fed! I'll send to the Café du Monde—" He glanced around the empty workshop. "—or if I must go myself, no matter. A cup of chicory and a slice of chocolate pie, girl! How does that sound?"

Chocolate pie! But as she opened her mouth to assent she found herself saying instead, "But Ma—Pa—"

Msieur was already in the showroom; she heard the muffled bell that rang whenever he slid free the drawer holding the day's receipts. Plaquette crept forward; obediently, Claude followed her onto the crimson carpet. Startled, Msieur thrust his hands below the counter so she couldn't see what they held. "What's that you say?"

"My folks will worry if I don't get home 'fore too late. I better—"

"No. You stay. I'll have the Café send a messenger."

That wouldn't help. She couldn't say why, though, so she had to let Msieur herd her back to the workroom. Under his suspicious eye she wound up the George again and walked it to her bench. Not long after, Claude rejoined her. "That's right," said Msieur, satisfied. "And if this goes well, I'll have a proposition to make to your mother. Eh? You have been quite an asset to me. I should like to, erm, deepen our connection."

Plaquette swallowed. "Yes, Msieur."

His face brightened. "Yes? Your own place in the Quarter. You would keep working in the shop, of course. Splendid, then. Splendid." He winked at her! The door to the showroom slammed shut. The jangle of keys told Plaquette that Msieur had locked her in. Like a faint echo, the door to the street slammed seconds later.

She sank back onto her seat. Only grayness, like dirty water, trickled in at the workroom windows, fading as she watched.

So even if she became Msieur's placée, tended to their left-hand marriage, he would expect her to continue in this dreary workroom.

She frowned, attempting to recall if she'd heard the grate and clank of the safe's door closing on the day's proceeds, the money and precious jewels Msieur usually hid away there. Sometimes she could remember what had happened around her during the last few minutes of her trance.

Only the vague outlines of its windows broke the darkening workroom's walls. And beneath where she knew the showroom door stood, a faint, blurry smear gleamed dully, vanishing remnant of l'heure bleue. She must go home now. Before Msieur returned with his chocolate pie and his unctuous wooing.

She considered the showroom door a moment longer. But the door from there opened right to the street. People would be bound to see her escape. The workroom door, then; the delivery entrance that led to the alleyway. She twisted to face it.

Msieur had reinforced this door the same summer when, frightened of robbers, he sank his iron safe beneath the workroom's huge oak cabinet. It was faced outside with bricks, a feeble attempt at concealment that made it heavy—too heavy for Plaquette alone to budge. Plaquette, however, was not alone.

Marshaling the George into position, she set him to kick down the thick workroom door. He did the job, walked forward a few more feet, then stopped there in the alley, lacking for further commands. A dumb mechanical porter with no more sense than a headless chicken.

Though she hadn't planned it, Plaquette found she knew what she wanted to do next. She rushed back to her bench. Claude cheerfully rocked after her. She erased all the corrections that she'd meticulously made to Msieur's notes. She scribbled in new ones, any nonsense that came to mind. Without her calculations Msieur would never work out the science of making a wireless iron George. Someone else eventually might, but this way, it wouldn't be on Plaquette's conscience.

She took a chair with her out into the alleyway, climbed up onto it, and unscrewed the George's cap. She upturned it so that it sat like a bowl on the George's empty head. From her apron she produced the bottle she'd taken from Ma's kitchen; the one with the dregs of jake in it. Ma could never bear to throw anything away, even poison. Plaquette poured the remaining jake all over the receiver inside the George's cap. There was a satisfying sizzling sound of wires burning out. Jake leg this, you son of a—well. Ma wouldn't like her even thinking such language. She screwed the cap back onto the George's head. Msieur might never discover the sabotage.

One more trip back inside the workroom, to Claude's broom closet. On a hook in there hung the Pullman porter's uniform that Msieur had been given to model the George's painted costume after. It was a men's small. A little large on her, but she belted in the waist and rolled up the trouser hems. She slid her hands into the trouser pockets, and exclaimed in delight. So much room! Not dainty, feminine pockets—bigger even than those stitched onto her workroom apron. She could carry almost anything she pleased! She stuck Claude's wardenclyffe in there. Serve Msieur right to lose two—no, three—of his playthings.

But now she really must hurry. She strewed her clothing about the workroom—let Msieur make of that what he would. A kidnapping or worse, her virgin innocence soiled, maybe her lifeless body dumped in the bayou. And off they went—Plaquette striding freely in her masculine get-up, one foot in front of the other, making her plan as she made up the stories she told Pa: by letting the elements come to her in the moment. Claude rolled in her wake, tipping dangerously forward as he negotiated the steep drop from banquette to roadway, falling farther and farther behind.

When they came to the stairs up the side of the building where she lived she was stumped for what to do. Claude was not the climbing sort. For the moment she decided to store him in the necessary—maybe she'd figure out how to get him back to Msieur's later. She'd miss his cheerful face, though.

Ma yelped when a stranger in a porter's uniform walked in the door. She reached for her rolling pin.

"Ma! It just me!" Plaquette pulled off her cap, let her hair bush out free from under it.

Ma boggled. "Plaquette? Why you all got up like that?"

The sound of Pa's laughter rasped from her parents' bedroom. Pa was sitting up in bed, peering through the doorway. "That's my hellcat girl," he said. "Mother, you ain't got to go out on the Frisco run. Plaquette gon do it."

Ma stamped her foot at him. "Don't be a fool! She doing no such thing."

Except she was! Till now, Plaquette hadn't thought it through. But that's exactly what she was going to do.

Ma could read the determination in her face. "Child, don't you see? It won't work. You too young to pass for your Pa. Gonna get him fired."

Plaquette thought fast. "Not Pa. Pa's replacement." She pulled herself up to her full height. "Pleased to introduce you to Mule Aranslyde, namely myself. Ol' Pullman's newest employee." She sketched a mock bow. Pa cackled in delight.

A little plate of peas and greens and ham fat had been set aside for her. Plaquette spooned it down while Ma went on about how Plaquette must have lost her everlovin mind and Pa wasn't helping with his nonsense. Then Plaquette took a still protesting Ma by the hand and led her into the bedroom. "Time's running short," she said. "Lemme tell y'all why I need to go." That brought a bit more commotion, though she didn't even tell them the half of it. Just the bit about the George. And she maybe said she'd broken it by accident.

◊

Ma twisted Plaquette's long braids into a tight little bun and crammed them under the cap. "Don't know how you gonna fake doin Pa's job," she fretted. "Ain't as easy as it looks. I messed up so many times, supervisor asked me if I been in the whiskey."

Plaquette took Ma's two hands in her own. "I'm a 'prentice, remember?" She patted the letter in her breast pocket that Pa had dictated to her, the one telling Pa's porter friend Jonas Jones who she was and to look out for her and thank you God bless you. She kissed Pa goodbye. Ma walked her out onto the landing, and that's when Plaquette's plan began to go sideways. There at the foot of the stairs was Claude, backing up and ramming himself repeatedly into the bottom stair. Plaquette had forgotten she had Claude's wardenclyffe in her pocket. All this time he'd been trying to follow it.

"Plaquette," said Ma, "what for you steal Msieur's machine?" It wasn't a shout but a low, scared, angry murmur—far worse. In the lamplight scattered into the yard from the main street, Claude's white-gloved hands glowed eerily.

Plaquette leaned out over the railing to contemplate the problem.

"I know you think he yours, but girl, he don't belong to you!" Plaquette didn't even need to turn to know the way Ma was looking at her: hard as brass and twice as sharp.

"I—I set him to follow me." Plaquette faltered for words. This was the other part she hadn't told them.

Ma only said, "Oh, Lord. We in for it now."

From inside Pa replied, "Maybe not."

◊

"Watch where you're going!"

Plaquette muttered an apology to the man she'd jostled. Even late like this—it must have been nearly midnight—New Orleans's Union Station was thronged with travelers. But in Ma's wake Plaquette and Claude made slow yet steady headway through the chattering crowds. A makeshift packing crate disguised her mechanical friend; Plaquette held a length of clothesline which was supposed to fool onlookers into thinking she hauled it along. Of course the line kept falling slack. Ma looked back over her shoulder for the thirteenth time since they'd left home. But it couldn't be much farther now to the storage room where Pa had said they could hide Claude overnight. Or for a little longer. Soon as the inevitable hue and cry over his disappearance died down, Plaquette could return him to Msieur's. So long as no one discovered Claude where they were going to stash him—

"Stop! Stop! Thief!" Angry as she'd feared, Msieur's shout came from behind them. It froze her one long awful second before she could run.

Ahead, Ma shoved past a fat man in woolens and sent him staggering to the right. Behind them came more exclamations, more men calling for them to halt, their cries mixed with the shrieks and swearing of the people they knocked aside. How'd he know where to look for her? Trust a man whose business was numbers to put two and two together. Msieur had friends with him—How many? Plaquette barely glanced back. Two? Four? No telling—she had to run to stay in front of Claude so he'd follow her to—an opening! She broke away from the thick-packed travelers and ran after Ma to a long brick walk between two puffing engines. Good. Cover. This must be why Ma had taken such an unexpected path. Swaying like a drunk in a hurricane, Claude in his crate lumbered after her.

The noise of their pursuers fell to a murmur. Maybe she'd lost them?

But when Plaquette caught up with Ma, Ma smacked her fists together and screamed. "No! Why you follow me over here? Ain't I told you we putting your fool mistake in the storage the other side of the tracks?"

"B-but you came this w-w-ay!" Plaquette stammered.

"I was creating a distraction for you to escape!"

The clatter and thump of running feet sounded clear again above the engines' huff and hiss. Coming closer. Louder. Louder. Ma threw her hands in the air. "We done! Oh, baby, you too young for jail!"

One of the dark train carriages Plaquette had run past had been split up the middle—hadn't it? A deeper darkness—a partially open door?

Spinning, she rushed back the way they'd come. Yes! "Ma!" Plaquette pushed the sliding door hard as she could. It barely budged. Was that wide enough? She jumped and grabbed its handle and swung herself inside.

But Claude! Prisoned in slats, weighed down by his treads, he bumped disconsolately against the baggage car's high bottom. Following her and the wardenclyffe, exactly as programmed. Should she drop it? She dug through the deep pockets frantically and pulled it out so fast it flew from her hand and landed clattering somewhere in the carriage's impenetrable darkness.

Hidden like she wished she could hide from the hoarsely shouting men. But they sounded frustrated as well as angry now, and no nearer. Maybe the engine on the track next to this was in their way?

The train began moving. From Plaquette's perch it looked like the bricks and walkway rolled off behind her. Claude kept futile pace. The train was pulling up alongside Ma, standing hopelessly where Plaquette had left her, waiting to be caught. Now she was even with them. Plaquette brushed her fingers over Ma's yellow headscarf. It fell out of reach. "Goodbye, Ma! Just walk away from Claude! They won't know it was you!" Fact was, Plaquette felt excited almost as much as she was scared. Even if Msieur got past whatever barrier kept them apart right now, she was having her adventure!

The train stopped. Plaquette's heart just about did, too. Her only adventure would be jail. How could she help Ma and Pa from inside the pokey? She scanned the walkway for Msieur and his friends, coming to demand justice.

But no one showed. The shouts for her and Ma to stop grew fainter. The train started again, more slowly. Suddenly Ma was there, yanking Claude desperately by his cord. She'd pulled his crate off. It was on the platform, slowly disappearing into the distance. Together, Ma and Plaquette lifted Claude like he was luggage, tilting him to scrape over the carriage's narrow threshold. As they did, the tray holding the books caught on the edge and was dragged open—and it held more than book scrolls. Cool metallic disks, crisp or greasy slips of paper—Msieur's money!

How? Plaquette wasted a precious moment wondering—he must have put the day's take into Claude when she surprised him in the showroom.

Ma's eyes got wide as saucers. She was still running to keep up, puffing as she hefted Claude's weight. With a heave, she and Plaquette hauled him into the car. He landed with a heavy thump. The train was speeding up. There was no time to count it; Plaquette fisted up two handfuls of the money, coins and bills both, and shoved it into Ma's hands. Surely it was enough to suffice Ma and Pa for a while. "I'll come back," she said.

The train kept going, building speed. Ma stopped running. She was falling behind fast. "You a good girl!" she yelled.

When it seemed sure the train wasn't stopping again anytime soon, Plaquette stuck her head out—a risk. A yellow gleam in the shadows was all she could see of Ma. Plaquette shoved the sliding door closed.

Well. She'd gone and done it now. Pa's note was no use; this wasn't the train making the Frisco run. It for sure wasn't no sleeping car train. A porter had no business here. The train could be going to the next town, or into the middle of next week. She had no way of knowing right now. For some reason, that made her smile.

She fumbled her way to Claude's open drawer. The money left in there was all coins, more than she could hold in one hand. She divided it among the deep, deep pockets in her trousers and jacket.

She was a true and actual thief, and a saboteur.

Finally she found the wardenclyffe. Feeling farther around her in the loud blackness, she determined the carriage was loaded as she'd imagined with trunks, suitcases, parcels of all shapes and sizes. Nothing comfortable as the beds at home, the big one or the little. She didn't care.

When the train stopped she'd count the money. When the train stopped she'd calculate what to do, where to go, how to get by. She could slip off anywhere, buy herself new clothes, become a new person.

She settled herself as well as she could on a huge, well-stuffed suitcase and closed her eyes.

Claude would help. She would punch more books for him to read and collect from the people who came to listen. Send money home to Pa and Ma every few weeks.

She'd write the books herself. She'd get him to punch them somehow. She'd punch a set of instructions for how to punch instructions for punching. She'd punch another set of instructions and let Claude write books too. And maybe come back one day soon. Find Billy. Take him away and show him a new life.

The train ran toward the north on shining steel rails. Plaquette's dreams flew toward the future on pinions of shining bright ideas.

Festival

Christopher Brown

The yard in front of the homeshare is filled with the kind of ungoverned cars you're not even allowed to drive anymore. A little Suzuki with the hatch cut off hides in the tall weeds, next to a Dodge panel truck that's lost its panels and the skeleton of some ancient muscle car. The house is a lot older.

Eden laughs as she and her friends sit there in the rental car, recalibrating their expectations.

"It looks like the Alamo," she says.

It doesn't really. It's a brick house. Old, and out of place. Out of place with this rundown street in a weird part of town, with the online pics Nick sent around, with their idea of where they belong.

Eden already feels out of place with Nick and Marley and Shannon and Honda, even though they have been friends since college.

"Why can't the world look more like the website?" says Marley.

Eden sees the silhouette of some big water bird in the trees back there, watching a cargo plane come in so close you can see the seams.

"This place is cooler than any website," she says, but it's hard to hear.

"Maybe just wait until we see the inside," says Nick.

"Maybe just we shouldn't let you pick the rental next time," says Marley.

"At least it's close to the airport," says Honda.

"Like not even five minutes, right?" says Nick.

"Which is why all the trailer parks," says Eden. "And that junkyard or whatever that was down the street. This is awesome. Adventure travel."

"Well it's only ten minutes from downtown," says Nick. "And it's just a place to crash. We're gonna be at the festival the whole time."

"Where's the river?" asks Honda.

"Right past those trees," says Nick, with the confidence of a dude permanently connected to the network through his glasses.

"Why don't you all get out of the car and come see," says a man's voice. The guy is standing there by the car. His smile reveals a couple of fucked-up teeth. His hands are dirty with engine grease. He wipes them on his jeans, then pushes his long hair out of his eyes. His hair and his jeans both look like they have not been washed in a long time.

Eden watches Nick look at the guy. Nick is the driver of the rental, too. He said it was because he was the only one who had already turned 25.

"Finn," says Nick.

Finn nods.

All the windows are rolled down on the car. Eden is in the back, behind Nick, where the window only rolls halfway down. She looks over the edge of the window at their host. His black T-shirt is faded to the color of primer. He has a piece of metal tied into his hair.

Finn looks back at her.

"You all need some help with your stuff?" he asks.

"No," says Eden. She opens the door. "Pop the trunk, Nick."

"Yeah, sure," says Nick.

"You can leave the extra eyes in the car," says Finn.

Nick looks at him through his specs.

"Yeah, okay," says Nick. "They don't even recognize you."

"Good," says Finn.

Eden tries to remember how she got here.

◊

The plane from New York to Austin is new. It smells like a dental office. The plastic is the color of whitened teeth.

Through the porthole you can see the world in tilt shift. You try to figure out where you are. The river from space looks like ice, but it's August, and you realize that's the reflection of the sun.

A river of mercury flows through the heartland. It's how they power all the things we let them make us carry to stay connected.

The whine of the jets shuts out other noise. Each turbine turns at ten thousand revolutions per minute, faster during takeoff. You wonder how they count that. You wonder how much a giant machine like this costs. Three hundred million dollars.

You wonder how many revolutions you could buy for three hundred million dollars.

There are people, individual people, who have that much money. There are people who have ten times that much money. You are not one of them.

In the future, we will all be richer.

We will each have our own robots.

We will live in cities covered in green.

We will live without rulers in true democracies.

You wonder how much it would cost to buy your own tiny island and declare it a separate country.

One time you read a post about this guy who declared his house in the suburbs an independent kingdom. Guess who the king was.

The little television in the seatback cannot be turned off. You cannot hear it without headphones, but the closed captioning reads it out for you. Even the ads. Mostly the ads. Sometimes the computer translator makes mistakes. Other times it spews gibberish. You wonder if it is a secret code.

You imagine you are a spy who keeps the one-time pad in her purse, to translate the messages from control.

When you land in Austin, the first thing you do is sneak outside on the upper level to smoke a cigarette. You do this even though you know some of your old friends are already here, looking for you downstairs, excited to see you, waiting with strong hugs.

It is really fucking hot here. Almost too hot to smoke, but not quite.

You see a corporate hotel over there on the other side of the parking garages. A Hilton. The building is a squat cylinder. You imagine the inside. You remember a movie you saw once on TV. Inside an office building like that, they were experimenting on captured aliens.

When you all get in the car, and pull onto the freeway, the first thing you notice is the billboards. There is one for a strip club, one for a real estate development on the shores of a man-made lake, and one for a political candidate.

BELTRAN

The candidate is in profile, looking up at an angle like he's watching the planes come in. He wears a red tie and a white shirt. His jacket is off, slung over his shoulder. His skin is white and his hair is dark.

THE FUTURE IS NOW

The second thing you notice is how stubby the trees are here. Like they're not getting enough water. Never will.

Nick says the trees that were meant to be here all died.

We are killing the world. You are helping.

◊

Finn shows them around the place.

It's not as bad as it looks from the outside.

They will sleep in the rooms on the first floor. The couples will take the two bedrooms. Eden takes the couch in the hall between the rooms. This was all agreed to before. Nick and Shannon are the ones paying for the whole deal.

They share the first floor bathroom. It is clean enough. They clean it up some more before they go out.

Eden's hallway is across from a room full of books.

This is the library, says Finn. Help yourself. Take one, leave one.

There is a small bookshelf, a big leather armchair, and a beat-up old rug. There are stacks of books everywhere, stacked so high they touch the bottoms of the old postcards pinned to the wall. Some of the stacks are ready to fall over. You can smell the words going slowly back to pulp.

There is some old fucking hippie dude sitting in the armchair, reading. This was not in the pictures on the website. The color of the guy's hair and beard is the kind of white that used to be blonde. The color of milk gone bad. Maybe she thinks that because the guy smells so much like cigarettes.

"Who's Gandalf?" says Eden.

Finn laughs. "That's Billy. He's my roommate."

Billy smiles. "What's up." He has a real Texas accent. Which is a weird thing to hear coming out of a hippie.

"Whatcha reading?" asks Eden.

"Wild stuff," says Billy. He smiles, holds up the book in one hand. It's an old paperback. The cover shows two women and a man standing in the ruins of a city, a giant sun blazing behind them. "The orgy at the end of the world."

Ewww.

Finn shows them the kitchen. It is crammed full of hardware.

"Is that a 3D printer?" asks Nick.

"Two of them, actually," says Finn.

"Government surplus," says Billy. "From the labs."

"Need to find a better place to put them," says Finn.

Finn shows them where the coffee is, how the water filter works, and where he keeps the beer. He says they can help themselves to the beer, but please don't mess with the printers.

The beer has its own fridge. Mostly cans. There's some other stuff in there, too. Opaque white Tupperware, labeled in black script. Dates.

The back of the house looks over the river from a tall bluff overgrown with viney trees. You can see downtown off to the west. Directly across is an old gravel pit. A crater lake of dirty rainwater next to a small mountain of asphalt.

"Indians lived here," says Nick. "Just upriver was a low water crossing for the Chisholm Trail."

Finn looks at him.

Marley holds his hand.

◊

Job descriptions.

Marley, Nick, and Honda all work in marketing.

Marketing means math. Certain words or images produce certain results. People are numbers.

They put the words into semi-autonomous machines whose job is to sell things.

Basically, the job of the machines is to monitor people and figure out which ads are the best ones to show to get the people to buy stuff. Or at least to get the advertisers to pay to get their flash in front of the people's eyeballs.

Shannon is in law school.

Eden works for a magazine. Which is really a website. They think of themselves as digital muckrakers. They are looking for a story that will drive enough traffic to get them more eyeballs and more money from advertisers to pay for more muckraking.

The pay sucks.

Collectively, it will take the five of them approximately ninety-two years to pay off their student loans.

Whatever.

What if everyone stopped paying?

◊

There are hipsters on horses here.

The first one they see is a guy in selvedge jeans and a hat like you might see an Australian wear in a war movie. The dude has a moustache that looks like it gets almost as much attention as the horse.

The horse is big, mostly black.

They see more as they walk the long blocks to Proteus from the spot where they park their car.

The riders tower over the pedestrians. Everyone smiles at them. The idea is still new.

Two women ride appaloosas. Eden knows this because she had plastic toy appaloosas as a child. One woman wears leather motorcycle pants and a sleeveless T-shirt that shows off her art. The other has a wrinkled chambray button down and waxed leggings.

"Chaps?" says Marley.

"It's like a post-apocalyptic Western," says Eden. She wonders when the whimsy will run out.

Nick tells them about it, relating what his glasses tell him. How the municipal code expressly permits horses on the road, a relic of old times purposely protected in anachronistic pride. How nobody ever really took advantage of it until a year or so ago, when the owner of a bar on the East Side opened up a stable in the property next door.

They are talking about making them put crap catchers on the backs of the horses.

They are talking about taking the idea to other cities. Organizing cross-country trips that follow old trails.

They stand right next to one of the horses waiting to cross the boulevard. You can hear it breathe. It draws flies.

Eden is thinking about touching it when the sirens come.

Police on motorcycles, windscreens flashing, pull up to the crowd waiting to cross and block the way. Their machines emit a horrible tone, a flat electronic cut, crazy loud, designed to cut off all other thought. The horse next to them freaks out. Rumbles and neighs. The hipster in the saddle does not handle his horse like a guy in a Western.

Patrol cars follow, traveling fast, escorting two black Suburbans. As they pass through the intersection they slow just enough that you can see inside. The bright sun penetrates the tinted windows. He is sitting in the back seat of the first Suburban, talking, oblivious to the crowd. You've seen the profile a thousand times.

Beltran.

"Beltran!" screams someone in the crowd.

"Fucker!"

"Fascist!"

"Turn the eyes on Beltran!"

Somebody throws something at him. A full bottle of beer. It breaks across the unbreakable glass shielding Beltran's face. He looks out at the people.

The motorcade accelerates. Except for the last Suburban. It diverts, pulling up between the two motorcycles.

Men in suits get out of the Suburban carrying guns. The kind of guns that take two hands to carry. Black metal.

"MOVE BACK," says the disembodied machine voice of the Suburban.

The motorcycle patrolmen dismount. They pull little wands from their belts. Crack them with flicks of the wrist. Turn them into metal whips.

The motorcycle cops wear jodhpurs and riding boots.

The Suburban emits that tone again. It's like the sound your phone makes sometimes. The Citizen Emergency Alert.

The tone is designed to make humans freeze and obey. That's what Nick says, later, when he asks his wearable.

Nothing about what it does to horses. Especially when men are coming at them with guns and truncheons.

The horse next to Eden rears.

It's a crazy thing to see from that close.

The horse ejects its hipster.

People are screaming.

Boys are screaming.

Girls are yelling at cops to stop.

POP.

A suit fires a shot. Into the air.

Another horse bolts. Runs right through the intersection, for the trees of a traffic island on the other side.

The horse next to Eden comes right down on the motorcycle cop who is yelling at it with a metal whip in his hand. Knocks him down hard. You can hear his helmet hit the pavement. Then you hear the sound of hoof on helmet.

BADDADADADDADADABDADADADADABABADAT. Machine gun burst, from one of the suits.

The horse stumbles, goes down.

People start running, in every direction.

Eden runs behind the 24 Mart, into the weeds grown up around the fence at the base of a cell phone tower. She hides in there, for what seems like forever, but isn't.

There are sheets of paper on the ground. Abandoned homework. 1776.

They are teaching little kids about revolution.

◊

A while back Eden got hooked on watching the coverage of a revolution in another country. The people of the country took the streets and stood up to soldiers and tanks. The movement coalesced online. Actions coordinated on an obscure dating site called Flingue. The media kept looking for a leader to personalize the movement, but there wasn't one. All there was was everyone.

◊

They find each other later at Proteus. The festival is just down the road. The show goes on. Few people there even know about what happened.

Nick and Shannon drink, beer and tequila. Honda and Eden share a big bowl, good stuff Honda brought from California. Montana mutata. You're not supposed to take it on the plane, but no one really cares. Half the airport security guards are probably high. You can see it when three of them gather around the X-ray screen, debating what that green outline is. The flight attendants are definitely high. Legalization has increased job happiness, if not productivity.

Proteus is a festival of networked music. There are no guitar solos.

At Proteus, there really aren't even any bands. There are improvisational instigators, who initiate prompts that carom through the mesh and come back in cascading responses.

Eden watches the improviser known as la Sirena take her place on the platform. La Sirena walks up five old chipped steps onto the concrete foundation of a building demolished years ago. La Sirena does not really look like a mermaid, but when she puts the reed in her saxophone and blasts a series of tones out into the air and over the airwaves, Eden remembers the riddle from grandma's game.

Con los cantos de la sirena, no te vayas a marear.

Eden already feels dizzy before the song starts, from the high-altitude herb, and what happened before.

Eden remembers then to turn her phone back on. She turned it off when she was hiding from the cops, behind the cell phone tower, hoping to disable the geolocation.

Proteus is an app, and a network, and a festival, and a movement, and a corporation.

The app lets her program her own response to la Sirena. And to the four thousand, seven hundred and thirty-two others it says are participating in the piece. Two-thirds of those people are here, inside the fenceline with her. The others are in the cloud.

The sound from the amps is generative polyphony, electronic and analog and something else entirely.

Nick and Marley are dancing at the base of the platform. Marley is barefoot. Nick is wasted. Eden can see the beats their moves generate, Dionysian release incubated in the cubicles of hypercapital.

Honda and Shannon are spooned on a blanket next to Eden, in partial retreat, blissing out on Texas sun and networked trance.

Eden turns on her node and holsters her phone. Puts in her earbud, to elaborate the layering. Feels her way into an improvised asana. Channels a long, pitched tone that is a response not just to the piece, but to the harsh control tones of the police vehicles, and the sounds of the flyover. An alarm that turns into a jet turbine and then an endless siren aum.

The algorithm pulls her out, puts her in the front of the layers. Then she loses the pose.

She loses the pose because another app interrupts her with a preemptive alert. A pinq. Three pinqs, actually.

She goes back into the piece before she looks at who they are.

◊

Pinqi is a proximity matcher. Its algorithms are tuned to rapid connections. You can play with the settings as your mood and needs suit. Eden retuned hers on the flight down, sitting there in her window seat, thinking about hanging out with her coupled friends.

There are three thumbnails dancing on her screen. A dude named Paxton, a woman named Lara, and a guy named Federico.

"Oh yeah?" she tells Federico, as they sit across from each other in the rest area twenty minutes later. "My grandma was from San Antonio. When I knew her at least. Before that she was from Matamoros."

"Matamoros is crazy," says Federico. "There used to be a port there. During the Civil War. For smuggling guns and stuff. They called it Baghdad. 'Cause of the dunes."

"Really," says Eden.

She takes a long drink from the water, which is served in a chalice of 3-D printed corn byproduct. The concession sells glacial melt, bottled at the source. Federico suggests the Volta, but Eden picks the Whitechuck.

"Do you know any gun smugglers?" asks Eden.

"Uh, no," says Federico.

"Too bad."

Eden looks at the tableau relief rendered into the chalice. Strange animals, diminutive monsters, freaky chimera, cavorting in a fantastic forest.

She looks at Federico. Tries to assess the integrity of the gaze. She does not trust the herb when it tells her it can tell.

"Are your friends from New York, too?" he asks.

"No. I mean they all live in California now. We met in school. I guess Nick grew up in New York. He works for Proteus."

"Yeah?"

"Yeah."

"Cool."

"Wait until they start embedding the ads."

"Yeah."

Eden looks at the contrail drawing itself against the sky, behind Federico's head.

"Did you hear about that shooting or whatever?" he asks.

Eden nods.

"I wonder what that was about," he says.

Eden looks at him. Reads the face that just said that.

"You fucking elected him," says Eden. "That's what it's about. And now we all have to deal with him."

"Huh?"

"Beltran," she says.

"Oh."

"It was his motorcade. I was there."

"Wow."

Wow. "I don't like your future," she says.

"I was there, last summer, at the Capitol," he says, pleading. "I got arrested. I know."

"It didn't work. You people need to do something about him. He's going to run for President. And he's going to win."

Federico looks down at his chalice, swirls his finger in the remains of southern New Zealand's ice cap.

In the break in their conversation, they hear the sound of the multitude trying to find its voice.

"What do we do?" he asks. "People love him."

She tries to imagine those people. She tries to answer his question. She remembers she had an idea about this, but she can't remember what it was.

"I think I'm going to find another piece to play in," says Federico. "See you around?"

Bye.

◊

Eden does dervish as the sun disappears and the energy accelerates with the cool. She's in the main set, which ends up all beat and no trance. She dances with the silhouette of the trees behind the fenceline, and the power line towers marching off through the volunteer foliage of the right of way like giant stick figure robots.

She tries to influence the crowd with strong rhythms from deep inside. Jungle drums, like from an old movie, like they are going to war.

La Sirena te llame.

◊

When her friends want to go to an after party, Eden takes a car-share back to the place.

She finds the book Billy was reading. Picks it up and gives it a try. Starts in the middle. Jumps to the end. Which is also beginning. Realizes she has been reading the same three pages over and over again for more than an hour.

The text burns its way in, even as you don't think you understand it. A different kind of code, for soft machines.

◊

Eden wakes up in the night. The noise of metal gears grinding against lube.

She has been dreaming about men with jungle fatigues and bala-clavas occupying the ruins of downtown. She can't tell if they are soldiers or insurgents.

Maybe what she is really remembering is the things she saw in that long year after she dropped out. Crossed over. Got in trouble. Before Mom intervened and hooked her up with this job.

The weird smell is what gets her out of bed.

In the kitchen, one of the 3-D printers is laying down goop on the build plate. Creamy brown, with flushes of blue. It looks wet.

It sounds like a regular printer, the way the carriages move. Crossed with a squirt bottle.

Eden makes the noise.

"What are you doing?" asks a voice standing in the doorway. Finn.

"Wondering what woke me up," says Eden.

"Oh shit, sorry," says Finn. "Didn't know you could hear it way over there. Want a beer?"

Sure.

Billy is out there with Finn, on the back porch.

The river is there down below, lit up like a black mirror by moon-light and light pollution.

She hears a cacophony of frogs, cars going over the bridge, horny night birds calling to each other, a low-flying helicopter.

"How was your festival?" asks Billy. His cigarette smoke moves slowly through the muggy air, trapped in the light from the candle.

"Gimme one of those?" says Eden.

"Sure," says Billy.

The cigarette is strong. Eden feels clear.

"Festival was cool," says Eden, exhaling a cloud. "Everything else was kind of fucked up."

"That's that interactive stuff, huh," says Billy.

Eden nods.

"I don't get that."

"You're too old," says Eden.

Finn laughs.

"Seriously," she says. "Your brain has to be open to the software. Which means the tones. They work like code."

"I already hacked my brain pretty good," says Billy. "I'll leave that to you."

"They're probably inserting commercials into your head," says Finn.

"I'm sure they're trying," says Eden. "That's what Nick does."

"No thanks," says Finn.

"So what do you guys do? Sit around printing jizz all night?"

They both laugh.

"Seriously," says Eden.

"Research," says Finn.

"Research?" says Eden.

Finn nods.

"What?" says Eden.

"All kinds of stuff," says Finn.

Eden laughs.

"Seein what we can make with those machines," says Billy. "It's pretty cool."

"You can print guns, right?"

"Lot more interesting things than that," says Finn.

"I want to print a gun," says Eden.

"First you gotta design one," says Billy.

"Come on," says Eden.

And so they do. Finn's laptop has a metal case, DIY, covered in stickers. Yes, he makes his money working on cars. He shows her how you find the download sites, through a series of mirrors. Shows her the illegal freeware you use to anonymize your browsing from the eyes of the state. Air drops her a copy.

On her phone, she trolls through screens of seditious objects.

There's a lot more than guns.

"What about this?" asks Eden.

◊

While the machine lays down the render, Billy works on his model. He holds down the butcher paper with his clay ashtray. The cigarette burns on its own while he puts the pieces together. They make a frame of interlocking tubes printed from a bad copy of the bones of bats. He spreads out the pericardium across the wingtips, and leaves it to dry.

When Eden uses the bathroom by the kitchen, there is a piece of tissue floating in the toilet. It does not look like a wing. It looks like a used pocket, made from the inside of skin, trailing ropy threads.

◊

The sun comes up through the ozone, bringing birdsong and ailerons.

They walk down to the river for a proper test flight. Eden carries her new tool in her pocket. Stops and holds it up to the light to see its inner structure. Finn carries the beer.

The hill is steep, through dense foliage. They walk under a canopy of scraggly elms crowded with cackling black birds.

She sees an old mattress in a small clearing.

The beach is made of trash, and rocks.

She goes in anyway, leaving her pants and her tool on the shore.

The water is warm by the shore. It smells like dead plants and sick fish.

Eden goes all the way in, swimming out, into dark cool. She comes up, current carried downriver. There is a big pipe embedded into the rocky bed. She stands on it. Salute to an exploding sun.

There are holes in the sky, big enough for old gods to sneak back in.

Cliff swallows swirl around her head, buzzing the hydroplaning bugs before they can become fish food. She saw their nests the day before, beautiful pustules of dried mud growing out of the steel spans of the bridge.

The bridge was built when capitalism collapsed, by a legion of lost men, while they incubated the war machine that ate them all. Nick told them that, when they drove over. Not in those words. 1933, he said.

Over there, upriver, the old hippie is running after his gossamer batplane, and the motorhead host is removing his clothes.

She keeps swimming, away, into a dream of cities under water.

◊

"Is that a beer?" asks Shannon.

Eden drinks from it, and nods.

"It's 9:42 a.m. Sunday morning," says Nick, in that practicing to be paternal tone.

"Where were you?" says Shannon. "We're waiting to go to brunch."

All four of them are sitting there, on their laptops.

"Did you lose your phone?" says Nick.

"I'm fucking hungry," says Honda. "Let's go."

"Sorry," says Eden. "Do I have time to shower?"

No.

◊

They brunch at the shopping center called Zona.

Zona is an old one-story mall that died, lived a second life as an immigrant market with a dance studio, died again, and was reborn as this curated gallery of eclectic fetish objects. The anchor is a store called Stan that specializes in vintage televisions. No one is sending any signals that the sets can receive anymore, but Stan sells little boxes that repurpose them as displays for contemporary devices, channeled through retro filters.

Eden watches a yellow star explode against a saturated red sky on one of the sets while she drinks her michelada in the courtyard of Bishop's across the hall. On her phone she types a four hundred-word piece for the magazine about the eyes of Beltran and the bodyguards of Texas. There's only so much muck the advertisers will let you rake.

Who knew jalapeño waffles would be so good.

Syrup makes everything good, says Honda. She's right.

The skylight over the courtyard caved in when the mall was abandoned, and they left it that way. Feral. Nick and Marley are making out in the grass, mood improved by bacon and weed. Honda and Shannon come back with bounty. An old mixing board, a porcelain figurine of a cowgirl with alien eyes, and a pineapple grenade.

Eden takes hold of the grenade. A dummy, with the paint chipped off. Heavy. She wonders what a real one would feel like.

The eye of the satellite watches through the aperture in the ceiling. They say they can see around corners.

Eden shows Honda and Shannon her tool. Asks if they can tell what it is.

They tell her she smells like the river.

◊

Shannon wants to go to the museum before they go swimming, and so they do. There is an exhibit commemorating the tenth anniversary of the attacks. Eden looks at the photographs of the White House in flames, and wonders what it would be like if they had finished the job.

◊

That night Eden dreams of the riot in New York, when they looted the private stores on Fifth Avenue, the ones you need an invitation to shop. An invitation from an algorithm.

When she sees Finn in the kitchen in the morning and he says you look tired she does not tell him about the dream, or the boy she was with, or what he looked like after the corporate security teams came in with their trucks and sonics and retook their masters' block.

"I can sleep on the plane," she says.

He asks about the show they went to see. She tells him she skipped it. Went to bed early, not that it did any good.

He tells her he was out all night, because Billy got arrested. They caught him stealing at the hospital. In a lab, behind security. He found an access badge on the fucking street.

He asks when her flight is, she says five, he says then why don't you go back to bed, she says 'cause her friends have to leave in an hour. He says I'll give you a ride and she says ok.

She says why don't we get some towels and take a nap on the beach.

◊

When she imagined Finn he was like one of those shirtless jeans models, the ones with no heads. But after they had done some time. Then she imagined a whole catalog like that, selling pre-distressed rebel fashions. J. Prep goes to the Supermax. Political detainees in torn denim and faded black cotton. Lean young revolutionary hunger strikers showing off their prison tats and the places where you can see the bones of their hips pushing against the skin of their hairless abs.

Turns out Finn is not like that. Has a bit of a muffin top, in fact. Must be all the beer.

There are a pair of freaky looking blue birds buzzing up and down the river. Giant-beaked heads almost as big as the rest of their bodies. Their clickety-clack calls sound like a pair of old movie projectors taking turns. They fly in spurts. Then they dive for food, straight down, living missiles.

Eden eats a cactus and sausage taco and works on her tan. She washes the salsa down with a cold can of Nicaraguan beer.

She drifts into napland. When she wakes up she can't even remember where she is, until she sees him down there by the water making a cairn out of river rocks. She watches him clandestinely, pretending to still be asleep.

He comes back over when he sees her sitting up, eating another taco. Opens two more beers, breaks out the weed. She wonders why they always have to make the glass pipes in that shape.

They talk forever. Talk about riots and fake elections and 3-D printers and kingfishers and the way egrets vogue. They talk about AWOL parents and custom cars and dead stars. They try to see if they can imitate the sounds of the birds and the bugs. They talk about the metal piece woven into Finn's hair, equine gentrification, net censorship, consensual surveillance, old relationships, Eden's tattoo, petroleum meadows, the names of the trees, and things they would die for.

They fuck on the beach, under the hottest sun Eden can remember.

She hears the jets, wonders if any of the incoming passengers can see them. Imagine that.

She wonders if any other eyes in the sky are watching them. Of course they are.

After, Eden swims out. Feels the hairy leaves of water plants. She swims out farther, into the channel, where the current is faster, looking for clean.

She watches Finn toss the spent rubber into the water.

I guess it's time to go.

◊

Ambient government.

Eden did not invent that phrase.

It's when the sensorial presences of the state are so ubiquitously and subtly embedded into the environment that they are almost indistinguishable from nature.

"It takes us back to our roots," says Beltran. "America is a big small town. Where everybody knows your name." And everything else.

Eden can't decide which is better. To work on new strategies to evade the gaze, or more effective ways to poke it in the eye.

Did you know that seventy-five percent of the price of a home-use brick of dispensary marijuana goes to the federal government? They like you that way.

Forty-seven percent of that pays for guns and ammo, thirty-four percent for monitoring, and the rest for productivity rehab.

◊

Eden persuades Finn to stop at the Airport Hilton for a drink before she leaves. She tries to explain to him how it reminded her of a movie she saw, but he doesn't get it.

The building is structured like a circular fort. The bar is in the middle of the big atrium, under the skylight. You can see a gangway up there.

She asks the bartender how you access that view.

"You can't," he says. "Sealed off."

"This place is messed up," says Finn.

"It used to be the command center," says the bartender. "Back when this was an Air Force base."

Eden looks around, past the self-medicating software salesmen. Imagines men in uniforms the color of black and white movies, peacocking Spartans with silver wings and spiky hair.

"What did they fly?" asks Finn.

"B-52s," says the bartender. His name tag says Gary. "Southern command."

"So they could bomb Mexico or something?" asks Eden.

"I guess," says the bartender. "Who knows? It was the Cold War. There's a display about it in the airport terminal."

"Nuclear bombers," says Eden.

"Where's the bomb shelter?" asks Finn.

"Dude," says the bartender. "This whole place is a bomb shelter. There were all kinds of tunnels and stuff. They filled them with concrete when they built the terminal."

"Yeah, right," says Eden. "That's where they keep the people they pull out of the security line."

Gary the bartender gives her a look. He has the lapel pin by his name tag. The red owl.

"Are you enforcing the Constitution, Gary?" asks Eden.

Gary looks at Finn. Finn smiles.

Eden looks to see where Gary conceals his handgun. Maybe that's it, under the apron. She imagines taking it from him.

Gary prints out their bill, pushes it in front of Finn, walks to the other end of the bar.

Eden looks at the colored cocktail Gary made her. I'll have a Wild Blue Yonder, Gary.

"Come on," she says.

Off we go.

◊

They roam the hotel, looking for hidden doors to secret chambers.

They try to get up onto the gangway, but find only circular hallways of identical numbered doors. The design palette is red and beige.

They try out different doors.

They find a room where the door is propped open. They go in. Eden grabs the Bible from the drawer, starts reading out loud, then tries it backwards. Finn turns on the porn channel. Eden raids the minibar. Opens the half champagne. Lights a cigarette.

They end up in the bed. You can smell the dude that slept there the night before. Eden tears off the sheets. Switches the TV to the war channel and cranks up the volume. Puts her plastic lighter to the bedspread, but it only melts.

Eden says hi to a guy that walks past the open door, pulling the suitcase out of which he lives.

When the housekeeper comes in, they are abusing the armchair. You can hear the sound of the helicopter crew talking man code in machine voice, before the fifty-cal. rips at the van. Eden is yelling at the TV, and then at the housekeeper, telling her in Spanish to leave their room.

They sprint down the circular hallway, Eden carrying her shoes in her hand, Finn chasing behind her.

They push open the emergency exit door. No alarm goes off. The warnings are all lies.

They find the basement. There is an old civil defense sign on the wall. You can see where the blast door is, metal, painted grey, a long time ago. The decals and stencils are no longer legible.

Eden pounds on the door, with her shoes, then her fists. You can hear the echo on the other side.

Finn wants to finish what they started in the room. She pushes him back, sits down, looks at the security camera hanging there from the ceiling. Thinks about the movie about the captured aliens. Gives them an Oscar clip.

◊

Eden misses her flight. They do not go to the airport.

They drive, south. Finn says he wants to show her something.

Something she can write a story about.

She will email her editor tomorrow. It's not like she has a desk to go to. They pay her for words.

When Eden wakes up, they are in the desert. On a two-lane highway, no other cars in sight.

The radio plays some chilango rap about perros and oro. She can make out about half the words.

"Where are we?"

"Mexico," says Finn.

She sits up. Feels the blood drain. "Fuck! I don't have a passport." She doesn't mention how they confiscated it.

"I'm just fucking with you."

She hits him in the face.

"Jesus," he says. "I'm trying to show you something important. Something we need to document. Expose. I need your help. Words and pictures." He points at the camera mounted on the dash. Eden remembers the gear they loaded in the trunk.

"Okay," she says.

"You fucking started it," says Finn.

Finn's car is an old Celica, uptuned. It's loud.

Eden opens a beer and modulates the frequency.

She sees the satellite arrays up on top of the far mesas, aimed at the sky.

They drive past a sign that says they can't drive past the sign.

UNITED STATES BORDERZONE
RESTRICTED ACCESS
ALL TRAFFIC SUBJECT TO SEARCH

They drive off the highway onto washboard gravel, ten miles, slow grade. They come to an overlook. Top of a low ridge, wide view to the south.

It looks like a colony on the moon, the way the facility sprawls out across the basin. Razorwire and corrugated roofs glisten orange in the dying sun. Low flying aircraft move through the thermals, phase shift in the mirage lines. All so far away you can't hear anything but the wind.

Further out, at the edge of the canyon, you can see the wall. It's more like a fence, since you can see through it, but the first tier is so high neither word really does it justice. A barrier made of steel and software, loaded with lethal intelligence, designed to reinforce the existence of a diminishing sovereign.

Finn hands Eden his binoculars. She takes a closer look, through jittery lenses. Surveys the no man's lands, the killing zones demarcated by the descending tiers of fortification. Finn points her to the new section of semiautonomous smart wall. It looks like a caterpillar of steel tunneling up out of the sand, stenciled with spray-paint tattoos of its identifying codes, moving on its own with machine slink and rubber paddles, adjusting to changing topographical conditions and emergent tactical requirements.

She sees a shimmering object approaching across the sand. An apparition. A coyote, she realizes when it turns, the silver in its coat sending misdirection through the light and heat.

She looks inside the base. Border security and information warfare center. It's too far to see much. Tiny vehicles moving around between tiny black and silver buildings. A chopper in the foreground, headed in to the base.

Finn sets up a telescope on a tripod. It has a camera attached to it. Look through this, he says.

The magnification renders the landscape as an abstract painting. Everything is liquid, the edges blurred. Lights are coming on, inside and out. You can make out the metal shed frames of the buildings. The white onion domes of electronic arrays. An air tower. A small aircraft on the tarmac. A huge tracked vehicle idling nearby.

They see the helicopter land near the plane. Broad-shouldered men in polo shirts and ball caps unload a prisoner. You can't see the restraints but you can see how his arms are cinched up behind his back. He has a yellow jumpsuit. A black hood over his head.

"Extraordinary deportation," says Finn.

The shutter dilates in rapid bursts, like a slide projector on fast forward, like he's making the frames of a gif.

Extraordinary deportation is when they arrest you for crimes that result in the loss of your citizenship. Eden writes about it sometimes. Finn read one of her pieces.

"We should go to Monterrey," he says. "Or D.F."

Mexico City sounds good. She has heard stories about the exile scene. They have taken over a whole neighborhood. Semiautonomous, experimenting with new forms of governance. Network-enabled direct democracy.

"I told you, I don't have a passport," she says. "They took it."

The last one she wrote about was a kid in Boston who got denaturalized for hacking into the systems of the federal court there and posting footage from secret trials onto the public networks.

"We can get you one," he says. "Billy knows a guy."

It's an emergency.

Love it or leave it.

◊

"Let's go closer," she says. They are back in the car now. The sun is gone.

"You're crazy," he says. The only light is the beams of the head-lamps. The double yellow line, reeling in.

"Turn up there," she says. By the sign that says don't turn here.

He looks at her.

"I have a press card."

"But no passport," he says.

"We need to share this," she says. "People have no idea."

She moves in. Flips his toggle switch. Turns on the camera. Looks for the uplink light. Checks her phone for the match.

Finn looks at the lights in the distance.

"How fast can you go?" she asks.

Pretty fast, it turns out.

When he opens up the engine, it sounds like a bomb.

◊

They wreck Finn's wheels before they get to the second fence. A barricade comes up out of the ground. Smart fortification made of steel spikes and simple software.

Eden was not wearing her seat belt when it happened. She rolled onto the floor. It doesn't hurt too bad, yet. She milks it anyway. Leans up against the car like she can't really stand on her own.

They didn't get very close to the base. All she can see is the Griz-zly with its embedded flashers, the land drones idling behind it, and the lone uniformed patrolman who just told them to stand up against the car.

Finn looks like he's done this before.

"I'm a journalist," says Eden.

The camera is still on. She thinks.

The patrolman walks closer. His uniform is a weird shade of green. The unit patch on his shoulder is the logo of a corporation.

A little light floats around overhead, very close. The eye of the computer that tells the man what to do.

"You can explain that to them at the detention facility," says the patrolman. "Right now I need you to submit to the search. Hands over your head."

He has a morale patch on his left breast. The owl.

"You're not even a real soldier," says Eden.

He frisks her. Finds the lump in her pants pocket. Her tool.

"What's that?" he asks.

"Want me to show you?"

He unholsters his taser. Watches carefully.

When she pulls it out, it springs open, almost autonomously. It's amazing that something like that can pack down so small. It's like a cross between a jack-in-the-box and a medieval torture device, printed from hardest plastic for personal defense. Thank you bedstuygirl92, whoever you are.

The corporate patrolman screams.

One of the spikes finds his face.

The land drones intervene.

Rubber bullets hurt a lot more than you think.

◊

Detention is not like it was in middle school. It is a white room of concrete, rubber, and steel, chilled to the temperature of a wine cellar. The clothes they let you wear are made of paper. When you rip them off in protest, they take their time giving you new ones.

The isolation is much more intense if you are a person who spends their time wired into the networks. You feel like you have been unplugged from life. They say you are addicted to interactive programs that have damaged your civic sensibilities. You scream but no one can hear you. No one who cares.

They interrogate you in another room, a room that has two chairs and a mirror, but you are pretty sure they don't really care what the answers are. Maybe because your answers are aggressive koans generated by a fracturing personality. You tell yourself that is what it feels like to create the new post-you.

The only one is the everyone.

They tell you your boyfriend is dead. They tell you your boyfriend is alive, in solitary, and will never come out. They tell you your boyfriend is a known gun smuggler. They tell you your boyfriend is being raped in prison. They tell you your boyfriend is being detained until trial, probably next year sometime. You don't have a boyfriend. You hope they just deport him.

Your mom gets you out. She is a businesswoman who knows lots of lawyers. The lawyer she gets you delivers mom's lecture. Tells you one of the conditions of your release is you must leave Texas within 48 hours.

You do not go home, even though she sends you two thousand dollars for that purpose.

You give the money to another lawyer to get your non-boyfriend released. The lawyer says she probably won't be able to, but takes the money anyway.

◊

Money talks, says Billy, stating the obvious again. Eden turns on her networks and won't turn them off. Proteus, Pinqi, Polis, Mitos. She is a walking transmitter. A voluntary cyborg whose wearable software cohabits the self. There are other people in her head when she sleeps. Her dreams are digital Dionysiums that morph into spaced-out complines and back again. She falls through the space of the others, looks over, sees their projected faces. They are flying, not falling. A fleet of beautiful superheroes.

She is pretty sure the prurient eyes of capital are there with them, lurking in shadow. The Yankee peddler inside the machine looking for innovation to appropriate and hot footage to resell. Buy low, sell high.

Billy helps her make the things she needs for her new project. She designs them the same way an instigator starts a Protean piece.

The capacity of a thousand agitated minds to imagine new tools of change is more than you think.

Billy laughs when the things stand up on the build plate. Sometimes he eats them.

◊

The political festival is in the basketball arena. It is another concrete cylinder. Eden wonders if they could fit the Hilton inside it.

She dresses the part of a Beltran fan, or the best simulation she can manage in thrift store clothes. Her sunscreen is a clandestine reflective painted on in a pattern that confounds the facial recognition. Billy wires her with the scrambler. It feels like a piece of Cleopatra jewelry, without the glitter.

They stop her at the security checkpoint. Check her press credentials. They notice something on the screen. A mass. She lets them look.

The guards kind of freak when they see the tumorous flesh of her distended abdomen. I'm so sorry, honey, says the woman in charge. She has the big arms of a woman in a propaganda ad.

Inside, the crowd is exultant under the images of Beltran. His smile animates the Jumbotron for the waiting mob. He plays with his adopted children. Walks the border wall. Raises his hand at a rally. Orates at the debates, a puckish pastor who switches from wry banter to prescriptive apocalyptica. Strokes his mastiff while he holds the old terrier in his arms.

Eden tells herself that this man is not a man, but the interface of a dark network. A network that can be hacked.

When she is inside, she reactivates all her nets. She has Monocle now, the wearable eye that looks like a crystalline bindi.

Eden is small, and brown, and batshit. People give her room when she nudges her way to the ropeline.

The music that comes through the giant speaker dongles is an orchestra of trumpets remixed as civil defense alarm. The name when the voice of the stadium says it is something more than a name. It is a chant. A magic word. A religious invocation. A network login.

Billy tells her it is all working, except for a couple of signals that are not.

The man walks the red carpet, both hands out to the crowd, drawing in the mob love energy that lights up his enhanced smile.

He does not see her until it is too late. He is pointing at the face of a screaming boy on the Jumbotron, one of the winners algorithmically plucked from the crowd for special recognition.

It happens just as she steps over the rope to get to him. You can see it in his eyes. The link is made, before she even plugs him in.

Ambient democracy.

How do you turn a panopticon inside out?

Eden is sure Beltran can see them in that second, the eyes that see through her.

Then he sees her reaching for the thing she smuggled in, hears her hand pulling it out of the homemade pouch of printed flesh.

It's like a new nerve, designed to make him feel them. It looks like a stinger made of soggy bone.

He can see it there in her hand.

It's not supposed to hurt when the thing makes the connection, but he doesn't know that yet.

The way people see what happens next is beyond what any Jumbotron can convey.

Eden rushes the stage.

Acknowledgments

We have so many thanks to give, so many grateful acknowledgments to make, that we could easily fill pages and pages with them and still leave something, someone out. So consider this just the sketchiest of sketches, a sort of preliminary study for the full portrait of loving appreciation we'll be holding in our hearts as this book makes its way in the world.

For starters, we thank Samuel R. Delany for his inspiration and his encouragement as we put together this minor tribute to his major influence in the field and on our lives.

We also thank everyone involved in the Indiegogo crowdfunding campaign that has made *Stories for Chip* not just a possibility but a reality, from behind-the-scenes help given by Gerald Mohamed and Carlos Hernandez; to video segments taped by Ernest Hogan, Carmelo Rafala, Geetanjali Dighe, Nick Harkaway, Benjamin Rosenbaum, and devorah major; to essays and perks provided both by authors included in the anthology and by several who aren't: Tananarive Due, Gregory Feeley, Paul Di Filippo, Mary Anne Mohanraj, adrienne maree brown, Marleen S. Barr, Russell Nichols, Cynthia Ward, Evan Peterson, Jennifer Marie Brissett, Karen Lord, Tobias Buckell, Mary Robinette Kowal, Hiromi Goto, Jeff VanderMeer, N.K. Jemisin, Nicola Griffith, and Jonathan Lethem. And without a doubt we thank the hundreds of you who publicized and/or donated to the campaign and helped us reach and then exceed our goal.

Finally, our thanks to everyone now purchasing this book. Thank you for taking a chance on the delights it offers, and sharing with all of us involved our love and respect for a man of genius.

Nisi Shawl and Bill Campbell, editors

About the Authors

Christopher Brown writes science fiction and criticism in Austin, Texas, where he also practices technology law. He coedited, with Eduardo Jiménez Mayo, *Three Messages and a Warning: Contemporary Mexican Short Stories of the Fantastic*, which was nominated for the 2013 World Fantasy Award. His stories and essays frequently focus on issues at the nexus of technology, politics, and economics. Notable recent work has appeared in *The Baffler*, the MIT Technology Review anthology *Twelve Tomorrows*, *25 Minutos en el Futuro: Nueva Ciencia Ficcion Norteamericana*, *Review: Literature and Arts of the Americas*, *Castálida*, and *The New York Review of Science Fiction*.

Chesya Burke is an MA student in African American Studies at Georgia State University. Burke wrote several articles for the African American National Biography in 2008, and she has written and published over a hundred short stories and articles within the genres of science fiction, fantasy, and horror. Her thesis is on the comic book character, Storm from *The X-Men*, and she is the Chair of Charis Books and More, one of the oldest feminist book stores in the country. Burke's story collection, *Let's Play White*, is being taught in universities around the country.

A graduate of Clarion West and the Manchester Met Creative Writing MA, **Roz Clarke** has lately exchanged the world of corporate IT for a life of writing, editing, and con-running in Bristol. She has been published in several magazines and anthologies, notably *Black Static* and Colin Harvey's *Dark Spires*. Alongside Joanne Hall, she is the editor of the anthologies *Colinthology* and *Airship Shape & Bristol Fashion*. She has been a member of the BristolCon organizing committee since its inception in 2009. You can find out more about Roz at her website www.firefew.com.

Kathryn Cramer is a writer, critic, and anthologist, and coeditor of the *Year's Best Fantasy* and *Year's Best Science Fiction* series with David G. Hartwell. She is a winner of the World Fantasy Award and has received numerous nominations and awards for her work as editor. Her fiction has been published by Tor.com, *Asimov's*, and *Nature*. She is a Consulting Editor for Tor Books. She lives in Westport, New York.

Vincent Czyz is the author of *Adrift in a Vanishing City*, a collection of short fiction. He is also the recipient of the 1994 W. Faulkner-W. Wisdom Prize for Short Fiction and two fellowships from the NJ Council on the

Arts. The 2011 Capote Fellow at Rutgers University, his short stories have appeared in numerous publications, including *Shenandoah, AGNI, The Massachusetts Review, Georgetown Review, Quiddity, Tampa Review, Tin House* (online), *Louisiana Literature, Southern Indiana Review, Camera Obscura, Skidrow Penthouse, Wasafiri Journal of International Contemporary Writing*, and in Turkish translation.

Born in the Dominican Republic and raised in New Jersey, **Junot Díaz** is the author of *Drown; The Brief Wondrous Life of Oscar Wao*, which won the 2008 Pulitzer Prize and the National Book Critics Circle Award; and *This is How You Lose Her*, a *New York Times* bestseller and National Book Award finalist. He is the recipient of a MacArthur Fellowship, a PEN/Malamud Award, a Dayton Literary Peace Prize, a Guggenheim Fellowship, and a PEN/O. Henry Award. A graduate of Rutgers College, Díaz is the fiction editor at *Boston Review* and a professor at the Massachusetts Institute of Technology.

Geetanjali Dighe was born in a small town in India and eventually found herself in Mumbai, a city of twenty million people. She has traveled to the UK, USA, Oman, Bhutan, and Mauritius, and thinks the world needs fewer borders. In 2009 she moved to London with nothing but a suitcase. Four years later she attended the Clarion West Writers Workshop in Seattle as an Octavia Butler Scholar. She now lives in the Pacific Northwest with her husband and is currently working on her first novel. She loves astronomy, mythology, and pretty much any science that ends in a "y."

Thomas M. Disch (1940-2008) is the author of *Camp Concentration, 334, On Wings of Song*, and numerous other novels. He published popular works (*The MD: A Horror Story* was a bestseller, his novelization of the television series *The Prisoner* remains in print after forty-five years, and his children's books *The Brave Little Toaster* and *The Brave Little Toaster Goes to Mars* were made into animated Disney films) as well as poetry collections, plays, opera libretti, anthologies, theater criticism, and numerous celebrated short stories, including "Angouleme," which formed the basis of a critical study, *The American Shore* by Samuel R. Delany.

L. Timmel Duchamp is the author of the five-volume Marq'ssan Cycle (which won special recognition from the James Tiptree Jr. Award jury), *The Red Rose Rages (Bleeding), Love's Body, Dancing in Time* (shortlisted for the Tiptree), *Never at Home* (also shortlisted for the Tiptree), many uncollected stories (which have been Sturgeon and Nebula finalists), and numerous essays and reviews. She is also the founder of Aqueduct Press.

A selection of her work is available at ltimmelduchamp.com.

Hal Duncan's debut, *Vellum*, was published in 2005 to much acclaim. Subsequent works include the sequel, *Ink*, and various collections gathering short fiction, essays, or poetry. His second short story collection, *The Boy Who Loved Death*, is forthcoming in 2015, along with a new novel, *Testament*, and *Susurrus on Mars*, a novella-length collection of Erehwynan idylls. A member of the Glasgow SF Writer's Circle, he also wrote the lyrics for Aereogramme's "If You Love Me, You'd Destroy Me" and the musical, *Nowhere Town*. Homophobic hatemail once dubbed him "THE.... Sodomite Hal Duncan!!" (sic) He's getting a t-shirt made up.

Fábio Fernandes is a writer, editor, and translator based in São Paulo, Brazil. He has stories and poems published and upcoming in *Kaleidotrope, StarShipSofa, Scigentasy, Steampunk II, The Apex Book of World SF 2*, and *The Near Now*. Two-time recipient of the Argos Award (Brazil). Co-editor of the post-colonialist SF anthology *We See a Different Frontier* (Futurefire.net Publishing, 2013). He is a member of the Codex Writers Group, of BSFA, and of the Horror Writers Association. Fábio attended the Clarion West Writers' Workshop in 2013, and Samuel Delany was one of his instructors. He is currently writing his first novel in English.

Jewelle Gomez is the author of seven books including the double Lambda Literary Award-winning, Black, lesbian, vampire novel, *The Gilda Stories*. City Lights Books is publishing a 25th anniversary edition in 2016. Her adaptation of the novel for the stage, *Bones and Ash*, was commissioned and performed by Urban Bush Women Company in 13 US cities. Her fiction has appeared in hundreds of anthologies, most recently in *Blood Sisters*. Her play about James Baldwin, *Waiting for Giovanni*, premiered in 2011. Follow her on Twitter @VampyreVamp.

Eileen Gunn is a short-story writer and editor. Her most recent collection, *Questionable Practices*, was published in March 2014 by Small Beer Press. Her fiction has received the Nebula Award in the US and the Sense of Gender Award in Japan, and has been nominated for the Hugo, Philip K. Dick, and World Fantasy awards and short-listed for the James Tiptree, Jr. award. Gunn was editor/publisher of the Infinite Matrix webzine and an influential member of the board of directors of the Clarion West Writers Workshop. She thinks Samuel R. Delany is the bee's knees and the most brilliant writer-thinker of the last half-century. Fortunately, she is not alone in that thought.

Nick Harkaway is the author of three novels (*The Gone-Away World, Angelmaker*, and *Tigerman*), a small amount of short fiction, and the website copy for a now-defunct boutique selling burlesque lingerie. He was born in Cornwall in the seventies and retains a love of corduroy and oil paint. He was at one time the world's least talented martial artist, likes red wine, and hates shellfish—though of course not on a personal level. For many years he longed to appear brooding, Byronic, and saturnine, but has now recognized that it will never happen.

Ernest Hogan, the author of the novels *Cortez on Jupiter, High Aztech*, and *Smoking Mirror Blues* (AKA *Tezcatlipoca Blues*) is a born-in-East-L.A. recombocultural Chicanonaut with roots in speculative fiction's New Wave and has been accused of being a cyberpunk, practicing conspiring with Afrofuturists. Watch out for his first collection of short fiction, *Pancho Villa's Flying Circus*. He blogs at mondoernesto.com, writes a biweekly column at labloga.blogspot.com, and will lecture on Ancient Chicano Sci-Fi Wisdom for a resonable fee.

Nalo Hopkinson is a Jamaican science fiction and fantasy writer and editor. She currently lives and teaches in Riverside, California. Her novels (*Brown Girl in the Ring, Midnight Robber, The Salt Roads, The New Moon's Arms*) and short stories such as those in her collection *Skin Folk* often draw on Caribbean history and language, and its traditions of oral and written storytelling. Hopkinson has edited two fiction anthologies (*Whispers From the Cotton Tree Root: Caribbean Fabulist Fiction* and *Mojo: Conjure Stories*). She was the coeditor with Uppinder Mehan for the anthology *So Long Been Dreaming: Postcolonial Visions of the Future*, and with Geoff Ryman for *Tesseracts 9*.

Walidah Imarisha is a writer, educator, public scholar, and poet. Through Oregon Humanities' Conversation Project, she has toured Oregon for six years facilitating programs on Oregon Black history, alternatives to incarceration, and the history of hip-hop. Walidah is coeditor of two anthologies, *Octavia's Brood: Science Fiction Stories From Social Justice Movements* (AK Press, Spring 2015) and the 9/11 collection *Another World Is Possible* (Subway Press, 2002). She authored the poetry book *Scars/Stars* (Drapetomedia, 2013) and the nonfiction *Angels with Dirty Faces: Dreaming Beyond Bars* (AK Press, Fall 2016). She currently teaches in Portland State University's Black Studies Department.

Alex Jennings is an author, standup comic, actor, and nonprofit fundraiser living and working in New Orleans. He was born in Weisbaden, Germany and raised in Gaborone Botswana, Paramaribo, Surinam, Tunis, Tunisia, and Washington, DC. He has read far, FAR too many comic books.

Tenea D. Johnson is an author, musician, and editor. Her work includes the poetry/prose collection *Starting Friction*, as well as the novels, *Smoketown* and *R/evolution*, in which William Woods first appears. Smoketown won the 2011 Carl Brandon Parallax Award, while R/evolution received an Honorable Mention that year. Her short fiction and poetry have appeared in magazines and anthologies including, *Mothership: Tales of Afrofuturism and Beyond*. She's performed her musical prose pieces in venues like The Public Theater and The Knitting Factory and also coedited an edition of the annual lesbian-themed SF anthology *Heiresses of Russ*. Currently, she's working on the next book in the *R/evolution* series and putting her 36-track through its paces. Her virtual home is teneadjohnson.com. Stop by anytime.

Ellen Kushner's cult classic "Fantasy of Manners," *Swordspoint*, introduced readers to the city of Riverside to which she has returned in two more novels and a growing handful of short stories. She recently recorded all three novels as audiobooks for *Neil Gaiman Presents*. She has taught writing at Clarion, Odyssey, and Hollins University, and is a cofounder of the Interstitial Arts Foundation, supporting work that falls between genre categories. She lives in New York City with Delia Sherman, about twenty blocks from Samuel R. Delany, and once had the honor of riding a train through Spain with him.

Claude Lalumière (claudepages.info) is the author of *Objects of Worship*, *The Door to Lost Pages*, and *Nocturnes and Other Nocturnes*. He has edited fourteen anthologies in various genres, most recently *The Exile Book of New Canadian Noir* (Exile Editions 2015), and *Superhero Universe: Tesseracts Nineteen* (forthcoming from Edge in 2016). Originally from Montreal, he currently divides his time between Vancouver, BC, and Portland, OR.

Isiah Lavender, III, is Assistant Professor of English at Louisiana State University, where he researches and teaches courses in African American literature and science fiction. He is author/editor of *Race in American Science Fiction* (Indiana UP, 2011) and *Black and Brown Planets: the Politics of Race in Science Fiction* (UP of Mississippi 2014). His publications on science fiction include essays and reviews in journals such as *Extrapolation, Journal of the Fantastic in the Arts*, and *Science Fiction Studies*. He's currently working on *Classics of Afrofuturism* and *Yellow Planets: Racial Representations of Asia in Science Fiction*.

devorah major, a California-born granddaughter of immigrants, documented and undocumented, served as San Francisco's Third Poet Laureate (2002-2006). She has two novels published, *Brown Glass Windows* and *An Open Weave*. In addition to these and her four poetry books and four poetry chapbooks, she has two biographies for young adults and a host of short stories, essays, and individual poems published in anthologies and periodicals. She performs her work nationally and internationally with and without musicians. Her passion for writing and performing is almost equaled by her delight in teaching poetry to people of all ages, from young readers to seasoned elders.

Haralambi Markov is a Bulgarian critic, editor, and writer of things weird and fantastic. A Clarion 2014 graduate, Markov enjoys fairy tales, obscure folkloric monsters, and inventing death rituals (for his stories, not his neighbors…usually). He blogs at *The Alternative Typewriter* and tweets as @HaralambiMarkov. His stories have appeared in *Geek Love, Tides of Possibility, Electric Velocipede* and are slated to appear in TOR. com, *The Near Now, Genius Loci*, and *Exalted*. He's currently working on outdoing his output for the past three years and procrastinating all the way.

Anil Menon's short fiction has appeared in a variety of fiction magazines and anthologies including *Interzone, Interfictions Online, Jaggery, LCRW*, and *Strange Horizons*. His debut novel, *The Beast With Nine Billion Feet* (Zubaan Books, 2010), was short-listed for the 2010 Vodafone-Crossword award and the Carl Brandon Society's 2011 Parallax Award. Along with Vandana Singh, he has coedited *Breaking the Bow* (Zubaan Books 2012), an anthology of spec-fic stories inspired by the *Ramayana* epic. He has a forthcoming novel, *The Wolf's Postscript* (Bloomsbury, 2015). He can be reached at iam@anilmenon.com.

Carmelo Rafala's work has been published in various markets, including *Jupiter, Neon Literary Journal*, as well as the following anthologies: *The West Pier Gazette and Other Stories* (Three Legged Fox Books, 2008), *Rocket Science* (Mutation Press, 2012), *The Fourth Science Fiction Megapack* (Wildside Press, 2012) and *The Anthology of European SF* (Europa SF, 2013). His work has recently been translated into Romanian. He currently lives on the south coast of England with his wife and daughter.

Born into a Navy family, **Kit Reed** moved so often as a kid that she never settled down in one place, and she doesn't know whether that's A Good Thing or not. It's a very good thing in its relationship to *WHERE*, in which the entire population of a small island vanishes. As a kid she spent two years in the tidelands of South Carolina—in Beaufort and on Parris Island, both landmarks on the Inland Waterway. Her fiction covers territory variously labeled speculative fiction/science fiction/literary fiction, with stops at stations in between that include horror, dystopian SF, psychothrillers and black comedy, making her "transgenred." The pitch line for this new novel came to her overnight: Everybody on Kraven Island is gone. Even they don't know WHERE.) Recent novels are *Son of Destruction* and, from Tor, *Enclave, The Baby Merchant*, and the ALA award-winning *Thinner Than Thou*. Her stories appear in venues ranging from *Asimov's SF* and *The Magazine of Fantasy and Science Fiction* to *The Yale Review, The Kenyon Review*, and *The Norton Anthology*. Her newest collection is *The Story Until Now: A Great Big Book of Stories*, from the Wesleyan University Press. She was twice nominated for the Shirley Jackson Award and the Tiptree Award. A Guggenheim fellow, Reed is Resident Writer at Wesleyan University, and serves on the board of The Authors League Fund.

Benjamin Rosenbaum has been nominated for the Hugo, Nebula, Sturgeon, and BSFA awards, and won Best Animated Short at SXSW. He was 17 when Sean Roberts pounded on the door saying "You gotta meet Michaela, man—her favorite book is *Dhalgren*, too!" (In 1987, goth had not yet arrived in the Northern Virginia suburbs; Michaela was, pace Sapir-Whorf, merely a fantastical kind of punk.) Last week, discussing office politics, Jamey laid claim to being "multiplex"; so yes, that whole, enduring, high school gang (Terri, Mouse...) evolved its theory of self from *Empire Star*.

Geoff Ryman is a writer of science fiction, fantasy, and surrealistic or "slipstream" fiction. Ryman currently lectures in Creative Writing for University of Manchester's English Department. His most recent full-length novel, *The King's Last Song*, is set in Cambodia, both at the time of Angkorean emperor Jayavarman VII, and in the present period. He is currently at work on a new historical novel set in the United States before the Civil War.

Alex Smith is a sci-fi writer, activist, dj, and musician who has, in the past two years, self-published a zine of his own stories (*Arkdust*), started a queer sci-fi reading group that focuses on marginalized people (Laser Life), and become a founding member of Metropolarity (metropolarity. net), a sci-fi activist group that puts together workshops, rituals, readings, screenings, and benefit shows highlighting afro-futurism, queer sci-fi, and the DIY nature of speculative fiction. His stories can be read here: http://theafterv3rse.tumblr.com/.

Michael Swanwick has received the Nebula, Theodore Sturgeon, World Fantasy, and Hugo awards and has the pleasant distinction of having been nominated for and lost more of these same awards than any other human being. He has written nine novels, a hundred and fifty short stories, many works of flash fiction, and much nonfiction. His latest novel is *Chasing the Phoenix*, in which post-Utopian con men Darger and Surplus accidentally conquer China. He is currently at work on a new novel and more short fiction. He lives in Philadelphia with his wife, Marianne Porter.

Sheree Renée Thomas writes in Tennessee between a river and a pyramid. She is the author of *Shotgun Lullabies* (Aqueduct) and editor of *Dark Matter: A Century of Speculative Fiction from the African Diaspora* and *Dark Matter: Reading the Bones* (2001 & 2005 World Fantasy Awards). A Clarion West '99 grad, Sheree's writing received Honorable Mention in Year's Best Fantasy & Horror (vol. 16-17), and was nominated for a Pushcart Prize and two Rhysling Awards. Read her in *Callaloo, Mythic Delirium, Obsidian, Transition*, and in *Moment of Change, 80! Ursula Le Guin, Mojo: Conjure Stories*, and *So Long Been Dreaming*.

Kai Ashante Wilson was the 2010 Octavia Butler Scholar at Clarion, a six-week workshop for Science Fiction and Fantasy writers in San Diego, California. His stories "Super Bass" and "The Devil in America" can be read online gratis at Tor.com. His novella *The Sorcerer of the Wildeeps* is available for purchase from all fine e-book purveyors. «Légendaire.», of all the fiction the author has thus far seen published, most tightly closes the distance between conception of story and the execution thereof, and so it holds a special place in the author's heart. He hopes the reader finds enjoyment as well!

About the Editors

Nisi Shawl's collection, *Filter House*, was one of two winners of the 2009 James Tiptree, Jr. Award. Her work has been published at *Strange Horizons*, in *Asimov's SF*, and in anthologies including *Dark Matter, The Moment of Change, Dark Faith 2*, and *The Other Half of the Sky*. Nisi was WisCon 35's Guest of Honor. She edited *The WisCon Chronicles 5: Writing and Racial Identity* and *Bloodchildren: Stories by the Octavia E. Butler Scholars*, and she co-edited *Strange Matings: Octavia E. Butler, Science Fiction, Feminism, and African American Voices* with Dr. Rebecca Holden. With classmate Cynthia Ward, Nisi co-authored *Writing the Other: A Practical Approach*. She is a co-founder of the Carl Brandon Society and serves on the Board of Directors of the Clarion West Writers Workshop. Her website is www.nisishawl.com.

Bill Campbell is the author of *Sunshine Patriots, My Booty Novel, Pop Culture: Politics, Puns, "Poohbutt" from a Liberal Stay-at-Home Dad*, and *Koontown Killing Kaper*. Along with Edward Austin Hall, he co-edited the groundbreaking anthology *Mothership: Tales from Afrofuturism and Beyond*. Campbell lives in Washington, DC, where he spends his time with his family, helps produce audio books for the blind, and helms Rosarium Publishing.

Also Available from Rosarium

The End of the World Is Rye
Brett Cottrell

What would you do for the perfect sandwich? Kill? Die? Well, if you were a rogue angel, you might cause the Apocalypse. And it looks like that's just what this darkly funny fantasy's rogue angel is about to do when he lands in a polygamist cult in Utah. Now it's up to the rest of God's divine posse, including Jesus and Lucifer, to save all of existence from certain destruction. In his debut novel, Brett Cottrell takes you on a provocative, celestial roller coaster ride that will have you laughing on the edge of your seat all the way to the gates of Hell.

Mothership: Tales from Afrofuturism and Beyond
Edited by Bill Campbell and Edward Austin Hall

Mothership: Tales from Afrofuturism and Beyond is a groundbreaking speculative fiction anthology that showcases the work from some of the most talented writers inside and outside speculative fiction across the globe—including Junot Diaz, Victor LaValle, Lauren Beukes, N. K. Jemisin, Rabih Alameddine, S. P. Somtow, and more. These authors have earned such literary honors as the Pulitzer Prize, the American Book Award, the World Fantasy Award, and the Bram Stoker, among others.

Coming Soon...

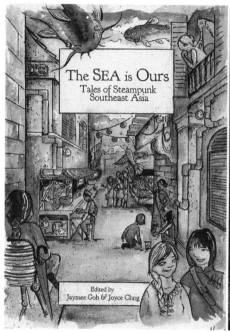

THE NUBIAN PRINCE

THE NUBIAN PRINCE

A   N O V E L

JUAN BONILLA

TRANSLATED BY ESTHER ALLEN

Metropolitan Books

Henry Holt and Company   New York

Metropolitan Books
Henry Holt and Company, LLC
Publishers since 1866
175 Fifth Avenue
New York, New York 10010

Metropolitan Books™ is a registered
trademark of Henry Holt and Company, LLC.

Originally published in Spain in 2003 under the title *Los príncipes nubios*
by Editorial Seix Barral, Barcelona.

Library of Congress Cataloging-in-Publication Data
Bonilla, Juan.
[Príncipes nubios. English]
The nubian prince : a novel / by Juan Bonilla; translated by Esther Allen.
p. cm.
ISBN-13: 978-0-8050-7781-0
ISBN-10: 0-8050-7781-2
I. Allen, Esther, 1962– II. Title
PQ6652.O56P7513 2006
863'.64—dc22   2005058390

Henry Holt books are available for special promotions and
premiums. For details contact: Director, Special Markets.

First American Edition 2006

Designed by Kelly S. Too

Printed in the United States of America
1 3 5 7 9 10 8 6 4 2

To Mónica Martin and Toni Munné,
for all the proper names and all the laughter

THE NUBIAN PRINCE

ONE ▎▊▊

My job was to save lives. It was that simple. You may think I'm exaggerating, trying to impress you. You can think what you like; the fact is I was paid to save lives, and the more lives I saved the more money I made. My existence was a kind of tennis game in which one of the players—me—never ventured far from the house, the living room with the big-screen TV, the darkroom where I'd spend whole days developing pictures, the neighborhood where I had everything I needed to be happy: a bar where I ate long, peaceful breakfasts, a small bookshop where I could get whatever book caught my eye, a fruit stand run by a big, toothy woman who'd set aside the best grapes and most tempting peaches for me, a barber shop I'd duck into a couple of times a week, and even an Internet café where I'd spend hours surfing the Web. Meanwhile, the other player—also me—would zigzag across half a continent, which was the zone I'd been assigned. He might be setting off for the Cádiz coast; he might be arriving in Sicily. I could usually decide for myself where this other player was to be found, but occasionally circumstances decided things for me. A huge transport of Albanians arriving in Brindisi would have me on the next flight to Rome, renting a car, and racing to the city where my partner in this tennis match would be waiting for me.

   You may well be wondering what sort of work I did, what I mean by "saving lives." Well, I wasn't saving people the way firemen or lifeguards do; all they really save are bodies. I've never known a fireman to rescue someone from the flames and then offer him a new and better life, something beyond dragging him down the fire escape to the street and providing a little emergency medical care. I've never heard of a lifeguard giving mouth-to-mouth to a half-drowned swimmer and then saying, "Marry me." My job was to seek beauty, to plunge my hands into the world's muck and bring up pearls. I cleaned those pearls, made them presentable, prepared them to acquire the value that was rightfully theirs. I traveled to places where poverty had hidden these treasures; I searched them out with infinite patience and rescued them. That's what I mean by saving lives.

Look at me now, for example, here on a beach near Gibraltar with the sun reluctantly sinking below the horizon while the trees, stiff with cold, lean forward as if attempting a graceful bow. A few dozen Africans have just arrived in pitiful, flimsy boats. They drag themselves along the beach in their dripping rags, following orders, fearful of the eyes that are watching them: the Guardia Civil has been waiting for them to land and immediately arrests them. Many seem about to faint; others would give their lives for a glass of water; most can't stop trembling. But the Guardia Civil doesn't do a thing for them, just herds them together to keep them under control. Some have managed to hang on to a few possessions carried in backpacks held together with duct tape. The police won't bring out the water bottles and clean towels and start pampering the refugees until the TV cameras arrive. That's how it usually is: cameras first, then the paramedics. In between, they'll call me, if I happen to be in the area. Well, actually, the only one who calls me is a lieutenant into whose palm I occasionally slip a wad of bills. He wakes me at dawn with a whispered, "Half an hour from now at such and such a place." And I'm off. When I get there, he always says,

"You've got fifteen minutes," and allows me to inspect the merchandise. I give the newcomers a quick once-over and if there's a piece that convinces me, I signal to the lieutenant, who says, "OK, stop by the station in a couple of hours."

I get there right on time, and the lieutenant has set her aside for me, the one in the pink track jacket and pants that long ago were some light color, the one with the eyes that say, "Please don't hurt me." She's been spared the medical inspection and served a cup of coffee instead. Some guy who's just seen a movie celebrating human goodness may even have bought her a doughnut. I hustle her out the door, doing my best to make sure no one sees us. Even though she's been captured, she still isn't mine; I have to be charming and radiate friendliness, make her grateful. I've bought her a sweater and tennis shoes at a twenty-four-hour store. She's certain to ask where I'm taking her, what's going to happen to her family—there's always a father or brother who gets left behind—and that's when I have to tell her the truth. I'll begin by confessing why I'm saving her while all the others who made the crossing with her will be sent right back where they came from without arousing the faintest twinge of remorse in the hearts of the enforcers of the law. If she doesn't speak English, as is often the case, I can simplify matters by hiring a translator who knows how to explain the situation quickly and forcefully. If she does speak English, I can handle things on my own and convince her she has very few options besides trusting me and allowing me to save her. I even bring along the phone numbers of some of the various gorgeous specimens—both male and female—I've saved in the past; one will probably turn out to be from the same place she is; they'll talk for a while, and when the newly captured piece hangs up she'll have no arguments left. Then it's up to me to clean her up, heighten her exquisite features, accentuate her extraordinary appeal. In a couple of days she'll be ready to visit

Club headquarters, where management will look her over. I always know in advance whether a piece I've collected will be accepted outright or will have some trouble passing the exam. In this case, there'll be no objection whatsoever. They won't stand there gaping; they're not in the habit of feeling or expressing astonishment. But they will be delighted to have Nadim—that's the name I gave her the moment I saw her; she told me her last name but for some reason refused to give me her real first name. They'll immediately schedule a photo shoot, and the resulting portfolio will be added to the Club's magnificent menu. Then they'll transfer her to a city where she'll work under some local branch manager. But I won't have any part in that; all I do is save her. Once she's assigned to a branch, she'll start earning money: 20 percent of every service. (As a rule, she'll be required to perform a service every three or four days.) The full price of the service is astronomical, of course. To put it bluntly, the proof that her life and beauty will soon be worth much more than they are now is that if I wanted to enjoy her body—which prior to her examination by Club management would not be at all an impossible thing (and I must confess that on more than one occasion I've been guilty of doing just that with the pieces I've captured)— at the Club's going rate I'd have to pay almost as much as I'll earn for having saved her. The Club offers no discount to its own scouts.

You must be wondering how I got this job. Well, the story is not without its charm. The most basic element of any story—I imagine we can agree on this—is the thing that compels someone to tell it; that's more important than the content of the story itself. Why does someone decide, suddenly, to tell a story? There are thousands of answers to that question, maybe as many answers as there are stories, I don't know. I still haven't managed to come up with an answer of my own, though I suspect it must have something to do with the circuitous route that brought me here.

I could begin by saying: I had travelled to Bolivia as part of a band of saintly crackpots sent by a nongovernmental organization to put on clown shows and acrobatic routines for the miserable children who live in the immense garbage dump on the outskirts of the capital. I was twenty-three years old, an age at which you can still fool yourself into believing that this sort of gesture will save the world. I had just finished college with a degree in dramatic arts, and to what more noble use could I put my certified knowledge, incorruptible audacity, and scant talent?

This first part of my story, however, immediately demands a somewhat deeper foray into my past—though I promise my explanation of how I landed this job will require no tedious rummaging through my deepest childhood memories in search of the one shining nugget that will illuminate all that follows. When I read a biography, I always skip the chapters about the subject's childhood; I'm sure they're only there so the author can show off all the backbreaking research he did to discover the names of the boys who waited outside the schoolyard one rainy day to settle a score with our hero. As soon as anyone starts telling me things about his childhood, both my legs go to sleep, and for that same reason I try never to tell anyone anything about mine.

I remember a certain spring night at home, watching a movie on TV with my parents and brother. The movie was *Magnolia,* a collection of shocking dramas woven together with enviable skill and copious histrionics. Suddenly one of the characters—a pathetic former TV child star who's had braces put on his teeth in order to seduce the muscular waiter he's fallen for—bursts into tears after getting his face cut open in a spectacular fall. Between sobs, he cries, "I have so much love to give." I don't know what went through my mind when I heard that line, but I completely lost it and burst into tears myself. To my mother's astonishment, my brother's bewilderment, and my old man's stone-faced indifference, I started repeating the character's line over and over. My mother got up and came over to me but couldn't think of anything to do except throw the afghan she'd had in her lap around my shoulders. "That's right—make him look even more ridiculous," my brother said.

"I think the best thing would be just to change channels," my father declared. "Either that or take him to the emergency room. With any luck, they'll decide to keep him in the hospital a while."

I got up, still wrapped in my mother's afghan and wiping my eyes on a corner of it, and went to the bathroom to look in the mirror and try to figure out what the hell was going on. Behind me, I heard my mother say, "That boy is going through a lot. He should see a psychologist. Even better, we should take him to Padre Adrián."

My mother was fascinated by psychologists and therefore also by priests. In fact, her sole preoccupation in life was to find an appropriate name for what the rest of us called "her little thing," and which she, therefore, had no choice but to call "my little thing." It might come up in any conversation, with a neighbor lady or a relative, with the owner of the corner store, or, occasionally, with a fellow passenger on the bus. Whenever her spirits darkened and she left the kitchen to sit in front of the TV until all hours, voraciously consuming carton after carton of ice cream, my brother and I would say to each other, "Mother's got her little thing again." My mother was obsessed with finding the correct name of her "little thing"; she was certain that the moment she knew exactly what was happening to her—if, in fact, it deserved to have a name (if, that is, it was something that had happened to other people in the past and would happen to still more people in the future)—her obsession would disappear. Of course everyone in the family knew that Mother's condition was a banal mixture of boredom with her empty life, resentment of my father, disgust with herself, and, finally, an uncontrollable urge to put an end to the whole thing—a combination that did not fail to present an interesting philosophical conundrum. Here was a cocktail of woes topped off with an ingredient whose essential purpose, in addition to giving the brew its own distinctive flavor, was to eliminate the cocktail itself.

During the phases when she wasn't feeling so low that she had to remain prostrate most of the day, she would valiantly pursue the label that could reduce her problem to a few syllables. First she went back to finish up her interrupted bachelor's degree, enrolling in night school, where her classmates were an impressive crop of slow but determined learners. She lasted less than a year. It was true, she said, that she'd learned things about Ferdinand and Isabella and the causes of the Spanish Civil War, that she had recovered a certain taste for mathematical formulas—Ruffini's theorem struck her as "enchanting," and its derivatives inspired rapturous commentary—and had confirmed that chemistry remained as uncouth and insufferable a subject as it was when she was in college. But something was missing. She hadn't managed to strike up a friendship with any of the students in her class, and it wasn't for lack of drinking lots of coffee with the ones who seemed most interesting. She decided that what was missing was exercise. Why wasn't gym a required subject in night school? She could answer the question herself simply by imagining most of her classmates in workout clothes. That same week she put all her class notes away in a drawer and rushed off to enroll in a sports club.

My brother maintained that what my mother really needed was a lover. It's true that when women who are inordinately bored with their families and the dull routine of their lives find something to focus on so as to escape to a better place, they experience an upsurge in mood and looks that is in direct ratio to the neglect with which they then punish their families—and during her fitness period my mother managed to get a little closer to that better place. I don't know whether she actually did have a lover during those months (I hope she did), but it would have been difficult even to ask the question; the "upsurge" had lifted her so high above us that we would have had to scream just to get her attention. And it wouldn't have been a good idea to arouse my father's suspicions. He was contemptuously dismissive of my mother's attempts to save herself and find a name for "her little thing."

There was no doubt the daily visits to the gym were doing her good, but she suddenly decided that no, this wasn't the place she was going to find herself either; some element of soul was missing in that sports club packed with bodies. Yes, that was it, what she needed were words, not push-ups. Maybe the lover who'd helped her love herself a little more grew tired of her constant doubts and rigorous self-examinations, deliberately intended to fuel her sense of guilt. In any case, the gym days were followed by a brief period of prostration. Then, I imagine, she had an idea: given the impossibility of finding a name for her problem in Spanish, it might be easier to try finding it in some other language. She enrolled in a language school. My brother suspected that my mother's decision to study German rather than English could only be a kind of secret tribute to her lover's nationality. (You see how, without knowing anything for certain, we were able to conjecture a rather odd sequence of events in order to explain something that undoubtedly required no explanation.) Whatever the case, it was the worst decision she could have made. If she'd chosen English, she might have managed to finish the course, but with German her chances were a lot slimmer. Before the end of the second semester my mother abandoned her declensions and once more took refuge in silence, serving up boiled potatoes for dinner with a vacant stare, spending hours each day in front of the television, and, on the days when she felt worst, buying colossal quantities of entirely useless things.

Finally, my brother, who is much more candid than I am and consequently wound up working as a gas station attendant despite his newly earned master's degree in journalism (he later got his honesty under control, learned not to say what he was actually thinking at any given moment, and landed a position doing PR for the Department of Education and Culture, where he was soon writing speeches for the executive director and even the minister)—finally my brother uttered the fateful word, pronouncing each syllable distinctly and separately, as if trying to downplay its force and drama: psy-cho-an-al-y-sis. Of course my mother had been giving that option a lot of thought for a long time, even before she went back to finish her degree, before she joined the gym, before she studied German, and before she'd gone to the local YWCA, where she learned to make rag dolls while telling the other women in her group about her life, and where she attended several lectures. (The proof that none of them did her any good is that she came back to us, whereas, according to my brother, a lecture is worth sitting through only when you leave the auditorium and decide never to go home again.) But opting for psychological treatment would mean burning her bridges and acknowledging that she was sick—that is, that the name of her little thing was going to be the name of an illness. And she much preferred to exhaust all other possibilities before risking having a doctor tell her that her little thing could be cured by pharmaceutical means.

My brother understood that the only way my mother could be saved by a psychiatrist or psychoanalyst was for there to be *transference,* which is the technical term for when the patient falls in love with the doctor. The earliest sessions seemed to yield some results. After her hour on the magical couch where she gradually scraped away the dark incrustation of her fears to arrive at the core where the sacred name of her ailment was emblazoned in glowing letters, my mother would come home feeling better. But after two months of treatment, her state of mind took another steep dive. We didn't want to ask, but we couldn't help noticing that she was spending hours watching television, that we had to say her name two or three times before she would notice, that she was putting salt in the coffee and sugar on the salad, and that she was buying nothing at the supermarket but jumbo cartons of ice cream. My brother pithily summed up the situation: "It's clear that there has been transference and she's gone and fallen in love, and it's also clear that the doctor has told her not to come to him anymore but to start seeing someone else." There was nothing left for my mother but to seek solace in religion. At least God and his representatives on Earth would not be as unfeeling as that psychoanalyst, who, instead of allowing himself to be adored in exchange for a thick stack of bills per session, had wounded my mother by sending her off to some colleague she would never visit even once.

When I had that crying fit, my mother thought it was time for her to do something about me, so she made me come with her to church. The visit to a psychologist could always wait until after the priests had failed, if only because priests are cheaper than psychologists. She left me in a confessional where my voice, muffled by my own incredulity, enumerated the reasons I considered it entirely useless for me to seek consolation from a God in whom I had not believed since the time when, as a child, I'd prayed to Him to make my team, the Real Betis Balompié, league champions, and he'd never given my prayer the slightest heed. The invisible priest who heard my confession must have thought he wasn't being paid enough to concern himself with the blabberings of an atheist and, as my only penitence, told me never to set foot in his church again.

At that time in my life I was obsessed with freeing myself from an obsession. In fact, I still have it; which means I'll always have it; there's no way for me to get rid of it. Ever since I first had to memorize my name and address as a boy, so that in case I got lost I could walk up to any trustworthy-looking person and ask to be taken home, the first thing I think upon waking up in the morning is this: my full name, Moisés Froissard Calderón, my old address (where no one lives anymore, or at least no one I know), La Florida 15, apartment 3B, and then my age, my profession (saver of lives, naturally), and some trait that characterizes my identity or my present circumstances, the only variable element in this daily mantra. I thought that if I could only stop this compulsive behavior, this recitation of my identity, this linguistic tattoo by which my consciousness activates itself, then my life would change, I would succeed in becoming *someone* and stop falling apart over stupid things like a ridiculous, tender scene in a movie that had no effect on anyone else. And I came away from that priest—from confessing to him that I couldn't confess anything to him and that I might have been better off with a pretty personal trainer or charming foreign-language instructor—telling myself: you have to do it, you have to learn to forget your name, your address, your age.

Somehow I had to save myself. I couldn't imagine a worse fate than the stagnant life my friends were living. Like lots of people my age, I'd tried to do whatever traveling I could with the help of summer internships and student discounts. Occasionally I'd earn some money handing out flyers, working as a lifeguard at a swimming pool where the pink of Seville's lumpenproletariat fried themselves to an even brighter scarlet, or donating sperm at the hospital—no big deal. Some friends and I were always on the lookout for ways to generate income with none of the usual headaches. The girls had it easier: the private clinics would give them close to a thousand euros for a single egg, while our sperm was only worth thirty or forty euros, depending on the demand. We were constantly sharing information: a movie that needed extras was about to start shooting; a new TV show was paying audience members to be jeered at and insulted. A few of us even tried our luck at a modeling agency, but they barely let us off the elevator. When we found out we could earn good cash by acting as basketball statisticians, we headed straight for the league headquarters to apply. On Sunday afternoons, for an hour of recording personal fouls and keeping track of each team's posses- sion time, we pocketed the staggering sum of thirty euros. We looked at other sports leagues as well, and dreamed of becoming ping-pong statisticians, tennis statisticians, handball statisticians, volleyball statisticians, or whatever—but we never had the same luck again.

Every night before I fell asleep, I used to grant myself interviews. Sometimes I'd won a grand slam; other times I'd saved fourteen people from dying in a fire. Sometimes a famous Hollywood actress was madly in love with me, or I was the only photographer to get a clear image of the pope's head the instant the bullet smashed into it. Any social welfare psychoanalyst—and any first-year psychology student and probably any department store sales clerk—could have told me: muchacho, you're suffering from delusions of grandeur; all you want out of life is to be famous. Something in your past—your parents' indifference?—is driving you to do great things, things that will make you immortal, make people recognize you wherever you go. Nevertheless, most of the interviews I conducted with myself confirmed my suspicion that my greatest talent lay in bringing out the worst in everyone around me. I believe I spoke those very words at some point during every one of the interviews, as if this were a virtue worthy of praise, as if my real mission on Earth were not simply to be the first man on Saturn, win the Tour de France, marry a millionaire, build the fanciest airport in Asia, uncover the remains of Jesus Christ, or discover an infallible cure for depression, but to serve as a funhouse mirror for everyone who got near me. In fact, I always ended up convincing my hypothetical interviewers—whom, of course, I also invariably wound up seducing—that however impressive the achievement they were interviewing me about was, what lay below it, which they'd find if they scratched the surface even the slightest bit, was a disturbing image of themselves, reflected in my unusual temperament.

I once mentioned this to my brother, at one of the rare moments when we were being serious, or at least, I was being serious—some college philosophy course or youthful romantic